William Henry Anderdon

**Antoine de Bonneval a tale of Paris in the days of St. Vincent de Paul**

William Henry Anderdon

**Antoine de Bonneval a tale of Paris in the days of St. Vincent de Paul**

ISBN/EAN: 9783741195341

Manufactured in Europe, USA, Canada, Australia, Japa

Cover: Foto ©Andreas Hilbeck / pixelio.de

Manufactured and distributed by brebook publishing software
(www.brebook.com)

William Henry Anderdon

**Antoine de Bonneval a tale of Paris in the days of St. Vincent de Paul**

# BONNEVAL.

Chap. viii.

# ANTOINE DE BONNEVAL:

## A Tale of Paris,

### IN THE

## DAYS OF ST. VINCENT DE PAUL.

By Rev. W. H. ANDERDON.

---

"Call it a moment's work (and such it seems,)
This tale's a fragment from the life of dreams:
But say that years matur'd the silent strife,
And 'tis a record from the dream of life."

COLERIDGE.

---

BALTIMORE:
KELLY AND PIET.
1867.

# ADVERTISEMENT.

THE name given to the hero in the following pages was chosen by fancy, though not without permission from the distinguished family to which it actually belongs. It may be well, however, to state, that a considerable portion of the volume was in type, and so fixed beyond recall, before the appearance of the graceful story entitled *La Comtesse de Bonneval*, which has been lately republished in a separate form from the pages of the *Correspondent*.

# CONTENTS.

# Preface.

HE period to which the ensuing story relates, constitutes one of those remarkable epochs in the history of civilization, which, like graduated lines upon the banks of mighty rivers, serve to denote the outbursts of their swollen fury in contrast with the narrower limits of their wonted course. The history of the Fronde is fraught with as much instruction and entertainment as that of any other period of the history of France—indeed, of any country. It was then that the impersonation of monarchical ambition, Louis the Fourteenth had attained to the zenith of his splendor. The insatiate rage for extensive dominion, with which nations are too often afflicted, had been, by conquest, reasonably gratified. With trade—that "calm health of nations"—came wealth, and with wealth, luxury. It was, in brief, an age in which the rank weed of libertinism flourished in its wildest luxuriance, whilst the State rejoiced to an eminent degree in the possession of all the elements of material prosperity. Louis Quatorze, Richelieu, Mazarin, De Retz, Conde, are names

familiar to the ear of the historical reader.  If it
be true that "History is Philosophy teaching by
example," then, indeed, should we derive an ample fund of political lore from the study of the
times included within the limits of the present
story.  To many the pursuit of such inquiry is at
best an irksome task; and he is deserving of great
praise, who, like the Author of Antoine de Bonneval, clothes the repulsive skeleton of tedious
narrative in the graceful drapery of rhetorical
elegance.  Like a skillful surgeon, he is deeply
conversant in the anatomy of the body politic.
He delineates with the precision of a master-hand
the salient points of individual character, indi-
cates the motives which actuate the principal actors
on the busy stage, and traces through private acts
the latent sources of public achievements, which,
to the casual observer, would otherwise remain
forever unknown.  To understand thoroughly the
history of any period, it is necessary to become
familiar with the characters of the few who invariably mould the destinies of the many.  And as
civil society is but an aggregate of individuals who
have sacrificed the capricious yearnings of private
inclination for the advancement of the general
welfare; so the measures by which the world is
governed are but a compromise between the interest and ambition of those who are fired with a
stern incentive to control, and whom the mass, as
it were, instinctively obey.  It was Burke who
declared that moderation in politics is not seldom

the truest wisdom. At the time of which the
Author treats, we behold a haughty monarch
flushed with the triumph of conquest, jealous of
his high prerogatives, dwelling in the midst of
the most luxuriant profusion, and ignorant or
studiously neglectful of the vital interests of his
subjects, until their miseries are conveyed to him
in the indignant language of remonstrance, to be
speedily followed by the defiant action of revolt.

On the other hand we find the body of the people viewing with a jealous eye the magnificence
and pomp of regal splendor. They taste not the
sweet flavor of that exotic—pleasure; they but
experience the goading sting of a laborious discontent. There is no middle class to serve as a
barrier in the fierce contest between the advocates
of extreme measures. Richelieu, with unprece-
dented daring, had destroyed, at one fell swoop,
the conservative element—had frozen the social
current of a powerful class, leaving them impotent
for good, but powerful for evil. Nor ought it to
appear strange that a house thus divided against
itself should suddenly fall. It is rather to be
wondered that it should have endured so long.
With a King with whom self-aggrandizement
seemed to constitute the principal object of life;
with a court and a nobility, whose sole idol was
pleasure, it may be readily conceived how the
helm of the Ship of State became entrusted to the
guidance of such a timid and indecisive pilot as
was Mazarin, and that such spirits as those of

De Retz and Conde, impelled by national pride, as well as by personal spleen, should have joined the mutinous crew in the capture of the vessel, or the destruction of the adventurous stranger amid the fragments of the wreck.

With these brief prefatory remarks, we would earnestly commend this tale of the Fronde to the careful perusal of the reading public, having full confidence that they cannot fail to discover in its pages an abundant source of profit and of pleasure.

# PROLOGUE OR EPILOGUE,

AS THE CASE MAY BE.

"Deem of it what thou wilt; but pardon me,
That I must bear me on in mine own way."
*Schiller : The Two Piccolomini.*

*Reader.* Well, but you don't expect this sort of thing to go down?

*Author.* What sort of thing?

*Reader.* Why, the kind of crude and shapeless concrete of chapters which you have chosen to call a story, and thrown into the press.

*Author.* Nay, courteous reader, I have only called it an incident. And an incident, be pleased to observe, in one of the most freakish, desultory periods that are to be found in the history of any country or time: when men of station, and some of them men of talent, owned no principle but their own wayward fancies.

*Reader.* Not forgetting the fancies of those yet more freakish ladies, whose humors had such an influence upon the affairs of state.

*Author.* Till, as I was going to say, they became dangerous, chiefly by perseverance in being wrong-headed. So that an incident in the Fronde may well be pardoned for being somewhat dithyrambic.

*Reader.* Even thus, you might have made more out of your materials, and produced a *book.*

*Author.* By going deeper? or by treating matters more popularly?

*Reader.* Either way, by being more interesting.

*Author.* Interest is a relative term. There are minds among us engrossed in their own departments of study,

1

who may yet feel it worth while, as a by-play, to occupy themselves for the space of two or three hundred pages on a sketch, however imperfect, of that period in French affairs less generally known than the reign of Louis XIV., yet paving the way for it, and—

*Reader.* Sketch? That is my ground of complaint: an able sketch is a good thing; yours is rather an indistinct dissolving view, in which politics fade into adventure, and adventure into religion; much like the enchanted mirror of your own hero, where there was nothing to grasp at, nor any abiding impression; where all begins in a mist, and ends in a *caput mortuum.*

*Author.* You hit me rather hard by that unexpected comparison. But you did not take me up expecting either an historical essay, or a thorough-paced novel?

*Reader.* I was in hopes you were going to make more of Mazarin, or again, of St. Vincent de Paul.

*Author.* The latter I safely leave in better hands :* the former I, for one, cannot think deserving of any great thought or trouble in the process of developing him.

*Reader.* Why not, then, borrow at least a little liveliness from M. Dumas?

*Author.* Thank you very much.

*Reader.* Well, it is too bad; you have not even a word of sentiment in it from beginning to end, except one rodomontade, which has all the air of a burlesque : scarcely one reader of the gentler sort, therefore, I can promise you, within the four seas of Britain.

*Author.* Alas, I must then fall back upon the worser half of humanity. But, *en revanche*, have I not a reasonable allowance of gunpowder, perils, and imprisonment? Do not swords flash, and carbines discharge themselves, through the pages; are you not captured in the forest, and locked into the Bastile? Why, pray, are all stories to be moulded upon one type, or to occupy themselves with one section of human interest, till every novel-reading master or miss knows, almost unerringly, what is coming at the last, however tortuously he or she may be conducted

* A Life of St. Vincent de Paul forms one of the volumes of the "Popular Library."

towards it? The cut-throats and their employers are killed off, together with the unsuccessful suitors: generally, indeed, they kill one another. Meanwhile the good, heroic, handsome, much-tried ones "live very happy afterwards:" and we are well aware of all these historical facts beforehand. The hero lies desperately wounded, or becomes utterly ruined, as the case may be; distress of mind brings the heroine to a brain-fever; the villains of the piece have it all their own way; universal blackness impends—*n'importe*, we sit it out with great composure, for we are not such simpletons as to imagine it is going to end so. The story winds and doubles about like a hunted hare; fierce gaunt greyhounds of misfortune and crime course it up and down; there seems no reasonable chance of escape; but while the inexperienced might pant with excitement and scream with terror, of course, at the right moment, poor puss "turns a corner jinkin," and is safe in her form.

*Reader.* The Bride of Lammermoor, for example?

*Author.* No; there are notable exceptions to prove the rule. Yet even with regard to those hapless Lucies and Ravenswoods who form the dark side of the canvas, certain conventional and dramatic unities exist, according to which their miseries advance to the conclusion. Characters of this class are labelled and ticketed for misfortune, and the *denouement* is a mystery to no one. They remind you of the axiom so ingeniously laid down by Mr. Puff in the *Critic*, that when the heroine of a piece goes mad in white satin, her confidential attendant is bound, in the etiquette and due adjustment of things, to go mad, by sympathy, in white muslin. To violate the rule would bring to every well-constituted mind a sense of incongruity more distressing than the tragical events that are involved in adhering to it. Now, however numerous the demerits of my small excursion into the realms of fiction, this at least I may say, that not one reader in three could tell, without peeping on, precisely what he was coming to. The road along which I conduct him may be flat and uninteresting, and the company upon it, if not tedious in themselves, yet ill-dressed and ill-interpreted. But it may claim the poor

advantage of a fog that conceals the distant view, until
you are nearing the halting-place itself. *Obscurus fio* is
surely no very arrogant pretension in a writer.

*Reader.* So far I readily grant that I do not see what
you are driving at; and this is always unpleasant to a
reader. Every one who claims attention in print, is supposed to have some definite aim in doing so. Even to *talk*
at random is not very creditable to the talker; and really,
he who casts such inconsidered ramblings into type,
comes under the sentence which Butler, in the preface to
his *Analogy*——

*Author.* Nay, it is you who are now manifestly getting
too deep for me. In an age when all books, good, bad, or
indifferent, provided they are not too solid, are greedily
swallowed by the much-devouring public mind, why may
not one nameless scribbler present you with a homœopathic
compound, diminutive in size, and of very mild ingredients,
which, if it does you no good, is not likely to do you any
serious harm? So, prithee, be good-humored for a short
space; sit you down, like Christopher Sly in the *Taming
of the Shrew*, and see the masque played out, with a
promise, that at least it shall not detain you long.

*Reader.* Well, then, like that judicious critic, I will
endure. "Comes there any more of it? 'Tis a very excellent piece of work,—would it were done!"

# BONNEVAL.

## CHAPTER I.

"'My father bless'd me fervently,
Yet did not much complain ;
But sorely will my mother sigh
Till I come back again.''

*Childe Harold.*

PERCHED on the brink of one of those volcanic rocks which occur so frequently in the central district of France, stands, or rather totters, the old castle of Bonneval. A secluded and gloomy position had the barons of that ancient name chosen for the principal stronghold of their family ; but their choice had probably been determined by its nearness to the valley of the Cher, then, as now, the main line of traffic between St. Amand and Clermont, as well as by the almost inaccessible strength of the crag itself. Only to be approached by a steep and winding path, rudely scarped into a series of irregular steps by the hand of man, it could easily be defended by a few determined men-at-arms against a far superior force of assailants from below. Both these motives for a choice of residence were well appreciated by the former lords of Bonneval, who, unless the report of the neighborhood greatly belied them, had spent their brief days in acts of lawless violence, and no less uncontrolled

1*

revelry.   Swooping down like birds of prey from their
eyrie on the substantial burghers travelling through the
valley, and, after the exaction of a liberal toll from among
those well-stored wallets and laden sumpter-mules, carous-
ing in honor of their successful foray, these bold barons,
like many others of their class, became the scourge and
terror of the country-side.   Dark deeds of blood, too, were
whispered by the peasants as connected with the frowning
old tower that rose above the mass of surrounding buildings, and had been used for the custody of prisoners since
the reign of Louis VI.   It was there that a baron of the
fourteenth century, Michel le Noir, of bad pre-eminence,
had kept the wealthy merchant Pepin of Bourges in
durance, and had twisted round his head the tough string
of an *arblast*, or crossbow, till his eyes well-nigh started
from their sockets.   It was from that lofty window that the
unhappy trader, compelled by his tortures to sign a bond
that flayed him of his wealth to the last ducat, had flung
himself in bitter despair into the ravine below.   And it
was there—but peace to the departed.   The old place has
long since been laid in ruins: a party of revolutionary
soldiers in 1793 sprang a mine under the foundations of
that tower, and sent a huge fragment of it thundering down
the crags.   The remainder, jarred and blackened by the
explosion, has been abandoned to the tenancy of the lizard
and the owl.   We will not take from it the only thing it
can now lay claim to,—the dubious obscurity of its past.

Not every thing, however, connected with the Chateau
de Bonneval was of this stern forbidding character.   One
of its later possessors, a courtier in the household of Francis
I., had made additions to the donjon-keep and curtain-
walls of his ancestors more in accordance with the taste of
his own day ; and a wing in the style of the *renaissance*,
after a kind of debased classical model, though built of the
dark basaltic material of which both rock and castle were
composed, yet lent a certain air of refinement to the
severity of the earlier portions.   A row of Corinthian
pilasters, relieving broad arched windows, with the usual
appurtenances of heathen gods and goddesses, and urns of
stone, and- pinnacles bearing a strong resemblance to

gigantic nine-pins, had been added, after the most approved style, by a fashionable decorator—the Wyatville of his day—summoned from Paris at the no small expense of the Sieur Charles. In fact, it was some little time before the diminished rent-roll of the barony recovered from the onslaught thus made upon it by the *haut ton*. But what must one not do for the sake of appearances? The nobility of Auvergne were not to be behind the world of Paris in progress and refinement; and so, on the whole, Baron de Charles was looked upon by the family as a man who had left to those that came after him an inconvenient debt indeed, but in a very praiseworthy cause.

It is now for his grandson, the young Antoine de Bonneval, lately appointed to a lieutenancy in the royal guard, and setting out to join the court at Paris, that so much bustle is going on in the principal yard. The household has been in commotion ever since the early dawn. All the young officer's equipments and provisions have been examined again and again by many a pair of careful eyes, from M. le Baron, and Madame la Baronne, and Pierre the gray-headed seneschal, who had tossed the young lord in his arms full seventeen years ago; and Marthe, the old family nurse, who, by dint of long care and spoiling, had come to look upon him almost as her own; down to Jean the underling in the *manege*, whose whole soul is centred on the coat of the roan Flanders filly, lest its condition should throw discredit in Paris upon the grooming of Auvergne. With the exception of Jean aforesaid, there were few of that busy and anxious group who had not shed some natural tears on the October morning that was to see the hope of the house depart from under its roof-tree. The father, it is true, deemed it incumbent on his dignity, as the representative of a line of stern warriors, to gulp his sorrow. His ancestors had ever served their king, and held places in his court; and now it was Antoine's turn also. Yet there was an occasional thickening in his manly voice, and a twinkle in his proud gray eye, to tell a close observer that the baron had to summon a good deal of stoicism to sustain his part becomingly. The lady-mother owned her feelings with less disguise; and as for poor old

Marthe, she relieved her employment by frequent outbursts of grief, which laid claim to so little philosophy as to extract a half-growl from Pierre, himself not very far from a similar weakness.

"So young, and so gentle and inexperienced !"—thus ran the monody of Marthe—"and he to go to Paris, where there would be traps and pitfalls laid for him at every step ! He would be fleeced of his money, and robbed of his good name, and hustled in the crowd, who have no more feeling for the name of Bonneval than if he were just one of themselves; and those cut-throats the Frondeurs, who lie in wait for every loyal gentleman, besides the other robbers on the road; and then the streams he must cross, swollen by these awful rains," and so forth *ad infinitum*,—for we have not space for the remainder of the good old lady's impassioned lament.

"Robbers !" echoed Pierre, in no amiable mood, as the idea was forced disagreeably on his own convictions; "I warrant our young lord is a match for any three of the fellows. He has not learned the art of defence from his noble father for nothing, I tell thee. Thou shouldst have seen him practise with his rapier against the quintain in the old tilt-yard—*ça, ça !* I never saw hand and foot keep better time; and I ought to know something of those matters, methinks," added the old soldier proudly.

"Well," rejoined Marthe, "my comfort is to see Martin and Jacques stand there in the court-yard, ready to mount, with their carbines and sabres; for they were bred up under the shadow of the old house, and would shed every drop of their blood before a hair of his innocent young head—bless him ! I shall cry my eyes out—is injured by thief or rebel either."

Meanwhile the baron had drawn his son aside, to communicate to him, after the worthy example of Polonius, a few maxims of parting advice. "You, see, my dear boy," he began, "the times in which we are at this present demand, certes, the greatest circumspection. You remember the letter I read to you a few weeks since from my old friend at court, the Marquis de Sennechamps. He describes all Paris as turned upside down by the fury of this

Fronde party. You have been so thoroughly imbued, my son, with the principles of loyalty to your sovereign, that I have no fear for your steadfastness in these troublous days. And over and above this, you will not forget that loyalty is entitled to its just recompense. This party will be crushed. Mark me: every one who knows France may safely predict it. Order will be restored; and the throne, which in the course of the present year has seemed even to totter, will stand on a firmer base than ever. Far from the name of Bonneval be all suspicion of mercenary motives," added the baron, with a certain solemnity of tone; "but when honors and rewards are to be distributed for faithful service done, why, in the scramble, Antoine, I see no reason against thy share being worth thinking of as well as another's. Yes, my boy," with a look of intense fondness; "and you, pride of my heart as you have been, may also become the restorer of this ancient house to its former fortunes:"—a glance at the old donjon-keep, and along the line of those later additions that had swallowed much of the fortunes to be so restored.

"Well," continued the father, after a pause, "another word I had, about religion; but it must be a brief one. There are two extremes, my Antoine—there are two extremes: for your father's sake avoid them both. You have a just horror of license and free-thinking—*bon*. I have to thank M. l'Abbe for his care of your instruction. But I am told there is another spirit abroad just now among some of the great people of Paris; a certain—how shall I call it?—unpractical extravagance in matters of devotion. Ah, what a world it is we live in, where people cannot avoid one evil without plunging into the opposite!" Here came a philosophic sigh, directed against all extremes. "A priest, they say, a M. Vincent, whom the Regent has made councillor of state, forsooth, is turning people's heads with such practices as, I am sure, my worthy uncle, the Bishop of Macon, never once dreamed of. They cannot be orthodox; nay, depend upon it, the thing smacks of the sourness of these Huguenot psalm-singers. The Archbishop should look to it. Keep thou the golden mean, Antoine, as thy father before thee, and meddle not with

such fancies. The religion of a gentleman; graceful
and easy; irreproachable, but not excessive : the measure
of devotion that sits well on a man who remembers that he
is not to be a monk, but a courtier; that is the *juste
milieu*—the thing for my Antoine to aim at. And now,
my son, I cannot detain thee : the morning wears away,
and there is old Pierre, with a stirrup-cup of Bordeaux,
waiting to catch a last word, and—and thy mother is also
on the stairs. Adieu, then, adieu, my brave lieutenant of
the Guard !" And the father, spite of previous self-school-
ing, bent over his son's neck; while the tears no longer
twinkled so demurely in the corners of his eyes.

In a minute or two after these last words, the archway
of the old castle rang sharply in answer to the spurning
hoofs of the roan ; while Antoine, emerging at full canter,
commenced the descent of the steep with a heedlessness
that caused more than one pair of eyes to strain after him
from the windows, and more than one heart to beat anxiously within. We will not at this moment look him too
curiously in the face, for the honor of manhood and the
military profession. Poor fellow ! it is his first parting
from the home that has nurtured him, and from the hearts
that hold him so dear.

## CHAPTER II.

### A ROUGH SKETCH.

"*1st Lord.* It is the Count Rousillon, my good lord,
Young Bertram.
   *King.*         Youth, thou bear'st thy father's face;
Frank nature, rather curious than in haste,
Hath well compos'd thee. Thy father's moral parts
Mayst thou inherit too. Welcome to Paris."
*All's well that ends well.*

HE has fairly commenced his launch into life, and it is
time for us to attempt our hero's portrait. Behold him
then, as, after a brisk gallop, whereby he has dispelled the
sadness of that morning's farewell, he reins up his favorite
steed, and carols to himself the butt-end of a *rondelai*
popular in Auvergne. He is no mean specimen of a scion
sprung from the old French noblesse; and there is a flush
on his embrowned cheek, and a lustre in his speaking eye,
that come partly from the excitement of his rapid riding,
partly from the anticipations of that new world to which
he hastens. Yet the features of Antoine de Bonneval,
taken apart, were far from being classical, and could scarce
even be described as handsome. It is a bold avowal, while
we aim at interesting our readers in the fortunes of a young
man on the threshold of life: but severe truth compels us
to deny to our hero, at the very outset, a quality without
which he may not carry with him the sympathy of the
majority of readers to the end of his career. There was,
however, no common degree of intelligence in a pair of
large hazel eyes, that seemed to vary in expression with
every changing mood; now flashing with youthful hope
and the high spirit of his race, now thoughtful, almost
beyond his years, then again revelling in that joyous per-

ception of the ludicrous and the grotesque which is so often
united with the highest qualities both of intellect and of
heart. The brow, boldly arched yet delicate, accorded
well with a forehead whose breadth and mould would have
satisfied the disciples of phrenology, had they or their
theories been then in existence. Add that the mouth,
scarcely shaded as yet with a dark moustache, gave perhaps
more salient tokens of feeling, of taste and refinement,
than of the sturdier qualities of firmness in purpose or
decision in view; and the reader is now in possession of all
that general philosophy would condescend to notice in the
countenance of the young soldier.

His clustering hair was loosely gathered in by a carna-
tion riband, from which it now partly escaped over his
shoulders in the disorder of his hard riding. It was still
a lingering mode in Paris, and yet more in the provinces,
for cavaliers to appear in their own hair; though the
thickly-curled exuberant *peruke* was making steady inroads
on this more natural arrangement, and was destined in a
few years to supersede it. False hair will be somewhat
slower in crossing the British Channel; although several
foreign fashions have already made that voyage, under the
patronage of Buckingham and other gallants of his stamp.
For at the period of our story the cause of the Roundheads
is gaining ground in England over that of their more joyous rivals, and "the unloveliness of love-locks"* has
already excited the fanatic zeal of those who perversely
denounce the graceful, even the natural, in costume or
manners as worldliness and irreligion. But when the
Roundhead dynasty shall have passed away, the love-locks
and long waving hair will exist only in the portraits of
Vandyke; for the restoration of monarchy will usher-in
the French peruke on the degenerate heads of Charles II.
and his courtiers.

De Bonneval's broad riding-hat of dark velvet, edged
on the rim with white eider-down, and looped with a small

* The title of a vehement pamphlet by Prynne, the noted Puritan,
in which he inveighs with great indignation against a fashion then
prevailing among the court-party, of nourishing one especial lock
of hair to a greater length than the rest of the chevelure.

stud of brilliants, was set with just that degree of declension over the left eye that gave a certain jauntiness of expression to the wearer, not altogether unnatural in one who has yet to spend his twentieth summer. There is no absolute wickedness in the half-shaded eye that looks out upon you from that covert; but there is a vast inclination for frolic and adventure, an abundance of animal spirits, and a determination to see and enjoy as much of life as his religion does not manifestly forbid. His gray jerkin, or *juste-au-corps*, large-sleeved, slashed on the arms, and laced with silver, fitted (as its name implied) closely to the form of the wearer, and was calculated to set off a light and active figure, which promised, should it attain to maturity, to excel as much in strength as now it excels in youthful elasticity and grace. Over the right shoulder, and depending under the left, hung a belt of stamped and gilded leather, distinct from the scarf of dark blue silk, whose folds partially concealed it. This sustained by a polished steel clasp the strong straight rapier of an officer of the guard, double-edged for some eighteen inches from the point, and inlaid on both sides near the hilt with various fanciful devices. A pair of rather long horseman's boots of Spanish doe-skin, with large spur-leathers over the instep, together with a richly laced cloak of stout material, completed our hero's travelling costume.

And so he rides on his way, thirty good paces in advance of the two stout arquebusiers whom his father had provided from among the trusty retainers of Bonneval. His seat on horseback is perfect: it has neither the stiff precision of the military officer, nor the ungainliness of the more irregular horseman; but firm, yet easy, and yielding to every movement of the animal, the rider seems rather to form the more intelligent portion of the horse than a distinct being: and the two, by their apparent unity of purpose with the evident supremacy of the rational will, might well have suggested to a poet's mind the fable of the half-human centaur.

Onward De Bonneval rides, flushed with hope and gladness; now putting the good roan to her full speed, as a tempting bit of level greensward invites to a gallop; then

2

drawing bridle, and laughing cheerily as he looks back, to
see that the horses of his followers, larger of bone, but inferior in blood and spirit, are unable to keep pace with him.
Art thou a horseman, reader? knowest thou the wild ex-
hilaration of that chivalrous and manly exercise? Mount
then, and accompany our hero upon his way. Cross with
him, at that frolicsome pace, the frontiers of Auvergne:
laugh with him aloud, and inhale the fragrance of this
genial October morning. The short springy turf is
rebounding, the new-fallen leaves of gayest hue are crisp-
ing under the rapid print of our hoof-tracks; while the
tempered sun lights up every tint of the autumn forest, and
glances on the spires of the quaint old town of Montlucon,
that lies right upon our path; and we ourselves—nay, for
the moment we are strangers to all that might mar that
exuberant gladness: unknowing of the world, its hollow-
ness and its pitfalls, untried by age, sickness, want, or
care; with life before us, and youth and hope to show us
the way; and hey for Paris and the court!

Was, then, our hero merely one of those numberless
butterflies that might be seen winging their way, year by
year, to the great flaring, devouring flambeau of the court,
till the next glance shows them writhing disabled, or feebly
and painfully extricating themselves from the flame, with
singed wings, dusky and blighted, to hide themselves in
the obscurity from which that fatal light attracted them?
Is he now riding on to Paris with no thought beyond the
enjoyment of the hour, to flutter his brief span, to twinkle
for a moment in the ray, till he shall be crushed or
scorched, swept up and forgotten? We would not do him
so much wrong: he has better qualities than this amounts
to. Not merely a high sense of honor, and a facile goodness of disposition; he looks beyond. He can respect self-
control, and appreciate it; and that is no mean characteristic in a period when the majority are setting up their
wayward inclinations as the idols before which to fall and
offer their hearts' incense; when all high aspirations, all
consistency of act, are laughed off the scene as bigotry.
His father was right in saying that the young man's early
training had predisposed him to good. The comparative

solitude of his home has maintained him in a state of inexperience and simplicity more than his years would warrant. It will make the first burst of the great world upon his dazzled senses the more perilous trial. And hence arises one chief source of our apprehension for his future. Side by side with these flowers of a good heart there grows "the nettle danger." He has a tendency to become dreamy; he spreads over things actual, the things of this work-day world, the roseate hues of his own imagination; and is apt to be dispirited and downcast when these fade again. He has, moreover, an intense love of beauty—of beauty for its own sake. Will this overpower him? Hitherto it has been in him the foundation of taste, and more; the spur to acquirement, the strong attraction to truth and goodness. But the hour is coming when he must run the hazards that attend such a character. Will the loveliness of earth have force to drag him downwards, and chain him to the ground? or will the attractions that centre there, real and undeniable within their own lower sphere, be outshone by the supreme blissfulness and beauty which descends to dwell with man, until it have transformed and fitted him for its native heaven? One or the other will surely be the case. An ardent imagination, an elegant, fastidious, and somewhat fanciful turn, like Antoine's, are perilous things to play with; and, like the tendrils of some parasitic plant, graceful, yet tenacious, are certain either to fasten on some strong support above themselves, and so climb upward, or to wanton and luxuriate upon the earth, losing themselves in their own exuberance.

Up to the present moment, however, the circumstances of Antoine's youthful days have stored his inner heart with a little household of cherished aspirations and purposes of good, such as the allurements of the mighty world will have some ado to put to flight. During the solitary rides which have formed his recreation among the romantic and even savage scenery of Auvergne, his thoughts have shaped themselves in many a dream, fantastic, prolonged, and delicious. But there is not one conscious scene of all that fairy-land that he would have hesitated to unfold to his father, or to the white-haired abbe, when his ride was

over. His visions have been always of the romantic and
the pure. He was the errant knight; he bestrode his
powerful charger, pacing down the woodland glade. And
lo! as the sunlight dies through the sequestered forest, he
hears the agonized cry of yonder noble maiden, hurried by
a band of ruffians to the castle of her father's foe. With
what a lofty battle-joy rushes on the youthful knight, in so
fair adventure to win his golden spurs! How does he
cleave the villains to the chine, unhorse the leader of the
band, compel him, as he bites the dust, to yield himself,
rescue or no rescue, and unhelm! Proudly doth he send
him, with shield reversed, to the baron's castle, to tell his
foul disgrace. Then to the gentle lady does he kneel,
pours out the vows of his unclaimed heart, and learns with
manly grief her troth erewhile bestowed upon some happier
knight. Ah, with what staid respectful tenderness on his
war-saddle he the fair enthrones, taking the rein to lead his
fiery steed, that champs with pride beneath that honored
freight! Thus, with a pilgrim pace and downcast eye,
cheering with courteous word his timid charge, he leads
her safe the pathless forest through, and up the rocky steep,
till his loud horn rouses the warder on the outmost tower,
and all is weeping thankfulness and joy. Then the rescuer
forlorn, his knightly devoir all fulfilled, plunges in mad
gallop within the trackless wood, turns loose his steed,
and, under the cold moon, hangs his paternal shield on
the scarr'd limbs of oak-tree thunder-riven; there, in his
darkling solitude of soul, with matted hair and armour
rusting dim, the salvage man, yet gentle in despair,
bemoans with constancy his hapless love; spending un-
counted vigils mid the forest silence, where distant rise
those castle-towers, o'erspread with rosy light at even, or
in the morning stately-gray: till on a time he meets a holy
frere, the hermit of yon neighboring forest-shrine, slow-
pacing homeward at the vesper hour, with beads and staff,
and pilgrim-sandal rude, while heavenly mildness lights
his clear blue eye:—

Such, then, was young De Bonneval; a dreamer, if you
will, because, for lack of living companions and tangible or
stirring interests, he has been forced to people inanimate

nature with fantasies. He is a dreamer, however, who
only needs some object really great to change his visions
into the wakeful energies of a life. One of a minority in
this listless and selfish world, he is capable of working,
living, ay, and spending himself, for whatever he shall
have tested as a worthy aim. As yet, he has none such
before him. His high spirits give an almost equal zest in
pursuit of each object that comes across his path; nor has
experience yet qualified him to sift out the precious from
the worthless, or to see things in their true proportions.
He takes them as they come before him, chasing them
with the inconsiderate zeal of an untrained sleuth-hound,
that follows every chance scent and quarry. This facility
of adapting himself to each position, and aiming at things
in turn, seems to give a pliancy and want of individual
direction to his acts. Such, however, is rather a defective
tendency of his character than any essential part of it; and
as it seems not to have been corrected by his training
hitherto, let us hope that after-trials, yes, if need be, after-
sufferings, may perfect the work. If these shall strengthen
and mature his purposes, and wean him from the counter-
allurements to which he now lies too much open, it will be
well. The day may come when he shall gain in concentration without losing in energy. He will then consolidate
the floating impulses that now spend themselves in
nothings, and rise into a greater man than any of the
mailed and plumed ideals of his present fancy.

# CHAPTER III.

> "Consider, that
> What his high hatred would effect, wants not
> A minister in his power :—I know his sword
> Hath a sharp edge ; 'tis long, and it may be said
> It reaches far ; and where 'twill not extend,
> Thither he darts it."
>
> *King Henry VIII.*

THE veteran courtier had not forewarned his son without reason.   Troublous times had already begun in Paris; and, like the sullen mutterings and flashes of a thunder-cloud, foreboded the near outburst of a more sweeping storm. The power of the French parliament had for some time been growing formidable to those whose interests were pledged to restrain it within existing limits.   On the one hand, the increasing importance of a sturdy middle class, and on the other, the well-deserved unpopularity of the great body of hereditary nobles, immersed in pleasure and neglectful of their dependants, combined to throw the balance of power more towards the base of the social column than was relished by those who formed the gay and graceful capital that crowned the summit.   Discontents among the yet inferior classes, the sons of petty commerce and toil, and a haughty jealousy on the part of the aristocracy, gave tokens of some decisive struggle, that would ere long decide this controversy by the final overthrow of one of the antagonist forces.   It was becoming evident, moreover, that not a clashing of accidental parties merely, but deep and abiding principles of action were engaged in the issue ; principles that had long been gathering strength on either side, and whose adherents might be broken, but would never bend.

In the life of nations (it is an old remark) certain cycles seem traceable, by whose law a more developed formation and power is given now to one element of a constitution, now to another. Thus the earlier patriarchal monarchy, and, next, the strong coercion laid by the chief of an invading horde upon his rude warriors and the subjects of his conquest, had yielded, each in turn, to the feudal system of the middle ages. That system, whatever its defects, however obvious the tendencies to oppression which unfolded themselves in the course of its working, proceeded at least upon a theory of mutually balanced relations between lord and vassal, of common interests, offensive and defensive, of well-recognized duties and restraints to lawless violence. And so, through cloud and sunshine, chequered by eminent virtues and great crimes, it had its day, and set.

Later, again, to a voyager on that advancing tide of events that lingers through no portion of its channel, a new vista in the annals of royalty opens soon after the dawn of the seventeenth century. What remains of the feudal growth yet existed in France were then demolished by the assaults of one vigorous unsparing hand. The genius and energy of Richelieu were almost concentrated on this sole enterprise. He aimed at exalting the throne of his master to a height hitherto unknown; but it was on the ruins of most other existing interests: it was after clearing away the accumulated traditions, usages, and unwritten sanctions of ages, and by setting arbitrary limitations to the fundamental laws of the kingdom, that he laid the basis of that new authority. He thus effected what has been well described* as a revolt of the crown against its subjects. The internal balance of power, that should have made France united and happy in herself, and formidable to her hereditary foes, was as effectually destroyed by this despotic change as by any revolutionary movement from below. In this kind of rebellion, no less than in its opposite, force was enlisted against right in the perpetration of

* M. de St. Aulaire, *Histoire de la Fronde*.

a great civil crime. And as in the world's moral government great outrages and wrongs sooner or later bring great
revenges in their train, so, while we look along the after-
field of history, the eye is arrested by one tremendous
counter-action, whereby the subject classes paid back with
interest all such previous insults and encroachments of the
crown. Richelieu established a Reign of Terror in his
day, and quitted the scene before that word had been appro-
priated by the opposite party. But could he have seen,
in the glass of the future, the powers that were one day to
rise and pass over the stage, even *his* determined spirit
might have quailed before the phantom of a retribution in
store, towards which the murdered liberties of the people
pointed in vengeful triumph. The problem was indeed
long in working itself out, and justice seemed slow of foot.
But justice came at last, in her sternest mood, and was
recognized; though she came not with upright sword and
evenly-poised balance, but in the guise of her sisters the
furies, with torch and snaky scourge. Neither did the
lesson lose any of its impressiveness because a century and
a half elapsed before it was read to mankind.

Richelieu's immediate policy, however, was less concerned with the masses of the people, who were afterwards
to become so dangerous to the social order, and whom he
may be said rather to have left out of reckoning than to
have oppressed by overt act. The condition of the serfs
and minor vassals was perhaps the last particular of the
feudal system he would have been active to disturb. His
mark was a higher, and in that day at least a far more
important one; for the importance of the inferior ranks to
the well-being and safety of a kingdom was not then a
fact so recognized as later events declared it. He was
the avowed enemy of the nobility of France, so far as
their rights or pretensions limited the expansion of the
royal power. Nor was he without reason, on his own view
of the political balance, in employing all the resources at
his command to humble and weaken this haughty class.
The governors to whom the provinces and fortified towns
of the kingdom had been intrusted, men of wealth and high
alliance, and frequently of talents equalling their ambition,

had assumed rather the aspect of independent princes than
of vassals to the crown, and exercised not unfrequently
the privilege of levying both imposts and men-at-arms
without any reference to the royal authority.

Against this dominant class, therefore, the genius and
determination of the cardinal concentrated themselves. It
was one chief object of his political existence to humble
the nobility under the footstool of his sovereign. This
being effected, he next turned his energies to undermine
the influence of the magistracy throughout the provinces
of France. Both these purposes were greatly advanced by
separating judicial causes from those of mere administration. Over the heads of a countless crowd of officials and
placeholders, many of whose functions had been purchased
from the crown under the earlier kings, and had become
hereditary and permanent, Richelieu erected a simpler and
more efficient organization, by creating a staff of commissioners or *intendants*. These were distributed throughout
the provinces, with jurisdiction over all matters of justice,
police, and finance. They were appointed absolutely by
the minister, they held their offices at his nod, and from
their decisions there lay no appeal but to himself. Greater
proof could scarcely be afforded of the power acquired by
this extraordinary man than the fact of his being able, in
the face of public opinion, and by the perpetration of a
vast and glaring act of injustice toward existing rights, to
annihilate by a blow the vested interests of no less (it is
said) than forty thousand families, possessed of the great
mass of commercial wealth in France, and united among
themselves by an *esprit de corps* much more tenacious than
had been that of the ancient barons. Yet this numerous
and well-organized body, extending through nearly every
rank of the community, from the merest underling to the
great officers of the *cours souveraines*, had no other
resource, on being thus superseded, than unavailing protestations against the hopeless bankruptcy to which the
policy of that one man had reduced them.

By these consecutive acts the constitution of France
became simplified, and assumed something that might be
termed organization. The metropolitan and provincial

courts, in whose ill-constituted system various departments,
judicial, financial, administrative, were mingled together,
and in which the rankest abuses had flourished for generations, were at once reduced to order by the cardinal's
sweeping reforms.   Happy would it have been for his
country, for his successors in office, and for the very throne
to whose interests he lent his great powers, if this cleansing
of the Augean stable of public corruption had tended to
adjust the claims of the various classes and offices existing
in France, and to establish over all an equitable and
enlightened sway.   But Richelieu never lost sight of his
one object.   In levelling arrogant pretensions, and clearing
away from the constitution the abuses by which it was
encumbered, he was but the more surely paving a royal
road for the establishment of a pure despotism, of which he
himself necessarily became the right hand.

Such bold successful strokes had changed the whole
aspect of French politics, when, about six years before the
commencement of our story, this most able minister, and
the earthly sovereign whom perhaps (like a second Wolsey)
he had served more faithfully than the Supreme Master
of all, both went to their account within a short interval
one of the other.   Richelieu, in dropping the reins of government from his dying hand, left a task of no slight
hazard to the successor whose grasp of them should be
less firm and commanding than his own.   Nor was Mazarin, to whom the widowed regent soon gave all her confidence, the man to step in effectively at such a crisis.   He
had neither resolution to pursue the unbending course
traced out by his predecessor, and to consolidate the
monarchy of Louis XIV. on the basis of Richelieu's
ideal ; nor the still nobler courage freely and generously
to restore the plundered rights upon whose ruins that ideal
had been raised.

A great and spirit-stirring occasion it was, certainly,
that offered itself on the concurrent deaths of Louis XIII.
and his minister.   The times seemed to demand a man
commensurate with them, and to shape themselves in
expectation of his advent.   It was the dawn of a new and
untried day in the history of France.   On one side were

the salutary warnings afforded by those risings against the policy of Richelieu, which he had been able only to stifle in blood. There was, moreover, the ominous precedent of a similar struggle in England, where the differences between a king and his parliament had assumed a fierceness and intensity that foreshadowed the darker events yet in store: a royal prisoner at Carisbrooke, an arraignment before a crowd of sanguinary rebels in Westminster, and a "gray discrowned head" laid low on the scaffold at White-hall. On the other hand, there were topics of encouragement abundantly sufficient to nerve a minister of loyal and public spirit to the fulfilment of his task. Among the nobles and the magistracy alike, in the midst of much that was corrupt and rapacious, men were discoverable who would have rallied round the cause of public order, anxious only for the due balance of power in the state, and ready to uphold the throne in its true prerogative, while sternly resisting encroachment on other and equally sacred rights. That throne had lost none of its real *prestige*, and France was still essentially monarchical.

The Church, too, possessed even at this period her bright examples of purity and self-devotion. Abuses existed, nay, abounded: personal corruption, public scandals, in the conduct, or the negligence, of the priests of the Most High. Quiet times had attended upon religion, and had come with inevitable dangers in their train. Tranquillity had lapsed into sloth, and sloth had bred moral evils and miseries in fatal luxuriance. Yet the general darkness that was now overspreading the land only served to throw out in more vivid brilliancy some scattered examples of zeal and holy life, beaming here and there as beacons to cheer the "men of good-will" in their voyage through a dreary period. There were the Vincents de Paul, the Oliers, with Tronson and the Sulpician school of divines; the priests of the French Oratory, founded by the pious Cardinal de Berulle; these and others, whether individuals or in community, constituted, during the whole of Mazarin's term of power, the lights of their generation, the salt that preserved an inert mass from the utter corruption to which it tended. Instruments for good, therefore,

lay ready to hand.   And the very weariness, the exhaustion of spirit, following upon unrestrained license and mad
self-will; the wretchedness haunting the steps of all that
rampant vice; the evil of the times, in a word, to which
the example of such men was an ever-present rebuke,
formed the element on which they would have energized
with tenfold effect, had the minister been gifted with perception to value them, or administrative skill to employ
them.   As it was, they worked individually, did great
things, and won their own incorruptible crowns; they
became so many centres of purifying influence, till they
left their names and their works stamped upon after-
generations.   But it was by a power inherent in their own
characters, or, let us rather say, given them from above:
it was certainly not by any influence lent to them by a
government incapable of prizing the rare, or wielding the
mighty, among men.

In the changes that attend public measures and public
opinion, conjunctures such as these afford abundantly the
materials needed by a hero, by a saint, by a statesman-
philosopher, to effect great things for the welfare of the
country he rules.   Mazarin, however, was none of the
three.   A foreigner, ill acquainted with the character of
the nobility and the people, unpractised in the constitution,
unable to speak correctly even the language,* of France,
his conduct was marked by the indecision that ever attends
a man when he is not sufficiently master of his subject to
prosecute one consistent view.   Amid the troubles attending his administration, and his great personal unpopularity,

---

* Numerous were the witticisms, contained in lampoons and pas-
quinades of the period, which represented Mazarin, by his Italian
mispronunciation of French, saying things the most grotesque and
mal-a-propos of the state-questions then in debate.   And, as to
affix the stigma of ridicule to the public men and measures in the
shape of a song or a bon-mot is among the most powerful means to
ensure their discomfiture, it is probable that these light shafts of
raillery told against the minister with a degree of effectiveness
resembling that of our own "Lillebulero" in the Revolution of
1688.   In either case, the effort of wit was, in itself, contemptible;
but it was caught up, multiplied, and invested with a damaging
power, because it chimed in with the general feeling at a moment
of great popular excitement.

Mazarin naturally reverted in thought to his own unten-anted palace at Rome, and to the tranquil existence he might still pass there, undisturbed by the factions of arro-gant nobles and disaffected citizens. Apprehensions, too, for his safety, more than once threatened during that turbulent period, were aided by the occasional qualms of a conscience seldom perhaps over-sensitive. Had he any right to remain where his presence only increased the dis-cord, the confusions, and therefore the miseries, of the time? Of these motives, the former were abundantly sup-plied, as the struggles of the Fronde proceeded in thier wayward and perilous excesses. The latter was repeatedly and urgently enforced by representations from Vincent de Paul. That holy and disinterested man again and again urged the Cardinal to make this sacrifice for the welfare of France and of the regency; and urged it with a degree of power which can spring only from acquaintance with the sufferings of the lower classes, and a deep passionate sym-pathy with their distress; and with a plainness which avoided offence only because it resulted from his well-known zeal for good, and was tempered by his habitual mildness and courteous deference.

It would indeed have been difficult to say which class of French society regarded the minister with greatest aver-sion. He maintained his place simply by the personal favor of the queen-regent; and, as far as acts may inter-pret motives, maintained it for his personal aggrandisement. Yet, so powerful were the appeals made to his better con-science by St. Vincent, that at one time he seemed on the point of yielding to the only right, or even dignified, course—a withdrawal from that government and country which he could not hope to benefit, and which his presence was perpetually embarrassing. His evil angel prevailed over this half-formed resolution. He could not determine, like the heroic citizen of old Rome, to leap with self-devo-tion into the gulf that yawned in the very forum, and threatened all interests alike; and while he lingered irreso-lutely in a position which he lacked the courage to aban-don, he saw that gulf widen visibly before his eyes, till it burst out, a volcano of devastating fury, submerged both

3

city and country in the fiery lava-streams of internal warfare, and at one time swept away himself, the prime author of the convulsion, upon its headlong, resistless torrent.

## CHAPTER IV.

### A CAPTURE.

"*1st Outlaw*. Fellows, stand fast; I see a passenger.
*2d Outlaw*. If there be ten, shrink not, but down with 'em."
*Two Gentlemen of Verona*.

"OUR young lord seems to have a mind to break our necks," grumbled Martin, as the change from woodland to a more dreary and uneven road brought no abatement in Antoine's riding; "and I am sure, at least, he has blown my poor chestnut."

"Chut! man," answered his companion; "didst not hear yon peasant say, half a league back, another hour's spurring would bring us within sight of Saint Amand?"

"Ay, but," rejoined the first, taking advantage of a broken ascent to draw his sleeve of buckram across his brows, that were glowing like burnished copper; "methinks I would not trust overmuch to what it might please such peasants to say. He had a strange look about him, that same: seemed more like one of the bandit-fellows that old contrabandiste—thou rememberest the Malaga he brought to the chateau?—used to tell us he had met with over the Pyrenees."

"*Allons*, then," cried Jacques, striking spurs into his jaded roadster, and forcing him up the remainder of the bank that had afforded space for this brief dialogue; "the

poor churls are half-starved by these times of ours; no
wonder they look as haggard as hawks. If you don't like
their looks, close up all the more to our young master;
there may be more of them hanging about, eh? Troth!
we had been wiser to go before him as a patrol, if it comes
to that."

Nor were the anticipations of the worthy pair altogether
groundless. The road, which, from the moment of its
leaving the valley of the Cher, had become broken and
irregular, now plunged down again into one of those broad
belts of forest-track, which, in such unsettled times as the
period of our tale, contributed more to the picturesque
interest than to the security of a journey. A turn round
a projecting mass of rock had hidden Antoine for a couple
of minutes from the sight of his trusty attendants, when
the confused sound of angry voices, followed by the report
of a carbine, served to advertise them, a little too late, that
their closer attendance might have been greatly to his advantage. To rouse the spent energies of their steeds by a
sharp application of the spur, to unsling their cumbrous
matchlocks, and blow at the tedious matches of their ban-
deliers, were manœuvres executed with as much rapidity
as the nature of the case admitted. But by the time they
had cantered up at their best speed to the scene of action,
the struggle was already over; and a glance sufficed to
declare it. One rough-looking fellow, half peasant and
half *larron*, had a strong grasp on the bridle of the roan,
whose wild plunges showed every determination to get free
from so unwelcome a neighborhood. Another, of the same
dubious appearance, armed with a rusty rapier that had
seen better days and worthier usage, was partly forcing,
partly assisting, Antoine to dismount; while our hero, his
sword-arm hanging feebly by his side, unable to refuse the
service of his unmannerly esquire, swung himself with
difficulty to the ground. The heir of Bonneval, however,
had evidently sustained his reputation during the brief
contest. His good sword-blade, broken short from the
hilt, lay on the opposite side of the road, while the pommel
still remained in the grasp of his disabled arm. A long
cudgel or quarter-staff, in the hands of a third ruffian,

who stood leaning on it with a look of grim satisfaction, explained the process by which this twofold disaster had come
about.   Three or four more gentry of a similar character
were armed with the common country scythe, attached
firmly to the end of a pole, which thus formed a weapon of
the most destructive and ghastly kind.   They had also
long knives stuck in the girdles of their leathern jerkins,
and were altogether a band of formidable appearance,
whose invitation to "stand and deliver," in the spot they
had chosen for their ambuscade, would not have been an
easy one for any horseman to decline.

It must not be supposed that Jacques and Martin failed
in playing their part manfully under all these circumstances
of disadvantage.   It is true that, what between unskilful-
ness and haste, they delivered an ineffectual fire the moment
they rounded the corner and came upon the scene of action.
But deliver it they did, with a hearty good-will; and were
proceeding to lay about them with their trusty swords,
when they were instantly surrounded, and, after a short
scuffle, disarmed and pulled to the ground.   Antoine, not
withstanding the pain of his swollen and disabled sword-
arm, and the uncertainty of his own situation, lifted both
hand and voice to deprecate any further violence to his followers.   But when the whole party had been once fairly
overpowered, no additional maltreatment was offered,
beyond some rough handling while they were dragged
forward by the collar towards one who seemed to be the
leader of the band.

This personage, since the termination of the brief contest, in which he had taken an active share, had with great
composure withdrawn to one side of the scene of action.
Seating himself on the steep bank, along which ran the
narrow lane he had chosen as the spot of his ambuscade,
and pulling from his pocket a written paper, he regarded
Antoine, who was now led up to him, with a fixed and
steady gaze.   There was a remarkable expression in the
man's whole countenance, especially in his eyes, which were
small, of the deepest black, and set rather near together
under a bushy overhanging brow.   It was a glance which
few who had once fairly met it would readily forget again ;

while it conveyed an impression that the person subjected to its keen scrutiny was being read by an intellect of no common discernment, and fixed in a tolerably retentive memory. The remaining features in this singular countenance, overgrown with hair of shaggy black, here and there slightly grizzled, seemed rather to indicate a high degree of firmness than any savage ferocity. Yet Antoine could not avoid feeling, as he approached him, that the milk of human kindness was not an ingredient entering largely into the composition of his captor; and that no feelings of compunction or pity would be likely to stand in the way of that stern determination to pursue a purpose once deliberately adopted, which characterised the man. His dress was of scarcely superior materials to that of the ruffians who surrounded him; but, unlike theirs, it indicated a scrupulous cleanliness, and even some degree of taste in the wearer. The hands also, large and sinewy as they were, had neither been stained nor hardened by manual toil. Altogether there was that about the leader of the band' which implied either that his present occupation had been assumed to prosecute some temporary purpose, or that, if it were indeed habitual to him, he must be a brigand of a different stamp from the ordinary cutpurse or highway robber.

It was in a voice deep, full, and deliberate, that the captain of the band now broke silence.

"By what name are you called, young sir ?" asked he, alternately eyeing Antoine and the document he held in his hand; "and whence, and whither, may you be journeying ?"

De Bonneval, in spite of the reluctance he felt to answer any question so authoritatively put to him, saw, after a moment's reflection, no good purpose likely to be gained by withholding a distinct answer.

"My name," he answered, returning steadily the gaze of the other, "is De Bonneval. I left my father's castle this morning; and should have been in Paris two days hence at the furthest, had my travelling experience been as great some quarter of an hour ago as it is at this present."

3*

"How mean you by that, *beau sire ?*"* inquired the captain, with no symptom of resentment in voice or manner, but a slightly perceptible banter at the boldness of Antoine's reply.

"I mean," returned our hero, without heeding the probable consequences of his words, "that had I reflected upon the chance of this road being occupied by gentlemen of your trade, I should have ridden abreast of my attendants ; whereby we had cut our way through your band, or pursued our journey over your dead bodies."

This unhesitating answer, and the tone in which it was delivered, produced an instant effect upon the circle of listeners. Some half-rose, with threatening gestures, from the lazy attitude in which, stretched upon the bank, they had been hearkening to the brief dialogue, or examining the workmanship of the weapons taken from Antoine and his attendants ; others, of a gayer mood, laughed aloud at the young man's fruitless vaunt, and turned their eyes inquiringly towards the followers for whom their young lord had just engaged such valiant things. They were seated on the opposite side of the road, with fallen countenances ; while two of the conquerors mounted guard over them with a scythe and bludgeon. The captain, however, repressed any further notice of the words just uttered : while he himself seemed rather propitiated than otherwise at the evident fearlessness displayed by his young captive.

"A forward springald, and a ready," said he half to himself, and with some approach to a smile about his compressed lips ; "and by that token, might almost be the right man, after all. Yet no," he added, with another glance at his paper, "the description varies too much for that ; and Gourville is always accurate in his accounts of men and things. The age might do ; but the stature and features—no. Yet he may know somewhat, and so put us on the right track. Hark ye, young master," he continued, raising his voice, and speaking with the same calm determination which had struck Antoine from the first :

---

* A term of high courtesy, anciently applied to knights and nobles, and retained in the language of this period on occasions of ceremony, or sometimes employed half-ironically.

"there are men of my profession"—he dwelt on this last word with a slight accent of irony—"who would have knocked thee on the head for such an answer as thine without more ado, as well as taken thy purse, which thou knowest to be safe within thy travelling-gear at this moment. Such things may serve to show thee, spite of appearances, that thou art fallen into the hands of men who are neither unthinking ruffians nor common thieves. For myself, a bold word ever finds favor with me as well as a brave stroke; the more if either be in a good cause, and in that respect I could wish thee a better. Now, mark me; answer faithfully, and to the best of thy ability, to what further questions I shall propose, and it may go more prosperously with thee than thou dost yet think. Thou camest from Auvergne; who are thy father's principal neighbors thereabout?"

Antoine paused for a moment, as his mind ran over the various possible motives that might have prompted this question. Finding none likely to involve any injury to the subjects of the inquiry, he named in succession four or five of the small seigneurs and proprietors of land in the immediate vicinity of Bonneval.

"And none of greater note? Bethink thee—stay," added the captain after a moment's pause, "let us go westward from thine own neighborhood into the Limousin. Knowest thou the castle of Turenne? Canst thou tell me whether any but the old seneschal and the few retainers have met there since the viscount has been absent in the German wars?"

Antoine was silent. He remembered to have heard that the Duc de Bouillon, elder brother of the great Turenne, and head of the family of La Tour d'Auvergne, had been paying some stealthy visits to his ancient fortress near Brives in the Limousin. These had been suspected of a seditious object; for the duke was well known as one of the most influential movers in the Fronde. Though deprived by the power of Richelieu of his hereditary principality of Sedan, he still possessed in the domain and viscounty of Turenne a feudal sway over several towns in the district, and no less than four hundred villages. The peasants

throughout this domain had been constantly practised at
their weapons; and it was reckoned that the house of
Bouillon would be able at a few days' notice to summon
some five thousand men of good service into the field.

Information had lately reached Mazarin that the armed
peasantry in the Limousin had been more regularly practised, and attending in greater numbers. The movements
of the duke himself had been partly ascertained; and notwithstanding his changes of dress and late hours, he had
been traced in several places by a vigilant spy, devotedly
pledged to the interests of the crown. This was the young
Comte de Noailles, a captain in the guard, whose family
possessions were contiguous to those of the Turenne, and
whom the cardinal had therefore selected for a secret
mission into the province, both to gain information and
secretly to counterwork the seditious movements already
on foot.

. This mission of De Noailles had become known in some
measure to Antoine; who in his more distant rides or
hunting-matches had fallen in with a cavalier, apparently
little older than himself, well mounted and armed, but with
no ostensible object for his visit to that part of the country.
He was acute, observant, inquisitive; and had bent upon
our hero a glance of some interest, as though he knew his
parentage and the loyal principles of his race. Antoine's
curiosity had been awakened by the occasional appearance
of this unknown cavalier. There was a degree of romance
and mystery attending him that tallied well with his own
disposition; and he had made inquiries of the people of
the villages through which the rider had passed, or at
the small hostelries where he had put up for the night.
Nothing could be gathered from these sources to solve the
enigma. It appeared that the stranger was of extreme
royalist sentiments, liberally supplied with money, and open-
handed even to profuseness; and that he was perpetually
making inquiries on the state of the country, the tone of
general feeling in the neighborhood, the dispositions of the
several proprietors and families of consequence, the martial
exercises of the peasantry, and similar topics. He had
castigated severely with his riding-whip mine host at a

little inn near Ussel, for expressing some sympathy in the progress of the Fronde; had drawn his rapier and kept a score of the stoutest frequenters of the said hostelry at bay when they took up the quarrel; and had flung among them a handful of broad pieces to salve some slight flesh-wounds received by the most venturesome. Finally, having gleaned all information on the subjects of his inquiries, he had taken one fine evening his powerful black palfrey, and vanished northwards, on the route for Paris.

Antoine revolved in his mind these various incidents, the latest of which had occurred only a few days before his own departure from home. Combining them with the questions now put to him, he came to the conclusion, that the ambuscade into which he had fallen was no ordinary scheme of highway robbery, but had been intended, though too late, to intercept De Noailles, and prevent the information he was carrying to the minister from being turned to account against the popular party. At all events, he felt that silence was the only course to be adopted, if he would avoid compromising interests which he had been trained to hold sacred. Silence, therefore, he sturdily maintained; and met without flinching, but without answering, the scowls of inquiry turned upon him by his captors. For some minutes there was a pause as deep among those who were collected on that lonely spot as if they had formed an inanimate groupe, designed by Salvator Rosa in one of his wildest and most savage moods, and hewn out by the hand of some rude sculptor from the rocks that lay scattered around the forest-glen.

## CHAPTER V.

### THE BARRICADES.

"A royal knavery, an exact command,—
Larded with many several sorts of reasons,
Importing Denmark's health."

*Hamlet.*

WHILE the hope of the Bonnevals is thus making uncomfortable acquaintance with the present realities of life, we
must ask the reader to go with us one step backwards, into
the month of August preceding the autumn in which our
tale begins. For Antoine, on his arrival in Paris (and to
Paris, notwithstanding appearances, we are pledged to conduct him), will find himself moving among events resulting
greatly from those which the Marquis de Sennechamps had
detailed in his letter to Auvergne. We shall proceed,
therefore, without ceremony to enter the sitting-room of the
old baron. Some little while after parting with his son,
he has proceeded to unlock a quaint ebony cabinet that
stands against the tapestried wall, and to extract the letter
aforesaid from among the documents preserved in that
repository. There are the title-deeds of several portions of
the Bonneval estate, tied up with whipcord, fishing-lines,
and other such irregular contrivances. A small packet,
secured by a twist of faded silk, contains half-a-dozen
letters that had passed between himself and Madame la
Baronne during the stately preliminaries to their union.
A few well-approved horse-medicines, and (truth compels
us to add) a charm against the evil eye, complete the in-
ventory of the cabinet. The baron then throws himself,
with a sigh inspired by the event of the morning, into an

easy-chair, or what in those days passed for such, to refresh
his memory with the despatch of his ancient friend at
court.   We are unable to present the marquis's letter verbatim to our readers, omitting only, as irrelevant to the
subject, some of that redundancy of compliment and courtly
phrase which added as much to the bulk as to the elegance
of the composition :

Paris, this 27th of August, 1648.

"Alas, my valued friend, what intelligence am I not
obliged to communicate to you!   Amid what evil days is
it our lot to exist, when the sacred authority of kings loses
its reverence among men ; its decrees disobeyed, its demands set aside, and its very threatenings disregarded!
Happy they who, called to a tranquil existence amid the
retirement of country pursuits, only hear from a distance
of the agitations, the anxieties, of hearts as loyal though
less favored than themselves!   I might quote to you our
favorite poets on this fertile theme ; but my heart is too
much oppressed with sadness, with uncertainty of the
future to which these late events are pointing, to permit
me to do more than furnish you with some brief detail of
the occurrences.

"Know, then, Monsieur, that all Paris has been in
revolt against that royal authority which had ever exercised
over it so vigilant and paternal a sway.   No sooner had
our arms been declared victorious over the hostile forces of
Spain than the blackest rebellion rose up from the midst
of us, to threaten the sacred crown just wreathed in such
shining laurels.

"In brief, a solemn *Te Deum* is proclaimed in Notre
Dame as a thanksgiving for the victory of Monsieur le
Prince at Lens.   The parliament comes in a body to assist
at the function ;—traitors! how my heart rose against them
as they stood gathered there in their long robes !   Numerous too, and with a look of determination on their plebeian
countenances such as I had never seen that class of persons
assume before.   To what are we tending?   And when
will these rebellious spirits learn that their proper attitude
is kneeling before the footstool of our ancient throne ?

Well; my consolation was to contemplate the regiment of
royal guards drawn up in double line from the Palais
Royal to the church; the sun glancing upon their polished
accoutrements.  They seemed to present a living wall of
unshaken loyalty against the treason of which that unhappy
day gave too undeniable symptoms.

"Their majesties arrive; all is in order, but the threatening looks of the commons continue; our royal mistress,
the regent, has an air constrained tranquillity, and our
ancient friend De Guitaut whispers to me his conviction
that something is at hand.  The *Te Deum* is chanted:
you know the solemn tones of that organ and the full voices
of the choir.  They seemed to add to my apprehensions,
and sounded like a burst of thanksgiving to be succeeded
by another storm.  The day too was sultry and dark, the
lowering clouds charged with thunder.  Somehow I could
not avoid recalling passages of the Abbe Cosse's last Advent discourses, which, to say the truth, had entirely
escaped my remembrance in the interval.  Ah, I recount
to you these details; but the catastrophe is at hand.

"On leaving Notre Dame, when the function was over,
her majesty passed by the spot where the Chevalier de
Comminges was posted with his division of guards, and
close to where I stood at the moment.  As he bent forward, and presented his sword on one knee, I heard her
say to him in a low voice, 'Go, Comminges; and may it
please God to assist you!'  The royal train passed; the
lieutenant remained on guard, and glancing around him on
his men, ascertained that each was in order, and standing
to his arms.  This action, though slight in itself, spread
the greatest consternation among the gentlemen of the long
robe—so valiant in their chambers of debate, so faltering
when confronted with actual power.  They saw at once
that something was on foot, and retired, or rather fled,
from the church without waiting for more.  The exempts*
advanced; but too tardily—they had not sufficiently com-
prehended the importance of seizing that knot of vipers

---

* A soldier of a rank rather above that of the mere private; and
*exempted*, as the name implies, from the duty of mounting guard,
though equally liable to other military service.

together; and the president Blancmenil was the only one
who remained in their hands. Comminges, meanwhile,
not finding the president Broussel in Notre Dame, had
pushed on to capture him in his own house; a lodging in
a narrow street looking out upon the Port Saint-Landry.
I can only give you the result as far as I myself witnessed it.

"I was returning home along the Quai des Orfevres,
musing upon the good old times when such insolence of
the parliament or the burghers would have been put down
with a strong hand, and the guilty have soon expiated
their presumption in the Bastille. Suddenly my progress
was impeded by a dense body of persons, chiefly of the
lower orders, who were emerging upon the quay from the
Marche-Neuf. They went tumultuously forward, their
numbers gathering every moment: they rent the air with
cries and imprecations. In the midst of them was seen,
moving with difficulty through the crowd, or rather along
with it, a coach, driven by a *mousquetaire* of the guard;
while one of his comrades kept his place beside him, and
menaced the populace with his drawn sword. Soldiers also
preceded and surrounded the carriage, using their utmost
endeavors, without actual violence, to keep off the increasing multitude. The hat and plume of the officer in command were seen moving along close to the door of the
vehicle; I observed his sword flash several times in the
sun, while with the flat of the blade he beat back those
who were pressing nearest. I stood close; I mounted on
a door-step as this tumultuous procession came towards me.
My anticipations were just; it was the brave Comminges
endeavoring to secure his prisoner.

"Meanwhile the rascal multitude gathered strength: a
few moments and Broussel would be torn again out of the
hands of authority. Nevertheless the brave lieutenant
pushed steadily on, making for the Rue Saint-Honore;
and the little band advanced with a cool determination and
unshaken discipline that for the present kept the disorganized rabble at bay. In that unlucky moment the coach
broke down, and further advance became impossible. The
cries were now redoubled: 'To the rescue! to the rescue!'
'Down with the soldiers; down with the tyrants who sent

4

them !' 'Rescue the father of the people, the defender of
our rights !' 'Death to the traitor Mazarin !' There was
a rush and a savage roar, and for a moment I thought
Comminges was down. But no ; he stems that angry tide
as steadily as ever : they give back again. I could scarce
contain my joy : ' *Vive*' rose to my lips ; when the scowling
glances of some unwashed mechanics who were near me,
with their greasy leathern aprons and begrimed hands,
made me sensible this was not the precise moment for any
needless display of loyalty. But what do I see ? That
consummate tactician Comminges has secured a second
coach that was passing over the Pont Neuf, has kept off
the uncleanly family of that 'father of the people' at the
sword's point, and has conveyed him safely into the fresh
vehicle. The cortege proceeds, in the midst of unheard-of
cries and tumult ; but it proceeds, and is soon under the
safeguard of the troops who were that morning ranged in
line to keep clear the Rue Saint-Honore for the passage of
their majesties.

"I afterwards learned, that with the greatest difficulty
the traitor was conveyed to Saint-Germains ; that the sedi-
tion reached its height as the rabble, with the guards and
their prisoner, were passing by the Palais Royal ; and
that menacing disloyal cries startled the court even in the
apartment of her majesty. The Marechal de la Meilleraye
is sent with two hundred soldiers to chastise the rebels ;
but such were their numbers and obstinacy, that he himself
and his brave troops would probably have fallen victims to
the popular fury had not Monseigneur the coadjutor suddenly issued from the gate of the archbishop's palace in his
rochet, and hastened to the spot. You know his credit and
influence with the populace : great, dangerously great, it
never was exerted with more salutary effect than in that
moment. I had again drawn as near to the scene of action as safety would permit. I saw the prelate from a
distance mount on the parapet of the Pont Neuf, and address the people with energy. It was a crisis in the fate
of the marechal and his troops. At first there were continued discordant cries ; at one time I thought the coadjutor would have lost his footing, and been precipitated

into the Seine. But he continued, waving his arms with vehemence, and exerting the full power of his sonorous voice. The cries sank into suppressed murmurs; at length came a deep dead silence. They are listening to him. He draws himself up to his full height, his very stature seems to increase as I trace his figure sharply cut against the sky. I like him not, that De Gondi, and mistrust him; but on this occasion he was great indeed, the very ideal of a noble and fearless energy. He descends from the parapet; he approaches the marechal, the crowd make way as he motions them with his arm. Gondi himself marches with De Meilleraye at the head of the two hundred; and almost before the insurgents have recovered from the spell of his subduing eloquence, the whole party are safe within the gates of the Palais Royal.

"Alas! this was but the second act of the drama with which yesterday evening closed upon us; and the courier departs before I have time to detail its concluding scenes. Let me endeavor to convey it to you in few words. At five this morning the parliament assembled, proceeded to deliberate, and passed a resolution insolently demanding the release of the prisoners. The burghers immediately rose again with greater violence than yesterday,. and in less than three hours' time no fewer than 100,000 men had armed themselves against the authority of our gracious sovereign. They have blockaded every principal thoroughfare, every street leading to the palace, with impenetrable barricades, formed of barrels filled with sand, piled one upon the other, firmly united by iron chains, and kept in their places by weighty fragments of masonry. I cannot give you an idea of the savage and disorganized appearance of this city, once the abode of all that was graceful, courtly, and gay. Bands of armed disorderly burghers are patrolling the open spaces, or watching jealously from behind their barricades; threatenings are on their lips, and defiance in their looks. The shops are closed; no commerce, no enjoyment, nothing is astir but open-eyed rebellion. There is a pause and a hush, as though every one were waiting for the next scene in a fearful drama. What will be the end? No one believes it will terminate here. As I write this, the report arrives that the Chancellor Seguier, carrying the royal commands to the parliament, has been stopped at the barricades; and after vainly attempting to effect a passage, torn by the mob from his *chaise a porteur* (a coach has been out of the question since last night) and forced to fly for his life into the Hotel de Luynes, where he secreted himself in a closet behind some tapestry. The chancellor of her majesty concealed like a rat behind the arras! Shades of my ancestors, repose happily that you have not witnessed times like the present! Meanwhile this audacious parliament has carried its petition to the Palais Royal: I saw them pass from my window,—traitors! a hundred and sixty magistrates, in their robes and caps of office, walking two and two. Had honest folks their will, these gentry would soon be chained two and two among the galleys at Marseilles. As it is, chains have fallen before them; and they are the only men to whom the barricades have afforded a free passage to-day. All Paris waits breathlessly to hear the result of their embassy. And waiting thus, I must close my letter.

"Send up thy son, my valued friend, and that without delay, that he may swell the number of loyal spirits in this city of ours. The sacred cause of royalty needs all its true supporters at such a crisis. I wait, then, with impatience to embrace thy Antoine, and to call myself his second father;—that youth whom I remember as a bright-eyed boy learning tales of chivalry at thy knee. A shade too serious, methought him; but that will disappear, if Paris recovers its tone from these cursed troubles.

"*Vivent* loyalty and gaity! twin-sisters are they, and never should be parted. But I sing songs with a heavy heart; remaining always, however, with devoted remembrances to Madame la Baronne, and the assurances of my most distinguished consideration to your honored self, Monsieur,

"Your constant friend
"and most humble servant,

"MARQUIS DE SENNECHAMPS."

A day later was written another despatch, herewith subjoined, and sent by a trusty hand into the neighborhood of Bordeaux to a man in the middle ranks of life, a small legal functionary, deprived by the late cardinal of an hereditary office in his native province, who had since then lived retired, and more than half-suspected of seditious principles:

Paris, August the 28th.

"Rejoice, ancient comrade! · The first act of the piece is played: a blow has been struck which will vibrate. through France, and unite with us the forces of the commons in every province. It grows, it develops, that just alliance against arbitrary power. The details will be given to you by our friend Etienne Charrier, the bearer of these few lines. Suffice it, that the tyrants have put forth their hands to touch the liberty, if not the life, of Broussel, the people's father and friend. But the people rose in their strength, and repelled the aggression. Broussel is again ours, and Blancmenil, and the rest; we have wrung them out of the hard hands of a government too paternal, forsooth, to give us back willingly such dangerous playthings: ha! the child has learned to know its strength; 'twill be hard if it submits to the rod and the lesson again. Those barricades! they afford a bright idea for the future, if this struggle between might and right shall continue, as continue it will. We are on the eve of great things, and all parties are preparing. Come thou to Paris; it is from the centre that this great movement must radiate forth. We need all thou art, and all that thou canst bring—heads, hands, purses, and sinews; none of the implements of war, moral or physical, can come amiss to us now. The struggle will open in the chambers, but it will be consummated on the field; and each true citizen must bring his quota for the good of his country, for the sacred cause of liberty,—

> 'Car contre tout esclavage
> Rien ne fault, sinon courage
> A soi-mesme d'etre fidele—
>     A soi-mesme!'

4*

Psha! thou knowest I am no quoter of verses; yet methinks I could now take the lyre of Tyrtæus, and sweep
it until my country's enemies fall before its impassioned
strains.   Rejoice with us; but above all come, and come
speedily.   Thine,

"CLAUDE SARON."

----

## CHAPTER VI.

### A YOUNG OAK ALL BUT BROKEN.

> "What hallooing and what stir is this to-day?
>   These are my mates, that make their wills their law,
>   Have some unhappy passenger in chase :
>   They love me well; yet I have much to do
>   To keep them from uncivil outrages."
> *Two Gentlemen of Verona.*

"YOUR answer, young sir," at length pursued the leader
of the gang, fixing his eyes again upon De Bonneval with
their former severity, on perceiving that our hero's silence
continued: "what say you of the chateau of Turenne?"

But Antoine was by this time convinced that it would
be the safer course for others at least, however perilous to
himself, that he should maintain an absolute reserve on
the state of affairs in the provinces.   He therefore simply
folded his arms with a look of quiet determination, and
signified in a few words that he intended to submit to no
further questioning.

"'Tis well," answered the other, without altering a
muscle of his countenance; "you have made your choice,
and you will abide by the consequences."   A movement of

much satisfaction pervaded the band, who had been listening attentively round them, at the result of the discussion.
All seemed to anticipate the instant immolation of the
daring youth who had ventured to cross the will of their
chief while so completely within his power. The more
ferocious among them were already approaching Antoine
with bent brows and threatening gestures, handling significantly the various rude and barbarous weapons which they
carried. Martin and Jacques, on their part, seeing that
matters were now likely to come to an extremity, began
with an awkward mixture of respect and alarm to remon-
strate with their young lord on the uselessness of sacri-
ficing his own life, and probably theirs, to a point of honor
which was utterly above their comprehension. The whole
group, which a few minutes before had been hushed in a
stern expectant silence, was now in movement, agitated by
various passions. On the one side was fear of death, and
a kind of surprised indignation at the cause that was bringing it about; on the other, savage exultation, fierce anger,
and thirst for blood.

Antoine alone, and the robber-chief, maintained their
calmness, and stood facing each other in the midst of the
circle.

"Silence!" broke in the latter, with a sweep of his arm,
at the same time drawing up his athletic form to its height,
and speaking in the deep full tones of command which
suited so well with his whole countenance and bearing,—
"silence, and bear back, my men; you understand naught
of this business. What!" he continued, looking round
on the savage forms that were still converging towards the
prisoner, menacing him with instant death, "would ye
sully a great cause by the shedding of needless blood, like
the ruffian bandits who will cut purses and throats for a
few poor florins in the dominions of some selfish despot?
But I speak to senseless ears," he muttered, checking
himself midway, "and the struggle for freedom hath fallen
e'en into such base peasant-hands as these!" Then abruptly changing his manner to one of the sternest command, he drew a heavy pistol from his belt; and stepping
with one firm stride between Antoine and his assailants, he

continued, with a voice slightly lowered, and spoken from
the teeth :—

"The first who draws a step nearer has parted with his
life. You know me, my men," he added, after a pause,
"that I am not given to many words; but seldom speak
without meaning what I say. Retire further back, all of
you; and you shall not be able to allege that I command
you without a reason. This youth,"—he indicated De
Bonneval with his left arm, while the right hand still
grasped the *petronel* or horse-pistol, ready for instant use,
—"has spoken frankly and boldly. Would that all on the
right side shared something of his spirit! He has refused
to answer questions that would compromise his friends.
Our prisoner he is, therefore; and that until he shall be
ransomed. Touch a hair of his head, ye senseless slaves,
and your ransom is gone. Mark you? Ay, now are ye
willing enough that he should live. There shall be a sop,
too, to stay you the while." He then turned round to
Antoine, and in the same quiet commanding tone bade
him to deliver up his purse.

As this was a demand that concerned himself only, the
young man had no hesitation in complying with it; and in
a few minutes he saw the whole of the little stock which
had been destined for the prosecution of his journey divided equitably enough by the captain among the disorderly and savage bandits with whom he seemed to be so
strangely associated. As if to show his indifference to this
part of the proceedings, the chief of the band then tied the
empty purse into a knot, and threw it carelessly among the
trees overhanging the bank on which he had been seated.
This was too much. The purse was a parting gift, had
been put into Antoine's hand by his mother almost with her
farewell kiss, and was embroidered by herself. A flush
suffused his brow as he watched that memorial of home so
contemptuously cast away by the hand of a robber; and
his firmness, which had stood proof through all the trying
scene of his capture and probable death, was moved by this
one trivial circumstance to a degree that did not escape
the notice of the captain. To the latter's glance of half-
surprised inquiry De Bonneval answered by a few words,

somewhat sullen withal, and certainly containing no entreaty—for such he would have disdained -for the restoration of his purse. None, however, was needed. The robber instantly rose from his seat, and beckoning one of his
subordinates to bring him the purse from where it was
dangling on a bough, presented it to Antoine, with a
courtly reverence that would not have disgraced any
of the most polished circles of Paris. He even slightly
raised his hat as he approached the young soldier with the
recovered purse in his hand, and said, in his full and
measured tones :

"I thought it had been, perchance, the gift of a be-
trothed; and even thus it should have met with worthier
usage. But better as it is, young man; better and holier
even than that. And shame fall on them, whatever their
politics or their creed, who would refuse to honor so righteous a feeling as you have shown. Ah," he went on,
speaking again to himself, but not withdrawing his eyes
from their fixed scrutiny of the young man's countenance,
"our country, the common mother of us all, lies bleeding
and in bonds; and some of her sons, that should put their
hands to the work of her deliverance, are more insensible
to her claims than this beardless boy to a trinket from his
mother's hand !"

In truth, the conduct exhibited by De Bonneval, from
the moment when he had fallen into the ambuscade, had
evidently won in some degree upon the captain's interest.
Upon his sympathies, we had almost said, but that this
impenetrable man seemed to possess no sympathies, or none
that he permitted to be discovered. His whole mind appeared engrossed with some absorbing object, that had still
to be attained. In those half-inward mutterings, which
contrasted so strangely with his prompt and energetic manner, he spoke of their object as one that demanded self-
devotion, and involved uncertainty, perils, perhaps death
itself. It needed no very acute guess to imagine this to
be, in fact, the advancement of the popular cause during
the impending struggle between the people and the crown.
Seemingly, the readiness with which he would, at a moment's notice, have sacrificed every thing, himself included,

for the promotion of this great cause, kept him indifferent
to the lives and liberties of others, except so far as they
might promote it, or stand in the way. Antoine had been
unable to detect, during the brief but trying interval when
his young life hung in the balance, any look or expression
from the other that might be termed compassion; and
when he rescued him single-handed, it seemed rather as if
urged by a stern sense of right that he had done so than
from any emotion of the heart. Like Roderic Dhu, with
his mortal enemy within the grasp of his power, he had
appeared to scan him with scrutinizing eye until satisfied
that the young man really deserved the respect which one
fearless heart is ever ready to yield to another,

> "And that stern joy that warriors feel
> In foemen worthy of their steel.''

Meanwhile the brief autumn day, that had been declining during these events, now drew rapidly to its close.
The tempered but cloudless sun of a fair October evening
peered horizontally through the stems of the forest, glanced
on the polished beech-trees, or the more rugged trunks of
the gnarled oaks and pines, with a ruddy light, illuminating the wild countenances and picturesque though savage
attire of the group below; then flashed upward, and sank
behind the distant hills of Poitou that bounded the undu-
lating woodland. The captain promptly announced that it
was time to arrange for the ransom of their prisoner, and
to repair to their place for bivouac for the night. Drawing
some writing-materials from a pouch at his side, he signified
to Antoine, in his own brief emphatic manner, that the
young man should reseat himself on the bank, and indite a
letter to his father at Bonneval. As this, however, was a
performance of which the state of our hero's sword-arm
rendered him incapable, the robber-chief himself assumed
the task; and Antoine was surprised to observe, that
although in the existing state of education in France the
penmanship of many even among the nobles was discredita-
ble enough, this man acquitted himself of his undertaking
with an ease and readiness which might have been envied
by many proficients in clerkly skill. In a bold running

hand, which bore the impress of the determination, and also of the degree of refinement, forming the character of the writer, the freebooter had soon achieved a dozen lines, in which the old baron was informed of his son's mishap, and recommended, as he valued the latter's personal safety, to send, within the space of four days next ensuing, the sum of two hundred pistoles by some safe hand, and deposit them within the hollow of an oak celebrated for its antiquity, in an unfrequented forest-valley about a league from the spot in which they were assembled.

"Every one hereabouts will know Le Chene Chauve," he remarked; "nor will it be the first time that nature has lent it as a banking-office to creditors whom the injustice of their fellow-men has forced to levy dues somewhat more peremptorily than in better times. See, fellows," he added, turning to Martin and Jacques, whom their rude sentries had in the meanwhile collared and led nearer to him,— "see that the request in this letter be promptly attended to, or it will fare the worse with your young master. Go yourselves to the spot; ye know the way, partly at least, and the rest can be learnt from the first peasant who meets you. Beware of bringing any other with you, or of whispering the purpose of your coming. Deal fairly with us, and you will depart unharmed, and maybe find a silver crown or two by the oak to pay your journey home. But attempt any treachery"—his brow contracted again, and his voice deepened as he spoke—"and there will be a brace of bullets apiece for your special benefit ere ye reach the tree. Other eyes than those of the squirrels will be upon you the moment you enter the forest. Now listen, as you tender your safety. When you return hitherward with the ransom, journey silently, as men who know themselves under surveillance; you are then in *our* territory. *We* are the regents,"—and a stern smile curled his lip,— "we are the Mazarins and *intendants* of this district. Remember, we need no *bourreau du cardinal*\*—no Laffemas;

---

\*Le Sieur Laffemas, intendant of Burgundy under the ministry of Richelieu, was known by this odious name, which he seems to have abundantly merited by the zeal and cruelty with which he executed the will of the uncompromising minister upon his political enemies.

we can perform the office indifferently well for ourselves.
Go straight to the oak; look neither to the right hand nor
to the left.   Deposit the bag containing this cavalier's
ransom in the hollow of the tree; whistle thrice distinctly,
and with a pause between.   Wait until your whistle is
thrice answered; then depart as you came, and look not
behind you.   And once again, I say, be exact, and beware; or your lives are not worth one of these withered
leaves beneath your feet."                .

So saying, he signed to his followers to release Jacques
and Martin, and restore to them their horses. This last
order was executed with some half-suppressed grumbling
on the part of the rapacious freebooters, who seemed to
reason that as all was fish which came into their net, so
nothing was too valueless to be retained within its meshes.
But their leader was not a man to be questioned in his
commands.   A minute investigation, therefore, took place
of the holsters on the saddle-bows, and of the wallets fastened *en croupe;* and this was followed by a scrupulous ap-
propriation of their entire contents.   The proceeding was
unobserved by the captain, who was then addressing a few
words to Antoine; though it deepened the rueful expression of countenance worn by the two proposed ambassadors
to the chateau: and then their travel-soiled and jaded
roadsters were again pronounced ready for mounting.   His
faithful attendants now cast a wistful look towards their
young master, as though they would fain have said somewhat on this constrained parting; but Antoine deeming
it more prudent to abstain from further words, contented
himself with waving his hand, bidding them make good
speed on their journey, and assure his father that he had
escaped with a slight bruise, and was in honorable keeping.

Glad enough to find themselves once more at liberty,
the two worthy retainers mounted nimbly into their saddles,
saluted their young lord with unabated respect, and then,
striking spurs into their horses' flanks, departed at a round
trot along the road by which they had arrived at this unwelcome place.   Antoine, now alone in the hands of his
enemies, watched their departure with a painful interest,
while the twilight deepened around them; and when they

had turned the angle of the projecting crag, and were hidden from view, it seemed to him for a moment as if hope had departed with the presence of the faithful men who would willingly have laid down their lives to preserve his own. He stood for a moment gazing after them through the darkness—counting, half-unconsciously, the sharp sounds of their hoof-strokes upon the rocky road, until they became undistinguishable in the distance. Then better thoughts came to his aid; and signing himself with the holy sign, he commended his safety, in a brief act of prayer, to the court of heaven, and turned with calm resolution to encounter whatever new vicissitudes might await him on this eventful evening.

## CHAPTER VII.

### AN ENTERTAINMENT AL FRESCO.

"They bid that lorn unlook'd-for guest
  To feel at home, and share their gruel ;
Nor he, good sooth, needs twice be press'd,
  But steps at once to meat and fuel—
Quite ready, on their couch of heather,
To keep out hunger and cold weather."
*La Fontaine's Fables.*

THE envoys to Bonneval being fairly started, and out of sight, the captain of the band gathered his men together, and placing Antoine securely in the midst, immediately struck up the western bank of the deep lane in which they had hitherto been holding parley. The robbers moved in as much order as the nature of the ground they traversed would permit, maintaining always a careful watch upon

5

their prisoner. This became the more expedient, as the
deepening gloom of the autumnal twilight was now increased by the shade of the forest through which they were
forcing their way; while the overhanging boughs, and the
tangled brushwood growing unchecked between the massy
stems of timber, rendered a very orderly progress next to
impossible, and every now and then presented a tempting
opportunity for some effort to escape. That such an attempt would have been utterly desperate, was obvious
enough ; for, unarmed, and ignorant of the bypaths of a
wood which to him was untried ground, while it seemed to
be a familiar haunt with his captors, Antoine could have
escaped only by miracle from being either shot down or re-
captured on the spot. Yet an impression of determined
resolution on the part of the young man had been produced
by all his demeanor hitherto, and the freebooters evidently
considered such an enterprise by no means out of the question. Constant and jealous, therefore, were the glances
bestowed upon him by the fierce eyes around, as he
marched calmly and silently in the midst of the band;
whilst those behind, or immediately beside him, kept their
rude fire-arms ready for instant use.

Antoine had never for a moment wavered in his purpose
of freeing himself at all hazards from the hands of the
robbers. At one time he had entertained a vague hope
that they might be induced to set him at liberty without
ransom, or at least upon his *parole*. His capture had
evidently, so far as their leader was concerned, been the
result of an error. He was not the person for whom the
ambuscade had been planted ; though this circumstance
did not prevent the inferior actors in the drama from
availing themselves of the good fortune which had thrown
another traveller in their way. The vigilant despatch
with which the young De Noailles had executed his retreat
from the Limousin had frustrated the good intentions of
the Frondeurs in his regard. He had already returned to
Paris, a successful and honored spy, and had given in to
Mazarin an accurate report of what he had seen and heard
of the movements of Bouillon and his dependents. The
springe, that had been set after the bird was flown, had

therefore only succeeded in snaring poor Antoine; who
thus incidentally, and without his own volition, became
early in his career a sufferer for the royal cause.

The hope, however, entertained by our hero, of being
freely set at liberty when the mistake of his captors had
become apparent, vanished from the moment when he found
himself compelled to choose between his freedom (or perhaps, as it had seemed probable, his life) and a revelation
which he had felt it dishonorable to make at any cost.
Had a doubt remained as to the captain's intentions regarding him, they would have been solved by the after-proceed-
ings resorted to for obtaining his ransom. And thence-
forward our hero made a settled resolution patiently to
watch for any opportunity that might be afforded either
to daring or skill to obtain that liberation by his own exertions which he had ceased to expect from the good-will
of others.

For rather more than half an hour the party wound their
way through the thickly-grown forest-tract; availing
themselves here and there of the narrow glades that opened
in the direction of their journey, formed by the fall of
some veteran monarch of the grove, or rendered practicable by the passage of the deer through the underwood.
The autumn moon had risen; but so dense was the leafy
screen extended overhead, that a few uncertain beams
alone struggled through, silvering patches of the leaves,
casting a weird light at intervals upon the gnarled stems,
and rather serving to show quaint shadows and broken
effects of moonlight on their path than to aid in the prosecution of the march itself. The robbers, however, though
occasionally at fault when the obstacles to their progress
were more than usually impenetrable, or when the trunk
of one huge tree so much resembled another in the darkness as to confuse their accustomed land-marks through
the forest, seemed sufficiently sure of their route to pursue
it without much deviation. A gruff expression of content-
ment from one or two of the band soon announced, as the
party emerged upon a little turfy spot clear of trees, though
partly overhung by a giant oak, that they had now reached
the scene of their bivouac.

Instantly the band dispersed, to make preparations for
passing the night.   Antoine remained on one side, closely
guarded by two of the number ; and threw himself exhausted on the short turf of the greensward, on which
the unbroken moonlight was showering calmly down.   A
hard day's riding, the excitemet of his surprise and subse-
quent capture, and the unwilling march that had closed
the evening, all disposed him to forget his cares and anxieties in sleep.   But the pain of his swollen arm, and the
cravings of hunger, which had been unsated, except by a
hasty traveller's repast at Montlucon, combined to keep
him still watchful; and thus he lay stretched on the natural
carpet of the forest, supporting himself on his unwounded
elbow, and moodily, though at times somewhat drowsily,
contemplating the scene before him.
     It was one in which Rembrandt or Caravaggio would
have taken delight.   The robbers, appearing and vanishing in their search through the surrounding thickets
for dry fuel, glanced momentarily, like so many spectres,
into the quiet moonlight, and were lost again ; but soon, a
heap of wood having been collected in the midst of the
open space, and a spark struck from the flints of their fire-
arms, there arose a bright tongue of flame that leapt and
played towards the overhanging branches of the oak,
startled the birds from their neighboring roosts, and lit
up in strong relief the wild and savage forms that were
busily engaged in feeding the fire.   Their features, seamed
and distorted by the habitual dominion of all the fierce
lawless passions of our nature, derived a more haggard and
repulsive aspect from the brands over which they were
bending; while the matted locks, grisly beards, and dark
fiery eyes, displayed by the group as they spread their
limbs to catch the increasing warmth, rendered it no difficult matter for fancy to transform them into avenging
demons, employed in the awful ministries of torment which
religion assigns to them in the regions of despair.   A cloud
of smoke volleyed upward into the clear heavens above ;
burning sparks ascended in a thousand fantastic eddies
from the crackling brands; and, to complete the wildness
of the scene, a large bat, disturbed from its torpor in the

old oak by this rude intrusion into its haunts, wheeled
upon noiseless leathern wings, circling around the heads
of the freebooters, uttering at intervals a shrill and foreboding cry.

The captain meanwhile, apart from the rest, was leaning, with his arms folded, against the tree that presided
over the little open space; lost in one of those thoughtful abstracted moods that seemed habitual to him when
nothing immediately called forth his energy into action.
There are countenances which, whatever their particular
turn of feature, impress the beholder with the conviction
that a history belongs to their possessors. In some cases
it is so because the lines of care, or passion, or wasting
thought, are legibly imprinted there, and remain as an
index of many sufferings experienced, many vicissitudes
endured, perhaps illusions dispelled, and obstacles van-
quished. In others, again, it is because an evident change
has been superinduced upon the original character, and the
struggle for self-mastery had not been made without leaving traces of the exertion. The face which De Bonneval
was now studying, not in idle curiosity, but with a desire
to read in it what might tend to his own liberation, was of
a kind that announced no common past history. To judge
from the aspect of that man, as he stood there in an attitude of complete repose, gazing into the cheerful fire, but
with thoughts far away from every thing that met the
eye, an accurate observer would have pronounced that two
separate elements dwelt side by side within him, and influenced his actions in turn. The thin lips and close-set
mouth told of prompt decision, of energy in act; while
they also implied that his anger might be as fierce and
destructive as his resolution was unflinching. Yet the
marble tranquillity of the mouth, so far as could be discovered through the bushy beard that shrouded it, seemed
to indicate a share of calm habitual thought, if it excluded
the idea of any tenderness of disposition. There was
nothing sensual in either feature or expression, but much
to tell of a proud self-command, of the supremacy of the
intellect and will over aught that was animal or base in his
nature, and of a spirit that dwelt too much in solitude to

5*

become enslaved to the more ordinary corruptions of mankind. Nor did the eye and brow belie the expression of
these lower features. Fiery, yet self-restrained, and
touched at times with a dark melancholy, without either
losing their vigilance or abdicating their authoritative look,
those keen deep-set orbs gazed into the fire-light, as though
they read in the casual fantastic forms of the leaping
tongues of flame somewhat to recall memories of things
past but unforgotten. Whether the visions that occupied
him were calling up feelings of remorse, or whether they
ministered to more grateful remembrances, it would have
been impossible for any observer to determine. Antoine,
as he reclined opposite to him, was riveted, he scarce knew
why, by the whole bearing of the man, and felt a kind of
longing to know more of the possessor of one of the most
striking countenances on which he had ever looked.

Bent on far different thoughts and cares, his band were
busily employed in preparations for their rude supper.
The materials for this were not very far off; for the spot
on which they were now assembled seemed to be an accustomed *rendezvous* during the intervals that chequered
their life of lawless adventure. Two of their number soon
emerged from the thick underwood, laden with the good
things of this life, which they had drawn from some secure
receptacle. Goodly portions of venison, together with
several hares and a string of wild-fowl, were followed by a
couple of those large leathern cases, containing either beer
or the sour wine of the country, which, from their resemblance to huge overgrown boots, where known in the dia-
lect of England by the name of *black-jacks*. Some man-
chets of coarse bread,—stale enough, it is true, and rather
mouldy from the nature of their forest-larder,—flanked by
a round cheese, which some nefarious transaction had
transferred from the cellar of a neighboring farm to the
commissariat department of the freebooters, completed the
good cheer. This they now spread upon the turf with
rough exultation ; and prepared to cook the meat after a
hasty fashion, with those ruffian jests bandied from one to
the other which it was evident a little spark would soon
kindle into fiercer quarrel. The want of carving-knives

was no embarrassment to their proceedings; for they readily plucked from their girdles the long sharp weapons that had known far less harmless employment. Forks, by a still more primitive arrangement, were supplied by those begrimed and sinewy hands, which an hour ago were so nearly being imbrued in De Bonneval's heart's blood.

The rude preparations for supper being now completed, the captain motioned to Antoine to take his seat beside himself at what might be called the head of the table. Much as our hero disliked the company, and critical as was his present situation, this was an intimation to which he was unable to pretend any decided repugnance. Hunger is a great leveller; and if, as the poet assures us, "wisdom comes with lack of food," it now brought to De Bonneval a well-considered and most philosophical conclusion. "These men," he reasoned with himself, "are villains and cut-throats,—conceded; yet it is a benevolent act, under the circumstances, to invite me to supper. Moreover, that broiled venison smells most invitingly. Venison? but then it belongs to the king: let me see. Ah, well; it is the fitter repast for an officer of his majesty's guard. Still, am I not sharing in their disloyal plunder? Nay, I am only eating it here in the king's forests, instead of in the guard-room of the Palais Royal. But I shall be sitting side by side with men who are Frondeurs and republicans,—I, Antoine de Bonneval,— and sharing their salt? True; but if you were benighted in the desert, and a Bedouin should ask you into his tent, you would not be binding yourself to his notions of *meum* and *tuum;* nor professing faith in Mahomet by supping with his disciple. Shall I really, though, be pledging myself to nothing? Nothing whatever; you will only pledge your hosts in a cup of reasonably good *vin du pays* out of one of those black-jacks. But I never ate and drank save with true loyal hearts? But then you have had nothing at all since Montlucon. Ah, I do not need to be reminded of that circumstance. *Allons, donc!*"

Thus, in the controversy between pride and hunger, the physical argument gradually prevailed over the intellectual, and had the last word. Antoine, therefore, all things

considered, obeyed the summons to the robbers' evening
meal with a better grace than he would have been altogether willing to own at Bonneval; and bringing the forks
which nature had furnished ready to his hands, and receiving again his hunting-knife as a loan during supper-time,
he played his part manfully in the demolition of the coarse
loaves and the broiled slices of his majesty's venison.

------

## CHAPTER VIII.

### THE CAPTAIN'S STORY.

"I do not know the man I should avoid
So soon as that spare Cassius. He reads much ;
He is a great observer, and he looks
Quite through the deeds of men ; he loves no plays,
As thou dost, Antony ; he hears no music ;
Seldom he smiles ; and smiles in such a sort,
As if he mock'd himself, and scorn'd his spirit,
That could be mov'd to smile at any thing."
*Julius Cæsar.*

THE man whom we have endeavored to present to our
readers, and who, occupying no better position than that
of a felon, seemed to possess qualities so much above his
present trade, had interested young De Bonneval to an extent which the latter might have been slow to acknowledge.
There were, in truth, points of real sympathy between the
two ; nor was this fact inconsistent with the no less broad
and obvious differences which separated their positions,

lines of conduct, social and political opinions. Both were
of unshaken personal courage ; and this itself is a quality
that tends instinctively to bind the sympathies of man to
man. Antoine had displayed a cool intrepidity which had
won him the respect, and in some degree the regard, of
the robber-chief. Dauntless himself, and of a kind of
bravery that can remain unshaken apart from the mere
animal impulse which so often goes by that name,—can
stand unblenching and wait the approach of danger or
death as well as rush blindly on to meet it,—he knew how
to estimate the same quality in another. Moreover, each
of these men, now become so strangely acquainted, recognized in the other an elevation of soul which, trained
though it had been in different schools and manifested in
very opposite directions, found something of an intelligible
response within his own breast.

When, therefore, their rude meal was at length concluded, and the captain, drawing somewhat apart, invited
Antoine to share the cloak which he had spread for himself
at a little distance from the fire, it was not without interest
that the young man anticipated some intercourse with his
companion of a more unreserved nature than the circumstances of the day had hitherto permitted.

And amply were those expectations fulfilled. While
the remainder of the band were paying their final homage
to the mighty skins of liquor, or settling themselves in
various attitudes around the fire to sleep out the night,
the robber-chief and De Bonneval engaged in earnest conversation upon many successive topics of interest. Each
found in the mind of the other an answering chord ; not
always in direct harmony with his own, but not therefore
the less suggestive, nor ministering less to the pleasantness
of their dialogue. As in music, so is it likewise in discourse. There are in the first, not only recurring octaves,
that ring out to each other immediately in clear response,
but also deflections, regular intervals, and subtle gradations
from key to key, and approaches to actual discord, that
mingle and intertwine to perfect the melody in its progress.
So too, in the intercourse of one thoughtful mind with its
fellow, it is as much the evolving of differences, salient

but not irreconcilable, demanding energy of argument to
sustain and breadth and reach of thought to test them,
that make the charm of free discourse, as thoughts that
actually chime together, and conclusions which have been
reached by a similar process of reason.

Such was the converse with which these two whiled away
the early hours of the night in their forest bivouac.  They
differed in the texture of their minds almost as much as
in the antecedents of their lives ; probably, indeed, as an
effect of those antecedents.  The younger of the two had
been as much in the way of books as his companion, though
his excursions into literature had not been very regularly
conducted.  His imagination, as we have seen, was the
department in his mind most richly stored ; in the severer
powers of reasoning he was less fully armed.  On the other
hand, his companion had been reading the great book of
human nature while Antoine was in the cradle; and had
read it, too, in the school of personal trial.  Men, and their
motives, and the tendency of those acts to which their
characters give birth, he knew ; not from the axioms of
philosophers or the description of poets, but from having,
in the conflict of life, been brought into collision with them
all, and made wise by the stern experience they had imparted.  The habit of his mind was to divest things of the
unreality, and therefore the illusions, in which they were
clothed at first view : a tendency clean opposite to that of
De Bonneval, who had been accustomed to throw around
them the halo of his own fancy.  In the one there was an
ideal love of goodness and beauty, a fond hope of finding
things as they ought to be; while the other broke in with
a sadness not unmixed with severity, and exposed them as
they *were*.  The one was capable of bursts of ardent indignation, when forced to acknowledge any where the existence of a meanness or a wrong.  His more experienced
companion regarded them fixedly ; with a hatred not less
intense, but less impassioned, and tinged with a calm
indignant sarcasm, as having known the counterpart of
such things ere now.

They touched on poetry and romance : and here Antoine
went off at score, for he was on his own ground; while the

other listened as to a reverie, which he could follow in
idea, though it made small part of his mental composition.
They touched on political science; and now it was the turn
of the robber-chief to unfold to the young loyalist such
views and principles as would have made the family circle
at Bonneval lift up their hands in horror. He spoke of the
limits which well-ordered states assigned to the power of
their rulers; of the due balance of authority, the claims of
the governed, the sacredness of those rights which each
man possesses as the citizen of a civilized community. He
showed, less from history than from the nature of things
and experience, how any aggression upon this lawful order
was as short-sighted as it was oppressive and unjust; how,
unless re-adjusted, it involved the decay and moral death
of the constitution thus invaded. He warmed into real
eloquence, he threw aside all his sternness and cold reserve,
while describing in outline that ideal state or polity which
philosophers have dreamed in their studies, and for which
oppressed indignant men have groaned under the weight
of their shackles. *They* bear the rule in it on whom their
Creator has bestowed the elements of command. Its aristocracy is that of nature and of gifts. The patents of their
nobility date from the first great deed of self-sacrifice they
have done for the public weal. Its armies are led by the
energetic and the truly brave : its laws are framed and ad-
ministered by the experience of men calm of thought, large
of heart. Its monarch must be one equal to his post : let
him fall short of his great vocation, he is thrust aside to
make room for his better. The best man, each in his place;
with the head to conceive, the heart to feel, the hand to
execute, what shall be for the welfare of the body. Do all
these qualities unite in one? that one rises to the throne
by a natural law; and sits there, maintained by the universal will. Are they found separately? they are distributed
into departments of government. Have they become viti-
ated in those who once possessed them? then are such
diseased members severed from the body they would corrupt; ay, though they be in the highest dignity and place.
The power, the life, resides in the community : it submits
to government for its own good. Woe, then, to those who

would tamper with the edge of this sword of authority—
who would wield it for their selfish ends! They are
traitors to the first power from which they drew it, and will
meet a traitor's doom.

"You speak, young sir," continued he, "as you have
been trained; but the words have not yet come from your
own intelligence.  You are at present the victim of a tradition.  The divine right of kings?  So said they in England; it was the jargon there, as here, of crowned heads
and court flatterers; and see what comes of it.  The prince
who of all others held to that antiquated dogma, and for
haughty absolutism might have been a disciple of Richelieu
himself, is now contending at a disadvantage with his parliament.  And that parliament; it holds to a great idea,
and has substantive right on its side.  The fanaticism, the
personal absurdities, of its members, have not wholly ob-
scured the truth they have distorted.  These men now
stand as representing, not the towns and provinces of England merely, but the middle rank and subject classes of all
countries alike.  They are successfully resisting, not an
individual, but the principle of oppression.  In their stern
energetic assertion of the rights of the governed they teach
a wider lesson than is at present foreseen : and we on this
side the Channel shall merit the name and the lot of bond-
slaves for ever, if we know not how to tread the way their
bold footprints are tracking out for us."

At length our hero, on the basis of unreserved communication now established between them, felt an uncon-
trollable wish to enlarge his experience of life by the
changes and chances that must have attended such an unusual character as the one before him.  He therefore pre-
ferred a request to the robber that he would relate to him
as much of his personal history as he might be disposed to
unfold to a stranger.  The other smiled his peculiar and
measured smile at this request, while he scanned the countenance of his young companion.  Then, after a pause,
gazing for a moment or two abstractedly into the fire, he
seemed struck by the idea that the narrative might serve
some purpose worth promoting; and without further hesitation he thus began :

"I was born, some eight-and-thirty years ago, close to the little town of Vaison, between three and four leagues from Orange. My father had inherited a small estate, with an old mansion of proportionate size, within two arrow-flights from the walls of the town; and there he resided, with a few farm-servants, who assisted him in tilling his slender patrimony. I believe the name of our family had been known for more than a century and a half in that part of France. They had not worn golden circlets on their brows, as yours have, *beau sire;* but they had rooted themselves firmly in the soil as sturdy and not unprosperous *roturiers;* and had borne arms too, not without credit, in more than one of the wars of their country. This last was the characteristic of my forefathers on which I used to dwell with pleasure. From the time when I first began to think, and listen to the conversation of the more experienced, I never remember feeling an emotion of envy towards my fellow-men for the mere circumstance of rank, or descent from a high ancestry. Power, I always fancied, I would willingly grasp; and station and wealth would have been not unwelcome as ministers to power. But the external trappings of name and family, on which I saw the hearts of others set with self-gratulation if they possessed, and with longing if they lacked them, never drew my eyes after their glitter even as a boy. It was the pre-eminence of a personal sway over my fellow-men that formed my day-dreams: for I had dreamed too," added the robber, his lips again curling into a peculiar smile, while his eyes steadily rested on the more imaginative cast of his companion's features.

"Well," he resumed, "as I grew up, this feeling of contempt for the outward distinctions between man and man increased within me, and settled into a kind of principle. I trampled upon the ordinary pride of mortals with a greater, perhaps a guiltier pride. But I am not speaking of guilt, and it is a point you may think it strange in me to touch upon. I loved to go and meditate among the crumbling ruins of old Roman construction, which had remained from the days of their rule in the land, when Vaison had been a Roman station. Often have I sat, with

6

Livy or Cicero in my hand, under the broken arches of
what was once their theatre, shaded by the rude massive
stone-work from the heat of our Provençal sun.   My
thoughts would then wander from the page before me to
other times and modes of feeling, which both the scene
itself and my studies suggested.   I seemed carried back
to days when country was a sacred name; when patriotism
lived, not in the declamations of fine writing, but in the
daily actions and ready sacrifice of living energetic men.
My young heart would leap and burn as I framed to myself, out of such studies, the characters of Cato and Brutus
and Cincinnatus and others of their stamp,—men staid and
awful, yet not unkindly withal; severe when brought into
contact with corruption and tyranny, unhesitating in their
chastisement of these, but in themselves warm-hearted,
simple, self-denying.   They became the heroes of an idolatry within me that was not fantastic nor transitory, because it was storing up in my deepest will the resolution
to imitate them.   With all the devotion of a young heart
I breathed, or rather meditated, a vow to become their
living disciple in this seventeenth century.

"The severity in which my mind was now cast, and
loved to dwell, was nurtured moreover by the solitude of
my early life.   My father, besides his farm, held a small
hereditary office in Vaison, which called him almost every
day into the town.   I scarcely saw him, except in the
evenings.   As he was rather proud of my early devotion
to study, and anxious that I should ultimately follow the
career of an advocate, he left me free from all manual
labor, and my time was at my own disposal.   My mother
had died a few days after giving me birth.   It may be
that this circumstance has greatly aided in determining
the character of my mind and life.   I have heard other
men speak of the softening influence which a mother's
presence, and the memory of a mother's words and looks,
have exercised upon them.   They have said how the well-
remembered tones of her voice, how her parting kiss, her
last request, her prayer for her child, remained upon them
undyingly, and came back fresh upon them in middle life,
with all their old power intensified by distance or the sepa-

ration of the grave. These things I have never known. I receive them by report, and try at times to create them by imagining what they must be to men of other, happier experiences than mine.

"I am wandering from my story. Motherless and companionless, I grew on from year to year; making no friends, uncertain whether I should ever find an opening to realize my day-dreams in act. It was not that I lived in a world of my own, or a mere creation of fancy; I was living, in heart and sympathy, in the realities of a past time. The beings with whom I held viewless converse had been men of actual flesh and blood, and had performed most determined tangible acts in their day. Their stern voices had been raised in the senate and the public assembly in the sacred cause of that ancient liberty to which they had devoted themselves; their strong hands had grasped the dagger when *that* was the only appeal that would reach the heart of selfish tyranny. And though their dust had long since filled the funeral urn, their deeds, their examples, their burning words, remained stamped upon those pages of history, which had become to me not a romance, but something more like a book of devotion.

"Yes, devotion! You may smile, or think the expression a profane one; but it expresses me truly. The love and heart-worship I gave to that antique virtue, that glorious and heroic stern simplicity, approached more nearly to a religion than any thing I had yet known. It might be paganism; but it preserved me at least from many of the soils of earth. Was it not better than vice? than the monstrous profanations of a religion, in which men profess to believe while their lives dishonor and blacken it in the sight of their fellows?"

The narrator paused a few moments. His eyes flashed, his lips were close set, his chest heaving, as he raised his clenched hand with a stern gesture. Cato the censor, if his awful shade had glided in to make the third in their discourse, would have glared approval on his modern disciple. "All this while," he resumed, "I was greatly unacquainted with the actual condition of things around me alike in Church and State. That there were corruptions

and oppressions, meanness, selfish cruelty, I heard in general. The name of Richelieu was whispered as a name of
terror when the report of any fresh arbitrary act reached
the provinces. But he was a power distant, and, on the
whole, moving in another sphere. That he should crush
the influence of the great nobility in Paris, and excite at
once the hatred and fear of the governor of Provence, in
no way immediately affected the few persons from whom
alone I learned any political tidings. The time had not
yet come when he should descend lower in the scale of
men in France, and aim his great blow at the vested interests of the middle rank.

"But it came, that moment: it came, and roused me
from the contemplation of the past, from which I had been
shaping my own future course. It came suddenly too, or
suddenly to me, who had not been watching the steps that
ushered it in. One evening my father returned from his
*bureau* in Vaison, a ruined man. He held, as I have said,
one of those minor offices of finance which had been so
commonly purchased throughout the country at an earlier
day, and passed from father to son. I had always had
suspicions of the lawfulness of these tenures, and of their
effect upon the public good. But I had lived, a growing
inexperienced boy, among my few books, and still more
among my own untested thoughts. I had not observed
the real working of that long-established system ; and it
was not till later that I became fully alive to its inherent
and baneful corruptions. I should have honored that
uncompromising man," continued the freebooter, rising
again into greater energy of manner, "who struck at it
one annihilating blow, but that his aim was merely to
level a thousand minor abuses in order to erect one more
gigantic and more crushing in their room. It was the
kingly power he sought to exalt; and he exalted it by
reducing to penury a countless number of families, who for
generations had enjoyed those offices as their own, by free
purchase, at least, if not by abstract right. It was the
kingly power, therefore, against which I vowed on that
my first entrance upon manhood to turn whatever energies
or influence I might possess. One short hour had seen

the courier enter Vaison and deliver the cardinal's *lettres-de-cachet*, which abolished my father's employment and sent him to his home a bankrupt. That one hour had also transferred me from the state of a studious dreamer into a *man:* determined to cope with the adversities of life, feeling within myself the powers and the force of will to do so. I closed my books; and rose up to meet the necessities of my position, and begin life in earnest."

## CHAPTER IX.

### CONCLUSION OF THE CAPTAIN'S STORY.

> "With that he shook the gather'd heath,
> And spread his plaid upon the wreath:
> And the brave foemen, side by side,
> Lay peaceful down, like brothers tried
> And slept until the dawning beam
> Purpled the mountain and the stream."
> *The Lady of the Lake.*

"Among those," continued the robber, "who, in my limited acquaintance with men, personified to me the very principle of tyrannical oppression, a deputy in our provincial *chambre des comptes*, or exchequer, stood foremost. Guillaume de Boisguerin was this man's name: he resided chiefly in Vaison, where he, too, had a bureau for one of those famed government-offices which were the bane of all the public administrations of that day. Corrupt they were in their very principle; and I have already confessed with shame that my father was a partaker in the evil system. Yet in administering even a corruption, the difference between man and man is extreme. De Boisguerin

6*

displayed in his method of conducting the office he held an
insatiable rapacity, and a disregard of the rights of others
where it was safe to disregard them, which, joined to his
undisguised contempt for all classes and persons undistinguished by gentle blood, completed the character of a
selfish petty despot in a responsible position.  From the
first, my spirit had been stirred against this mean hard-
hearted man.  I referred his personal vices, perhaps
unduly, to those of the system he represented ; and the
constant sight of him, and the accounts we received almost
daily of his oppressions and injustice, tended to rivet in me
those opinions which you, young sir, as a trained loyalist,
have doubtless already denounced in your mind as republican or revolutionary.  Be it so.  I think even you would
have thought less kindly of the absolute authority of monarch or minister if it tended to the exaltation of such a man
as De Boisguerin.

"For exalted he became.  My father, as I have said,
was ruined by Richelieu's harrying, at one fell swoop, that
nest of petty offices which my forefathers, and those of so
many other families of the middle rank, had feathered for
themselves in bygone generations.  It was a great blow,
and came more suddenly upon himself than upon others
who had foreseen the administrative reforms projected by
the minister.  My father had already reached the decline
of life, and was unable to stand the shock.  His health
failed ; it became evident to me that, even should he live,
he would be incapable of turning to any other employment
for the scanty remainder of his days.

"I do not know that there had ever been much real
sympathy between the old man and myself.  I had lived
in a solitary world of my own thoughts, shut up and centred in an ideal past ; and the day-dreams of ancient
republican virtue, which had almost become my life, found
no more response in my father's mind than in that of
others who surrounded me.  He was of a placid *insouciant* turn, content to enjoy his office and let the world
go by him.  Thus there had always been a gulf between
us, which severed me from any true converse ; though it
hindered neither our kindliness. nor my determination to

perform all filial duties towards him. But when our misfortunes made it plain that henceforward the burden of maintaining the struggle of life for both was to fall upon me alone, I was the more roused to meet the necessity of instant and strenuous exertion.

My dislike to Monsieur de Boisguerin was extreme. There was reason enough in it, certainly; but even my favorite philosophers, and still more, I know, your priests, would have bid me conquer the feeling, so far as it amounted to real antipathy. I had not the self-control to do so, nor even to avoid showing what I felt. He had observed this on some occasions when I had been thrown into his society. His pride revolted at the notion of a mere youth, and of a rank inferior to his own, exhibiting towards him the independence of manner (to say the least) which I on my part took no pains to conceal; he repaid my scorn to the full, and was enabled, from his position, to show towards me all the haughty superciliousness of a superior. Thus there was established between us, on personal grounds, a settled enmity; and it was fed by the antagonism of our political views, which the troubles of the times could not allow to slumber. Soon, too soon both for him and for me, came a third topic of hatred; and then mere silent animosity blazed out into vengeance. It changed the whole of my life—and ended his.

"A certain mystery had always hung over the cause of my father's loss of his office. Others, it is true, had been deprived nearly at the same time, or were daily expecting it. Still, his case was by no means the most flagrant in our province, and yet it was among the first dealt with. He was not of an observant character; yet he said once and again that some one must have performed an unfriendly office towards him with the cardinal, or with some of his creatures. Upon my mind the conviction flashed irresistibly, and almost from the first, that an enemy had done this. Who was that enemy? Something told me that I need not hesitate in assigning the authorship of this injury to the man who had excited so deep an antipathy within me. It was De Boisguerin, whispered an inward conviction. I waited only for proof. My mind

was fully determined to exact from him a signal retribution
in case of my more than suspicion proving correct.

"The proof came soon enough; and was sufficient, at
least to a mind so predisposed to receive it.   And yet I do
not know," continued the robber musingly, and scarcely
so much addressing his companion as soliloquising to himself,—"I do not know, even after the lapse of so many
years, that there was any essential failure in the evidence.
There was De Boisguerin's undisguised hatred of myself;
there were his threats of taming my pride, reported to me
by more than one mutual acquaintance; then the news
that a temporary commissioner had been appointed by
Richelieu to manage my father's *bureau* and receive its
emoluments; the unguarded words of insolent triumph that
broke from this man when the citizens of Vaison expressed
their surprise at so unexpected a turn, and their sympathy
with my father; and then, when the *lettre-de-cachet* arrived
in the town, and all were in expectation to know who was
the unwelcome stranger, the execration that broke from
the bystanders, and the look, not of surprise, but of gratified malice, that lighted up his sinister countenance, as the
town-clerk read out the name of this same enemy, this
detested, and now triumphant, Boisguerin !

"No! he brought the vengeance down upon himself; it
was less my hand than his own bad deeds that sent him to
his account."

The outlaw paused in his narrative.   His thoughts were
plainly absorbed in that past time of which he spoke; he
was not giving a connected account of it, but recalling
inwardly the events themselves.   De Bonneval saw at a
glance the catastrophe that remained untold.   There was
a fierceness flashing from the eyes of the narrator which
indicated that nothing less than a desperate deed had
avenged his wrongs upon the aggressor.   He did not,
however, seem disposed to resume his history, but remained
with looks riveted with more than usual intentness upon
the now decaying fire.   The lips, strongly compressed, fur-
rowed his gaunt countenance with lines of moody thought;
and as Antoine sat gazing on him through the deepening
gloom, a thrill came over the young man's heart.   It was

not fear; and something in the manner of the bandit, and the course of his story, forbade its being utter repugnance: it was a mingling of many emotions. There, within a few feet of him, sat an acknowledged murderer; and his words had come sounding through the darkness, and falling upon the ear of one young and inexperienced, and at that moment absolutely in his power. Antoine, as we have said, though brave, was imaginative; his spirits, therefore, were not shielded by that passive insensible courage which results mainly from a want of the imaginative power. His quick perception was readily open to emotions of horror, while he was intrepid in actual danger. But to his excited fancy at that moment it seemed as though the spirits of, perchance, numerous victims, disembodied by the hand of that ruthless man, were gathering round them in the gloom, the ghastly witnesses to his confession, the awful commentary upon that tale of guilt!

After a while, the other continued, but in a hollower tone:

"A fugitive, with blood upon my hand, and—what in those days was worse than blood—the crime of having assailed the person of an *intendant* appointed by the minister, I passed at once, with no word of farewell, from my father's roof, from all the accustomed homes of my thoughts, beyond the pale of society. I was an outlaw, who had done with the sympathies of his kind. I was a Cain: I was thenceforth to be an Ismael. What was the future to me? a blank to the heart; and to the hand an uncertain existence—homeless, perilous, criminal. Such has it become. So far De Boisguerin has been avenged."

There was another long pause. The head of the robber sank, and a slight tremulousness was perceptible in his voice, which hitherto had maintained its stern deliberate calm. Antoine felt little disposed to speak. No other sound broke the stillness which each was filling with thoughts dark as the night itself, except the heavy breathing of some of the band, stretched in deep sleep round the expiring embers, or the occasional bark of a fox, or mournful hoot of the owl, from the recesses of the forest.

"Enough!" at length exclaimed the outlaw, rising

vigorously to his feet, and raking together a few embers
with the point of his sheathed weapon, "and more than
enough, *beau sire!* You have heard more of my autobiography than I usually impart to my acquaintances. My
friends, I would have said; but that a bandit," and he gave
a ghastly smile, "has no friends. Well, other chapters
of the history remain untold; some that would thrill you
to hear; some that might, perchance, awake a kindlier
interest for a man who believes himself more sinned against
than sinning. It grows late, and we must snatch some
few hours of sleep; for to-morrow I carry you betimes to
another of our *rendezvous* at some distance, to wait for
your ransom, before I move up nearer to Paris.

"And do you know," he went on, slowly pacing up and
down before the fire, which he had raised again to a light
flame, and then stopping before Antoine and leaning upon
his sword—"can you guess, why it is that I have taken
such an unaccountable interest in you, and have so opened
my heart to you, young man? Listen; I will tell you,
that you may not"—he smiled again his peculiar, half-
reluctant smile—"report the Frondeurs of the provinces
to be a set of romantic gentlemen, fanciful in their sympathies, and given to sudden friendships, like your fantastic
Parisian gallants. It is not without a reason," said he
after a pause, and fixing upon De Bonneval a penetrating
but softened look, "that I have been thus drawn to you.
The sight of you carries me back, not to my own youth,
for nothing could well be more unlike; but to another,
long since laid in the earth, whose fate was once partly
interwoven with mine. Hear it in a few words; and then
no more.

"An enterprise, somewhat like that which has placed
you in my hands, had not been so successful. I was
wounded and taken. After a slow recovery, which I owed
to a vigorous constitution, and in no wise to the care of the
prison authorities, I was brought up for examination. Had
I been recognized as my father's son, my life had been for-
feit without reprieve. As it was, the present case was
clear; and I scorned defence or entreaty. I was condemned for ten years to the galleys at Marseilles. They

chained me to a vile malefactor, from whom my whole
soul recoiled with loathing. We worked together, hand
to hand, for seven long months. It was a living death to
me, such as I had read of as practised by the barbarity of
ancient times. This punishment was almost beyond my
endurance. It sometimes lashed me into fury, sometimes
drove me to the brink of despair. I marvel why, under
such intolerable torment of mind, I never lifted my hand
against this hound in the leash, or against myself.

"But I was at length released. The sirocco had been
blowing strongly during the summer-heats. Whether it
came charged with the breath of pestilence from Africa,
or whether it merely enervated frames that had been
already worn down and predisposed to disease, I know not.
Constant and degrading toil," and the robber drew himself up to his height, while his eyes flashed fire at the
remembrance,—"toil, and under the severity of the task-
master, unwholesome food, scant clothing, and, more than
all, the wearing action of the mind on the body, for those
at least who have *minds*, or can retain them amid such
bondage : these are all excellent tamers of the strength
of man ! They tame even the ferocious brute to whom I
was chained. He sickened, and refused to labor. They
deemed him obstinate, and applied the lash. He howled,
and gnashed his teeth ; but his day of work was over. He
was released just in time to die. I heard but a part either
of his agony or of his blasphemies ; for the sirocco had
struck me also, and I was borne senseless to the hospital.
On coming to myself, I lay stretched in the last stage of
feebleness on a pallet, miserable and squalid, surrounded
with dying wretches like myself. That was a sight that
might have taken out of most men's breasts the pride of
life or the zest of pleasure. A crowd of gaunt emaciated
forms, neglected, hateful, and hating all around them,
revealed by the sickly uncertain light of a large building,
that was half-hospital, half-dungeon. They tossed in the
restless thirst of fever, or cursed and raved in madness, and
gnawed their chains, or lay still in hopeless prostration, or
were already stiffening in death. A loathsome spectacle !
and the atmosphere through which you viewed it was

charged with the fœtid taint of disease. I grow tedious while I recount to you a time which is so deeply burnt into my own memory. Carry it in yours, young sir; and tell some of your dainty cavaliers at court—tell those in whose hands now lies unused the power to alleviate suffering, and lead crime to repentance by treating the criminal as a brother-man—as a cure for their sloth and selfish enjoyment, tell them, I say, to go and meditate in such a scene as the galley-hospital at Marseilles.

"We were neglected by all—by all but one. Yes, there was *one* form that moved amid the horrors of that lazar-house like an angel of light; watched and followed by the weary eyes of the suffering felons whom he tended, for whom he seemed willing to spend and to be spent. I speak not of him as he is known throughout France; as the founder of institutions, the councillor of princes. With these things I have little to do; and yet, wide-spread must be his name if it has reached even *my* secluded haunts, and my lawless path in life. But I speak of him as he was to me and my fellow-sufferers, criminal and outcast though we were, in that gaol-hospital. Do you know the man I mean? There is but one name at this moment in France that corresponds to the outline I have given."

"Vincent de Paul!" readily answered De Bonneval, to whom the reputation of this holy priest was familiar, as it was to all who had any knowledge of what was passing either at court or in the provinces.

"Ay, Vincent de Paul," rejoined the other; "the friend alike of high and low, the honest, fearless reprover of pride, the minister of mercy to all who any way needed it; the one unselfish god-like man, whose sole example might atone for a thousand of those ordinary deeds of wrong—"

He paused abruptly. Many emotions were struggling within him; he turned slowly on his heel, and strode into the darkness beyond the reach of the fire-light. Antoine watched him intently as he returned, and paced to and fro with his arms folded and his broad hat drawn over his brow, taking no further notice of the young man. It was De Bonneval's first initiation into the fearful contest that may be waging between the whisperings of good and the

passions of evil within the human bosom. He had read of
such things, and had even written themes upon remorse,
and a sonnet to the power of conscience, which had been
highly approved by the old abbe his tutor. He now witnessed the conflict passing before his eyes, and upon no
ordinary battle-ground. If there had been elements in
the robber's character to attract him from the first, that
attraction was not diminished now that it became evident
that he could respond, not only to the naturally noble and
generous, but even to the self-devoted heroism of Christian
mercy. Antoine sat by the flickering fire-light, his head
resting on his hand. He was musing upon what he had
just heard, and speculating on the man who had given him
such strange passages from his history. Was the example
of Vincent, and the memory of his deeds of charity, the
one bright spot in the outlaw's mind; or did these ally
themselves with other memories of which he had not
spoken? Again; how was it possible for a man such as
this, who, with all his resoluteness, could be so deeply
moved at the casual remembrance of a saintly character, to
pursue his present life of crime, perhaps of blood? What
wayward inconsistencies must be fellow-lodgers within that
breast! how must he be racked with the memory of having,
even once, come across a soul that breathed around it the
atmosphere of heaven; while he was himself under no pal-
liation of ignorance to shelter him, but open-eyed and
prominently, treading the highway to hell! His story, too,
was incomplete, and contained matter for speculation, if
De Bonneval would fill it up satisfactorily. It had never
been explained why the robber had so taken to him; and
Antoine, after revolving it in his mind, could only conclude
that his own features or manner had casually reminded his
captor of some younger fellow-sufferer at Marseilles, whose
illness, perhaps whose death, had been cheered and allevi-
ated by Vincent's works of mercy.

Turning again from this, our hero began to forecast how
far he could hope to use the softened mood of the robber
to effect his own liberation. It might be, he thought, that
the interest he had awakened in this stern man's breast
might induce him to set him free, at least on *parole*, before

7

the ransom arrived. It might at least procure him an
easier pardon, if he should himself make the attempt, and
fail. But no; a second glance at the tall resolute form
stalking before him to and fro dispelled both these illusions.
He felt that, whatever might be the present good-will of
the outlaw, it would never lead him beyond his first determination, and would at once disappear before any attempt
to evade his power. And this, though it did not alter De
Bonneval's firm purpose of adventuring it, realized to him
the extent of the hazard he was preparing to run.

Meanwhile, finding that no further communication was
to be expected from the robber, and overcome with weariness, the young man performed his brief devotions, and
then prepared himself for sleep. His silent companion
waved to him a courteous good-night; and the last thing
of which Antoine was conscious, as with half-closed eyelids
he looked out upon the wild scene before him, was the
motionless form of the other, dimly shown by the light
of the fire as he stood near it with folded arms, and
features composed into their usual cast of grave and stern
deliberation.

---

## CHAPTER X.

### THE ESCAPE.

"Fly, good Fleance; fly, fly, fly!"   *Macbeth.*

DAWN broke on the following morning gray and chill; and
the light that found its way slowly to that secluded spot in
the forest-lands of the Bourbonnais where our hero is now
lying, awoke him from an uneasy slumber. He opened
his eyes; and, with the cautious watchfulness which he
had assumed in order to effect his purpose of escape,
glanced stealthily around him. His two immediate guards
had sunk to a deep sleep, one on either side of him; and
the relaxation of the sinewy limbs, from which their wea-

pons were drooping, and the strong heaving of their mus-
cular chests, showed that *they* at least could oppose no
obstacle to his design.   But their place was supplied by a
vigilant robber seated opposite, who, with his matchlock
across his knee, had stationed himself by the decaying fire,
and was raking together a few of the wood-embers to keep
off the chill of sunrise.   It was evident that the slightest
movement on Antoine's part would at once rouse this man's
attention.   He therefore directed one more searching
glance round the little space in which the band had been
assembled on the preceding night, and then closed his eyes
again, and lay ruminating on what he had observed, and
maturing his plan.

Of the remaining robbers, three or four lay stretched
around the fire in various attitudes of slumber.   With the
habitual precaution of men of their class, they had kept
their weapons closely within their folded arms; and the
few who were provided with muskets had carefully preserved the locks from the night-dew by covering them
with the lappets of their jerkins.   The captain was nowhere
visible, though De Bonneval could not doubt that he would
be found within immediate call.   One man, therefore,
alone remained at that moment to cope with; and as a
bright idea flashed into our hero's mind, he felt that no
time was to be lost in executing it.   Let but one or two
more of the robbers awake, as they would when the light
strengthened, and his chance was gone.

Antoine was not of a character very apt to calculate
dangers, or to pause upon a resolution once formed.   He
now, acting a part for the first time in his life, pretended
to awake as naturally and quietly as he could, and went
through a little pantomime of yawning, rubbing his eyes,
and shivering with cold.   With a gesture, intended to imply that he was unwilling to disturb the rest, he motioned
his request to the savage seated by the embers of the fire
to be allowed to draw near and warm his limbs.   A surly
nod was the only answer; while, as Antoine approached,
the other significantly examined the lock of his weapon,
as though to warn him of instant death should he attempt
either violence or escape.   Antoine took little notice of

this sinister movement. His whole attention was at that moment fixed on a small glade or opening in the thicket, not immediately behind the man, but at an angle over his shoulder, and seeming to afford a more practicable outlet to the scene of the bivouac than the difficult passage by which they had entered it the night before. On the probability of that opening really leading out of the forest depended Antoine's entire chance of freedom ; and now, thought he, with a mental ejaculation of prayer,—now for one bold attempt to gain it!

He approached the fire gently, and with a submission of manner which cost him something to assume ; and crouched down immediately opposite the sentinel, taking care neither to sit nor kneel, which would have rendered it more difficult to gain his feet in a moment. The fire had burnt so low, and they were both so near its margin, that he was separated from the robber by a space of less than four feet. All Antoine's energies were now strung up to this one effort. In less than a minute he would be either dead or free. Commending internally his soul to God, he smiled with as much careless good-humor as he could simulate in the face of the robber, whose eyes remained fixed half-suspiciously upon his countenance. Then Antoine, making as though he were rubbing his hands together over the decaying brands, filled them both with the fine white ashes that were crumbling hot from the fire ; and instantly, without trepidation of nerve, by a sudden movement of his arms, and with steady aim, flung both handfuls straight into the robber's eyes, shot like an arrow down the opening glades, and vanished in full flight.

Completely blinded, and bewildered by this unexpected manoeuvre, the bandit started to his feet. His first impulse was to grasp at his musket ; but this had fallen among the embers, where the fuse igniting, sent the report of the discharged piece reverberating through the forest. Antoine, as he fled with all the speed of foot he could command, heard the loud cries of pain and rage vented by his adversary, mingled with the rough importunate questions of his now-awakened comrades. Hope strengthened in his mind, and nerved him to yet greater exertion, as he remembered that the robber could give no exact description of the course the fugitive had taken, and that the band must necessarily be dispersed in their pursuit. Moreover, the forest-alley which he had chosen, unlike the tangled passage of their late march, was well defined and practicable enough, and wound among the stately trunks of the forest-trees in a manner favorable to his escape; enabling him to dodge his pursuers, even should they succeed in nearing him, while it rendered a fair shot at him hardly to be gained. Two matchlocks had been discharged during the first moments of the surprise, the balls of which he could hear whizzing their way into the branches close beside him; and it was evident from the rapid sound of strong footsteps, and from the deep oaths, muttered with a growl such as might have come from the aboriginal bears of the forest, that several pursuers were on his trail. Still, the paucity of fire-arms among the band, of which three had already been discharged without mischief, and the young man's own confidence in his tried wind and speed of foot, presented altogether no contemptible chances in his favor.

With the speed of the wind, therefore, Antoine pressed on, resolved to sell his life dearly, should it come to the worst; but resolved in the first place to escape, and with good hope of doing so. He knew not how far he had fled, nor in such a crisis could he measure time. The track he followed now plunged down an abrupt descent into the bed of a sluggish rivulet just before it widened into an impracticable morass; then the fugitive, extricating himself from the slime and tangled weeds, toiled up the opposite bank by aid of the projecting roots of the pine and ash trees that overhung it. Then, without a moment's breathing-time, he was off again at full speed through the windings of the deep forest; but not before the report of a gun, and the swan-shot that came pattering among the broad leaves like a sudden hail-storm, announced to him that he had been in view of his pursuers, and indebted for his life to their imperfect aim.

But gradually, from the confused sounds of the trampling behind him, one footstep seemed to Antoine's sense to
7*

detach itself, and grow more and more isolated and distinct.  It was leaving the others behind ; its rapid echoes
came faster and faster upon his ear.  Another hundred
yards, and the feeling came over him, spite of himself,
that it was gaining upon him.  Moreover, he scarce knew
why,—there was no ascertainable reason,—yet the conviction shot through him that this powerful yet elastic
tread belonged to no other than the robber-chief.  Onward
it came, with the speed and precision of a fate, and louder
still, and nearer.  De Bonneval, whose strength was becoming exhausted, though his pace had not yet slackened,
was beginning to calculate whether it would be better to
turn sharply into the thicket whenever the first favorable
spot presented itself, and thus either elude his pursuer, or
die desperately in his covert like a stag at bay.  But no.
If, indeed, that tread behind him (for the others were by
this time at a safe distance),—if that remorseless and
unvarying yet most active footstep, whose sound was beginning to strike a vague feeling of despondency into his
heart, did indeed belong to the man who commanded his
inferior mates, then Antoine had seen enough of his keen
observation to despair of thus eluding his pursuit.  To
press on, therefore, was his sole resource ; and then, at the
last gasp, to turn and face his foe.  And scarcely had he
sprung forward with renewed ardor in his flight, when he
found himself rapidly descending a narrow sloping lane,
overarched with thickly interlaced branches, and debouch-
ing out of the forest upon the more westerly of the two
main roads leading northward towards Bourges.

The afternoon of the preceding day he had been travelling with his attendants along the right-hand or eastern
of these two roads ; and now, having in the meantime,
partly led by his captors, partly fleeing from them, traversed the intervening forest-tract, he had emerged unexpectedly upon the other.

A horseman was riding with his face towards Paris,
some ten or twelve yards in the rear of that spot where
the foot-lane opened on to the road, when Antoine at full
speed shot down upon the highway.  The horse started and
plunged at this sudden apparition ; but his rider sat him

firmly, and, spurring up to our hero, asked him what was the matter, that he was travelling at such a mad pace, and with such wild disordered looks. The young man was by this time utterly spent, and could hardly gasp out a few words to reply, that he was pursued by robbers, and fleeing for his life. Then, looking in the face of his friendly questioner, and seeing from his broad unlooped hat and long plain riding-cloak that he was a priest, he was just able to add, as he sank on his knees before him, and smote his breast:

"Father, my time is come: I confess all my sins, known and unknown, with a hearty sorrow. Give me absolution, and then ride on and save yourself; for the enemy is at hand."

And, as if to give effect to his words, at that moment there was a crackling of the boughs that interlaced across the mouth of the steep footpath leading from the forest, and the athletic form of the captain of freebooters darted down into the road and confronted them. In his hand he held a long sharp two-edged poniard, with which he advanced towards Antoine without a moment's hesitation.

"Hold!" exclaimed the priest, with a voice and manner as authoritative as his own; "thou shalt do no murder!"

Antoine was too well acquainted with the character of the man thus addressed, to suppose the exhortation would have any effect upon him. His own strength was gone; and, being incapable of any exertion to defend himself, he prepared for instant death. He was still kneeling before the priest, with his hands crossed on his bosom; and had closed his eyes, not in fear, but expecting at once the words of absolution and the stroke of the poniard, and composing his soul for its passage into eternity.

But none of these things came; and on raising his eyes once more he was astonished to see the priest and the robber looking silently at each other, and totally regardless of him.

Sick and faint with his struggle for life or death, De Bonneval leaned half-swooning against the bank, and wiped with a feeble hand the clammy perspiration from his brow. The revulsion by which, after his desperate race.

and its all but fatal ending, he had been plucked back from
the icy grasp of death, and seemed to have at least a respite
afforded to him, was well-nigh too much for a frame that
had lately undergone such various trials. His brain swam
round, his head sank upon the twisted root of a tree that
crowned the bank ; and there he remained for some minutes, a scarcely conscious spectator of a scene that was in
itself sufficiently remarkable.

The aged priest, after the momentary surprise of seeing
a second figure dart from the wood, had met the robber's
eye with a glance of recognition.; and then, bending on
him a look in which there was more of sorrow than of
sternness,—though he seemed also to possesss a power over
the other before which that fierce man could not but bow,—
he at length spoke. His voice was deep and full, yet
there mingled in it also a winning sweetness; and the
authority with which he spoke harmonized completely with
the evident humility and self-forgetfulness that marked his
whole demeanor.

"Claude. my son ! or can I still call you by that name?
on what unholy errand are you now bent ? Speak—have
you forgotten the past ? or do you hold in your memory
the sultry toil, the heavy shackles on the quay at Marseilles, and the promises spoken to him who caused the
sick man to be unfettered, and nursed him as his own
child ?"

"I have forgotten nothing, father," answered the bandit, in a tone so deferential and a brow so clouded with
self-reproach, that Antoine, though at that moment an
unobservant witness, might well have doubted whether he
was indeed the person whose prompt ond stern decision had
so impressed him ; "nothing have I forgotten of all *that*
past. Would that I could either have blotted out those
words from my remembrance, or lived to fulfil them truly !
But what would you of me ? Father," he exclaimed with
sudden emotion, and throwing himself in his turn at the
feet of the old man—"you, to whom I owe the preservation
of a life—nay, more than the mere worthless life itself:
you who reclaimed me once, and have at least prevented
my relapse into crime from being the pit of infamy it might

else have been,—command me; your wish is law. This
young man—you ask his life? it is too small a boon.
Accept it for those hours of consolation, of returning hope,
which have remained to me in my darkest times, as the
one bright ray in my existence. I had destined him to
vengeance; but he is yours."

He had already sheathed his poniard; and now, recovering somewhat of his usual manner, he stepped gravely
to the bank, and, taking Antoine's hand with an air that
almost approached to friendliness, led him towards the
priest. The latter had in the meantime dismounted, and
tied his horse to a tree. He met Antoine half-way, em-
braced him with a voice and manner of the most tender
interest, exhorted him to return thanks to the Father of
mercies for his unlooked-for preservation from death; and
then, leading him to his horse, undid a small wallet which
he carried at his saddle-bow, and insisted on the young
man's swallowing some portion of a restorative cordial, and
recruiting his strength with the simple fare that formed
the provision for his journey. At a sign from him the
robber-chief also drew near; and the two then walked
apart some few paces upon the road, leaving Antoine to his
own reflections.

These were of a very mixed character. He was too
much alive to religious impulses to allow him, as soon as
his strength returned, to neglect that part of the old man's
exhortation which charged him to make an act of thanksgiving for his escape. This having been done simply and
fervently, he next turned to the consideration of his present
prospects. Would the robber, who had abstained from
taking his life at the intercession of this unexpected advocate, restore to him also his liberty? Would he have
sufficient influence over the rest of the band on their arrival,
sufficient control over the first moments of their fury and
revenge, to secure even his life? Then, how was he now
to prosecute his journey? The idea of a lieutenant of the
guard entering Paris travel-soiled and footsore was sufficient to call back some little blood to his cheek from the
deadly pallor of his swoon. Yet the poor roan was still
in durance, and miles off, on the other side of the belt of

forest. Lastly, he thought of the ransom, and the two
hundred pistoles that were to be deposited in the Chene
Chauve; and felt alternately glad and sorry, at the very
imperfect and (by this time) untrue bulletin which Martin
and Jacques would soon be giving of his fate on their
arrival at Bonneval.

Meanwhile the rest of the band did not appear.   Either
they had given up the chase to their leader, as more capable of prosecuting it with success, or, what was fully as
probable, had taken advantage of his absence to engage in
some other enterprise more nefarious than he would have
sanctioned.   And so it was that De Bonneval, now
recruited, and once more fit for action or travel, had leisure
during nearly a quarter of an hour to watch the figures of
the two men, both such recent and unexpected acquaintances, as they paced slowly at a little distance upon the
forest-road, across which the risen sun was now slanting
his beams in unclouded splendor.

It was a singular contrast that was afforded by the
appearance and demeanor of those two, as their dialogue
proceeded.   The elder, tall and still vigorous, though his
looks denoted that he had already exceeded his seventieth
year, strode slowly forward with that deliberate firm step
to which we attach a character of decision, as far as character is marked by the gait and gestures of men.   His
action, too, simple and energetic, showed the earnestness
with which he was enforcing his wishes upon the other,
and the mastery which his mind had acquired over that
of his lawless companion.   The robber, on the other hand,
walked by his side with a step as firm as his own, but a
manner subdued by the moral power of the aged priest.
His head was bent, and his looks cast on the ground.   At
times they paused in their walk, and the elder would lay
his hand upon the freebooter's arm, with a look of almost
paternal affection in his mild gray eyes, or point upwards
to heaven.   Antoine felt well assured that much more than
his own fate and prospects was being discussed between
them in their prolonged conference.

At length it seemed to be concluded.   Vincent de
Paul,—for it was he who had thus providentially saved our

hero's life,—ceased speaking. He stayed yet a moment opposite to the freebooter, gazed fixedly into his countenance, and then slowly, and with a mien so simple yet so majestic that young De Bonneval could have believed he saw an apostle before him, the priest folded the robber in his arms. He seemed to whisper some parting words in his ear as his head rested upon the shoulder of that stern man, whose frame shook with emotion in the embrace of the other. In another moment the robber-captain had bent upon one keee, and kissed reverently the hand of Vincent, who rapidly made over him the sign of benediction, and then approached the spot where Antoine was standing. The freebooter remained motionless in the midst of the road with arms folded, his eyes still following the form of the venerable priest, who now, in a few kind words, but with that indescribable authority which seemed to reside rather in the mind than the outward manner of the old man, insisted upon Antoine's mounting his horse. Gathering the folds of his riding-cloak about him, he strode on a few paces before the animal, looking back at times, and encouraging the reluctant young officer to keep his steed (which, in truth, was none of the best) on the stretch of an active walking-pace. Thus they proceeded a few hundred yards, until they reached a small eminence from which the road slanted downward, so that a dozen steps more would have hidden the scene of Antoine's late deliverance from sight. Then Vincent turned; and, motioning his companion to precede him, looked back upon the outlaw, who still remained gazing after him. Raising his hand, he once more made towards him the sign of the cross. It was responded to by a deep reverence on the part of the other; and then the latter began slowly, and, as it seemed, dejectedly, to re-ascend the hidden path that led him back to the rendezvous of his band in the depths of the forest.

## CHAPTER XI.

### AN HOUR AMONG THE GUARD.

"Sir, here is newly come to court Laertes : believe me, an absolute gentleman, full of most excellent differences, of very soft
society, and great showing ; indeed, to speak feelingly of him, he
is the card or calendar of gentry." *Hamlet.*

"You are late at court, friend," said Louis de Montauban,
a lieutenant in the guard, junior to all but Antoine, on the
morning after our hero had presented himself at the Palais
Royal. The two young officers were sauntering up and
down the pavement before the quarters of the guard in the
left wing of the palace. "That unlucky capture," he proceeded, "has deprived you of some stirring scenes that
have been passing here while you were getting your wrist
pounded with a cudgel, or lying in doleful captivity on
the forest-leaves, in custody of two valiant ploughmen.
Nay, nay," continued the heedless young soldier, laughing, and passing his arm within that of De Bonneval, whose
blood began to mount into his cheeks : "I was but in jest ;
we know all about it, you remember. Has not that solemn
apothecary, Du Clos, just pronounced that, with all his
strengthening cataplasms, you will scarce wield your rapier
for another week to come ? Doubtless you fought like a
lion rampant against that pack of marauding wolves, or
with the desperate valor"—he rattled on, as his natural
turn for satire again got the upper hand—"with the chivalrous daring, I say, that made the grave knight, in the
Spanish romance that so delights Marsillac, do battle with
the windmill ! Don't be angry, now : I only meant that
had you been here, you would have seen sport. Why, you

might have been in time for the barricades! No, I forget, time trips along at such a pace in this good city of ours; *that* was all but two months before the disgrace of poor Delisle made the vacancy that summoned you from your paternal nest. But, *faute de mieux*, you would have had a kind of farce or interlude after the melodrama of Broussel's affair—that pompous little Abbe de la Riviere, fretting and storming because some side-wind of court intrigue was wafting the red hat away from his expectant brow. He a cardinal! it would be too excellent a jest ever to come to pass, I fear. And then the persevering way in which he worked upon his master, the Duke, to take up this mighty cause; and to see him trotting in his *soutane* between the Luxembourg and this place, the moment the court had returned from St. Germain's, while we were all laughing in our sleeve (and some of us pretty openly) at the little man, knowing his toil was all in vain:—and then the offended pride of Monsieur at the disappointment of his favorite little abbe, and the dignity and moderation of our royal mistress—it was as good as any comedy.

"Then, sir, the scene changes," continued Louis, suiting the action to the word, "and things grow more serious. The Duke studiously absents himself from court; a play is represented at the Palais Royal, at which all the world, or all that is not Orleanist, is present. Monsieur has departed meanwhile to St. Germain's to visit Madame; and at the Luxembourg they have their entertainments to themselves, and keep a court of their own. Long faces are seen at our theatricals; all the gaity and grace of M. le Prince, all the witty trifling of his *petit maîtres** cannot cheer up some of the old political stagers: that grave absurd Le Tellier looks as if he never meant to enjoy himself again. Things grow still worse; it is buzzed about that the Dukes of Mercoeur and Beaufort have offered themselves to the service of Monsieur; others of less note flocking there also. Our whole regiment is kept under arms, and the

* The knot of young nobles attached to the person of Conde were so called, because, like the *Importants* before the commencement of the Regency, they arrogated to themselves an undue degree of weight in the political questions of the day.

8

guards are doubled at every post. Strange speeches are
in all men's mouths; statists begin to hint uncomfortably
at such a possible thing as civil war, and—hark! as I am
alive, there is the first tap of the drum, while the guard
turns out: and see, the porters are pulling away at the
great bolts and chains of the palace-gate. Who can be
coming? O, the fatigues of military service!" cried the
gay young lieutenant, throwing himself into an attitude,
with a mock sentimental air, as he advanced with a galliard
step to take his post in front of the gentlemen of the guard,
who were forming hastily into line under the inspection of
their veteran captain, the Comte de Tremes.

Louis de Montauban was a young man of good family
in Gascony, who on the strength of a short year's acquaintance with the great world of Paris, and a seniority over
Antoine of some eighteen months of age, and of nearly
half that time in the guard, had undertaken the office of
*cicerone* to our hero on his launch into life. His Mentor we
could scarcely call him, without doing injustice to the
character of the Grecian sage; for any thing less steadying,
or, to say truth, less improving, than the influence of young
Louis over his companions, could hardly be imagined.
Gifted with a certain readiness of speech and vivacity,
which, united with no common assurance, might pass
current for wit, he sustained that character in many a trial
of repartee with men who were by far his superiors in all
true mental endowments. His sarcasm was piercing, and
rankled in the breasts of those against whom it was launched;
for it was no less cold than keen, and evidently unlit by
any spark of good-feeling or *bonhomie*. He rather liked
Antoine, as far as he had seen him, and as far as he liked
any one: that is, he found in him a mixture of originality
and of simplicity which it amused him to draw out; and
at the same time discerned that he was both talented and
impressible, and therefore a promising pupil in that great
school, the world, into which he determined to initiate him.
It was already obvious, that, since he chose to take this
trouble, he was a person likely to exert no slight influence
on the character of our hero.

Antoine, whose disabled arm exempted him for the

present from any duties as guardsman, watched from a distance the movement taking place among his comrades, and the arrival to which they were preparing to do military honors.   A few moments after the beat of the drums had called them to stand under arms, every man of that small picked body was motionless in his place.   It would have been a study for the physiognomist to pass along the rank that stood drawn up there, and read the countenances presented to him in succession.   For richness of dress, for the completeness of their equipments, and the habitual ease and familiarity with which they handled their arms and performed their evolutions, each soldier might seem a mere repetition of his fellow.   But in all that lay beyond that outward uniformity, there was a world of difference between man and man.   This guardsman had served under Conde five years ago at Rocroi, and again at Nordlingen.   It was at the former engagement he received the wound that scars his embrowned cheek, and gives a fiercer twinkle to his determined eye; while it obtained for him the honor of his present promotion.   His counterpart, standing next to him, an equally good specimen of the manly soldier, began life as a peaceable burgher, was unsuccessful, found himself a ruined and childless widower, and was enrolled on the recommendation of Vincent de Paul in the honorable corps in which he now serves.   The third is of Huguenot extraction: his father had been among those whose disturbances were allayed by the edict of Nantes.   He has been excused, and that too, by Vincent's intercession, from marching to Mass with the rest of the corps, and he religiously keeps in his pocket a small ill-printed copy of Clement Marot's metrical version of the Psalms.   But *his* day is coming also; a fever-fit will lay him low some eight or ten months hence; and while he finds the need in that hour of some more efficacious spiritual remedy than metrical psalms, the tender care of the Sisters of Charity and Vincent's own frequent visits will open out a better channel for his religious instincts, and lead him safely into the Church.

· The great gates of the Palais Royal yielded to the efforts of the lackeys who were pulling at them with all their

might, and turned, though somewhat unwieldy, and "grating
harsh thunder," on their hinges.   Running footmen appeared in the portal, ushering into the courtyard the
leading horses of a coach-and-six.   Both men and horses
moved at the long swinging trot, to which they were
trained, and, crossing the paved court with no little clatter,
drew up before the inner portal that led immediately to the
reception apartments of the regent.   The guard, recognising
in the rich liveries of green velvet the attendants of
Mazarin, presented arms to the occupants of the coach from
the moment when that cumbrous vehicle first made its
appearance.   But when the door was opened by the
attendants who crowded around it, the first who planted
his foot upon the heavy iron step and alighted, was Gas-
ton, Duke of Orleans.*

Instantly the beat of the drum changed, and the swords
and halberds were lowered to a still more respectful salute
than had been intended for the minister.

Orleans having descended from the coach, immediately
stopped, and with an air of good-natured courtesy gave his
arm to the cardinal, who, placing his jewelled hand lightly
on the duke's richly embroidered sleeve, accepted the
proferred assistance with many expressions of respect, and
they ascended the stairs together, the duke still retaining
his precedence.   There was, however, a third person still
to alight ; and one for whom Orleans, looking over his
shoulder with a careless smile, waited a moment on the
stairs.   This was the Abbe de la Riviere ; a man who,
without talents or weight of character, had succeeded in
persuading his weak and fickle patron that his society was
necessary to his lighter hours, and that the honor of the
Duke himself was in a manner pledged to advance the
interests of a man whom he had once fairly taken by the
hand.   With the usual obstinacy, therefore, of a narrow
mind, and the recklessness of a proud one, Orleans had for

*Madame de Motteville gives a special account of this visit, the po-
litical importance of which consisted in its being the first decided
step to an adjustment of the rivalries existing between the Palais-
Royal and the Luxembourg, which had been threatening to compli-
cate the civil war with additional incidents.

some time identified his own credit and influence at court
with the promotion of his favorite abbe to the cardinalate.
Thus it was, that a person, very insignificant in himself,
now stood in a position of importance through the mutual
jealousies of those above him ; and on the success or failure
of his own designs seemed to depend a coalition which
could alone preserve France from the curse of civil war.

On the present occasion, it must be confessed, the abbe
had done signal good service in effecting at least a temporary reconciliation between Orleans and the Queen.   He
had long been on the side of peace, and anxious to stand
well with the cardinal-minister.   He had, in consequence,
incurred the ill-will of those among the high nobility whose
policy had been to render the duke's palace of the Luxembourg the head-quarters of a discontented faction.   La
Riviere, perceiving that his own interests were to be
advanced by a continuance of peace, and perhaps actuated
by better motives also, had for some time negotiated with
Le Tellier, to bring about a better understanding between
his master and the regent.   And on this day he has
repeated a visit which he paid yesterday to Mazarin, and
has discussed with him various articles of agreement
between the* high contracting parties.   The minister,
delighted with the prospect of such a *concordat*, has accompanied the little abbe to the Luxembourg ; and together
they have persuaded Orleans to take a decisive step, and
returning with them, and presenting himself at the Palais
Royal, to declare his reconciliation with Anne of Austria
and his royal nephew.

No sooner had the occupants of the cardinal's coach
entered the palace than the guard of honor disbanded
again, and Louis was at leisure to rejoin his new friend.

"This is excellent," he remarked in a tone of great
satisfaction ; "do you not honor me as a magician who
has conjured up these high mightinesses by talking about
them ?   Now we shall have gayer times again in Paris, if
they can only be induced to understand each other, and
let the world run smooth.   Why, I protest, we have had
nothing here ever since the barricades but gloom, mistrust,
and politics, and perpetual bickerings.   I have been more
8*

than tempted to ask for leave to join one of Monsieur le
Prince's active battalions, and take a turn against the
Spaniard. There is some life to be seen there, at all
events; and it is *life*, friend," he added, clapping De Bonneval on the shoulder,—"life is the thing to see, after all.
Your philosophers call it experience ; I call it enjoyment.
Perhaps we mean the same thing ; for what is to enjoy
but to experience ? Grave men say that a life of pleasure
dissipates the mind ; I say no, it greatly enlarges the ideas.
In my state of pupilage there was one passage in history
which greatly took my imagination : and I will now
expound it for your benefit, my good neophyte."

He assumed a solemn and stately demeanor, to represent a professor delivering a lecture from his chair, and
proceeded :

"You must know, then, that among the ancients there
was one nation pre-eminent above the rest of mankind for
the profoundest philosophy, as well as the most practical
conduct of life. This race of philosophers inhabited the
Upper Egypt, and spread in after-times the light of their
discoveries to Greece and Rome, from whence, after the
taking of Byzantium, it penetrated to the schools of western Europe."

The young officer paused, and scanned his companion
with a mock gravity, to observe the effect of this sudden
display of erudition. Antoine, in fact, could not but be
amused at the light-hearted desultory talk of his brother-
lieutenant. The want of his life had been the want of a
friend of his own age with whom to interchange ideas,
especially of the gayer and more fanciful kind. Louis, in
spite of the misgivings inspired by his conduct, seemed the
kind of person to supply this want. That he had entertaining qualities none could deny. If (which was also
true) he generally contrived, after the few first sentences,
to transgress the line which separates all that may be said
without offence in sprightly conversation from all that may
not, Antoine was willing still to hope the best. It might
be mere liveliness and harmless play of fancy ; he might
not half mean what he said ; might be saying it merely to
startle a young provincial by his town-bred freedom. He

had certainly given vent to more undisguised wickedness
in a few hours than De Bonneval had heard before in a
lifetime ; and the latter could not avoid contrasting the
tone of the young guardsman's conversation with that of
the robber-chief in the forest.  That man was externally
an outcast from society, and lying under the edge of the
law ; yet his intercourse with himself had been marked by
a perfect absence of those vices of the tongue in which De
Montauban so freely indulged.  Antoine often pictured to
himself, as Louis rattled over topics he had best have passed
in silence, the stern rebuke he would have met from those
dark searching eyes of the man under whose ignominious
scaffold it might have been De Montauban's lot to keep
order among the rabble.

Still, our hero, who was of a frank and trustful nature,
waited with confidence for the better part of his new friend's
character to develop itself.  It was wiser, he reasoned, not,
by any marked rebuke, to excite still further the other's
spirit of contradiction.  At this time certainly there seemed
no reason why he should not listen to the promised trait of
wisdom on the part of the ancient Egyptians.

"These sages, sir," continued the reckless soldier, on
seeing that he had secured attention, "with the humility
which distinguishes the truly wise, felt mistrustful of their
own decisions in matters of practical importance.  They
desired to look at things from all sides.  Having in view
the variations to which the human judgment is liable,
resulting from such circumstances as animal spirits, a cheerful or a depressed view of life and events, and the alternate
predominance of the imagination or the judgment, they
introduced a custom worthy of a great and thinking nation.
Whenever a plan of action deeply affecting their interests
had to be discussed in their assemblies, they used to—"

"What ?" inquired De Bonneval, amused and expectant,
as his companion paused with mock solemnity.

"Let us not use so vulgar a word as intoxication,"
proceeded Louis, "or suppose that such was the whole
account of that ancient national device.  But they were
accustomed simply, by a process of elation which might
have been so designated by the unthinking, to remove that

over-caution which would mar the boldness of their first
conceptions of the subject in hand.   Thus carried beyond
themselves, their powers enlarged by that mystic touch of
the ivy-garlanded thyrsus, they rose to plans of action
which, apart from such assistance, they might have
regarded as gigantic or unreal: Then, after an interval,
returning from these altitudes to a more normal state, they
asked Prudence to give a verdict on the suggestions of her
bolder sister Fancy.   The counsels of Minerva tested and
modified the enthusiasms of Dionysos.   Now this may be
called a philosophic habit of regarding life and action from
opposite sides; and thus I prove my thesis in favor of a
course of pleasure being likewise a course of the most
exalted wisdom."

So saying, the professed scoffer left our young hero to
ruminate by himself on the wisdom and practical advantages of intoxication.*

## CHAPTER XII.

### ON MOTIVES.

"For why ? because the good old rule
Contented them—the simple plan,
That they should *get* who have the power,
And they should *keep* who can.''
                              *Wordsworth's Rob Roy.*

THE princess on whom had devolved a charge so burden-
some as the conduct of a regency amid conflicting interests
and pretensions such as then disorganized France, afforded
an instance of the degree to which even the well-inten-

---

* It seemed necessary to the development of a character like that
of Louis (supposing such an one to be introduced at all) to allow
him, at least on some one occasion, to speak for himself without interruption.   But it is earnestly hoped that no expression, either in this
or in any other part of the story, will be taken in any way to
diminish that hatred and fear with which vice, under any form or
circumstances, must ever inspire the Christian.

tioned are liable to misapprehend their own powers, or, no
less fatally, to misplace their confidence. Anne of Austria
was gifted with no inconsiderable capacity for sustaining
the burden of government, which the death of Louis XIII.
had committed to her hands. She inherited, however,
from her father, Philip III., a haughty determination of
will, and from the traditions of the Spanish court a somewhat exaggerated estimate of the royal prerogatives, and
the sacredness attaching to every declaration of the royal
mind. Nor had these characteristics been modified during
the period of her nearly thirty-years' reign as queen-con-
sort of France. The very despotism of Richelieu, oppressive as it had become to herself, had only deepened in her
mind the principle of ultra-royalism, which was afterwards
one chief cause of the misfortunes attending her own
regency ; since, whatever self-aggrandizement accompanied
it, that relentless oppression of the cardinal-minister had
been exerted ostensibly, perhaps purely, for the maintenance
or the advancement of kingly power.

How comes it that the widowed regent, left guardian of her infant
son at a time which, beyond all others, demanded a steady
eye, a firm hand, and a sound and clearly-seen principle
in government, showed neither perception of the wants
of the time, nor any disposition to call to her councils men
who would have supplied for her own defective views.
Such men, indeed, cannot be said to have existed in any
abundance among the classes of the high nobility, from
whom alone that haughty queen was likely to select her
advisers. The *gens de la robe*, who might have furnished,
had she sought them there, high statesmanlike qualities,
powers of organizing the finance and administration, and
calm far-sighted views for the best interests of crown and
people,—these men were in her eyes simply a class to be
thwarted in their wishes, to be beaten back in their encroachments.

How comes it that power over our fellow-men, when
not wrought out through our own exertions, but placed by
Providence in our hands in the shape of wealth, rank, and
the machinery of command, so often tends to close up the
heart and narrow the mental view, defeating the end for

which it was bestowed, as it disables us for its wholesome
or legitimate exercise? Is it that power itself brings with
it an intoxication against which the wisest and most moderate scarcely preserve themselves, and under which feebler
brains are ever sure to reel? Or is it that the Supreme
Wisdom decrees to maintain the balance which constitutes
this world a scene of probation, by often accepting the will
at the same time that He withholds the occasion for its
exercise, and, while He sets bounds to the dominion of
evil, restraining the good also from being wrought too
completely, or by wholesale?

From whatever cause, the page of history contains little
else than a succession of characters and events, in which
the reader has to deplore either the maladministering of
power intrusted to selfish unworthy hands, or the lack of
it in those who would have wielded it for the right, and
for suffering mankind. Thrones are set up by usurpation,
and cemented in blood; and they who occupy them wax
and swell amid the wrongs, the sufferings, to which they
owe their rise; while the incense of adulation steams up
around those self-imagined deities whose nod is law. Then
from all sides of their footstool spring up corruptions as a
natural growth of the soil, and attain a rank luxuriance;
and with corruption comes its attendant cruelty, and there
ensue in turn the overthrow of justice, the undue concentration of wealth, the ruinous despotisms of an oligarchy,
desecration of the sanctity of homes and hearths, and wide-
spread vice and public calamity. At length the day
comes round when nature is permitted to avenge herself.
She rises in her strength, and in the hoarse tones of indignant suffering summons Violence and Havoc to the work
that must be done; and the balance is overset that should
have been restored; and puppets are broken instead of
being merely cast aside, and history looks on, and calls
the deed a Revolution. The ground is cleared; all things
begin afresh. Power has been wrested from the hands of
selfishness long dominant and all but venerable; and it is
now wielded by selfishness elated, maddened by its new
acquisition; there are struggles and counter-struggles, till

despotism re-appears and is again enthroned; and the same events run round in another cycle.

The annals of nations,—what are they, but this dark story told again and again under varying forms? O, for the advent of some blessed one, whose strong hands shall also be pure, and his rule a maintenance of his subjects' rights; one long war against self within and around him; an unwearied upholding of the supremacy of laws divine! Prince or peer, the one office differs from the other only in the dimensions of the circle; in either case, he radiates forth benedictions, and is blessed in his deed. Suffering looks up, and feebly hails him; corruption and wrong fly before his tread. He gathers brightness for the starry crown awaiting himself, while he raises the present lot of others; and becomes nothing meaner than a type of Him for whose last coming earth cries aloud, and the whole creation groaneth and travaileth in pain together until now.

As if with settled design to afford in his own person a contrast to any such blessed character, Louis XIV., from the time when he assumed the reins of empire, commenced the demigod in right earnest, and was worshipped on his throne. The reign of self, whatever modifications it may receive from the immediate spirit of the age, is ever the antagonist power to the divine kingdom upon earth. It was so at the period of our story, and that which succeeded it. The selfish preference of the regent for a mean unworthy minister, deservedly unpopular, and incompetent to the high trust reposed in him, prevented the reins of government from passing into better hands, and thus, by continuing an intolerable evil, ushered in the Fronde, which purported to be its rude but needful remedy. During the Fronde, again, the reckless spirit of self played such fantastic tricks before high heaven as convulsed France to her centre, and were only saved from being contemptible, inasmuch as they were perilous and deadly:

"A wild and dream-like trade of blood and guile,
Too foolish for a tear, too wicked for a smile."

And when the power of the young king had become once established, mankind saw but a change of scene in the

same unworthy melodrama : the plot of the piece was maintained consistently, though scenery and dresses developed
into something more gorgeous, and the tinselled and
painted characters moved through their parts with a more
imposing step.   Self, the self of one grand egotist, and
the selfishness he engendered in his countless parasites,
was still the pivot on which the whole revolved.   The
tedious etiquette of Versailles became a rubric, or rather a
religion : and to have thwarted the inclinations, or with-
stood the nod of the autocrat, would have been as if an
inhabitant of Thibet should doubt the divinity of the Great
Lama, or a citizen of ancient Rome had refused to sacrifice
to the genius of the deified Augustus.

Throughout the long and prosperous reign of Louis
XIV. we look in vain for something to relieve the monotony of that absorbing egotism which may be described
as his dominant passion.   In the ordinances of his court,
Louis framed and consecrated a kind of solar system, in
which planets and satellites of various orb and brilliancy
revolved uniformly around their central sun.   If ever
idolatry was established upon earth, and inaugurated by
general consent, it was when, among the splendid crowds
who thronged the levees, and ministered to the selfishness
of the *Grand Monarque*, each man worshipped his own
private interests in worshipping his king.

Yet a St. Louis in Versailles at that day, as also a St.
Edward or an Alfred at Whitehall some few years later,
would have had before them a wide field for good, and
one capable of yielding a rich and blessed harvest.   They
would have found, indeed, a country drained of its
resources through the flood-gates of war, torn and exhausted
by internal discord, and all the desolation attendant upon
the fierce lawless passions of civil strife ; and therefore, all
the more would they have been surrounded by willing
instruments to aid in re-uniting and consolidating the elements of public happiness, while they secured, for the
general good, the complete restoration of the kingly power.
A glorious and thrice-blessed task would it have been for
such a monarch to seize, and to impress on those around
him, the stern lessons taught by rebellion and bloodshed ;

troubles which his just authority had quelled, and of which his mild enlightened rule was to prevent the recurrence. Cromwell and his Ironsides would not have been in vain, had they taught Charles Second the long-forgotten truth, that kings, if they would render a good account of their stewardship, must reign for the well-being of their subjects. De Retz, and the turbulent spirits he put or kept in motion, would have done—not a good work, but a work overruled for good, had they served to convince the young Louis that the middle class, and masses of his people, had sacred claims on his care, and rights which he must acknowledge and respect. The coronation at Rheims in 1653, the landing at Dover in 1660, would then have been the opening of a new and happy era in the history of the kingdoms which these two men were called to govern.

Such were doubtless the fond anticipations of many minds in France and in England at the critical periods of which we speak. They were doomed to a bitter disappointment. Stuart and Bourbon alike, once firmly seated on their thrones, forgot any such wholesome impressions as might have been made by the trials of their earlier years. The annals of their respective reigns, amid much that engages the notice of history in the shape of foreign success, stand blotted with the records of personal vices, of lavish expenditure and dishonorable embarrassment; while the servile literature and court language of their day represented the details of their notorious excesses as above all scrutiny, because performed by the demigods of its heathenism, and even as themes for a sycophant and disgraceful jargon of mythology.

From the weary task of following such a state of things we are, however, saved; and need but glance at it so far as it throws a retrospective light on the period of our story, which contained the germs of it, and served to usher it upon the scene. Antoine is no hanger-on of the court of Louis XIV. We rejoice to remember it for his own sake, and for ourselves his biographers. The struggles of the Fronde are real, though not always dignified. They are disgraced and travestied by the light reckless conduct of many who engage in them. Still, they represent some-

9

thing of a principle, though their vicissitudes often seem to
be the mere sport of caprice, and to be moved by nothing
deeper.    The period that succeeded the coronation of Louis
stands as a type of little that can interest the thoughtful
student.    It is a bold word; seeing that his long reign
was invested with such a factitious splendor : but look
closer at it; test it by any wholesome or permanent
standard—its brilliancy is spangle, its tone a falsetto.
Strip that imperious puppet, on which the eyes of an
adoring court are fixed, of all its externals, its lace, its
nodding feathers, and paste-diamonds; uncase it of what
old Lear—stern tutor in the science of reality—would have
called its sophistications ; come to "the thing itself;"—
what have you obtained ?    Is it the sterling hero, the truly
great king, gifted with the gift of command ? is it the
man who wields his power with an end in view beyond
himself, and who dares and energizes, denies himself and
suffers, because all these things are demanded in an
eminent degree from those who hold the high places of the
world ?    Bah ! the poor starveling soul, that emerges
unclad from its wrappings as you proceed, dwarfed by its
egotism, enervated by the habitual intoxication of its
vanity, is not worth throwing away words upon.

But have we, in mere criticism, forgotten the progress
of our narrative ?    Nay, gentle reader, a tale is never the
worse for its digressions, unless they are wholly irrelevant.
And we have wished to explain, in this circuitous mode,
why Mazarin will not re-appear in Antoine's chronicle.
You have seen the grace with which he can alight from
his coach ; the bland smiles he can dispense to those who
bow before him.    Be content; you have witnessed the
best phase of him.    These are his chief accomplishments,
except, indeed, that end of ends, to which all other
things with him are means subservient—the art of amass-
ing money.    Let him go, nor stand upon the order of his
going.    We dismiss him the more willingly, because of
the deep grudge we owe him for having tended to make
the young monarch what he afterwards became.    If the
character of Richelieu be an historical enigma, that of
Mazarin is as plain as day.    And for our part, having no

vocation to imitate the Flemish painters, we love not to depict, with their pains and fidelity of detail, any thing so minute, so mean and ordinary, as would be the portrait of that "pin-point of a soul."

## CHAPTER XIII.

### PRO REGE, LEGE, AUT GREGE?

"Thy deeds, thy plainness, and thy late exploits,
Have made thee fear'd and honored of the people:—
Join we together for the public good;
In what we can, to bridle and suppress
The pride of Suffolk and the Cardinal."

*King Henry VI.*

UNDER the avenue of old elms terminating the gardens of the Archbishop of Paris, two men walked with leisurely steps, engaged in earnest conversation. It needed scarcely a second glance to show that both were of a refined and courtly presence. Yet, though the dress of either was of rich materials, arranged in the height of the prevailing mode, there were differences whereby any one skilled in the costume of the period would have recognized the elder of the two as an ecclesiastic. The broad hat was worn without either brooch or feather, while the large falling band of costly lace was arranged with a slightly more formal air than that of his companion. Truly, the mode in which the silk and three-piled velvet were shaped and arranged differed less than a severe criticism would have approved from that of the other's gay attire. Nevertheless their graver hue, together with the absence of rapier and poniard, those invariable accompaniments of any layman of gentle rank, designated the wearer as one whose

taste for magnificence was held in check by the canons of
the Church.   Not so, however, the expression and air of
the man thus habited.   Paul Gondi de Retz, nephew and
coadjutor of the Archbishop of Paris, was of a deportment
yet more secular than these half-dubious vestments.   No
ordinances, ecclesiastical or secular, were of force to control the daring impetuous spirit which manifested itself in
that eager tread, and the fire of those small but luminous
eyes.

Older than his present companion the prelate certainly
was ; yet even he had some years before him ere he should
see his fortieth birthday.   It has been remarked by a historian of the period,* that during the commotions of the
Fronde, most of the men who, from rank or character,
bore the foremost part in public life were in the prime of
their years and energy, as the ladies, whose selfish spirit of
intrigue kept alive the disorders of the times, were in the
zenith of their beauty.   The effect of this coincidence was
visible throughout the struggle, and gave it a character at
once of license and of picturesque and semi-chivalrous
variety.   The spirit of Richelieu had passed away from the
scene.   Grave and commanding it had been, with all its
manifest faults, with all its possible crimes.   He was gone ;
and his sceptre had fallen into the hands of a man with few
qualities to render him either feared or respected.   A cardinal, though not a priest, with a mixture, therefore, of
the lay and the ecclesiastical character most unfavorable to
the consistent bearing of either, Mazarin was essentially
wanting in the qualities of his predecessor.   Under his
feebler administration, bold ambitious minds rose elastic
from the repression of Richelieu's iron hand, scoffed at the
subtle temporizing policy by which the Italian minister
endeavored to soothe or to win them, and plunged their
country into the confusions and disasters of one of the most
capricious wars that stand recorded in European history.
It was not until those unbridled passions had run their
course, and been tamed through very weariness, that the
developing qualities of the young king asserted their

* M. de St. Aulaire.

supremacy, and France again became tranquil under the sway of her natural ruler.

The prelate's companion was Louis de Bourbon, Prince of Condé. Inferior in birth to no subject of the realm, excepting only Orleans, the king's uncle and next of blood, Condé far exceeded him in all those qualities which tend to make a man a powerful adherent or a formidable antagonist of his sovereign. Trained equally amid the hardships of warfare and the refinements of court-life, his naturally great abilities had, however, been cultivated by the care of his mother, a princess worthy of her relationship to the great Montmorency. Polished in demeanor, ready in wit, the *hauteur* that was his by birth and temperament only lending him a more irresistible fascination when he chose to condescend, this young prince wore the laurels he had won in battle with so careless a grace, that it might seem as though his splendid achievements at Rocroy and Nordlingen lived in every remembrance but his own. Yet in his most disengaged moments there was a prompt decision, an impetuosity and military sternness, that served to caution his associates against trifling with one who possessed so many of the awful attributes of the lion, together with the generosity and dauntless courage of that lord of the forest.

To his former triumphs he has added the lustre of his recent victory over the Spanish forces at Lens; and he has within these few days arrived in the capital to take his share in the great political drama in which he is destined to play so prominent and so changeful a part.

They are beyond comparison the two boldest, ablest, and most dangerous men in Paris who are now debating together on the aspect of public affairs. The timid and even trifling Mazarin stands dwarfed in the intellectual scale by the side of the coadjutor, whose daring reckless spirit of intrigue would have required an antagonist of the commanding qualities that expired with Richelieu to cope with and keep it in check. And for Condé, greatest of his illustrious line, what captain in the field, what prince or courtier in the presence-chamber, or amid the chivalrous exercises practised by the nobility of martial France, can

9*

be placed in the balance against him? Turenne is wise
and experienced, intrepid in action, calm in military judgment; but with Conde, the full tide and rush of battle, the
rapid skilful manœuvre, seem as the very element of his life.
He is never more himself, never more light-hearted or free,
than in the stress of extreme peril, when the fate of an
army is hanging in the balance. What may be the last
moment of his life seems also the moment of his keenest
enjoyment  Marsillac, again, and Fontailles, are witty,
polished, faultless in that *tournure* of manner which goes so
far to establish a court reputation. Yet all the while there
is about Conde a keen intuitive perception, and a kind of
lofty grace, which, in spite of some austerity of natural
temperament, together with his devotion to the details of
military service, might have raised him, had he been so
minded, to the very pinnacle of fashion and wit. Look on
that slender commanding figure, shown as it is to still
greater advantage by contrast with the shorter and, and to
say truth, rather ungainly form of the prelate by his side.
Study those eagle features, on which, with all the tokens of
indifferent health, there is no shade of lassitude to tell that
the weakness of the bodily frame has subdued the vigor of
the commanding spirit lodged within. The lips, just
shaded by a slight moustache, with a predominant and
habitual expression of firmness and thought, might relax
without difficulty in the play of conversation, or pour a torrent of lofty, even of impassioned eloquence. And the
whole character of this striking physiognomy is crowned by
a brow, delicate and serene, nobly arched over a full penetrating eye, and seeming to indicate a forehead of equally
fine proportions, were it not concealed under the ample
curls of the peruke recently introduced as an almost essential part of the dress of every man of rank or fashion.
Should our readers be farther curious respecting the costume of this distinguished warrior, we will record for their
benefit that his doublet and nether garments are of a rich
white silk, slashed so as to exhibit a crimson lining of the
same material, and plentifully frogged and embroidered
with gold. The hose themselves are wide, according to
the fashion of the period, and confined at the knees by

large white roses. The stockings of pale pink silk are met upon the instep of the wearer by shoes of the whitest Spanish leather, with high red heels, squared at the toe, and garnished with roses of ample dimensions. Some of the gallants at court are now indulging in a kind of false heel, so adjusted upon the boot as to produce a sound like that of castanets at every step, and supposed to lend a grace to the stately movements of the minuet or the court promenade. But the great Conde is not given to such gauds; and, indeed, whether from pride, carelessness, or military simplicity, generally appears dressed rather beneath his rank than in any extreme of fashion.* At present he is in *grande tenue*, having just come from court; and therefore it is that he also wears the full silk scarf, crossing his breast and knotted on the left side, and that the decoration of the Ordre du Saint Esprit hangs round his neck beneath the rich collar of point-lace that Vandyke would have loved to delineate; while he wraps the ample carnation-colored cloak round him as a defence against the fog-damps of the autumnal day. His gilded coach, instead of his more favorite war-horse, stands waiting for him under the high garden-wall; you can hear the jingling of the bits and trappings on the six Flemish cream-colored steeds.

An unseen spectator of the interview would have remarked, that while the bishop's whole air betokened a

---

* Thus, even afterwards, when he had become one of the most brilliant ornaments of the court of Louis XIV., Madame De Sevigne has the following amusing passage upon the appearance of Conde at the marriage of his nephew, Conti, in 1680:—''I will tell you the greatest and most extraordinary piece of news which you can learn; and that is, that the Prince was shaved yesterday—actually shaved: this is not an illusion, not a thing said at random, it is a truth; all the court were witnesses to it; and Madame de Langeron, seizing her opportunity, when he had his paws across like a lion, made him put on a vest with diamond button-holes; while a valet-de-chambre, also presuming upon his patience, curled his hair, powdered him, and at length compelled him to be the handsomest man at court, with a head which threw all the perukes into the shade. That was the prodigy of the marriage.''

That Conde, however, notwithstanding the above passage, actually wore a peruke about the period of our story, is attested by a very fine contemporary portrait in the collection of engravings in the British Museum.

resolution already formed, the deportment of Conde indicated more of struggle, even of indecision, than usually
belonged to a character so impetuous and an intellect so
clear.   He now strode forward for several paces, as though
marshalled on by some apparition of his excited fancy.
Now again he would pause in his walk, fixing his eyes
with keen attention on the countenance of his companion,
who, with more collectedness, yet with great force and
expression, urged upon him the topics of their protracted
interview.   At another time he would lunge with his
sheathed rapier against the trunks of the old elm-trees as
he passed them, or snap some of the smaller branches, and
scatter their withered leaves to the chill air; then, impatient with himself at having betrayed such symptoms of
disquiet, he would fold his arms with a dignity more
habitual to him, and time his measured steps to those of
the kindred spirit at his side.

It was indeed no unimportant decision that the great
Conde was at this time summoned to make; nor was it an
unskilful advocate who was now pressing it upon him.   The
events of the few last months had been calling imperatively
upon men who occupied a far less prominent sphere than
the prince, to take their part without reserve in the struggle
at hand.   Hitherto he had dutifully maintained his place
beside the throne, to which, as well by blood as by personal
principles, he stood so near; and the regent had reckoned
the hero of Rocroi as one of the stanchest supporters of
the rights of his royal cousin.   But Conde, besides his
character of prince of the blood, was the possessor of fatal
gifts, which rendered it difficult to enact the part of a faithful subject with any consistency.   The very splendor of
his talents, his impetuosity of will, his fearlessness, rapid
combination, ability in command,—that union of qualities
which had secured his military triumphs and made him the
idol of a devoted army,—all tended to loosen him from the
only position consistent with duty to his sovereign, and
urge him headlong into open revolt.   These tendencies had
not passed unnoticed by Mazarin, and had begun to disquiet the mind of the regent herself.   The former had long
been aware that he was regarded with little favor by either

of the princes who sat with him in the royal council: in
the minds of both there were distinct feelings operating to
his disadvantage. Orleans, we have seen, had lately been
exasperated by the refusal of a cardinal's hat to La Riviere. The disappointed ambition of the subordinate had
worked strongly on the pride and jealousy of the patron;
motives which combined against the minister whom both
suspected of having exerted his influence to thwart their
design. Conde, who had placed the real barrier to La Riviere's advancement by asking the hat for his own brother,
the Prince de Conti, inherited from his father a feeling of
ill-will towards Mazarin; while his own temper accorded
but little with the cautious temporizing policy which the
cardinal was inclined to pursue towards the now all-but
insurgent commons. Mazarin, however, still hoped to
attach the young prince more firmly to the court-party.
Since his return to Paris, the tumultuous, ill-regulated
meetings of the parliament had indisposed a man of Conde's
temperament to espouse the popular cause. He perceived
the fallacy of his former endeavors to stand well with
both parties, which had seemed to lend the authority of his
name in some measure to the advances of the Frondeurs.
To strengthen him the more in these loyal dispositions, the
cardinal spared no arts of flattery or persuasion. Accommodating himself with the facility that belonged to him
to the temper of the man whom he desired to gain, he
engaged for the future to pay unlimited deference to his
wishes in the council, if he would step in at this crisis to
defend the rights of the throne, assume the command of
the army, and lead it against the parliament and the
rebellious capital.

On the other hand, all the rhetoric of the coadjutor was
now employed in engaging the prince to cast his sword
into the popular scale. Owing his present dignity to the
favor and patronage of the queen, Gondi had commenced
his career as an adherent of the royal cause. But *the Day
of the Barricades* in the preceding August had rendered it
impossible to one in his eminent position, and with so great
talents for popular agitation, to stand aloof from the interests of the magistracy and the commons. On that memor-

ble day he had indeed rescued from the fury of the populace the Marechal de la Meilleraye, with his detachment
of guards. But on his return with the marechal to the
Palais Royal to report the insurrection as more serious than
had been apprehended, the coadjutor had received from the
queen a rebuff which fired at once a train already laid in a
mind naturally active, intriguing, and ambitious. "There
is revolt," said the haughty queen, breaking in sharply
upon his representations, "in imagining the possibility of
revolting ; and his majesty will take effectual measures with
it.   I understand you, Monsieur le Coadjuteur," continued
she, her eyes sparkling with anger, and all her previous
suspicions of his disloyalty roused as he began to represent
the only effectual method of calming the people; "you
would have me give Broussel back to you!   I would
rather,"—at the same time menacing the throat of the
prelate himself,—"I would rather strangle him with my
two hands."

It is the curse of royalty to be doomed never to hear
the truth from the obsequious crowds that surround it;
and the obliquity of its own view is confirmed by the
answering looks of those with whom a crowned head is
incapable of doing or saying wrong.   These imprudent
words, uttered in an excited moment, but evidencing too
probably a fixed determination to make no concessions,
even of a just and reasonable kind, may be said to have lit
the torch of civil discord, and given birth to the Fronde.
Gondi, thus menaced by the regent, and become a mark for
the courtly jibes of the unthinking sycophants around her,
returned in a fury of indignation to the archbishop's palace.
From that hour the court-party lost an able negotiator, and
had to reckon a formidable enemy: for De Retz, now
relieved from any such scruples as might have restrained
him, threw himself headlong into the cause of the malcontents ; and finding ample development for the natural bent
of his character, while he fed his personal revenge, made
himself felt as the very life and soul of those insurgents
whom he had apparently wished to reconcile with the
throne.

But for a purpose so settled as that of the coadjutor had

now become, there needed some one to head the popular party, and lend it the influence of commanding talents, energy, and the splendor of a name. Otherwise, as Gondi's political foresight told him, the reluctant concessions which had been wrung from the regent by a sturdy determination and a growing influence on the side of the parliament, might soon be rendered valueless again by the disunion or military incapacity of the opposition. A more personal motive may also have influenced the high-born and court-bred De Retz to seek some ally from that class of society in which he himself moved. Nothing could well be more contrary to his natural bent and the habits of his life than to appear as the associate of a party formed of the magistracy and burghers of Paris, and in opposition to a court which his own brilliant though misused qualities had contributed to adorn.

Thus both parties at this moment vied with each other in eagerly soliciting the alliance of the Prince de Conde. And it is during one of those anxious discussions which he renewed again and again with the coadjutor, the present sharer of his debate, but his future sworn antagonist, that we find him walking in the formal avenue of the arch-bishop's garden.

---

## CHAPTER XIV.

### UNDECIDED STILL.

"The gentleman is learn'd, a most rare speaker,
To nature none more bound ; his training such,
That he may furnish and instruct great teachers,
And never seek for aid out of himself. Yet see,
When these so noble benefits shall prove
Not well dispos'd, the mind growing once corrupt,
They turn to vicious forms, ten times more ugly
Than ever they were fair."       *King Henry VIII.*

THE true political character of De Retz is a debatable ground in the history of the seventeenth century. It has been as much contested by writers of different views as the

body of Patroclus by the incensed Greeks and Trojans.
Some have not scrupled to compare him to the Cataline of
old Rome; others, and those his contemporaries, have
described him as possessing little of the concentration,
determined purpose, or thoughtful and over-mastering
ambition, which go to form the hero of a great conspiracy.
They have allowed him no further aim than that of a
brilliant notoriety; poor counterfeit of a solidly earned
reputation.  Far from the lofty though often erring design
of reconstructing an effete order of things on some basis
that might give hope for the future, Gondi represented,
according to these writers, no principle of patriotism, nor
even simply of revolution.    Dangerous, but without
decision, he seemed content to throw society into disorder,
and bring its several classes to a collision that had well-nigh
proved irremediable; he felt rewarded, if only the troubles
of the times might serve to bear himself upward into some
prominent position, or feed a personal grudge against the
regent, and a paltry vanity of measuring himself against
the ascendant minister.   Others, again, there are who speak
of him as a man of enlightened spirit, partly drawn aside
by the wild turbulence of the period, yet acting under a
dominant sense of the perils to which the State, and even
the monarchy, lay exposed by the progress of despotism.
Such panegyrists may, it is true, have been swayed in
their judgment by the singular charm of that style in
which the Cardinal de Retz composed his autobiography.
in the later years of his checkered life.  A writer among
the most brilliant, as he was also one of the most per-
suasive speakers, of that or any other period in France,
was not likely to let such faculties lie dormant when he
had to set forth his justification to the world.

The truth, perhaps, lay between the extremes of favorable opinion and censure.   Gondi was a man of eminently
popular and attractive qualities, nor ever backward in
exhibiting them.   His may be said to have been a the-
atrical cast of mind, and himself the foremost personage in
his melodrama of life.  Excitement, strong contrast, novelty
of incident, striking positions, all that looks well and lights
up well on the stage, tricked out his political career.   This

mental craving for effect and variety was met and answered
by the fantastic burlesque and semi-tragic action of the
Fronde movement.   It is of no avail to ask what De Retz
would have become had the years of his vigor been
cast in quieter times.   As it was, he did what others did
around him, only with greater intensity.   He played his
part, which could not fail of being a noted one, amid
scenes in which the earnest and the trivial were strangely
intermingled; lived and glittered in the society to which
his birth and talents, far more than his episcopal office,
invited him ; and thus shared deeply in its extravagances,
intrigues, and (as his own confessions inform us) its follies
and vices also.*

* The autobiography which Cardinal de Retz employed his latter
years in compiling, has transmitted to posterity many unedifying
details of this period of his life.   It is a strange spectacle of wayward inconsistency to see a man professedly retired from the world
to transact in solitude the great business which the vicissitudes of
an impetuous turbulent life had deferred until its close, and from
thence inditing to some lady of rank a memoir such as this.   Yet
the exhibition of himself involved in it appears only as the concluding trait of that dominant passion for notoriety which had pursued
him during his whole career.   Meeting with an indolence as habitual
as itself, and incapable, therefore, of spurring him on to any consistent exertion, or gaining him an honorable position in the history of his country, his all-engrossing desire to be notorious vented
itself in a meaner channel, and thus gave to the world the details
of his own more than questionable adventures.   "Vanity," says
La Rochefoucauld, in a characteristic portrait which he has left us
of his former ally, but which the caustic tone of the writer would
induce us to take with some abatement,—"vanity, and they that
led him, induced him to enter upon great undertakings, almost all
of which were inconsistent with his profession.   He excited the
utmost disorders in the State, without having had any formal
design of mastery in them.   It was not in order to supplant Cardinal Mazarin that he declared himself his enemy ; his only thought
was to render himself formidable to him, and enjoy the false vanity
of opposing him.   Indolence is his natural bent ; nevertheless he
labors actively in matters that press upon him, and carelessly
reposes when they are concluded.   He has great presence of mind,
and knows so well how to turn to advantage the opportunities
offered him by fortune, that it would appear as if he had already
foreseen and desired them.   His qualities are for the most part unreal ; and what has chiefly contributed to his reputation is, the
skill of placing his faults in a fair light.   He dexterously avoids
the discovery that he is but superficially acquainted with any thing."

10

Such was the remarkable man whom we left just now under the avenue of elms, assailing the hero of Rocroi with a well-directed battery of arguments and motives for casting his lot into the growing fortunes of the Fronde.

"You are convinced, then, Monseigneur le Coadjuteur," said Conde, after a long pause,—for he was aware that the whole of his future career was now in the balance, and he had schooled his fiery spirit to a patient review of the arguments of his companion,—"you are convinced that the course of action to which you urge me has nothing in it contrary to honor or religion ?"

"For religion," answered the prelate, "your highness may solve your own scruple, without formally adopting me for your spiritual guide." A very slight smile curled his features as he spoke ; for the disorders of Gondi's personal life, if not positively notorious, were too much suspected to admit of his being consulted by many as a director of consciences.

"The answer lies," he continued more earnestly, "in the very attributes of One who alone is self-sufficing ; alone rules supreme by an authority that emanates from and centres in Himself without external aid or limitation. No human throne can be erected on a basis absolutely independent, without trenching upon prerogatives not granted to earth. An infinity of checks, of mutual relations and reciprocal duties, has been interposed by the Supreme Will ; and thus the most time-honored, the most consecrated monarchies, rule, indeed, by the support of lawful arms, but chiefly after the precedents of righteous laws. This just and hallowed order of things has been undermined in France. Absolute power has been grasping at the lion's share. The balance is overweighed ; and it needs but the additional weight of that sword in the scale,"—he glanced at the sheathed weapon which Conde had plucked from his scarf, and waved occasionally in the heat of the discussion,—"it needs but that, and your disciplined battalions from the Flemish frontier, to see this order of justice finally overthrown."

"Monseigneur," exclaimed the prince, stopping short in his walk, and drawing himself up to his height while he faced the uncompromising speaker, "how am I to understand such expressions?"

"Your highness," said the other calmly, "will understand them in nowise as they are intended, if you find therein matter of offence. My meaning is simply, that the progress of events in the court and government of this country from the time (to go no farther back) when your most eminent kinsman acquired the ascendency consequent on his talents for government—"

"Talk not to me of Richelieu," abruptly interposed his high-spirited companion; "the late cardinal might have been trebly the relation of my wife, or my own, without those private ties pledging me to approve his policy. But the *throne* you speak of, Monseigneur—it is the throne of my ancestors. I am Louis de Bourbon," his nostril slightly dilating as he spoke, "and may be pardoned for an emotion of jealousy when any thing seems to trench on its prerogatives."

"We are here discussing principles rather than personal inclinations," replied De Retz, quietly yet firmly; "and by those principles we are to shape a course of action on which depends all that we both have, nay, all that we both are. Does your highness suppose," he added, his impetuous spirit kindling as he went on, "that *my* feelings, if I allowed them to play unchecked, would not urge me, would not hurry me onward, to decide the question for myself without another consideration? Can I forget,"—and the tones of his flexible voice, at the thought of the indignities offered to him on the Day of the Barricades, became deep and almost guttural,—"can I ever forget that on that eventful day, when I had saved at the risk of my own life the envoy of my sovereign from instant death—plucked him, sir, from the hands of an infuriated, ay, a justly excited mob; kept them at bay by the utmost exertion of an influence honorably acquired through sympathy with their previous wrongs, and restored him in safety to the palace whence he had issued upon his bootless errand,—that in that very moment I received from the hands that should tend every subject of this realm with a paternal care—"

The prelate strode forward many paces in silence ; but his breast was heaving, and his eye flashing, with suppressed emotion, while he thus suddenly conjured up again before himself the details of the unforgotten insult which had ranked him among the enemies of the royal cause.

Conde's own proud and generous spirit thrilled in answer to the chord which had been thus deeply stirred in the breast of the other. Never, perhaps, had he felt more swayed towards that cause in which the coadjutor had already embarked than during the few moments in which the latter, leaving the region of argument, simply laid bare to him the workings of a lofty sensitive spirit smarting under a manifest wrong.

"I have forgotten myself," resumed the coadjutor after an interval, "and am giving you, Monsieur le Prince, no goodly specimen of the philosophic temper in which so great a question should be reviewed. Let me now take up the thread of my answer to the questions you do me the favor to ask. How, then, can a just and constitutional resistance to the despotism which is gathering over our heads be otherwise than consistent with our honor ? Where will you find loftier sentiments, or more worthy of a noble breast, than in those great philosopher-historians of ancient Rome, who, while they chronicled the subjection of a whole empire lying prostrate under the feet of an individual despot, echoed, so far as the terrorism of the times permitted, the indignant wail of that mighty national heart amid its helpless thraldom ? Are those great writers to speak in vain to men whose impulses are as free, whose sense of honor is as high, and to whose necks,"—he carefully noted the effect of his words as he proceeded with a somewhat slower emphasis,—"the foot of absolute power is stealing as unerringly, as though their liberty, their most sacred interests, hung upon the breath of a Caligula or a Nero ? For myself," he continued, after a pause, "I trace out in me something of their departed spirit ; and sooner than thus lay all that belongs to me as man—my inalienable birthright—at the feet of my fellow-mortal, I would with Cato, or even with Brutus—"

"Noble Roman," interrupted Conde, with a subdued

and playful irony, "let us not be either beyond or behind
the age in which our lot has been cast.   The true hero, I
apprehend, is he, who without placing himself by any
strained imagination in times or circumstances that have
bestowed on others, not on himself, an occasion for developing the heroic temper, moulds and uses the elements that
lie ready to his hand as no inferior character can mould or
use them.   You and I are not living under the shadow of
that temple of Jupiter Capitolinus, from whose altar rose
up so many secret vows to liberty amid the smoke of sacri-
fices ostensibly offered to the genius of the emperors.   We
are in France, and in France since the influence of feudalism has re-organized the political world, and in France,
too, since the decay of that same feudalism has opened an
avenue for the progress, not of popular, but of monarchical power.   Deceive not yourself: the tide, notwithstanding some temporary fluctuations, sets ultimately that way.
Moreover, we both belong to the privileged nobility of our
country; and we are thereby marked out as natural supporters to the throne.   Why should I cast my sword, or
you, Monseigneur," with a slight glance at the semi-eccle-
siastical dress of his companion, "your crosier, into the
same scale which contains the very dregs of the populace,
and—what suits my fancy quite as little—the selfishness,
half-cunning, half-insolence, of those *gens de le robe*, your
burgher middle-class?   I confess to you, that since my
return to Paris, the first idea which possessed me, that
of becoming the restorer of public rights, has well-nigh
subsided before the vulgar contests and arrogant pretensions that have met me on all sides.   I feel a natural
attraction towards a nobler end.   It seems given to me to
uphold in its hour of need the royal authority, to which
Providence has allied me.   You tell me it has aimed too
high; I see it now in danger of being trampled under foot
by a factious rabble.   Choose; for it is but a choice of
two things.   Shall we have over us the ancient legitimate
crown of these realms; or a many-headed monster, whose
ignorance and caprice have none of the elements of government, and whose fickle despotism would overpass that of
the most absolute monarch?"

10*

"Your highness," replied De Retz, "may be allowing
your naturally clear perceptions to lie at the mercy of a
too trenchant haste.   The choice is not so absolute as your
impetuosity would represent it.   For twelve hundred years
France has been a monarchy; but her monarchs have all
the while been limited by law and custom.   Those limitations have not, it is true, been recorded in statutes or in
charters, as in the neighboring kingdoms of England and
of Arragon; nevertheless, from the earliest times, wisdom
has traced out her middle line to preserve us alike from a
lawless king and an unbridled people.   I do not pretend
that this middle path has been accurately trodden at all
times; it has been rather a tendency, an aspiration, than a
blessing always realized.   But it has been acknowledged
as a principle, in the very power assigned to parliaments by
the French constitution; it was, moreover, the principle on
which the wisest of our monarchs, our St. Louis, Charles
V., and Louis XII., and Henry IV., each in their day, cir-
cumscribed their own power within the ancient landmarks.
With the late cardinal (you will pardon my again referring to this) a different order of things commenced.   His
was a long and absolute reign; for need I say that the
ascendency won by his genius over the mind of his royal
master virtually placed the sceptre of France in his hands?
And during that long reign, the kingly power, as represented by the ruling minister, advanced towards becoming
the only element of the State.   One by one, the bulwarks
erected by our forefathers against the march of despotism
fell before him.   What else was the appointment throughout the provinces of his *intendants* of justice, police, and
finance, nominated by himself, removable at his sole pleasure, by whom he held the reins of every department of
the public service?   What else was that other master-
stroke of *centralization* (I like to speak of things, Monsieur le Prince, by their mildest names), whereby he
changed the whole judicial constitution of France, deprived
the parliament of all cognizance of political trials, transfer-
ring that important power to his own commissioners?   You
and I, prince, were boys when the Comte de Chalais was
condemned by these men, and the Marshal de Marillac

pleaded for his life before them, and would have pleaded
in vain, had not the parliament stepped in.   Do you not
remember, again, when those creatures of despotic power
executed two unhappy men in the dead of the night in one
of the squares of this very city of Paris,—bowstrung the
slaves and flung them forth at the command of that same
grand vizier, who ruled as absolutely on the Seine as his
brother potentate on the Bosphorus?"

They had approached in their walk the high garden-wall
separating the archiepiscopal residence from the adjoining street, and were on the point of turning back again,
each sufficiently occupied with his own reflections, when a
tennis-ball, thrown from above, suddenly bounded against
the angle of the wall, and rolled towards Conde's feet.   At
the same moment, the head and shoulders of a man were
to be seen appearing above the coping-stones.   The intruder seemed to have no little difficulty in holding his
exalted position, so strenuously did his hands maintain the
uncertain grasp that was necessary to keep him from falling; while he was evidently objurgated with much earnestness by the prince's attendants from below.   Notwithstanding this, the features of him who had thus become an
unobserved listener in the discussion were marked by an
expression of considerable intelligence and easy good-
humor.   He looked like one who was confident of the
reception he would meet with from those whom he had
not hesitated to disturb in their conference; and apparently enjoyed the jest of having startled the coadjutor by a
sudden surprise, and nearly hit the hero who had escaped
so many missiles of a more formidable kind.

"Gourville!" said the prince good-humoredly, when
he had recognized his assailant, "this is a new way of
enforcing a challenge, unheard of in the articles of war.   I
must teach thee a little military etiquette.   I am engaged,"
continued he, turning to his companion, who stood by,
nowise gratified by this interruption, just when he had half
won his important ally,—"I am engaged to play a match
with Marsillac at the Luxembourg; and, in truth, I had
well-nigh forgotten it in the interest of our discourse.   So
he sends this impudent fellow," with another look of pa-

tronizing good-humor at the valet, who had now perched
himself securely astride on the wall, "to remind me of the
challenge; and the rogue thinks he cannot do it better
than by giving me a contusion. *Garde a vous*, discourte-
ous enemy!" and he stooped to pick up the ball.

Just before delivering it, however, at Gourville's head,
his eye was caught by some writing on the leather. It
was, in truth, villanously enough executed; nevertheless
Conde was able rapidly to spell out the following words of
caution: "*Close with nothing; the time is not yet.*"

De Retz, foiled in the master-stroke he had been
achieving, was in too abstracted a mood to note this circumstance; and the prince, snatching a large pebble from
the gravel-walk, and merely saying in the same careless
tone that he should reserve the first missile to be, like
Guillaume Tell's additional arrow, a *corps de reserve* in
need, cried out, "*To Philip's right eye, ha!*" and sent the
stone whistling towards his challenger. Gourville watched
its approach with the utmost coolness, and an air of high
satisfaction at the success of his manœuvre; ducked with
consummate address to avoid the stone as it flew over his
head, and then, with a parting grin, slid down the garden-
wall and vanished. The next moment, the sound of his
fall, and a suppressed laugh from the attendants who were
watching his movements from without, showed that he
had not accomplished his descent as skilfully as he had
clambered up, or that some practical jest on their part had
occasioned his discomfiture. Conde joined heartily in the
laugh, and then turned to the coadjutor with a mute but
courteous apology for the interruption.

It was difficult to renew a discussion which had been
so suddenly and so unexpectedly broken. De Retz, however, was not a man easily baffled, and he was on the point
of recommencing; but Conde (and we doubt not our readers heartily sympathize with him) seemed by this time to
have become weary of the subject. He hastened, therefore, to conclude it by a final remark.

"You have referred to past things, Monseigneur le Coadjuteur; and I am aware that much remained in store for
you to quote. Enough,—let the dead sleep; we have no

man now to put forth a hand of power like that which lies
in the dust of Notre Dame; there lives no second Richelieu.
Had he left a successor in France," added he, endeavoring to break off by giving the discussion a lighter turn,
"where would all such prelates have found themselves by
this time, as endeavor to beguile princes of the blood
and stanch royalists from their allegiance? Cinq Mars,
De Thou, Moret, and the rest, did not half so much in
their day, and yet paid for their doings dearly. Nevertheless, be assured that I forget nothing of the topics we
have debated together. They are matters to be maturely
weighed. To decide them hastily might peril,—I will not
say our lives, for when did a soldier or (giving another
indescribable glance at his companion) a priest value his
life at the call of duty?—but our honor and our duty themselves. Meanwhile the afternoon wears,

> 'And Phœbus waits not on the strife of men.'

No," added he jestingly, "not whether they concern la
haute politique, or the vicissitudes of the tennis-court—a
no less royal game!" So saying, and with a courtly
reverence, he turned to retrace his steps down the garden-
avenue. De Retz laid his hand earnestly on the prince's arm.
"One word, Monsieur le Prince," he pleaded, "and I
have done. All I have had the honor to mention to you
exhibits a fatal tendency; manifested, openly avowed,
under the dominion of Richelieu; unchanged at the
present day, spite of the reluctant concessions of the regent.
We tended *then* towards absolute monarchy; we tend to
it now. The difference between the two periods is simply
this; formerly you had an able minister guiding the actions
of a feeble king; now you have a minister who is indeed
personally contemptible, but with the vantage-ground of
an example borrowed from that great man of whom he is
an inferior copy. And you have a young king to whom
every day adds something in development of intelligence
and strength of will, and who will soon force Mazarin from
the timid policy to which his own natural indolence inclines
him. Hard times appear to be reserved for those lovers of
freedom who would fain restore the balance of constitu-

tion in their native land. The regent is a host in herself
on the side of absolutism, and pursues her course with the
reckless inconsideration of a woman, and the imperiousness
of a woman who wears a crown. Parliament may vote
resolutions, the people may raise barricades: what are
obstacles like these to the onward force which the monarchy has gathered to itself during the last years? There
will be troubles and convulsions, and the kingly power
will but consolidate its strength amid them all. Louis
XIV. ascends the throne of his ancestors; and if the opening germs of character now traceable in him bear their expected fruit, we shall live to see nobles and burghers alike
fettered to his triumphant chariot-wheels. And oh, my
prince," he exclaimed, flashing out with one of those bursts
of enthusiasm which made his earnest speaking so persua-
sive, "upon *you* now lies the glorious task of reducing
these dangerous conflicting elements to order! All eyes
are turned upon you: those of your royal relatives and
their minions with some apprehension; those of the enslaved commons with a growing hope. You are the man
of the court; I dispute it not. Your gifts, your station,
your renown, combine to lay all its honors at your feet.
Let me say a bold word—aim higher still: *become the man
of the age.* The times demand you; France calls aloud
upon you: France, ever proud to claim you as her son,
now implores you to become the restorer of her dearest
liberties. Throw yourself into this unnatural breach that
yawns between king and people, with the same intrepidity,—ay, let me speak out my whole thought,—with
a yet loftier courage than impelled your breast against the
Spanish pikes in the most obstinate of your foreign battles. The moment is now; but let it pass, and it returns
not. Richelieu off the throne, the young king not yet
seated; a crowd of banished ones returned, and in their
right places once more; free play for every lawful right
and hallowed usage; the less privileged classes ready with
just demands in their firm hands:—there is a pause of
universal expectation. Whom do I see advancing to inau-
gurate that moment and fulfil its mission? It is a Bourbon; a princely Bourbon!—he comes to vindicate the

noblest privilege of rank and blood, to throw his invincible shield over the oppressed, to equalize again the balance which the self-aggrandizement of his family had been unduly weighing down. Honor to him, that noble spirit! Blessings on him, that wise and self-renouncing benefactor! His brows, shaded already by the proud though barren laurels of so many triumphs in the field, are thenceforth encircled by a far dearer wreath—the civic crown bestowed by a rescued and a thankful people!"

## CHAPTER XV.

### A COLLISION ON OPPOSITE TACKS.

*Gregory.* Do you quarrel, sir?
*Abram.* Quarrel, sir? no, sir.
*Sampson.* If you do, sir, I am for you: I serve as good a man as you.
*Abram.* You lie.
*Sampson.* Draw, if you be men. Gregory, remember thy swashing blow.
*Benvolio.* Put up your swords; you know not what you do.
*Romeo and Juliet.*

"Keep to thine own side, friend—villain! what art thou coming hitherward for? Back, or we shall cut thy traces for thee; back, I say, at thy peril!"

So shouted, with many a malediction subjoined, the driver of a splendid though ponderous coach-and-six. The massive vehicle, occupying no inconsiderable space in breadth, was being drawn at a round pace by its team of superb bays, which would have been considered in our degenerate times (such as men and horses now are) as model specimens of the powerful cart-horse. They thundered at a heavy trot along the paved causeway of the Rue du Faubourg St. Denis, which led from the heart of the city to

that pleasant suburb.   The Faubourg St. Denis was a frequent thoroughfare for the great, the idle, and the dissi-
pated, seeking to throw off their state cares, or recruit
their spirits by a brief airing in the country, whose quiet-
ness had no permanent attractions for them.   This seemed
the purpose for which those six "storm-footed" bays, their
manes and tails fantastically plaited up with ribbons of
showy hue, were now making the richly emblazoned vehicle rumble along the broad street with an impetus that
caused the ill-fitting glass to rattle in the house-windows
on either side.   The lady who occupied the principal place
in the carriage appeared greatly to need the refreshment
of country air, or whatever better restorative could be found
for the languor of a mind and body subjected to the hard
slavery of the world.   She was partly reclining, with a
restless pettish air, on the luxurious cushions of the roomy
coach ; the black half-mask, which ladies of fashion then
often wore in public, was dashed aside, and showed a countenance strikingly noble indeed, and beautiful, but possessed
with an expression of weary discontent that told unmis-
takably there was no peace within that fair exterior.   Ah,
Genevieve de Bourbon, it demands some mightier remedy
than the fresh air of St. Denis to restore tranquility to a
bosom so capable as yours of appreciating the truly beautiful, of loving the only God ; and yet so miserably diverted
from either as you are at present.

It needed all the objurgations of the coachman, of which
we have given some mitigated idea, and all the clamor of
the attendants who invariably accompanied a coach of
quality, to rouse Madame de Longueville from her gloomy,
perhaps her self-reproachful, reverie.   The cause of this
untoward incident in her drive soon became obvious, as she
raised herself with an effort, and, resettling her mask,
looked from the carriage-window.   At the turning of a
corner, at which a side street opened into the main thoroughfare, another coach-and-six had encountered her
equipage.   This unexpected stranger was indeed proceeding
at a pace more moderate · than that which the attendants
of the duchess knew best suited the impatient spirit of
their lady.   Yet, partly from the unmanageable length of

traces by which the leaders with their postillion were separated from the four-in-hand behind them, partly from the want of skill in one, or both, of the rival coachmen, the new-comer threatened to impinge upon the Longueville squadron; or, as a seaman would have expressed the accident, to "run in upon its starboard quarter." Hence arose those clamorous exhortations with which the stranger was greeted, and which grew all the more vehement and wrathful (such is the nature of man) as it became obvious that the assailant was, after all, the party more sinned against than sinning. Dire was the confusion of tongues as the two equipages, each impelled at a speed which their drivers could not slacken on the spot, unavoidably neared each other. Almost at right angles they hurtled on: there were a few moments of confusion and shouting on the side of the Longueville escort; while the other coachman now strove in grim silence to perform the desperate manœuvre which alone remained to him—that of executing a *demi-volte*, sheering in close to the side of his antagonist, and shooting astern round the corner. But for this the duchess's charioteer had allowed no sufficient space; and here lay the cause of the now inevitable accident, and of his towering rage. Both parties, however, struggled manfully; the horses were thrown upon their haunches, and reared wildly, while the street resounded with their prancings. The next moment, one hind-wheel of either carriage came in collision with its opponent with a crash that almost rent them from their axles; and so they remained firmly locked together.

Then began a fresh torrent of eloquence; but this time the former orator was fairly eclipsed by his rival. He in his wrong place! he had held to his side of the street all along, if that clumsy ignoramus, who did not deserve to drive a *bourgeoise* to church on a rainy Sunday, had not brought his lumbering vehicle in the way. He bidden to give place! as if the coach of the De Marillacs had not the right of road with any chance-comer. And here staid the rhetorical charioteer; in part, because his eye had by this time glanced on the armorial bearings of the house of Bour-

11

bon and Montmorency* quartered with those of Longueville on the panels of the coach he had run into; and no
less because personal defence became necessary against the
vigorous assault made upon him by the whip of his antagonist. The latter, if he had shown himself deficient in
the skill to avoid their mutual disaster, had no lack of
muscle or good-will in exacting from his supposed aggressor the penalty of a sound horse-whipping. Nor, it must
be confessed, did he fail in that other great quality of a
combatant—unflinching endurance in sustaining from the
opposite party blows as heavy and as well-directed as those
he was inflicting.

Swords meanwhile had leaped from their scabbards;
and the attendants, who numbered four or five on either
side, ranged themselves, with threatening looks, for a conflict: no unusual occurrence in the streets of Paris in those
disordered times. There was every symptom of an instant
and a bloody fray. Madame de Longueville, who on other
occasions could play the heroine on a large scale, startled
by the shock of the collision, and roused suddenly from
thoughts that had been far away,—guilty thoughts, it may
be, which always make cowards of their entertainers,—
now lost entirely her presence of mind. She screamed, and
threw her arms wildly from the carriage-window. The
sight of her distress only served the more to inflame her
retainers; who were rushing upon their antagonists with a
determination to avenge this insult upon the dignity of the
house they served, when all were hushed at once by a voice
from the opposite carriage.

"Peace!" said—in a low sweet tone, rendered a little
tremulous by the agitation of the moment—a lady in
widow's weeds, as she threw open the door of her coach,
and stood on the step. "Peace, my friends!" said she a
second time, looking round on the angry countenances and

---

* Anne-Geneviève de Bourbon, Duchesse de Longueville, was the
daughter of Henri, Prince de Conde, and of Marguerite de Montmorency, a sister of the great duke of that name, and heiress of
great part of his possessions after his execution. Madame de
Longueville was, therefore, sister of the great Conde, and of his
brother, the Prince de Conti.

bared weapons of the dozen of excited men, on the verge of shedding each other's blood.

There was something in that voice that thrilled and yet allayed the listeners. The sword-points dropped towards the pavement; the less sanguinary but not less wrathful combat of the two potentates in mid-air ceased likewise. There were heaving breasts and flashing eyes; but actual hostility was suspended.

The speaker was a lady past middle-life,* whose countenance bore evident traces of that self-mortification which, by subduing the natural to the spiritual man, builds up an undecaying shrine for eternity on the ruins of the fleshly tabernacle. There was a calmness in her eye which harmonized well with that pale cheek, and that composed and simple though dignified bearing.

"Michel," said she at length, turning to the principal valet, who with an abashed countenance was already sheathing his sword, "are these the lessons you have learned from the scene of misery and death we have so lately quitted in yonder street: to be as forward to offer violence as to repel it; to rush into eternity, and to drag thither also the soul of a fellow-mortal, your victim? Will

---

* Louise de Marillac, niece of the Marechal of that name, was born in 1591; and married Antoine Legras, secretary to Mary of Medicis. Even during her husband's lifetime she devoted herself to works of mercy, especially to that of visiting and tending the poor in their sickness, with the most heroic victory over the natural repugnances of one so delicately nurtured. On the death of Monsieur Legras, in 1625, she redoubled her fervor in these and other good works. Having been committed by Mgr. Camus, Bishop of Belley, who seems to have been her relative by the mother's side, to the spiritual direction of St. Vincent de Paul, she became one of the principal co-operators of that zealous and apostolic man in the successive works he undertook for the relief of temporal or spiritual misery. She may be regarded as having, conjointly with himself, founded the Order of Sisters of Charity, or *Sœurs Grises;* and when her saintly director commenced his efforts on behalf of the foundling children of Paris, Madame Legras hired a house for them in the Faubourg St. Victor; and, as she had been formerly styled the mother of the poor, so now she became the mother of the foundlings. After a life thus employed in personal mortifications, and the most energetic devotion to works of charity, Madame Legras died in 1662.

not madame," continued she, addressing the Duchesse de
Longueville with a courtly inclination, "do me the favor
of instructing her people to assist mine in extricating us
from our common though unexpected misfortune?"

Thus appealed to, Madame de Longueville again leant
forward in her carriage. No greater contrast could well
be than that afforded by the two high-born ladies who
thus, in a manner, confronted each other. In the one
were united all the graces of youth and unrivalled personal beauty, together with that perfection of manner
which is rather the unconscious result of habitual intercourse with noble equals than of any distinct process of
culture. These qualities, heightened and exhibited by
a dress rich in the extreme, did not fail to constitute a
striking and brilliant picture to the eye. The fair hair,
confined by strings of costly pearls, and breathing the
rarest perfumes; the blue eyes which, whenever awakened
from their habitual dreamy languor, could flash out with
sufficient fire to vindicate their kindred with the eagle
glance of Condé; the noble grace of contour and movement; these might have furnished court-poets with simi-
litudes, and have been sung to the strains of the rebeck
in the garden-alleys immortalized by Watteau's pencil.
And there was all! In that assemblage of rare gifts one
was wanting; the one that could alone harmonize the
rest, or give them value, except to the mere dull eye of
sense. Beauty there is, and gracefulness, and a noble
confiding trust in others, and a power of self-sacrifice
for those whom she believes as mentally noble as herself.
Alas! these very things have disorganized the inner
kingdom of the heart, dethroned the supremacy, though
not silenced the voice, of conscience. They have
robbed her of that one priceless gem—the grace, *par excel-
lence*, which, descending from the Supreme, and echoing
the harmonics that surround Him, moulds human actions
by laws higher in their source, more beautiful in their
operation, than results in mere turn of gesture and manner, or lines of outward proportion or form. But to be
endowed with human gracefulness, and exiled from grace
divine; a whited sepulchre, fair and garnished without,

and within a pray to death and corruption; to attract the
eyes of men, and be an abhorred thing in the sight of
heaven; the cynosure of a crowd of fellow-sinners, and a
sorrow to one's guardian-angel; to have the world in the
fulness of its glitter, while the jewel of great price—the
peace of the soul—lies in the hands of that soul's exulting enemy—what is this? It is to be a Duchesse de
Longueville!

Calmly regarding her, with a touch of sorrow,—for
they had been acquainted in those days when the young
Princesse de Bourbon, fresh, untried, with pure and noble
aspirations, was a frequent guest of the Carmelite Sisters
in the Faubourg Saint-Jacques,—Madame Legras was
still standing on her carriage-step. High-born, graceful, intellectual, with the evident stamp of breeding, and
much that constitutes the charm of society, this lady outshone the other in that peculiar undefinable manner,
refined at once and sympathetic, which forms the endow-
ment of those whose hearts are detached from self, and
can therefore be all leisure and considerateness to those
around them. It is the genuine though rare quality;
while mere conventional elegance is but the poor copy, the
inadequate substitute. A writer who was then rising into
eminence, and who, but for his Jansenism, might have
been saint as well as philosopher, had observed that
human politeness does but conceal the human self, does
but suppress its manifestations; while Christian charity
tends to its annihilation.* Such a manner, so winning, so
subduing to inferior natures, results perhaps in every case
from the combination of high qualities, belonging at once
to the natural order and to the supernatural. It was possessed in an eminent degree by Madame Legras. You
could not approach her without feeling yourself within the
sphere of a being of no ordinary mould; of one superior
to the average of great ladies, or even of good ladies.
There was an unconscious dignity amid all her sweetness,
less, perhaps, a relic from early training and associations in
the world than from present familiarity with the highest,
the most ennobling contemplations. And this was united

* Pascal.

11*

with a humbleness of mind that startled you as you approached it, from its depth and reality, and with something of the engaging simplicity of a guileless child.   Contradictory as such qualities might have seemed before experience, yet in Louise Legras, as in so many other of the followers of Him who impersonated "the majesty of meekness," they coexisted naturally and without effort.  Those who saw her most frequently found it hard to say whether they were more awed in her presence by the tokens of elevated sanctity that beamed round her, or attracted by her unassuming gentleness and sweet sympathetic charity.

Long before we have completed our sketch of two characters thus brought into strange juxtaposition, and while they were exchanging some few words of courtesy, the lacqueys on their part, with hearty good-will, now that peace was restored, had succeeded in disengaging the cumbrous vehicles, and all was in order for their continuing their respective routes.  At that moment the low wailing of an infant, awakened probably by the jolting and various other rude noises attending the accident, was heard from the coach of Madame Legras.

There was a movement of surprise, and some curiosity, among the party, at a sound so unexpected.  The lady turned with one of her bright smiles, and calmly said, in a tone of affectionateness that thrilled upon the ear, "Hush, little one! is it for thee to disturb with unseasonable complainings a peace so happily established?"  Then addressing Madame de Longueville, in a tone that reached her only, she continued: "Ah, *chere amie*—if I may still call you so—the time has been when I could have asked you with so much pleasure to come with me and visit our house of foundlings in the Porte Saint-Victor!  It is thither I am carrying this poor little creature, whose first experience of a miserable world is, to be abandoned by nature in order to be adopted by grace.  Let me not detain you longer from your airing.  But may that good time come again!  Yes, dear Lord, may it come soon!" added she fervently; and as she raised her face to heaven, the tears fell over her worn cheeks.

"Onward, sirrah!" exclaimed the duchess, conscience-startled, and venting the anger of her self-reproach upon her luckless charioteer, as she bowed her *adieux* to Madame Legras. The coach swept majestically by at a long trot.

"*Au revoir*, brother," muttered the coachman of the latter lady, in a subdued growl, which reached, however, the person for whom it was intended; "and next time we meet, remember to keep thine own place, and not accuse other folks of getting out of theirs."

"And if I do not make my whip curl round both thine ears, thou varlet," returned the rival Jehu in renewed ire, and shaking aloft the threatened instrument, "thou mayest call me the driver of a market-cart in Brittany!"

So parted, with gestures and intonations worthy of a place in the Iliad, the incensed and reluctant charioteers, each upon his way.

"Sister Marie Pauline," said Madame Legras, turning, as her carriage proceeded, to the *sœur grise*, or religious of the Order of Charity,—established by Vincent de Paul, not only in Paris, but in many of the provincial towns of France,—who was seated by her side, with the foundling infant in her arms, "do you not remember those few words of our dear father when he assembled Madame de Miramion and some others of us in the church, to plead the cause of these deserted children? You were there, I think? And I could not help half-quoting them just now to that unhappy lady."

"Imperfectly I remember them, madame," replied the staid and humble religious.

"*Fi donc!*" returned the lady playfully; "such words are not spoken every day, and should be treasured in our memories. I see him now before me," continued she with earnestness, and clasping her hands together, "the light streaming upon his venerable white hair, and surrounding his countenance with a halo which it needed not; for there was a radiance on those features that seemed caught as a reflection from the unearthly glory. At his feet lay several of the foundlings who had been received into the hospital of the Porte Saint-Landri; others were in the arms of the sisters who surrounded him. The sobs and plaints of these

little unconscious sufferers were already enough to move
our hearts ; nor was it needful to enter into details of the
horrors to which they were too often subjected, and which
were well known to many of us.   Think, sister, of these
unoffending ones, these frail tabernacles of immortal spirits,
being exposed in the cold, in the night, on the steps of
street-doors ; as an alternative on the other side of which
was murder, and murder without baptism !   Think—I
tremble to repeat it—of their being sold for twenty *sous*
to the first bidder ; sold to those from whom they were
to draw, not nourishment, but contagion and death : sold
even"—she paused, and went on with an effort—"for
inhuman and magical operations, or to furnish such a
sanguinary bath as the heathen emperor meditated, a
direful unholy cure for the leprosy wherewith heaven had
smitten him !"

The religious simply closed her eyes with a thrill, and
pressed the little one who had been rescued from such a
fate more closely to her bosom.

"Then it was," continued Madame Legras, "that the
apostolic old man rose up in the midst, and with a manner
simple, yet awful in its dignity, pronounced a few words
from which sprang to life our house for foundlings : 'Look
to it, ladies,' cried he, 'whether you also in turn will
abandon these little innocents, whose mothers you have
become in the order of grace, after their abandonment by
their mothers in the order of nature.   Cease for a moment
to be their mothers, that you may become their judges ;
their lives and their deaths are now in your hands : I am
going to take the votes.   It is time to give sentences upon
them.'   Ah, who could withstand such an appeal, uttered
by one so holy, and with the evident power of Him in
whose name he speaks every word ?"

"Blessed are they, madame, who say and do all things
for God," was the simple aphorism of the *sœur grise*.

"On, on ; faster, faster !" impatiently exclaimed Madame de Longueville, already half a mile beyond the Porte
Saint-Denis.   Her coachman urged his horses into a hand-
gallop ; a cloud of dust reeked up from the road, and

vollied round the carriage : fit emblem of the trouble and confusion that reigned in the breast of its occupant.

"Faster, faster," she still murmured; "and yet, to what purpose?" She sank back again. "Who can fly from their own thoughts, from their own wounds? It is *here*, it is *here*;" and she clasped her hands, to press them convulsively upon her aching bosom.

———

## CHAPTER XVI.

### AN OASIS IN THE DESERT.

"One of those divine men, who, like a chapel in a palace, remain unprofaned, while all the rest is tyranny, corruption, and folly."
*Walpole.*

YES; Madame Legras had not exaggerated. Among fluttering crowds of pleasure-seekers, and mighty Nimrods of ambition, votaries of self in a thousand various forms ; among abbes who were scheming for the mitre and the hat, or squandering themselves upon the literary trifle and the frivolity of the passing hour,—one man at least there was whose career and example stood out in marked contrast with the evil generation among whom his lot was cast. His was a will firm enough to withstand, like some immovable rock, that full-flowing tide of iniquity ; and his was a heart capacious enough to embrace, not Paris merely, nor France, nor civilized Europe, but humanity entire, in the earnest energy of its love. And so great was his influence upon the society no less than the government of France during the reigns of Louis XIII. and of his son, and through the intervening regency, that it would be unpardonable to attempt any sketch of that period without bringing Vincent de Paul again upon the scene.

Viewed in any aspect, the history of St. Vincent presents
a great moral phenomenon.  A poor priest, of mean extraction, who in his youth had tended sheep; friendless and
lowly, on the *landes*, or sandy plains, of Acqs; becomes
the centre of several important organizations,—important
politically, no less than to religion,—and the leading man
of his day, in the front rank of all that is really noble and
self-devoted.  He does not achieve greatness, as so many
have done before him and since, by the force of commanding talents, or at the bidding of a dominant ambition.  He
literally has greatness thrust upon him against his will ; he
cannot escape from the height of his position but by aban-
doning the interest of those to whom he is the guide to a
better world, and whose welfare is dearer to him than all
besides.  You discern him on his long voyage through
life, buoyantly cresting the proud world's topmost waves,
embarked with Cæsar and his fortunes, and not without a
hand upon the rudder itself; while his whole bent, and
every exertion of his energetic will, lie counter to that
same world's powerful seductive stream.

Yet here and there, on the moving panorama of history,
though in few instances more prominently than in this, we
may see a marked figure stand out in like manner from the
rest.  He so passes over the changeful scene as unconsciously to draw after him the eyes of observers.  He is
distinguished from the throng of triflers around him by a
concentration of the will upon one great object, giving him
a power he might not have inherited from nature, and
stamping him even in the eye of the philosopher, perhaps
also of the historian, as a remarkable man.

On the map of a district or a county run devious lanes
and by-paths in abundance, high-roads or bridle-ways
meandering, crossing, falling into one another : a tangled
network of traffic flung over the face of the land.  They
lose themselves, too, where the barren moor abruptly cuts
them off and the lane dwindles into an irregular horse-
track, or where the marsh renders them impassable, or the
straggling hamlet forms their ignoble bourne.  It is a picturesque confusion, and essentially natural.  Birds of song
love to haunt such spots, dreamers wander on and lose

themselves in reveries among them; men of art come to note with their poor imitative skill the wild irregularities, the graceful deviations and turns of feature, in that varied scenery. But it is with a far different interest that we mark the few straight determined road-lines stretching from point to point across the chart, as unerring as the flight of some strong bird, going right at the goal as they make for great successive halts; attaining this, thence shooting off to that, more distant. They leave their track well defined over the breadth of a province; those old military grooves, along which have rolled the pride and the power of armies long in the dust. Through all places alike, desert or populous, they hold right on, towards some ancient war-post or camp now sunk within turfy mounds, or grown into a provincial city. Through it they plunge and cleave—known for some hundred yards as the Watling Street, or the Foss Way, or the Roman Wall; then out again through the North Gate, away into the open country, stretching far and free from castrum to castrum; now thronged with way-farers, where a modern thoroughfare has adopted and widened the line; now left as a green solitary passage sheer through the wood; ploughed over at intervals, disjointed, yet unswerving still, turned aside never, nor ever wholly lost. Even such difference is there between man and man. The weakling, in his devious passage through life, graceful as may be its several scenes, novel and varied in its windings, fruitful in fancy, replete with interest in the after-narrating, is but the sport of its circumstances as they arise, the prey of its allurements as they offer. But he whose will, strongly bent on good, forms the guiding principle of his course; who tracks his undeviating way, yielding to no seduction from the paths that open on the right hand and on the left,—that constant steadfast man, less gifted, it may be, with the fatal brilliancy that misled his unstable brother, is yet graced with all the charm of consistency, and possesses the surest pledge of real abiding power.

When, therefore, we discover St. Vincent seated and writing in the roomy but scantily furnished apartment of his house of Saint Lazare, we may be sure that he is occu-

pied very differently from the crowds of intelligent and
educated beings who are breathing at that same moment
the air of Paris; and who, grave or thoughtless, toiling or
at rest, are simply pursuing their own fancies, and worshipping their own selfish aims.   It is to relieve a suffering, it is to gladden a distress, to enlighten an ignorance,
to remove a doubtfulness, to save from a sin, that Vincent
is at work there.   And as he bends over his writing; you
may see from the expression of his features how his whole
heart and soul go along with his occupation.   It is an old
man whom you are looking at; he sits by that little bare
table, without fire or carpet in his room, and clad, notwithstanding the severity of the season, in a cassock worn thin
with age.   He has seen more than threescore years and
ten of a world of toil, and passed them all in hardness of
living.   A youth of poverty, a middle life and age of
labor for souls, have inured him, indeed; but they have
combined, with rigorous penances, his "care of all the
churches," and a saint's constant sighing after his liberation to immortality, in tracing those furrows along his
cheeks, and wasting that spare frame.   But his brow is
unwrinkled, and tells of tranquillity and content reigning
there within; while the light in his eye, and the habitual
smile that plays on his speaking lips, seem almost to belie
the white hair which those long years of labor have
blanched in their fruitful passage over his head.   A well-
worn breviary lies on the table beside him; a small crucifix, towards which he occasionally glances with an ardent
look, as though to direct his intention in performing the
work that engrosses him, is placed immediately opposite.
Some few books of theology occupy a shelf, or lie upon one
or two of the chairs which form almost the only furniture of the apartment.   Against the wall is placed the
prie-dieu, or kneeling-stool, for the old man's devotions;
his manifold occupations never hinder his spending large
portions of his day in prayer, and he recites the divine
office on his knees.   Over this hangs a small picture,
devotional rather than of artistic merit, representing the
Mother of Dolours with the Incarnate Word dead in her
arms; a rosary, with a small reliquary attached, is twined

around the frame. Doubtless, under the *prie-dieu*, were we to search, or perhaps hidden within the hard couch in the adjoining room, we should discover the discipline of small cords with which the man of God is daily accustomed to subdue the flesh to the spirit, and to teach his inferior nature,—he who needs the warning so far less than others,—lessons derived from the Passion of the Redeemer, and the punishments in store for sin hereafter.

The writer was not destined to continue his employment long undisturbed. A modest tap at the door soon announced an interruption, and there appeared one of the *sœurs grises*, accompanied by a lay-sister. Both were in the habit of their order, with hands folded in the ample sleeves of course serge, and faces partially veiled by the large and very ungainly head-dress which Vincent has appointed as an essential part of their costume. The sister is come from her superior with some message to him whom they all regard as their common father in Christ; something to be undertaken for the good of their house and the advancement of religion, or some case of distress for which he may exert himself with the wealthy and the great. But she has only just made her reverence, and is proceeding with her message, when a quick, determined footstep, with the jingling of spurs and the clash of a rapier-scabbard on the stair, is heard ascending; and with hardly the interval of a hasty tap on the door, the head of a cavalier, shaking choice perfumes from his elaborate *chevelure*, suddenly presents itself, with a good-humored, half-saucy laugh.

"Ah, *mon pere*," cries the intruder, "engaged? But not from me, I hope. I have stolen away for a quarter of an hour from the palace; and have no objection," added the richly-dressed young man, advancing into the room with considerable assurance, though not without a certain deferential air towards the saint,—"not the least objection," pursued he, as he laid aside his rapier, "to acknowledge to these good sisters that I am come for confession; on which plea I hope they will let my business claim precedence."

"Ah, truant!" exclaimed Vincent, rising—a bright
12

fatherly smile beamed on his expressive face as he folded
the gay cavalier in his arms—"and where have you been
all this while? Confession? Yes, indeed; and the first
thing you will have to confess is this, that you have nearly
forgotten your poor old father and servant in Christ, and
how anxiously he has been expecting some tidings of you,
you wandering sheep! with your *tete de mouton*, too ;" and
he pulled the curled locks of the other till the young noble
gave a half-comic grimace of pain.

"Sister Marie Françoise," then said Vincent, turning to
the religious, who, with her companion, had witnessed this
little episode with the air of quiet amusement that befits
even the most recollected on all becoming occasions, "commend me to the mother superioress, and say, with my
respects, that I hope to be with her a short hour hence.
These spoilt children of the world," continued the old man,
laying his arm upon the shoulder of the last comer,
"expect to be humored, and petted also, by the Church,
under pain of their insisting on ruining their souls out of
sheer spite to us; and Monsieur le Vicomte here knows
me to be too old a fisherman to lose any off the hook again
that venture within the cast of my line. *Au revoir*, then,
sister: be good enough to go round by the Quai des Orfevres, and see that poor Madeleine Henrieau, whom you
have attended so well through her protracted agonies. Prepare her for my coming, and for the Sacraments; for I shall
take her on my way, when I have looked in at the conference which is now being held at the Jacobins. And stay,"
added he, stepping to an *escritoire*, whose mean appearance did not betoken the guardianship of much treasure,
but from which he took a heavy purse of gold; "that I
may not mix together things temporal and spiritual when
I come, give her yourself this *louis-d'or*, and tell her to
pray for Monseigneur the Coadjutor, for it comes from his
generosity through my unworthy hands. And now, my
beloved son," continued he, no longer with his former play-
fulness, but with even more marked tenderness of manner
and expression, as the door closed upon the Sisters of
Charity, "have you indeed offended our dearest Lord?
Praise be to His long-suffering! He has still spared you

to tell me so. Let us begin, that you may be the sooner reconciled to Him again."

At this moment the clatter of a horse was heard galloping along the paved street, and reined up suddenly at the *porte cochere* of St. Lazare, while a trumpet woke repeated echoes from all the houses around.

"What is it, brother?" demanded Vincent, whom nothing ever disturbed, though the arrival of some one was now producing a sensation below. What is it?" he again asked of the porter, who had hastened up to his room, but had not ventured beyond knocking and waiting for a reply. "A message from her majesty?"—for such was the announcement he received through the door;—"it is well. Beg of the courier to have the complaisance to wait a brief space in the guest-room; see that he wants for no refreshment this house can afford him. At present," he continued, turning to his penitent with a fond look, and motioning him to the *prie-dieu*, "I am myself charged with a message from the King of kings; and the human must give place to the divine. We will render to Cæsar the things that are Cæsar's, as soon as we have rendered to God the things that are God's."

## CHAPTER XVII.

### EARS POLITE.

"Oft have I heard of you, my Lord Biron,
Before I saw you; and the world's large tongue
Proclaims you for a man replete with mocks,
Full of comparisons and wounding flouts,
Which you on all estates will execute
That lie within the mercy of your wit."
                                        *Love's Labour's Lost.*

AND Antoine? We have not lost sight of him amid the other characters that have passed over our scene; and we now resume the part of Pylades to our Orestes by accom-

panying that modish personage to some of the brilliant
*reunions* which divide with his duties of guardsman the
young lieutenant's time. Not, however, to waste needlessly
our own and that of our readers in the employment, we will
record one special evening on which he bids us follow him
to a *conversazione* at the Hotel de Rambouillet. At the
period of our story, and for some years afterwards, with the
exception of an interval during the height of the Fronde,
the Rambouillet was the centre of all that Paris afforded of
noblest, most intellectual, and, let us add, most exemplary.
In that age of chartered license, the possession of great
natural qualities often became an admitted title to their
open and reckless abuse. Wit, courtliness, courage and
military talents, high birth, splendid fortune, statesmanship,
as well as poetry and grace and beauty, were all too generally enlisted on the side of evil. It was, therefore, a
refreshment to the moral sense to find one palace at least,
and one illustrious circle, witnessing to the truth, that it
was possible, and might be as pleasant, to cultivate the
*belles lettres* without making them handmaidens to licen-
tiousness, and to exercise wit otherwise than by outraging
religion and good conduct. Very willingly do we bend
our steps to spend an hour in the Hotel de Rambouillet.

Antoine, preceded by two richly-dressed lackeys with
flambeaux and well armed, turned out of the Rue St.
Thomas du Louvre into the court which led to the principal staircase of the hotel. On the pavement of the court,
two or three well-supplied bonfires of resinous pine-wood
were blazing to dispel the damp fogs of a winter's evening;
while along the ample flight of stairs leading to the suite
of reception-rooms were ranged several domestics in the
livery of the house of Angennes, the broad glare of whose
waxen torches lit up in strong relief the features and dresses
of such of the company as were already ascending to the
saloons. Among these De Bonneval recognized several of
his court-acquaintances,—for the receptions of the Marquis
de Rambouillet were thronged with the *elite* of the Parisian
world; but he also observed others mingling among the
titled and high-born whose distinctions had been conferred
on them rather by the republic of letters. These, with the

A TALE OF PARIS. 133

exception of a court-poet or two, were chiefly unknown to
Antoine; for we have misrepresented our hero, if the reader
imagines him to be bestowing much of his precious time on
literature or the sciences.  Indeed, he was so struck with
the medley formed by those whom he had seen moving in
the highest spheres of Paris, and those whose faces were
entirely new to him, that he paused for a few moments on
the landing of the staircase, and watched the different
groups as they crowded up towards the spot on which he
was standing.

That middle-aged man, in rich and rather tawdry attire,
who mounts the steps with a certain air of gasconade, is
George Scudery, the dramatist; he has long quitted the
guards, and has been working with indefatigable perseverance for the theatre.  The great object of his present
ambition is to be admitted a member of the Academy of
France.  Had his former patron Richelieu been still alive,
he might easily have attained that summit of his hopes;
so greatly had he pleased the cardinal by a vigorous cri-
tique on one whom Richelieu considered as his great literary rival, Corneille.  But Scudery's *Observations on the
Cid* have proved less immortal than the work of genius
which they assailed; and now *The Death of Cæsar*, or
some of his numerous tragi-comedies, must win for him
a disputed niche among the academicians.  The imperial
Roman, however, would not have been much consoled
in dying by the exaggerated bombast in which the dramatist's perverted taste had set forth his closing scene.  It
was truly, to use the quotation of the learned and caustic
Abbe Menage, from a poet then beginning to be known in
France, "Great Cæsar dead, and turn'd to clay!"  Ah,
here comes Marsillac, late and leisurely as usual, sauntering up the broad stair to pay his compliments to the lady
of the house.  He will trifle away an hour in aphorism and
repartee, delivered with the easy grace of a mere man of
fashion, yet containing so much of shrewd meaning, and
such keen observation of men, that the hearers will carry
away the impromptu maxim as a text for their more deliberate observations of life and character.  This is a more
congenial atmosphere to the future Duke de la Rochefou-
12*

cault than the stir of active politics; and he attains to no
higher position in *that* department than to be an eminent
theorist and a very subordinate actor. He is formed, or
has formed himself, rather to loll in the stage-box of the
great drama of life, to take snuff, and criticise with that
searching gray eye, and see the play played out before
him, than to mingle with other characters upon the actual
scene. But we must now press on to the crowd of literary
and scientific notables who are surrounding the ladies in
yonder saloon.

It is, in truth, rather an awful circle we are approaching—a very *chambre ardente* of literary reputations. The
ordinary scandal, which forms, together with politics, the
staple of conversation among the *coteries* of Paris, is banished by a tacit convention from the evenings at the Rambouillet. But it seems as though this general armistice,
during which characters sufficiently lacerated at other
times may repose without apprehension of a fresh onslaught, only gives leisure for a more desperate series
of skirmishes and single combats in the literary arena.
Deadly is the encounter of wits; merciless are the thrusts
given and exchanged among these votaries of the full-
armed Minerva; all the more, because so polished and
keen, and delivered with the grace and precision of experienced masters of defence.

There was one presiding genius, however, whose influence was always exerted on the side of conciliation and
harmless wit—the fair Julie de Montausier. The marriage
of the Marquis de Rambouillet with Catharine de Vivonne,
in 1600, had been the date from which these *reunions*,
afterwards so celebrated, and maintained through political
changes for more than sixty years, first commenced. Their
daughter, Julie de Rambouillet, became celebrated among
the distinguished personages who thronged her father's
assemblies, for noble qualities alike of mind and heart.
She had now been married about three years to Charles de
Sainte-Maure, Duke de Montausier, the son of an ancient
family in the Touraine, himself a distinguished marechal,
and one of the devoted loyalists who preserved their allegiance to the royal cause unbroken through the troubles of

the Fronde. Twenty years later, Louis XIV., grateful
for the duke's fidelity, will have appointed him governor
of his son, the almost infant dauphin. Montausier will
then acquire yet higher reputation at a court composed for
the most part of servile flatterers, by his lofty, unbending,
and even austere rectitude. But though his pupil died
before coming to the throne, literature at least is inebted
to the duke for having promoted that edition of the classics
so well known as *in usum Delphini*.

"I appeal to you, Monsieur le Marquis," said Julie de
Montausier, turning to an elderly courtier, who was leaning over a chair without taking any prominent part in the
conversation : "you shall enlist on my side. There is a
very anti-Spanish party in vogue just now. I am not
meaning to be political, madame," she continued, smiling,
and with a glance towards the Duchesse de Longueville,
whose look betokened that the last words had not passed
unnoticed ; "but speaking quite innocently of the literature
of our warlike neighbors. I maintain the Spanish to be one
of the grandest tongues the world has ever produced, and
that we shamefully neglect it in our national self-sufficiency.
What can be finer than the vigor, rude though it is occasionally, with which Calderon gives us his original but
well-intentioned ideas? For my part, I think the Saracen
element in that language lends it an agreeable relief ; res-
cues it from the effeminacy which might be charged against
the softier Italian. It is like the sonorous tones of a trumpet compared with the breathings of shepherd's flute.
But here is that incorrigible Menage, who will not give
in to me, opposing my ideas with all his Della Cruscan
lore, and firing a battery of Italian that silences my defence altogether. Now we regard you as one of the
'*patres conscripti*' of the Academy ; so what say you?"

The Marquis de Racan, thus appealed to, thought he
could not do better than recall to the fair disputant a
reported saying of the Emperor Charles V., that French
was the language of conversation, Italian of sentiment, and
Spanish of religion.

"For my part," said Madame de Longueville, with that
degree of fashionable languor in her voice and manner

which gave to her occasional awakenings into energy all
the surprise of novelty, "I hold the Italian to be the divine
among languages. If our geographers had not placed
Olympus in Thessaly, I could maintain that Pallas and
Juno conversed together in the purest Tuscan ; and to us
mortals, it breathes the very spirit of the *dolce far niente*,
which I take to have been the prevalent occupation on
Olympus itself in those good old times."

"Excepting the memorable occasions when goddesses
descended on the rainbow to take an active share in the
combats of some favored hero upon earth," remarked, with
a profound bow, the poet Chapelain, who now joined the
circle.

"On which occasions, Monsieur Chapelain, they doubtless performed their part as valorously as your own long-
expected Pucelle," returned the duchess.

The poet, who was currently reputed to have been
engaged for some thirty years on this effort of his muse,
seemed rather staggared at the lady's repartee ; but recovering himself, he managed to say with tolerable grace,
that if his heroine had been some time in completing her
equipment, it was that she would have to encounter such
a phalanx of criticism and wit whenever she appeared.

Fresh accessions to the company turned the course of
conversation, which was suffered to flow easily in any
chance channel, like some sparkling stream that leaps
gaily, now in this direction, now in that, according to the
form and position of the objects among which it takes its
careless way. Two characteristics, however, marked the
conversation throughout : it was more distinctly of a
literary turn than was usual, and it maintained a very
unexceptionable character. This was understood from the
commencement of the *reunions*, which afterwards became
so celebrated, to be a primary law of their continuance.
In process of time, it is true, the carefulness with which
every thing was avoided that could debase the standard of
polite intercourse became exaggerated into a tone of affec-
tation, until it brought upon these well-intentioned ladies
the relentless satire so well known as *Les Precieuses Ridi-
cules*. Yet it must also be acknowledged that a lash such

as Moliere was capable of inflicting was a penance over-
severe for what was at the most an error of discretion ;
an error arising from a better principle than probably the
comedian and satirist was well able to estimate.   But Moliere, at the period of our story, was only knwn in the
provinces as the leader of a band of strolling players ; and
the society of the Rambouillet culminated at its zenith,
unconscious of the man whose keen shafts of ridicule were
afterwards to effect its downfall.

"And where have you been all this age, prince ?" continued Julie, as Marsillac, with that union of nonchalance
and courteous deference, which sat so well upon him, glided
into the circle : "you are positively deserting the Muses ;
yes, all the nine ; for I do not suspect you of taking the
pains to cultivate even Terpsichore more than her sisters.
Is it Bellona"—with a scarcely perceptible glance around
her—"who detains you from Helicon ; or have you found
a classic name and rite whereby to propitiate the spirit of
ennui, to whom so many of us have long sacrificed in dumb
worship ?"

"If I have neglected the tuneful Nine, madame, at
least permit me to reserve all my homage for the Tenth,"
replied the prince readily.

"Expressed like a true courtier ; but I must not appropriate a title which you know all our little world here
lays at the feet of Mademoiselle Scudery.  Besides, if I
were to accept the compliment, would you not give me a
place among the other classes of fools, who are to figure in
those caustic experiences which Gourville says you will
one day give to the world ?  And why have you not
introduced your friend all this while ? for I see you have
been at the unusual trouble of standing sponsor to a new
face to-night.  Monsieur de Bonneval, did you say ?—and
in his majesty's uniform I observe : quite right, for many
reasons.  We are cosmopolitans here ; we belong to the
republic of letters, and own no form of government but
the poetic unities and the canons of taste and criticism.
In ancient Athens, you remember, they used to boast of
their freedom from all narrow prejudices and sour-faced

distinctions—you can give us the passage in Thucydides, Monsieur de Bonneval ? No ?"

Poor Antoine had not learned enough of courtly dissimulation to enable him to look any thing but blank at the sudden question ; while Marsillac's observant eyes watched his countenance for the answer, and lit up with a good-natured amusement at the evident honesty of his confusion.

"Well," pursued the lady, "if the Abbe Menage, there, was not so deeply engaged in discussing etymologies with my husband, I would have my revenge upon him by asking him the question. And yet I fear I should carry off no victory ; he would tell us in a moment whether it was in the funeral oration of Pericles, and on what leaf of the manuscript in the royal library. And apropos of that majestic old historian and philosopher, what think you, prince, of the account he gives us of the controversy between the deputies from Athens and the Melians in the fifth book of the Peloponnesian War ? As I was reading it the other day (always, you know, in Seyssel's* translation), my mind reverted unconsciously to you, and—"

"Deeply flattered," replied the prince, bowing till the curls of his ample peruke moved forward on his shoulders ; "and in what particular did you so honor me, madame ?"

"Why," replied the fair wit, "those unhappy Melian citizens—I will not say plead, but reason for their liberties and lives in such a sententious caustic tone of hard sense, and show such terse good reasons for being permitted to continue an existence, which the whole controversy proves to be a tissue of selfishness and crooked expediency :—they insist, sir, with such philosophic perseverance on still occupying the *terra firma* of life, denuded of its flowers, and with its wholesome fruits trodden down, that, while I said involuntarily, All good powers forbid that my friend should have to defend his life at the bar of any who deliberate whether they shall take it—"

"A sentiment very unlike Thucydides ; for which I

* The earliest French translation of Thucydides is that of Claude Seyssel. Paris, fol., 1527.

return my best thanks," interrupted Marsillac, with another of his mock elaborate bows.

"Well, so far it was a departure from my classical character. But in the case supposed, you would enact the defendant, I am sure, if you condescended to play the part at all, very much like those same world-knowing Melians. It would form an interesting chapter in philosophy to read. And yet," she pursued, in a more thoughtful tone, "all this is getting beyond our usual trifling. Ah, what times are these, when we cannot wear for five minutes the gay mask of Thalia, without the scene changing around us and presenting the severer features of her sister Melpomene!"

## CHAPTER XVIII.

### FRESH LIONS.

*Armado*. Men of peace, well encounter'd.
*Holofernes*. Most military sir, salutation.
*Moth* (*aside*). They have been at a great feast of languages, and stolen the scraps.
*Costard*. O, they have liv'd long on the alms-basket of words.

*Love's Labour's Lost.*

IN other parts of the saloon also the conversation had been vigorously sustained. It seemed as though that very darkening of the social atmosphere, which now overcast Paris with forebodings of some convulsion at hand, did but render more enjoyable the present interval before the tempest, as we come forth to bask in the last friendly gleams of a declining sun when he is about to sink behind

an ominous bank of clouds. Troubles were gathering over
the court and its adherents : a bad spirit was abroad working unchecked ; parliament and mob were progressing
from step to step in disaffection ; men began to speak of
the rights of the people and the balance of power—phrases
hitherto unheard of in France ; the leaders of the army
itself seemed wavering ; and thoughtful men of all classes
waited some change,—how thorough, or how permanent,
who could foresee ? Calculating on the morrow was a
gloomy employment of time ; why not enjoy the moment
as it flew ? So reasoned they in the circles of pleasure and
dissipation, alike in the Palais Royal and in the Luxembourg ; and the principle was acted upon also in that
literary *coterie* among whose guests we are numbered this
evening.

"Madame has only to continue in the same edifying
strain," said the poet Isaac Benserade, with the slightest
perceptible irony in his manner, "and we shall unanimously
concede to her a character for high devotion."

His words were addressed to a lady still in the bloom
of youth, who, from the footing on which she mixed in
society, evidently occupied the position of a married woman
of rank. She was seated near the capacious marble
chimney-piece of the saloon, surrounded by courtiers and
*literati* of various grades, and playing with one of those
ornamented fans which have come down to our degenerate
times, with their elaborate designs, semi-pastoral, semi-
heroic ; their shepherds in full perukes, buskins, and silken
jerkins of pale pink, or with corslets and rustic flutes ;
their shepherdesses with high-heeled slippers, attendant
cupids, crooks tied up with ribbons, and similar conventional emblems.

"Madame de Sevigne, however, is among the last to
abdicate a character for devotion," observed, with rather
an emphatic gravity, a speaker of middle age, and very
pleasing countenance ; "for we are never in danger of forgetting that she bears the name of Chantal."

"Certainly, Monsieur de Saint-Sorlin," replied the lady
in a tone of some slight embarrassment, and still employed
with her fan, "to have a near relation who is so undoubt-

edly among the blessed as my father's mother, ought to have no slight effect on the remainder of the family. Yet I fear it must be acknowledged that in my case—" a graceful gesture, supplying the remainder of the sentence, expressed that the lively lady was not conscious of any such family likeness in things spiritual to the Baroness de Chantal, as Monsieur Desmarets de Saint-Sorlin had been good enough to imply.

"Not that the accomplished author of the *Visionnaires* himself has always worn the cap of a doctor in theology," remarked Benserade, by no means pleased at this change in the current of conversation; "for I think the only claim that ingenious drama lays to divinity in any shape is the patronage it obtained from a cardinal."

"True," answered the other gently, and with perfect calmness; "and remarked, monsieur, with the keenness we have so often admired in you. To have known the unhappiness of a life that is furnished with no better aim than a pursuit of literature for its own sake, may well enhance the pleasure of having found, and endeavoring to follow, a juster path; not perhaps to Parnassus, but I trust, towards a better place, of which the Muses dreamed not."

"Excellent!" interrupted Madame de Sevigne, recovering her spirit from the brief act of self-reproach into which Saint-Sorlin's former observation had thrown her. "Really, monsieur, from the patience of your answer, one would have thought that you, and not your friendly opponent, had been the author of that sonnet on Job.* And apropos of sonnets," she added, to turn the theme of discourse into a smoother channel, "have we not all sustained an irreparable loss in poor Voiture? The fatal urn? as Horace complains: its billets are inscribed also with names dear to the Muses; they are drawn in their turn; and Parnassus mourns, but cannot resist the intru-

* Benserade and Voiture, as rival poets, had carried on a literary contest, which was sufficiently celebrated in their day. The former had produced a sonnet on *Job*, the latter one entitled *Urania;* and their comparative merits divided the world of criticism; though the palm was ultimately given to Benserade by Madame de Longueville.

13

sion of the Fates. Poor Voiture, how we shall all miss
him!"

"He is gone, madame," said the incorrigible Benserade,
"to explore those realms of Urania, which Polymnia so
well taught him to describe."

"Confess now, Benserade," said the Abbe Menage
laughing, as he joined the circle, "that you have felt about
our friend Voiture's visit to Urania somewhat as Numa
may have felt on the apotheosis of Romulus—as a removal
greatly to the advantage of both parties. Well, in truth,
I, who am no poet, regret him chiefly as one of the great
benefactors to the French language—"

"And would only be too delighted to step into his poor
friend's shoes as a member of the Academy," remarked that
tedious romancer La Calprenede, in a whisper to his neighbor the Duke de Chenonceaux, who nodded condescend-
ingly, without at all understanding the allusion. Menage
had failed in his election as an academician mainly on
account of his unpleasing and caustic vein.

"He has done much," pursued the abbe, "and in the
track of Malherbe, both to polish our tongue, and by the
same process to bring out the energy and precision which
it has inherited from its mother-Latin. I only hope some
true votary of the Muses will be at the pains to collect and
publish his letters; for they would doubtless prove a standard of polite writing."

"Is not that Bussy de Rabutin who passed just now
into the further saloon?" asked Le Sieur Montet of the
Comte d'Aubijoux, in a whisper. "I saw him salute his
cousin, Madame de Sevigne, as he went by."

"It looks like the turn of his shoulders, I think," said
the other; "and yet there is hardly self-confidence enough
about the man whom I see bowing to the Bishop of Grasse
for Bussy."

"Ay; but," returned the first speaker in the same
under-tone, "he has never been quite so well looked on,
you know, since his attempt last summer to carry off the
young widow, Madeleine de Miramion, by force, and marry
her against her will, though she is *devote*, and marked
with the small-pox besides. Her large fortune, I suppose,

was Bussy's great attraction. But it did not succeed; and
either the plan, or the failure, may perhaps make him a
little shy for the first few times of his re-appearance here,
where we are so *preceiux*, and all that sort of thing. In
truth, it *was* an extreme case. You must have heard of
it; it made so much noise at the time. She was only
rescued by a knight of Malta and his company, who
escorted her carriage into Sens."

"Ah, indeed," replied d'Aubijoux, with a slight yawn,
and a look of the most ineffable ennui; "well, perhaps I
did. But so many things are making a noise just now;
Mademoiselle Scudery, for instance, who is talking Hebrew,
I believe, or English, or some other barbarous tongue, on
that sofa. And as for people being carried off against their
wills, I am here myself, a living victim of the process.
Nothing would satisfy Marsillac but I must come, and see
what he calls the world of conversation: so Gourville put
me into a *chaise-a-porteur*, and two strong fellows transported me straightway; and here I find myself. Does not
that amount to abduction, I want to know?"

"Monsieur de Bonneval," said La Sevigne, looking off
from all her satellites, and espying our hero as he saun-
tered from group to group of the gay, the learned, and
the witty, "will you not join our circle? Here are bards
enough to sing all the heroic deeds you may perform in
the guard: unless you should turn composer yourself, for
then you must prepare for the *odium poeticum*, which
teaches all birds of song to peck one another bare of their
plumage. But it is gratifying to find you improving your
mind in such a classic assembly. You come from Auvergne, do you not? Can you tell us anything of an
experiment which has been tried at Puy-de-Dome, to prove
that it is not the abhorrence of a vacuum, as we have always
been taught, but the mere weight of the air, that raises or
depresses the barometer?"

Antoine, for the second time that evening, was obliged
to acknowledge his ignorance in matters of literature and
science.

"Why, I believe," said the Duke de Montausier, who
stopped for a few moments at each successive knot of his

father-in-law's guests, "the experiment is not considered as
conclusive for the new theory; but it has been conducted
by a very remarkable young man, who, if he lives (which
his extremely weak health is said to render doubtful), will
make the world hear of him before he quits it."

"Indeed?" inquired the lady; "and who is this unknown, but soon to be so well-known, and (most wonderful
of all!) this actual living subject of Monsieur de Montausier's commendations?"

"A son," replied the duke, "of a worthy gentleman
whom I have met in former days; of a Monsieur Etienne
Pascal, at one time president of the exchequer at Clermont.
The father is a man of great cultivation, especially in the
mathematics, in which he has made no ordinary researches.
In the course of his studies, indeed,"—and a slight smile
curled Montausier's lips as he spoke,—"he received the
commands of the late minister to make himself acquainted
with the interior of some fortifications near the Porte Saint-
Antoine; but pressing business, calling him into Auvergne,
deprived him of that opportunity of enlarging his experience
in architecture." The elder Pascal had, in fact, been
forced to secrete himself in his native province, to avoid a
warrant issued by Richelieu for his incarceration in the
Bastille, from his supposed share in some meetings in Paris
against the cardinal's arbitrary measures.

"But the young man," continued Montausier, "bids
fair to eclipse his father both in the pure sciences and in
philosophy. He seems to have been a mathematical
prodigy from his very cradle. And now, madame, as you
say, he has come to wonderful conclusions, by taking a
barometer up those mountains of Auvergne, on which I dare
say young Monsieur de Bonneval has often followed with
equal zest the partridges and hares. Ha!" continued the
merciless duke, noticing Antoine's ingenuous confusion;
"you observe that the healthy exercise among those bracing
regions has at least given a color to his cheek. Would
that he could lend a little of it to poor young Pascal, whose
wasted features and keen glittering eyes made me think,
the only time I ever saw him, of a refined Damascus blade,
too sharp for the narrow sheath that enclosed it."

"Pascal," echoed Madame de Sevigne, with rather a musing air, "have I not heard that name lately from Monsieur Nicole, or some other of the learned solitaries of Port Royal; and, if I remember, in connection with Jansen's *Augustinus*, which they said he was beginning to read and admire ?"

"Yes, possibly; that is, I really hardly know," replied the duke, with a momentary embarrassment; then, with a courteous bow, he continued, "we are your galley-slaves, fair Calypso, and shape our course at your bidding; yet are we not steering a little near the pointed rocks of theology ? They lie on the one side, I believe, while the whirlpool of politics foams on the other."

"On Scylla strikes the luckless wight who fain would leave Charybdis far,"

rejoined the lady laughing. "Whose translation is that, my translator-in-chief ? Or perhaps it is only elegant triflers, like Anacreon, whom the Abbe de Rance condescends to render into his mother-tongue ?"

She turned, as she spoke, to a young man of very graceful mien, and pleasing intelligent looks, dressed as little like an abbe as any one could well be without descending altogether to lay attire. His coat of dark velvet was adorned with a profusion of gold, and buttons heavy with the same material; his locks, curled and perfumed, seemed to be arranged purposely to set at naught ecclesiastical rules and public opinion alike. His shirt-sleeves, of the finest cambric, which the fashion of the day showed freely below the slashed and open arms of the *just-au-corps*, were confined at the wrist by two large emeralds; while a brilliant ring of great value sparkled on his hand.\* There was not about him a trace of the future restorer of a severe monastic rule to the rigor of its pristine observance. In truth, the young De Rance had now entered upon that career of license and gaity, for which he was afterwards to find so many long years of the most austere self-discipline too

* Histoire de la Trappe, etc., par M. Casimir Gaillardin. Paris, 1834.

13*

scanty an atonement. He has still some eight years to run
in his present course of perdition. Then a day will come
when, priest as he is, and a scandal to his sacred calling
even in that relaxed state of society, he will return to Paris
after a brief absence, and enter suddenly the apartment of
one whom he had left shortly before in all the bloom of
her guilty attractions. Loathsome disease has meanwhile
been there, and death has come, and even horrible muti-
lation; and they have done their work upon that once fair
form. He recoils at the sight; the work of grace in his
heart has begun. Is this "the end of these things," so soon
and so foul? What, then, is earth to him henceforward
but a place of penance, in which to find some spot where
he may consecrate himself to silence, to prayer, humble
manual labor, almost supernatural hardness of living
and humility, in expiation of that bitterly-lamented past?
The abbey of La Trappe, in a cheerless sequestered part
of France, has fallen, through his own neglect, and that
of his predecessor in the benefice, into frightful disorder.
He has hitherto known little of the place, except that, non-
resident, and careless of its spiritual condition, he has
drawn from it a considerable revenue to swell his pluralities,
and to squander upon self and sin. This, then, shall be the
chosen scene of his penitence. He will divest himself of a
charge which his scandalous neglect has already betrayed,
and enter that restored community as a humble novice,
which, as a worldly abbot, he had allowed to become a
waste and an abomination upon earth.

We have introduced an incongruous theme into the gay
and brilliant saloons of the Rambouillet. But who would
not have been beguiled into it by the sight of that young
abbo of three-and-twenty, so gifted, yet so perverse a
spendthrift of his best gifts? There he stands, leaning
lightly against the tapestried hangings, exchanging with
those around him the quick raillery and the well-turned
compliment, as though death and eternity were never to
make themselves felt, piercingly felt, and, once for all, in
his inmost conscience. Yet we may leave him safely in the
hands of his guardian-angel; for, unlikely as it now appears, he will be a brand plucked from the burning. Those

features will gain a higher and nobler grace of expression from the sweet austerity of his after-years.

"No, Monsieur De Rance despises anything so cumbrous as hexameters," said another young ecclesiastic, rustling in purple silk, and whose diminutive tonsure was lost amid the exuberance of his fine and carefully-arranged hair. This was the Abbe de Montreuil, a year or two older than his brother-trifler, and well-known at the Rambouillet for his small verses, facetiæ, and epigrams. "For my part I do not wonder," he continued; "I begin to have a horror of poetry that exceeds the fourth stanza, or prose that runs into a second volume. How dreadfully voluminous is the literature of our day becoming! Here was Monsieur la Calprenede, who quitted us within the half-hour: not content with having inflicted on the world his *Cassandra* in ten volumes, he has just introduced us to *Cleopatra* in twelve! Mercy on us, for which of our sins have we merited such a lengthened infliction? But so it is; authors are like singers—once let them commence the display of their powers, and you never come to the end of them."

"An ingenious comparison most ingeniously borrowed from Horace," observed the poet Sarrasin. "Confess the theft, Monsieur l'Abbe, or I will quote against you his other dictum about the quarters where the best wines were always to be found."

"And where?" asked De Montreuil incautiously, not perceiving the snare his rival wit had spread for him.

"At the supper-parties of priests, was it not?" said a lady who had hitherto been an amused listener to the fencing around her. She was seated near Madame de Sevigne; and, except in the high breeding, and in the look of intelligence which they possessed in common, no greater contrast could be imagined than that afforded by these two ladies. Madeleine Scudery had passed her fortieth year, and was remarkably plain in feature and appearance. But these personal disadvantages, though rendered more striking by the contrast they afforded to the galaxy around her, were lost in the charm of her wit and conversation. Her cultivation of mind, and the extent of her acquirements, were such as to merit for her, in the society of the Rambouillet, the current title of "the Tenth Muse," which we have already heard Marsillac offer as a courteous homage to another of the lights in this intellectual firmament.

"I answer the challenge of our friend Sarrasin," she resumed, "because you, my dear abbe, are much too chivalrous to be offended by any quotation from a lady, even when she cites an irreverent old heathen poet, who doubtless was a much better judge of wine than of the habits of the clergy."

"Well, Monsieur de Montreuil," said Madame de Savigne, "I leave you in the hands of your foes. You can claim no mercy from me, after your fierce assault upon my poor old favorite, La Calprenede. Ah, here comes the real Tragic Muse"—for just then Corneille stepped into the circle—"to put to flight every thing that is either frivolous or tedious in our unconsidered sayings, and to replace the sock by the buskin!"

"And Mars himself, the subject of all the Muses' songs," added Monsieur de Montausier, as Conde joined them almost at the same moment, "haply to bring us some tidings of grim-visaged war. No, I forgot myself," he muttered, with a kind of caustic good-humor, as he moved to greet the new-comers; "the only assault and battery heard within these walls,—and earnestly enough at times to gladden Bellona herself, and half-rouse the sleeping Erinnys,—is the strife of tongues. What were those lines, monsieur," asked he, putting his arm within that of Corneille, and strolling with him towards the further saloon, "that I found you the other day rendering into French verse from some English dramatist?"

"They ran thus, Monsieur le Duc," answered the poet, perceiving his allusion, and amused at its appropriateness; "but I can only give you my poor version, after having protested, in the name of all Parnassus, at your so vaguely referring to the immortal Shakespeare." He then recited, in an undertone, to Montausier's quiet, and perhaps somewhat cynical enjoyment, what *we* possess in the original:

"Have I not in my time heard lions roar?
  Have I not heard the sea, puff'd up with winds,
  Rage like an angry boar, chafed with sweat?
  Have I not heard great ordnance in the field,
  And heaven's artillery thunder in the skies?
  Have I not in a pitched battle heard
  Loud 'larums, neighing steeds, and trumpets' clang?
  And do you tell me of a woman's tongue,
  That gives not half so great a blow to th' ear
  As will a chestnut in a farmer's fire?"

———

# CHAPTER XIX.

### APOLOGETIC.

"Nothing to content you
Our true intent is."                 *Midsummer Night's Dream.*

WHAT says my friend?   The discontinuous tale
Lingers: now wayward leaps, now dives obscure;
And, unities alike and usage scorn'd,
Poor in adventure, poor in mental vein,
So scantily reveals the being true
Of him we would present, that stranger-like
You pass him in the throng, unrecogniz'd
By voice, or feature, or denoting mien.
    And ye bid us then portray
The steps of that smooth downward way
That leads, with deadly syren strain,
    Pleasure his victim-garland weaving,

And all the Graces in his train,
The gallant's tread, so sprightly-vain,
  To where perdition's dark wave heaving,
Whirls him to gulfs of endless pain !
And ye would list the music swell,
And see the lightsome revel glide
Through yon gay vestibule of hell,
By all earth's beauty glorified !
Yes ! watch the maze of twinkling feet,
As o'er the polish'd marble fleet
  Youth and earth-born pleasure ;
Plumes are nodding, jewels gleam,
Heroes lay apart the sword,
While to hautboys breathing sweet
Lady bright, and puissant lord,
Sweep—a living sparkling stream—
Onward to that brink abhorr'd !
And changeful as a changing dream
  Floats the courtly measure.
Would ye see the boy, scarce tried,
Caught, entangled in the tide,
  Helpless all, and drowning there ?
One by one in fitful throe
Mark his young aspirings go,
Yielding to that moral death,
As the far-spent swimmer's breath,
  Struggling faintly, melts in air ?
Dark the tale, yet—

CRITIC. Enough, in all conscience ! I raised a very
natural objection to the conduct of your story in prose ;
but when, to mend the matter, you rush into doggrel—
*do manus*, I submit : the remedy becomes worse than the
disease. If "all Bedlam or Parnassus" is to be let out,

I must prefer the patient in his ordinary asylum-jacket, to seeing him tricked forth, like Lear, "fantastically drest in weeds," howling to the elements. So let us descend from the buskin to the travelling-shoe again.

SCRIBLERUS (*unstayed by the interruption, though some-what diverging*) :

The soul, to whom in vain her angel-guide
    Whispers, as each new peril claims a care,
Then spreads his wing, up to the Throne to glide,
    And mournful lay th' accusing record there—

How large a thorny store for after-time
    Plants that poor wretch unconscious, with free hand ;
Till ·Vengeance, startling her smooth course of crime,
    Tear the false veil, uplift the scourge and brand !

Thrice happy they, to timely warning true,
    Who gaze on sin, then constant speed them by ;
Shuddering, yet thankful, that such dismal view
    Hath bid them fondlier court fair purity.

Yet be the next rank in the blessed theirs,
    Who reap experience healthful from their pain :
He, on whose path now turn our idle cares,
    Such good estate shall yet, methinks, attain.

Hark to that plaintive song ! while all around
    Woo him with smiles, he knows himself forlorn :
The still small voice *within*, at moments drown'd
    By din of earth, has ne'er been quite o'erborne.

At yon high casement leaning, all unheard,
    Weighing the present by the things that *were*,
Out from his depths of being, wildly stirr'd,
    Th' untutor'd strain he flings on the night air:

"Is mine the heart that erst
Echoed great Nature's voice in joy ?
Whence this death-change ?—the man hath slain that boy,
      And all seems murder-curst.

      Pure forms of young delight,
Fled are ye, or obscur'd awhile ?
O, yet again to see your beaming smile
      Flash on my spirit's night !

      Encompass me and save :
Not dead, for still I wake to grieve !
There looms a battle-day in store must leave
      Me conqueror, or slave."

CRITIC (*his hand on his chin*). Hm—Well, I suppose
you may put it in ; I don't know that it is much worse
than the rest. It might all be committed to the Thames
without fear of conflagration.

# CHAPTER XX.

### THE RIGHT HAND AND THE LEFT.

"Forward the right-hand huntsman spurr'd,
   Mildly to check, and gently warn ;
The left, with mocking laugh and word,
   Urges the deed of ruthless scorn ;
The baron spurns that gentle pleading,
   And follows where the left is leading."
                          *Burger's Wild Huntsman.*

ARE you happy, then, my Antoine, after your nine or ten weeks' experience of these brilliant circles? We do but echo your own conscience in asking the question and answering it. No; there is a void in the very best part of your soul : and the soul acknowledges thus much to herself, though you would not for all the world,—or all Paris, which is the same thing,—that Fontrailles or Marsillac, with their attendant wits, had the least hint about it. Fair remains every thing around you ; graceful to the eye and to the fancy ; smooth on the shining surface : but happy in the midst of it you are not.

Yet few young men, it must be acknowledged, for several years, have launched upon that glittering ocean with fairer prospects of a pleasurable voyage. You are appreciated; nay, that is saying too little. There is, thanks to your country-education, a something that might even make you the fashion. Finished as you are in training and accomplishments, there is about you a *je ne sais quoi* of originality—a down on the untouched plum—which would have disappeared, and left you a cheaper article, had you been sent earlier to the Paris market. As it is, any thing fresh, provided it be piquant, and susceptible of refinement, comes with the charm of welcome novelty to that great world. Ennui herself, the tutelary genius of the

14

court, raises her languid head to look at you; detailing,
part in amusement, part in admiration, those *naivetes*,
those shades of provincialism in accent and manner, which
you carry off with so good a grace.  You have a chance
of becoming the rage before you have attained your
majority, and what more can you desire when this is
within your grasp?

Why, then, are you forced, whenever you are alone, to
acknowledge that all is not well within?  You do not quite
know; you could not put it into words; yet the reason is
plain enough.  No one is well who is missing his vocation.
He hears a voice within that summons him to tread a
higher, surer path, to become thoroughly what he was
designed to be, yet fails to correspond with that impera-
tive call.  This is simply your case, my poor boy.  You
are coming short.  You have not perhaps fallen down such
gulfs of evil as have shattered and ruined so many about
you; yet even this will be, unless you walk more heed-
fully.  If life, in the very byways and secluded corners
of a world of probation, is filled with pitfalls,—if the easy
downward road opens out at every point upon our several
paths, and invites us wherever we may be treading, then
are those dangers multiplied in a capital and in a court;—
multiplied tenfold to you, my easy unsuspecting Antoine,
in an age of such license, and a court so disorganized, and
yourself only just out of your teens,—a creature made up
of imagination, caught by glitter, thirsting for adventure,
and with Louis de Montauban at your elbow.  I fear for
you, and for what further may develop itself in the
progress of this faithful chronicle.  Were it not for two
things, I know not but I might throw down the pen and
cease to follow you, as we close our eyes instinctively when
a poor insect flutters nearer and nearer to its inevitable
fire-doom.  But my two topics of consolation are strong
ones nevertheless—that Vincent de Paul has his eye upon
you, and that you are yourself half sickened of the world
ere you have well tasted its intoxicating draught.  I rest
my hopes on your own better self, and that priest's ardent
persevering charity.

· Yes, Vincent de Paul and Louis de Montauban now stand

as visible representatives of the good and evil angels of Antoine's life. The young courtier himself, as he recalls the
impressions which their several influences have left upon
him, is strongly reminded of the ancient myth of Her-
cules, placed in the midst, listening to the alternate arguments of Vice and Virtue. De Montauban has acquired
over him all that sway which a resolute will and adherence
to a principle of action, good or bad, gain in the long-run
over a character more rudimental and less compact. There
is an unblest completeness and individuality about one who
bears a seared conscience, and with whom the light that
was in him has become darkness. He is a consistent, a
concentrated being; he has no weak points of misgiving,
no qualms or pauses in his course; and as a consequence of
this, he acts upon others with a fearful instantaneous power.
Such men are instruments ready to the hands of the enemy
of all. The very fall which deprived them of innocence
and peace seems, Antæus-like, to have endued them with
a terrific energy for the perversion of others also. In the
steps of that master, to whose service they have surrendered
themselves, they seem to walk their rounds in quest of
human prey, restless ever and raging within, "seeking
whom to devour." Young De Montauban could not yet
be called a finished specimen of this semi-satanic class of
being; but he had tokens of being a hopeful pupil of the
school, in training for still greater lengths of energetic
wickedness.

This was Antoine's evil angel. Vincent, on the other
hand, who, with all his manifold engagements, had leisure
for every one's needs, and went about each purpose of good
with the same entireness as if he had nothing to do beside,
had more than once come across our hero's path. There
was something at once so venerable and so engaging in the
whole manner of the aged priest, and so much of paternal
interest in his calm look, that the young man had been
almost tempted to open to him the thoughts that were
harrassing his mind. Why had he never so determined?
Perhaps the knowledge that the almoner, with all his
suavity and consideration, with all his practical experience of life, was strenuous in his advice, may have chained

Antoine's tongue.   Perhaps a step so decided as that of
consulting a priest, whose whole tone and being was in
marked contrast with the worldly abbes and prelates about
the court, would amount to more than he was prepared for.
It was a kind of moral Rubicon; and once crossed, would
pledge him to a line of conduct thereafter.   He stood once
and again upon the brink; he tried to scan the look of the
country beyond; but he lacked nerve at present to make
the plunge.   Your time is coming yet, friend; meanwhile
we are compelled to leave you in the hands of the opposite
party.

"I cannot for the life of me make out what you mean?"
said De Montauban, yawning, while Antoine, pacing up
and down with him in an alley of the palace garden,
sounded him to see how far he might hope for sympathy
in his restless search after happiness.   "What more,
in the name of all that is *ennuyant,* can you want than
you either possess or may reasonably hope for?   Youth,
personal advantages, command of money, opportunities of
seeing and enjoying life, and life such as it is here in
Paris; then, the prospect of active service in the way of
street-fighting, and knocking of refractory shopkeepers on
the head, should his eminence continue to thwart the
Parliament; or else distinction in foreign service, if the
Fronde subsides without an eruption; thanks from the
regent and the young king, laurels, promotion, showering
in upon you!   You exchange your old baronial coronet for
the circlet of a count; nay, what know I? prince and duke,
if you will, like Wallenstein, who only began as a page
at court.   Your father, quitting this earthly scene in a
transport of proud felicity at your fame, makes way for
your enjoyment of the hereditary possessions, and you
rebuild the old chateau till it is as large as Chantilly; and
you are governor of your province, and go a-hunting with
a little court at your heels.   The worthy provincials,
admitted on state-days to walk through your grand apartments on tip-toe, absolutely bow down and worship the
prince's portrait that hangs at full length in the reception-
room.   Ha! I see you there," he pursued, reckless of De
Bonneval's vexation: "I see your highness staring out

from the canvass. What a polish on your cuirass, and in the very turn of your instep! What command in that baton, pointed with so noble an air! What luxuriance in the curls of that peruke; and, O what solemnity in the fullness of those cheeks and chin!"—and the satirist looking at the discomfited expression of the present Antoine, while he dilated on the glories of the future, burst into a peal of laughter, till he was forced to hold his sides as the tears rolled down his convulsed features.

It was plainly of no avail to take Louis into council. He could no more understand what was passing in his companion's mind than the deaf man could realize a strain of music by mere description. Antoine was turning from him with some discouragement and no little indignation, when Louis, as if struck by a new idea, grew serious at once, and, stepping close to De Bonneval, with his eyes fixed on his face, laid his hand on the young man's arm, and said, in a lower and graver tone: "Hark you, comrade; I angered you once by a jest which you received as reflecting on your courage, and that I meant not. But what I am now about to say, I *do* mean; and you see that I can cease to speak lightly on occasion. You have courage to exchange thrusts in single fight with any cavalier in Paris, or with any German or Spaniard of them all. Your hand would be braced, and your eye steady, and your foot firm, if the squadrons of the archduke's best cavalry were charging down upon the guard, making the solid ground shake beneath their hoofs. But there are other adventures to which a brave man may address himself, and demanding of him yet greater nerve. Antoine de Bonneval, have you a heart for these?" The other gazed at him, not comprehending his meaning.

"This future," pursued his companion in the same tone of earnestness, which, so unusual in one volatile to excess, had something impressive to Antoine's mind, while he felt fascinated by the glitter of the other's gaze,—"this dim unknown future, towards which we are whirled so rapidly, are *you* the only one, think you, whose breast has yearned, has panted, to discover the secrets it has in store? This thirst after happiness, with the uncertainty of its posses-

14*

sion, and of the term of its enjoyment,—are there no means
upon this earth of ours to assuage the craving and to end
the torturing suspense ?"

There was a pause, and the victim of the unhallowed
suggestion that was to come felt his heart beat faster, while
the utterance of De Montauban grew yet slower, and his
voice sank to a whisper: "Is there no way to pierce, has
no hand ever lifted, the dark veil ?"

Antoine shuddered at the question. He well knew
that, among the other unlawful practices of the time, it
was not uncommon to consult such professors of necromancy as possessed a real or pretended power to reveal
the future. With the vague sense which at times possessed him, that he was not on the path for his own happiness, he had more than once contemplated such a means
of solving the uncertainty that oppressed his spirit. It
now seemed as though the suggestion of De Montauban
had conjured up before him the phantom of a thought with
which he had often dallied, and which, though he shrank
from contemplating it, he had never wholly abandoned.
His brow contracted, his chest heaved ; he looked fixedly
at the man whose words had chimed in so ominously with
his own half-formed purpose, as though he almost expected
to see in him some token of the great enemy, from whom
he could not doubt the suggestion had emanated.

"Nay," remarked the other, as though in reply to the
thought, and carelessly executing a pirouette on his heel,
"I did but think to perform a kindly office, by showing a
perplexed benighted traveller his way out of the wood,
and he stares at me as though I were Will-o'-the-Wisp
inviting him into a quagmire ! Consult not Lomelli, nor
any of his fraternity, if thou darest not bear their verdict ;
remain content, knowing nothing ; and 'tempt not the
Babylonian numbers,' as we used to say at school. Only,
they that know nothing, when they might, can dare but
little, methinks, when they might also. And who can
tell, friend, what thou mightest dare hereafter, if thou
didst but know to-day ?" So, humming, a court-minuet,
and with a step of exaggerated gravity, De Montauban
took himself off through an opening in the tall clipped

hedges bordering the alley, into a side-walk of the garden, from whence our hero, left to his own dark musings, heard him whistling a lively air.

The marksman had a shrewd guess, however, that his shot had told. In Antoine's fevered state of mind, such a hint was not likely to be ineffective. He put aside the idea again and again; he fought against it as a temptation; he endeavored to smile it away as an absurdity; he would even persuade himself that De Montauban had merely wished to try his courage by suggesting it, or to draw from it, after he had fallen into the trap, some fresh matter for raillery. Still it recurred, and *would* recur to him. Unexpectedly, and in a moment; when he was on guard at the palace, or waiting in the antechamber; in dejected moods, on starting from a troubled slumber, or even when among the gayest and the most brilliant, that same thought would flash vividly across him. The secret of his future life, the answer to these vague and aimless self-questionings, lay within his reach, and he might put forth his hand, and grasp, and read it. It seemed almost to look him tauntingly in the face, and to borrow from Louis' voice a tone of mockery. Like the mysterious veiled statue in the Egyptian temple, the legend on whose pedestal promised a vision of Truth to him whose bold hand should lift the veil, so did his own shrouded future seem to stand before Antoine, and upbraid him with irresolution for not making it his own.

Meanwhile the young man's altered demeanor had not altogether escaped the notice of the court. The more frivolous laughed as they observed his uncertain step and clouded brow, thinking it sufficiently explained by some such fancied or transient affection as often formed a theme for their light sarcasms, and wore the mask of a tragic despair till it ended in a jest, and was forgotten. Or perchance his inexperience had been practised upon by some veteran gamester, and he had lost at one of the tables of hazard a larger sum than the heir of a not over-wealthy provincial noble could well dispense with. The graver sort, with whom politics formed the leading idea, looked at him with anxiety, as one whose loyalty might have been

160          ANTOINE DE BONNEVAL:

tampered with by the agents (and they were many and
various) of the Fronde. That party had gained strength
under the surface of a hollow and deceitful calm; several
men of note had succumbed to one or other of the motives
that allured them to its standard. A thirst for liberty, a
restless desire of change, or a conviction that some uncompromising change was needed in order to break up an old
corrupt system, and to distribute the general welfare more
equitably,—these and worse inducements were secretly
swelling the ranks of a faction which was soon to become
actively formidable. Antoine's affable disposition and love
of inquiry had brought him more in contact with some
members of the Fronde than was altogether approved of
at the Palais Royal. He had more than once been present
at assemblies frequented by members of the *Cours Souveraines*, parliamentary deputies, advocates, and members of
the learned professions,—*gens de la robe*, as they were
slightly called by the court circles. From these men, and
from the burgers, out of whose ranks they were chiefly
recruited, De Bonneval had heard, with some amazement,
but with an increasing interest, the same arguments which
he had first encountered under the forest-trees during the
night of his captivity. And though his devoted loyalty
remained unshaken, he was obliged to feel that more was to
be said on the popular side than he had imagined possible.
Corruptions, he could not deny, existed in all departments
of the public service, and told balefully on the happiness
of the subject. The court was indifferent to these things;
and they who ought especially to have righted them were
absorbed in their personal pleasures or ambition. The
groanings of oppressed men became daily fiercer, if not
louder, and assumed something of the tones of that righteous indignation which pours into the ear of Heaven its
claim for retribution.

The casual expression of some such ideas on our hero's
part had been reported in high quarters. His acquaintance with the Prince de Marsillac, and the influence which
that brilliant talker seemed to have gained over him, had
not diminished the apprehensions to which his conduct gave
rise. And thus, when his thoughtfulness increased, and

he was to be observed pacing up and down by himself with his arms folded on his bosom, they who did not set him down as crossed in affection or as ruined at play, more than half suspected him as tainted with the growing political heresy.

There were two, meanwhile, who watched the young man with a deeper insight into his mental struggle. He who represented the evil principle exulted with an unblest triumph at the effect of his suggestions. Vincent de Paul, on the other side, if he did not precisely fathom the temptation that was pressing upon him, seemed by a kind of intuitive perception, whenever they casually met, to give him, unasked, a fuller measure of his paternal sympathy. Something of more than common force was contending in the breast of the young soldier; that was evident. Whether it were the unlawful knowledge he hoped to gain from the sorcerer Lomelli, or any other of the manifold allurements to evil presented by the capital and the court that was now enticing him astray, Antoine's name, and the dangers he was running, lived in the daily prayers of the servant of God. Vincent whispered them in his Mass, he reverted to them as he opened his breviary, he offered up for them his fasts and apostolic labors and penances. Earnestly he asked on the young man's behalf, and often; it remains to be seen whether in the end he obtained for him or no.

## CHAPTER XXI.

### DARKNESS VISIBLE.

"This town is full of cozenage—
As nimble jugglers, that deceive the eye ;
Dark-working sorcerers, that change the mind ;
Soul-killing witches, that deform the body;
Disguised cheaters, prating mountebanks,
And many such like liberties of sin."
*Comedy of Errors.*

BATTISTA LOMELLI, the professor of occult sciences whom
Louis had mentioned to De Bonneval, had established
himself some few months before in an obscure apartment
overlooking one of the narrow streets that ran through an
ancient unfrequented quarter of Paris. Yet, mean and
even difficult as was the access to this chamber of mystery,
the anteroom of the sorcerer was resorted to by many of
the noble, the gay, and the influential of the period. So
universal is the yearning of the human heart, racked with
uncertainty and disappointment, to withdraw the impervi-
ous veil that hangs before the unknown future, that it
cannot be surprising if, in an age such as our story is concerned about, when the injunctions of religion were openly
set at naught by a great number who constituted society,
and professed to belong to the Church, means were
employed, though recognized as unlawful and impious, to
obtain a transient glimpse into what was to come.

In the dusky outer chamber, therefore, of the Floren-
tine, hung with faded tapestry, and furnished with a few
seats ranged against the walls, might be seen, with more
or less of disguise, according to the nature of their inquiries,
or the degree of credence attached to the adept's pretensions, a various and strangely-assorted company. Hither
came the cavalier, bent on ascertaining the success await-

ing him in some pursuit of his frivolous or guilty life;
hither, also, came the spendthrift and the gamester,—the
one to discover some golden secret for repairing a wasted
fortune, the other to acquire a lucky number that would
rule the throws of his dice or the turning of his cards.
Ladies, too, masked and concealed in large flowing man-
tles, not unfrequently stepped from unblazoned coaches,
attended by valets in plain attire.   Their rank might be
that of the highest nobility of France, or they might belong
to the families of the magistracy, or the burgher-class: are
they attached to the court, or taking part with the Fronde?
Or are they members of the almost effete party of the Importants, or neutrals, awaiting the issue of the struggle
that is so evidently at hand?   Such speculations passed
through the minds of the cavaliers, who made way for
them with a gesture of mute courtesy, or handed them,
with ill-suppressed curiosity, to one of the seats in the
waiting-room of this silent company, until their turn should
arrive for passing into the consulting-chamber and the
actual presence of the sorcerer.   Meanwhile we are occupied only with our hero, and with the result of his own
plunge into the dark waters of futurity.

Antoine, then, his heart still agitated with the emotions
of the long conflict with himself that had ended in the
triumph of the worser side, slowly paced the anteroom,
absorbed in uneasy thought.   It so chanced that at the
moment he was its only occupant, and had leisure to
debate with himself, unobserved, the errand on which he
had come.   That its object was an unlawful one, he could
not attempt to hide from his convictions.   He had been
too well instructed in religion not to be aware that the
dread inquiry on the threshold of which he stood was a
direct tampering with the powers of evil, and a sin against
the first of the commandments.   The only remaining
tribute he would pay to the supremacy of conscience was
a vain attempt to persuade himself that, once master of the
tremendous secret of his destiny, he should be the better
enabled to shape the course of his remaining time to the
true end for which it had been bestowed.

"Yes," he half exclaimed, as his fevered imagination

conjured up the various possible revelations of life or death
which the sorcerer's experiment might make to him : "let
me but solve this dread uncertainty, and know the worst,
or at least that which is appointed—the inevitable.   Conscious of all that is to come, I shall then brace myself to
meet it undauntedly.   If I am not now in my right
sphere, the knowledge will enable me to gain an entrance
into it ; if I am, to pursue it without hesitation or self-
reproach."   It was a sophistry that the young man was
attempting to palm upon himself; nor could he fully succeed in doing so.   Alas! he was not the first, nor will he
be the last, who "see the best, and yet the worst pursue ;"
who, unable to still the voice of conscience, or divest
themselves of their sense of the right path, and the wrong,
at least close their ears to its pleadings, and plunge forward on a way which they know to end in death.   Perdition will contain no more piercing remembrance than the
knowledge which the lost possessed, even in the moment
when they succumbed to evil, of the true nature of the
acts that have wrought their condemnation.

From such absorbing reveries De Bonneval was roused
by the movement of a dark red curtain of damask that
hung before a door at the farther end of the apartment.
Turning short in his walk, he confronted, though at some
distance, a tall spare form, dressed in an ample simarra of
purple stuff, furred about the sinewy throat, which was
left bare.   A glance alone was needed to tell Antoine
that he was in the presence of the mysterious person whose
powers he had come to employ.   But without allowing
him time for observation, Lomelli made a rapid, and, as it
appeared to the young guardsman, rather an imperious
gesture, to indicate that he should follow him into the
inner room.   No sooner had he done so than he dropped
the curtain again, and disappeared.

De Bonneval was naturally fearless; and moreover he
had often heard the mysterious powers claimed by the seer
treated with ridicule ; yet he was conscious of a slight diz-
ziness in his head, and of a certain tingling in his limbs,
as he prepared to obey this sudden mandate.   The moment
was now come to which he had looked forward, for which

he had prepared; yet, had he then stood uncommitted, he felt as though he would have drawn back from the adventure, even on the threshold. It was not any mortal danger that he apprehended; it was more. He was to become an intruder into the presence of the unseen, and to demand an answer from the unrevealed. What mysterious spiritual influences would be at hand—what mighty powers of evil meet, perchance over-master and possess him! But he shook himself free from such irresolution, and, without making the sign of the cross, or arming himself with the safeguard of prayer,—he felt it would have been a mockery on that unlawful adventure,—strode up towards the end of the apartment, thrust the curtain rapidly aside, and found himself in a moment in total darkness.

Instinctively Antoine drew his rapier, and holding the point before him in a posture of defence, while he brought his cloak forward over the left arm, still advanced, but with caution. He had not made many steps before he became aware of the flickering of a faint bluish flame, which came from a small chafing-dish raised a little from the floor, and placed in the centre of the apartment through which he was groping his way. Keeping his eyes intently fixed on this spot, he paused, equally ready to repel any sudden violence, or to continue a spectator of whatever else might follow. The restless flame quivered lightly among the bars of the cresset, now all but expiring, then shooting upward with a stronger flash; during which De Bonneval could trace the strongly-marked and attenuated features of the Italian, his dark eyes gleaming, and his face showing of an ashy paleness in the changeful light, directly confronting him.

Stronger and yet more strongly that lambent tongue of unearthly fire flashed and played upon the surrounding objects; till Antoine, his eyes becoming gradually accustomed to the loss of the broad daylight in the outer room, could observe that the chafing-dish of wood-embers that fed the flame rested on a small iron tripod, occupying the centre of a circle of some ten or twelve feet in diameter. This circle was drawn in white chalk, with careful exactness, on the bare tiling of the floor, and contained various

15

geometrical devices traced in the same material, to whose
meaning he could discover no clue. Within its circum-
ference, and placed at such an angle as allowed the light
to play freely upon it, stood a broad mirror, framed in a
style that showed it to be both of antique date and foreign
workmanship, whose polished and faultless surface reflected,
with a degree of accuracy then very unusual, every object
presented to its focus. A human skull and a short sword
of double edge and wavy blade, such as were brought by
travellers who had penetrated among the tribes of the far
East, completed the number of the objects shown by that
uncertain flame.

Antoine stood for several minutes firm and motionless,
surveying these various strange details; until the light
in the cresset, playing now on this side, now on that, convinced him that Lomelli was indeed the only other occupant of the chamber, and that the sorcerer was standing
before him, weaponless, with folded arms. A cast was
upon his expressive features that betokened rather deep
melancholy than any hostile or treacherous intent. Once
assured of this, our hero dropped the point of his rapier
to the ground, slowly sheathed it, and then stood, returning gaze for gaze upon his mysterious companion. In the
looks of the one there was a calm sad fixedness and concentration, as of a man who had nothing further to hope
in life, nor any thing to apprehend that he did not already
foresee. In those of the other there was wonder, uncertain
foreboding, and restless impatience for the event of his
dread experiment.

At length the younger broke silence. With a courteous
inclination, "I come," he said, "worthy sir—"

But Lomelli instantly threw out his lean arm, bare to
the elbow, and placed one finger upon his compressed lips
with a gesture that awed De Bonneval into silence. He
then quitted the spot where he had been standing, and
advanced towards the young man, motioning him to place
his right hand within his own. Antoine shrank at the cold
clammy touch of that hand, as the fingers closed around
his wrist with the tenacious pressure of the serpent when
he darts from his ambush to lock himself securely round

his numbed and helpless prey.   Antoine felt himself within
the grasp of a power greater than any he dared summon
at that moment to meet or to resist it; a power whose
origin and nature he more than mistrusted, whose possible
extent he shuddered to contemplate, but whose exercise
he had invited by his own act and deed.   It was not of
heaven, it was not of earth.   It worked in darkness,
claimed no connection with any thing hallowed or lawful,
was proscribed even by human authority, and shrouded
itself in mystery, breathed of death and hell, and pointed
to them.

Thoughts such as these shot through his dizzy brain,
while Lomelli, holding him firmly by the hand, bent his
piercing eyes upon his countenance, as though he would
read there any symptom of irresolution in the man who
had come so deliberately within his grasp.   But irresolution there was none.   Antoine would know his future at
any cost.   What that cost might be his heart sickened
within him to imagine.   Still he would go on; he would
go through with it.   Never had his will seemed so strongly
set upon a clearly known evil.   It was as though he had
been launching his light bark upon the edge of a current
of mysterious powers, recklessly dallying with their
strength, pushing out into the attraction of the stream.
Now he was sucked in by the vortex, and borne along
upon the torrent that seemed to laugh hoarsely around
him; he was become the sport of a giant might, as a
feather or a foam-flake, engulfed amid the tossing crests
of the billows, the multitudinous whirling and onward
roar, and hurled without resistance toward the dark abyss.
Can he now stop short?   Can he disengage himself from
the eddy, and make his way back to the shore from which
he madly parted?   Or is the will yet free?   Would he
now do so if he could?   No, he is resolute; he has
fastened himself on his unlawful project; he will pay the
price, but he will attain it.   He therefore returned the
gaze of those dark searching eyes with a look equally
steadfast; and, hand locked in hand, the seer and the
seeker advanced towards the fated circle on the floor.

Suddenly the countenance of the Italian changed, and

his whole form seemed to shrink into itself. He dashed
Antoine's hand wildly from him, and staggered back
several paces, cowering towards the further end of the
chamber. His whole attitude was like that of a lithe and
agile panther, confronted, overawed, by a human antagonist. His eyes remained still glaring upon the form
of the young soldier, as unable to avert them from an
absorbing yet agonizing object. At the same moment
Antoine felt that something was lighty pressing upon his
breast beneath the hand he had clenched there to still those
unwonted flutterings of the heart for which his pride had a
moment before rebuked him. At that light pressure *he*
too started, and a flush overspread his cheeks, which had
become deadly pale during the few minutes since we saw
him enter the darkened chamber.

Ah, Françoise de Bonneval! when on the day of the
first communion of thy cherished son,—that day for which
thou hadst waited and prayed with all a mother's longing
patient piety,—when, on that happy morning, thou didst
tremblingly bind round thy Antoine's neck the relic of his
patron saint, brought from the shrine at Padua, and didst
exact from the boy, kneeling thus before the altar, and
fresh from the moment of Divine communion, a sacred
promise to wear it always, whatever might befall him, could
thy tender scarce-mistrusting heart, then beating over him
with all a mother's blessing, have looked onward to a
moment so fearful, so dark as this?

The whole of that remembrance flashed over de Bonneval, and he paused. It was the last whisper of his guardian-angel, pleading with him by motives of nature and
of grace. But even such whispers, so mighty, so awful
in their thrilling tenderness, may be drowned in the hoarser
tones of passion and crime. The human will, bent desperately on a bad purpose, can overleap every barrier, can
rush to every excess of evil,—ah! and can prepare for the
victim it sweeps away with it a rack and a furnace in every
depth of after-anguish. The moment of grace is presented, and it passes. Antoine hears the call; but no, he
plunges on. In a moment of frenzied madness he tears
open the bosom of his vest, snaps the frail cord that secures

that sacred relic, flings it with violence into the outer chamber; and then grimly, with clenched teeth and tightened lips, with a fire in his eyes that had burnt out all their former expression of joyousness and hope, he turns again to Lomelli, grasping the lean hand of the adept as though he would have crushed its every bone.

Was it his excited fancy, or did the sulphurous light indeed flicker that moment with a livelier motion on the grinning outlines of the skull? and did the dark hollows of those sunken eye-holes look out upon him with a meaning, and the fleshless jaws quiver with a gibe of horrible triumph? and, hush! was it nothing save the moaning of the autumn wind that stirred and whispered round the old arras of that fatal chamber?

---

## CHAPTER XXII.

### THE VEIL REMOVED.

*Hamlet.* You go not, till I set you up a glass
Where you may see the inmost part of you.
    *Queen.* What wilt thou do? Thou wilt not murder me?
Help, help, ho?                                        *Hamlet.*

WHEN the strangely-assorted partners of this dark scheme were standing within the circle, directly opposite to the steel mirror, the Italian, whose eyes had never wandered from those of the young man, fascinating them with a glance like that of the basilisk, at length moved his lips in a whisper. Distinctly, yet with suppressed guttural hoarseness, the words fell upon Antoine's ear, while a gesture warned him not to utter a word in reply.

15*

"You would know the history of your life," said the whisper. "Listen, and answer not. Behold what is to be shown ; beware you utter neither word nor exclamation. Your past, your present, your future, will appear to you. The veil is lifted once for each five years. Prepare !

As he spoke, a low strain of music arose, and gathered strength, and with a wave-like vibration floated through the apartment. It seemed rather as though the atmosphere itself had been endued with breath and made itself audible to the ear than the result of any effort of skill. Nor did the sounds resemble those of any musical instrument with which De Bonneval was acquainted. Thrillingly sweet did they creep over him, those faint ripples of sound ; and as they ebbed away, fading in cadences that were all but stillness, or stole forth again in gradual approaches, like some scarce perceptible breath of air that stirs the loosened chords of a lute, they brought to his spirit voices from the dim and buried past ; they made his earliest years live to him again with an awful distinctness, though he was unable to determine how the remembrances poured so forcibly into his mind, or to trace the subtle connection between the outward vibration and the mental sight. Insensibly, however, this connection forced itself upon him, and grew stronger with the strengthening sounds. He seemed to hear the history of his own by-gone days narrated to him by a voice which itself belonged to the past, while it appealed irresistibly to his present being. Recess after recess in the chambers of memory that had been long closed—blocked up by the accumulations of after-years—the very avenues to which had been lost and forgotten, now epened out again with that vivid reality which often hangs round the dying pillow of the old man, and prattles to him of the scenes and sports of his boyhood, while all the energic life that followed is blank oblivion. Antoine was again, for the moment, as he had been at five years of age.

When the first chords of that voice-like music made themselves heard, the clear surface of the mirror gradually became clouded, and disordered shadows, radiating irregularly but in swift succession from the centre of the polished

steel, shot off and vanished at the outer edge, like the tumultuous bubbling rings of water flung forth on all sides from a
throbbing fountain, that broaden and die upon the margin,
while others chase them and subside in turn.   After the
lapse of a few moments, however, and while the mysterious
sound of the music seemed to grow more and more articu-
late, the young man distinguished in the mirror some
slight flashes of light, which soon became steadied, and at
length concentrated themselves in one spot upon the surface.   This light was not reflected from the flame in the
cresset, which had died down, as before, to a feeble glimmer, but seemed to be radiated by some unseen power
from the mirror itself.   Another moment or two, and the
component parts of a scene had grouped themselves upon
the polished metal, tremulously at first, then motionless
and distinct.   Antoine recognized it at once.   There was
indeed his mother's room in the old Chateau de Bonneval;
the high antique chamber that looked out upon the fosse,
down the slopes of which, in formal but not ungraceful
parterres, grew the favorite flowers she loved to gaze upon
from the mullioned window.   There was the tapestry that
had been patiently achieved by a maiden-aunt of the old
baron's; a strange medley of representations, sylvan and
sacred : the Judgment of Solomon, the court of Assuerus,
the interview of Rebecca with the steward of Abraham;
and awful-looking countenances of tall camels, and grim
attendants to match, were intermixed with hunting-parties
in full cry, gallant cavaliers on thundering Flemish steeds,
winding portentous horns, and huge boars at bay receiving
on their tusks the fierce hounds that rushed upon them
open-mouthed.   There, too, was the massive chair, carved
with the family cognizances, and surmounted by its coronet.   And who is the lady seated there, graceful and
gentle, whose beauty has assumed a slight matronly cast,
though she has scarcely yet passed the bloom of her
youth ?   Or who is that fair-haired child, who rests his
little hands upon her knee, and looks up earnestly into her
face while she bends above him, and winds her arm over
his shoulder ?   See, her cheek almost rests upon his brow,
and she seems to whisper into his very heart such words

of holy tenderness as cause his clear bright eyes to glisten
in answer to the tears of motherly love that are filling her
own.   Then she raises her hand towards heaven ; she
points to the crucifix that hangs against the tapestried wall,
and the child kneels down by her side and folds his hands
reverently in prayer.

Antoine gazed upon the scene, riveted by a thousand
dear remembrances.   His heart swelled, and a softened
look stole into his eye.   Fondly he watched the thankful
expression of that lady's face ; he recalled in her features
and air the early half-ideal recollection of his mother that
had been impressed upon him before advancing years and
sickness had touched that form or streaked those tresses
with silver.   And then, as he read the countenance of the
child at her knee, turned upward with a look so awed, and
yet so loving and trustful, to the image of the agonized
Redeemer, while the lips seemed parted in childish supplication to that Divine Heart of love—ah ! the thought
shot through him, could it be his very self on whom he was
now gazing in this moment of deliberate crime ?   Was he
not fear-stricken and abashed at standing before the image
of that child, all radiant in the strength of innocence, and
united in spirit with the great Author and Centre of all ?

Fain would he have retained that sweet yet most sad-
dening picture before his eyes ; he even bent forward and
advanced his hand towards the mirror on perceiving that
after a brief interval the lines were becoming less distinct,
and the hues fading away.   But no ; the magic scene is
vanishing again ; it melts from the eye like unsubstantial
foam that is flung upon the thirsting sands of the wild sea-
beach.   Another moment, and there is nothing but the wayward strains that sigh and swell and fall again fitfully, and
the lurid flickering of faint light, and the dark eyes of the
sorcerer bent unwavering upon his countenance, while the
disordered shadows course each other once more over the
surface of the mirror.

Then the sounds breathe out with greater vigor.   It
is as though a cheerful breeze were stirring among the
tree-tops of some leafy avenue ; and, mingled with these,  .
Antoine could fancy that he heard broken sounds of merry

discourse and rough jesting, with the pawing and snorting of steeds, and a few impatient flourishes upon the hunter's horn. Flashes of light are seen again upon the steel; the outlines of another scene peer forth, gradually strengthen, and at length stand fixed. It is still at Bonneval. There is the inner gateway of the old castle, leading out upon the paved court, guarded by the entrance-tower. The favorite gray of the baron is held by the only groom who can manage him, and tosses his dark flowing mane, impatient for the morning's hunt. Around are falconers, with their birds hoodwinked and perched upon the wrist, and prickers with fleet hounds straining against the leash, and other retainers grouped here and there, all with the badge of the house of Bonneval displayed on the left arm of their jerkins of russet and blue, the old ancestral colors. And the baron himself comes forth: a genial form, somewhat stately withal, in hunting-dress, and full ten years younger than on this night. His foot is in the stirrup, he all but swings himself into the saddle of the rearing snorting gray; when a boy comes bounding down the flight of stone steps, and clings to his father's arm, eagerly preferring some request. It is his tenth birthday, and why may he not join the merry hunt this morning? The father pauses; but while a fond look of pride and affection lights up his features as his eyes rest upon his son, so animated in every movement, pleading there with flushed cheek and kindled glance, the petitioner is gently denied. The gray bears off his stately rider, and the whole hunting-train, with a flourish upon the horns, with tramp of steeds and baying of hounds, sweeps out of the court, and that boy is left alone. He stands upon the steps, and looks sorrowfully through the vacant gateway. The autumn air lifts the light curls that cluster round his open brow, and plays with his rich scarf and plume. Antoine sees himself again; he remembers well the day of that boyish disappointment. Deeply moved at the distinctness with which every trivial circumstance is pictured to him, he stands riveted; but the scene is already fading: it is gone; and the mirror is rapidly clouded as before.

And now the changeful music that had ushered and

interpreted the successive pictures in this strange drama
pauses, sinks tremulously, then rises again as by an effort,
reluctant and slow.  Something is to be represented which
those evil powers would fain not have shown.   There is a
longer pause, too, in the formation of the coming scene ;
the clouded surface is wildly agitated, the shadows disperse more slowly.  Antoine feels that the hand of Lomelli,
which, lean and wasted though it was, had hitherto returned
the firm grasp of his own, became tremulous within
his, and clammier than before.  With his other hand the
sorcerer veiled his eyes close; and in that position he
remained until the scene had faded again from sight, as not
daring to look upon it.   At length the music, after several
unwilling efforts, that were followed by indistinct and
troubled-murmurs, gathered itself into a solemn pealing
organ-strain ;  and Bonneval, who had felt, he scarcely
knew why, more awed during the suspense than at either
of the previous representations, became aware that the
flashes of light in the mirror which now began to show
themselves were grouped so as to represent the tapers upon
an altar.   It is the fifteenth anniversary of that same boy's
birthday ; it is the day of his first communion.   There
he kneels in the little chapel of his father's castle.   The
cheerful sunlight that pours in through the ancient storied
windows, tracing their holy figures in quaint outlines and
liquid tints upon the floor, falls on the features of the
father composed into reverence and thankful happiness,
lights up his gray hairs, and sheds a halo round the countenance of another who is more deeply happy and thankful
still, and who holds the hand of that little sister, since laid
to sleep in the cathedral of Notre Dame de Puy in the
Velay.   She, too, takes her part in the general joy of that
quiet hour of thanksgiving.   The venerable chaplain in
his rich vestments has just closed the tabernacle upon the
altar ; the youth, with head bowed down and closed eyelids, still holds his clasped hands beneath the linen-cloth
spread before him on the altar-rails ; the post-communion
of the Mass proceeds.   All is brightness; all is love and
hope.   Ah! time it is that the scene should pass again
into shadows : let us not dive into the breast of the be-

holder, nor scan the remorse that harrows it. Let the
altar vanish, and the tapers be quenched; and let darkness come over those countenances that are beaming with
a radiance from heaven : he on whom ye gaze, he for whom
ye give thanks, belongs to those memories no longer.

And now the strain of music, as if relieved from the
compulsion of dwelling for a moment on such a scene,
dashes off into a thousand wild frisks, that meet and clash
and drown one another, whirling around De Bonneval on
every side, and telling only too vividly of his present court-
life. Snatches of familiar airs are suggesting such of the
fashionable and, in truth, dissolute and profane songs as
were most in vogue amongst his companions. They change
at intervals into the more regular measures to which cavaliers and high-born dames would move in the courtly dance
through brilliantly-lighted saloons ; and then they return
again into their former unbridled wildness. All speaks of
pleasure, of confusion, of self-seeking reckless gaiety ; and
the lights come readily into the polished mirror, and blaze
out from the many chandeliers and sconces represented in
the scene now before him,—a well-remembered state-ball
in the Luxembourg, at which the world, with all its intoxicating power, had wooed young Antoine, and almost without resistance. He recalled the pleasurable sense of life
begun, and begun with the most flattering prospects, that
had played round his heart on that evening, as he saw
himself surrounded by young companions ready to show
him the way to all that Paris could afford of worldly pleasure ; himself attracting the notice of the high-born and
the powerful, prominently in favor at court yet kindly,
regarded also and distinguished by those who led the
opposite faction and ruled in the world of *haut ton*. Enchanted by the witchery of music and the mazy dance,
bewildered by the rapid motion and blaze of light, the
syren of self-love whispering into his ear that all was now
before him, and that his present voyage down the smooth
stream of life would glide in unbroken sunshine,—

"Youth in the prow, and pleasure at the helm"—

De Bonneval had perhaps never been nearer than on that

particular evening to embracing finally the present good,
and surrendering the hopes and struggles for eternity,
which his court-life had been weakening within him.   And
vividly did the remembrance of all he had felt and hoped
and dreamed on that evening now come over him again ;
till the music of the dance, growing fainter by degrees and
slower, died out with the paling shadows of the late brilliant and courtly scene.

All has been revealed to him that belongs to the past
and to the present.   Will he, after this, have a heart to
tempt the future also ?   Will he not let this suffice, and
retire convinced of the sorcerer's power ?   Such seemed
the question asked by the fixed dark eyes of Lomelli.   De
Bonneval merely answered by a gesture of impatience for
the next revelation to appear.

The music swelled forth again ; and now Antoine, his
expectation wound to the utmost pitch, bent forward and
held his very breath, his eyes glaring intently on the mirror.
His heart beat audibly.   He felt his hair slightly bristle on
his head: the moment was come; his future would immediately be known to him.   Much he had already gone through :
those images of the past had wrung his heart with anguish ;
the preternatural power in whose presence he stood awed
and chilled him ;   it was only counterbalanced by the fever-
ishness of his strong determination to go through with it,
and know all.   He afterwards marvelled how he had been
strong enough to sustain this harrowing trial ; how it was
that his brain had not reeled, and his senses deserted him.
Even now he knew that he could not bear much more.
Yet bear it he would as long as strength remained.   The
future, the future ! the veiled and awful future, that he has
panted to know,—for the knowledge of which he has
incurred so tremendous a guilt,—let it appear !   Let it but
appear !

Forth swelled the music in a grave and measured strain,
and gathered strength, and proceeded.   Antoine listened
with an ear quickened, painfully acute, as though he would
anticipate by divining from its every note the revelation
that was to be made upon the mirror.   But that strain
baffled his efforts to draw from it any conclusion.   Grave

and measured it was, without expression of sorrow certainly, but with nothing either that denoted exultation, as, "unhasting, undelaying," it wound and swelled upon its way. There was a character now about the voice-like music that suggested fullness of life, and thoughtful intelligence, and steadfast maturity, and calm disciplined power. It was unlike either the playful air of spring, or the howl and rushing of the wintry blast; it resembled the tempered breeze that sails through the woods in early autumn, ere it has shaken down their first leaf, or so much as touched their glories with one golden presage of decay.

And what sees he as the shadows disperse on the polished steel? What is it that meets him there, and causes in him that start, that involuntary shudder? We know not, and for the present we cannot know. It is nothing horrible, for there is no terror in his riveted look as he gazes; neither can it be aught that is simply pleasurable, for his eye lights not up, his lips smile not. But it is something unexpected, something foreign hitherto to all his thoughts; it has gone deep into his heart, and is stirring it to its depths. Whether it be in disappointment, or with any feeling allied to thankfulness, that Antoine covers his face with his hand, and moves a step backward, we cannot guess. His fate is read to him; he is in possession of his secret.

There was a pause. It may be that De Bonneval, with the burden of the future resting upon his present consciousness, would now have retired from a trial of nerve that had grown too much for him. Something told him, however, there was yet another revelation in store. What will the next five years have brought? He almost read it beforehand; his heart presaged it, and it came.

Again the disturbed shadows were fleeting over the mirror; again that music rose. Slowly and solemnly it rose, and without prelude struck into a long-drawn sequence that smote at once upon De Bonneval's heart. He had heard it for the first time as he followed the corpse of his young sister to her resting-place in the aisle of Notre Dame du Puy. He had heard it occasionally as a funeral had wound its way through the crowded streets of Paris; on All Souls' Eve he had heard it again in the
16

court-chapel.  Note after note the solemn strain pealed
upon his senses with a separate and repeated knell.  It was
the office for the dead.

The words of the Church's hymn rose to his remembrance, awful, passionless, but startling as the archangel's
trumpet, while that dirge-like and plaintive strain wound
through the cadences of the ancient death-chant :

> "Tuba mirum spargens sonum
> Per sepulchra regionum,
> Coget omnes ante thronum.
> *       *       *       *       *
> Quid sum miser tunc dicturus ?
> Quem patronum rogaturus,
> Cum vix justus sit securus ?''

Antoine waited to hear no more, nor needed.  Dizzy and
faint he turned, he staggered from the mirror ; his senses
were fast leaving him.

Hastening steps traversed the ante-room.  The door
was suddenly forced open ; a broad stream of daylight
poured in upon the chamber of iniquity and all its unhallowed furniture.  The tall figure of a priest shone out in
the midst, and made the sign of the cross.  "In the name
of God !" he exclaimed, in a strong clear voice.  It was
answered by a shuddering moan that ran round the tapestried hangings.  Lomelli had disappeared, and Antoine
fell senseless into the arms of Vincent de Paul.

## CHAPTER XXIII.

### BETTER THINGS IN STORE.

"Come, while heaven lends us grace,
Let us fly this cursed place;
Lest the sorcerer us entice,
With some other new device.
Not a waste or needless sound,
Till we come to holier ground."        *Comus.*

GENTLE READER, have you the courage to follow our friend into the solitude in which he now exists? You have accompanied him through several prosperous and adverse scenes of his career; you have stood by while he was in imminent danger of losing his soul; will you look in upon him now that he is at length bent on saving it? It is no reflection upon your spirit to ask whether you can dare this; for in truth Antoine is undergoing an ordeal from which many a stout heart would shrink that never quailed in the moment of outward peril. He is alone with his own conscience; and that is not always agreeable company. He stands face to face with his past; he is questioning it, and receiving a dread reply. Where is he? His bodily presence is to be found in a small chamber in the house of Saint Lazare, where the priests of the mission, the special congregation established by St. Vincent, are living in community. You will find him in No. 15, if you ascend the staircase to the first-floor, and pass along the right-hand corridor. Do not knock at the door, however: you see that small paper upon it, to notify that the occupant is "in retreat," and cannot be spoken with.

In retreat he is and has been ever since we saw him carried forth from the sorcerer's apartment. The night-air had revived him after a brief interval; and when he unclosed his eyes, he found himself in a carriage with Vin-

cent de Paul; his head reclined upon that saintly bosom,
while the old man was busied in a thousand tender cares
to restore him to consciousness. In this he was zealously
assisted by the attendant priest who sat opposite. Antoine, when he came to himself, observed that the coach,
which was rolling easily and rapidly along, bore evidence
in its decoration and arrangement that it belonged to the
royal suite. He could not avoid expressing his surprise,
and turned his eyes inquiringly on the face of the Almoner,
still bent upon him with the same expression of exalted yet
simple benevolence. But Vincent returned a half-playful
answer, and parried the question. Antoine learned afterwards, what was well known to many among Vincent's
familiar acquaintance, that the use of the royal carriages,
together with any other such means and appliances as might
diminish the fatigue of his self-denying labors, was often
pressed upon her holy adviser by the Regent of France.
In most cases such offers were steadily declined; he seemed
determined to wear himself out in poverty and hardship
no less apostolic than the labors of his daily life. On this
occasion, however, he had accepted, if not solicited, the use
of a coach and attendant lacqueys, together with a couple
of exempts, who had mounted with Vincent to Lomelli's
apartment. He had represented these arrangements as
being important to the interests of a person in considerable
danger, but whose situation he was unable to explain more
distinctly at the moment.

Another question then rose to the mind of De Bonneval, though it did not cross his lips  How had Vincent
become aware of his unlawful design? That the good
priest could have held any communication with De Montauban on the subject, appeared to him the most unlikely
of conjectures; for Vincent, affable to all, and winning by
his attractive manner the affection as well as the respect
of many at court who could not be persuaded to follow his
personal example, was yet unflinching in his fatherly
rebukes, whenever the occasion called them forth. Louis
had more than once felt the weight of these, and, spite of
his wayward assurance, had felt it keenly; and Antoine
too well knew the character of his friend to suppose him

likely on this occasion to have made any communication
which might have reached Vincent de Paul. Was it, then,
possible, he asked himself, that in a moment of remorse
the young soldier who had tempted his companion to the
great crime he had just committed had himself fled to the
holy priest to acknowledge his share in the dark scheme?
and had the confessor urged his penitent, as the only
reparation in his power, to permit the use of the knowledge
acquired under the sacramental seal? This would have
been, on Vincent's part, a natural result of the confidence,
if made to him. But Antoine could scarcely reconcile the
idea of Louis, such as he knew him to be, with the making
of such a voluntary confession at all. He was well aware
that the young guardsman lived neglectful, not only of the
precepts of his religion, but of the idea of religion altogether. If Louis did not openly ridicule the doctrines of
the Church as much as he despised her obligations, it was
partly because his indolence and devotion to pleasure dis-
inclined him to the burden of argument, and partly because he wished to stand well with all who could in any
way further his interests or contribute to his amusement.
Vincent was known to have great personal influence with
the queen; and one who sat at the council-board with herself, Mazarin, and Le Tellier, was always in De Montauban's eyes a person to be regarded, even while he represented no intelligible idea. It was true, moreover, that
the young man, whose passion was to see life under every
phase, had widened his experience of late in several
unlikely directions, and had come across ecclesiastics as a
variation to his other freakish adventures. He had introduced himself, for example, to the Jesuit fathers in the
Rue Saint-Antoine, and held a controversy on metaphysics
(sufficiently shallow on his side, it must be owned) with
the Pere Roberval. He had accompanied the princess-
palatine to the Convent of the Visitation, and sustained
his part in a conversation at the grille with the superioress,
who had vainly endeavored to make some good impression
on her worldly visitors. And, riding over one fine day to
Port-Royal des Champs, he had dined there, self-invited,
with the half-dozen learned and distinguished men who
16*

were leading a life of retirement near the Convent of the
Mere Angelique; devoting themselves to studies which
resulted in their pledging themselves to the heterodoxy of
Jansenism. Then, on his return to Paris, De Montauban
had heartily amused his gay companions by the account he
gave of Arnauld's thoughtful austere countenance as he
sat peeling a potato; and of the sudden interruption to an
argument which Nicole was maintaining on a passage of
St. Augustine by Saci's choking with a herring-bone. He
described graphically how Le Maitre had given the com-
mentator some smart blows between the shoulders to prevent suffocation; and how Launcelot had poured down his
throat a cup of thin sour wine.

Some of these various escapades of his wild friend came
into Antoine's remembrance as he pursued his journey in
silence; but they did not assist him in solving the enigma
on which he was pondering. Wearied at length with the
speculation, and exhausted, both in mind and body, by all
that he had undergone, he leaned back in the coach, and
gradually lost all consciousness in slumber.

Our narrative, as the indulgent reader has discovered,
is, upon the whole, of the desultory kind. We are perpe-
trating neither a tragedy nor an historical romance, and do
not hold ourselves to be bound very strictly by the unities.
The ancients fabled that the Muses were the daughters of
Memory; and old Herodotus, whose veracity we are feebly
endeavoring to emulate, inscribed his nine books with
their several names, in token that he aimed at harmony of
arrangement as well as liveliness of fancy. We aspire
not to such classical severities; and as poor Antoine's
history is neither cast in syllogisms, nor distributed into
cantos, we shall convey him with little ceremony from the
coach in which he has sunk to sleep, and instal him in the
small chamber in Saint-Lazare where we have announced
him to be prosecuting his retreat. We beg our reader to
picture to himself the wise tender care with which Vincent
watched over the alternate exhaustion and moodiness of
the young man whom he had thus rescued a second time,
and from a more fearful peril than before. He must suppose that when Antoine awoke, it was by the sudden stop-

ping of the coach at the gate of Saint-Lazare; that, while his benefactor freely offered him the use of the carriage to convey him to the palace, he at the same time invited him to spend at least that night in his house, and recruit his wasted spirits by some hours of perfect repose. Nor will it require any stretch of fancy to picture to oneself how, the next morning, at break of day, Antoine was roused from a broken sleep by the form of Vincent standing before his bed; how, in consequence of his inquiries, a long conversation ensued between them; how the venerable old man enforced upon his guest the necessity of an immediate and effectual repentance for his sin, and recommended him for this purpose to follow during a certain number of days the spiritual exercises of St. Ignatius, under his own direction, or that of any other priest in the community of Saint-Lazare whom he might select as his guide. He engaged at the same time to send a messenger to the palace to announce that Antoine was for the present a guest in his house; and thus to remove from the young man any feeling that he was deserting his post, or forfeiting his honor, by that brief absence from court.

*Apres cela*, if our friendly reader either knows already what is meant by a spiritual retreat, or has no wish to inquire, we will ask him in courtesy to skip the following chapter. We would not inflict upon him a topic which he may feel irrelevant to the telling of a mere story. He will acquit us at least of having introduced into our "littel geste" over-much religion of any kind. Antoine has been hitherto a spirited young fellow, making rather a sensation at the French court,—in fact, a dashing officer of the guards. Though he has come up from the provinces with a better-regulated mind and firmer principles than many whom he has met in Paris, and has kept some of these treasures still undamaged, yet we have seen him enter with eagerness into the amusements of the great world, and without escaping many of its vanities. Maybe, for we cannot tell, he has not come off unscathed by worse still; and certainly the last of his actions has been a fall into grave and deliberate sin. Still we do not feel bound to keep our poor hero in that condition. We are not, indeed,

going, when his retreat is over, to make him revisit the
court a frocked and sandalled monk, startling his former
companions with any miracle of change from his previous
self.   Such things have been ere now,—sudden, most surprising, permanent revolutions in the whole state and character of a man; as though the magnetic needle should
whirl round upon its axis, and point steadfastly to the
south.   But mostly, in conversion, grace works by a gentler and a less sudden action, remodelling a character upon
much of its former outline, though in more excellent proportions, and of purified material.   The soft and yielding
remain gentle to others, while they acquire a Christian
hardness towards themselves; the impetuous become energetic in well-doing, yet receive a new element of tenderness and consideration.   De Bonneval, too, will undergo a
change; for in truth a change is needed.   The employer
of necromancy is not in a state to die, nor to live with any
blessing.   He must come to a halt, and strike into a new
path altogether, for he has been treading the way of perdition.   And for such a purpose quiet reflection is needed,
and retirement, and prayer; such opportunities of review-
ing his own heart in the light of eternity, as he could not
command in the Palais Royal.

Therefore is young De Bonneval now in No. 15, in the
right-hand corridor of the house of the Missioners of Saint-
Lazaro; and some such process it is that we are going to
witness in him.   Let those who feel no interest in observing it wait for us awhile outside the door.

## CHAPTER XXIV.

### RECULANT POUR MIEUX SAUTER.

"Then, soul, live thou on thy companion's loss,
And let *that* pine, to aggravate thy store;
Buy terms divine, by selling hours of dross;
Within be rich, without be gay no more
So shalt thou feed on death, that feeds on men,
And, death once dead, there's no mere dying then."

*Shakespeare's Sonnets.*

ANTOINE rose late on the following morning. A great task was before him, and he meant to address himself to it with courage and energy; yet he had much to do to overcome the languor induced by the reaction of his present quiet, after such a tension of the whole man as he had lately endured. He shook himself free from this, however, and began the first day of his retreat with an earnest will to make the most of the brief time that was to elapse before he must be summoned again to court.

And there he kneels by that *prie-dieu* against the wall of his chamber, his temples supported on his outspread hands, his eyes fixed on the open book lying before him, or raised to the small crucifix that hangs on the bare wall, or closed in still communion with Him who seeth in secret. It is the spiritual exercises of St. Ignatius, arranged for a retreat of eight days, that he is studying. His form is motionless; but there is "that within which passeth show." Let us endeavor to read our friend's thoughts as they pass before us in a kind of moving panorama of that wondrous week. Unlike all other days on earth, they seem to borrow something of the fixed undistracted intuition of truth and its consequences, which is an attribute of our coming eternity.

Yes, eternity, and nothing short of it, has now become
the subject of De Bonneval's thoughts.  His whole future
here, and that boundless future beyond, when the drib-
bling stream of life shall have passed into the shoreless
ocean, all is hanging in the balance, and those few days
will determine the sway of the momentous scale.  He feels
it.  The turning-point of his life is come.  One thing or
another he must be, nor aught between them.  He has
tried *that* too long.

What, then, was he created for?  With a question so
searching opens the work of his eight days.  He once was
nothing, and had been simply nothing for an eternity.
Time began; but he was not.  Angels, men, were created;
passed out of nothingness into existence; fulfilled their
end; still he was not.  That one individual existence,
that one self, with all the marvellous faculties that were
to clothe it at a future day, lay slumbering among mere
possible creatures.  Man fell; sin entered into the world,
and death by sin; the curse descended, and worked
towards its fulfilment; crime and misery began to run their
course.  Society was formed; the patriarchal tradition of
truth was handed down from saint to saint, from sage
to sage; men grouped themselves into communities;
kingdoms rose and sank again.  There were wars, con-
quests, revolutions, fresh dynasties, decay of empires.
Still no thought of him.  His own line of ancestors at
length began to emerge above the level, and grew in
power, and the family was gradually counted among the
ancient ones of the land; and the line lengthened out yet
more, until the moment came when it was *his* turn.  He
was to begin to be.  The nothing passed into something;
it became a being,—a being endowed with powers, inher-
iting a destiny; a creature with reason, and surviving
death, gifted with mighty fearful gifts—conscience, free-
will, the yearning for its own happiness and good, and
the yet undeveloped sense that that good was centred in
the knowledge, the love, the service of Him who had
decreed its being.  And that creature, so constituted,
but clouded with ignorance, subject to interior weakness
and liability to fall, now passes under the operation of a

sacrament, and acquires a fresh store of additional gifts.
Grace is imparted to it, supernatural strength, an illumi-
nation above the light of reason, and the rudiments of
faith.   It was immortal ; it is now baptized : it was the
heir of reprobation ; it is now the adopted child of a loving heavenly Father.   It commences its course—its one
decisive irrevocable trial—and for what?   What is the
end and object of all this complex machinery ?   That being
exists, and is what it is, so gifted by the hands of nature
and grace, simply that it may learn here below the knowledge, the love, the service of its God, and hereafter be
rewarded by the fruition of His presence in bliss.

It is thou, Antoine de Bonneval.   Pause here, and
ask thy own soul how this great end has been hitherto
fulfilled in thee.   A boyhood of comparative innocence ;
that is so far well.   A youth of day-dreams, in which
there is nothing greatly amiss : thou hast been protected,
young sir, hast gaily trodden the edge of many a hidden
precipice, where thou sawest nothing deadlier than the
blossoms and the verdure, but where many a footprint
has disappeared, before thy time, down the abyss.   Now
comes thy real launch into the world ; thy court-life, what
hast thou to say of that ?   Is it not time to be something
better,—to begin to be what thou wert designed to be
from an eternity past, what will shape thy well-being for
an eternity to come ?

It was an era in De Bonneval's life, when he set himself
steadily to face that question.   He dwelt upon it ; he suspended his answer, till he had gathered into his soul something of its length and breadth.

He examined it by the past.   How little had the pleasure, the excitement, the vain successes of his frivolous
career, brought him any true satisfaction, even in the hour
of their brimming enjoyment!   There had been a void
when the tide of its waters was at the full ; there had been
a darkness in the soul when outward things seemed bright
as bright could be.   He recalled the feeling well.   It had
partly isolated him amid society ; had made others occasionally think him strange ; saved him thus, perhaps, from
much he might otherwise have fallen into.   De Montauban

had not been the only one whom he had timidly sounded
on this unsatisfied craving after something better, nor the
only one who had endeavored to rally him out of the
eccentricity of such an idea.   In vain,—that feeling had
still haunted his heart.   Go where he would, a something
told him he was not yet in his spirit's home.   He plunged
into gaity; he would out-laugh that whisper, he would
out-sing it, would drown it in any mad recklessness at
hand.   It was a call from heaven, and it whispered on.
It had lured him hitherto by its hallowed fascination.
Now, within the four walls of that chamber, it is speaking
to him in yet clearer tones; for it speaks to one who is in
solitude, to a listener who begins to breathe the prayer
that ever draws a fuller response from the oracle of truth—
"Speak, Lord; for Thy servant heareth."

Still that question :—has he been fulfilling the end, the
only end, for which he exists?   An hour passes; and
another, and a third is on the wane.   Still Antoine is face
to face with that great question, grappling it.   Wax not
impatient, O giddy world! blow not thy clarion so loud,
shake not thy jingling reins; or, if thou wilt, ride onward,
and leave us altogether.   Dost grudge him a few poor
hours to answer that which embraces infinity?

He tests it by his present convictions, as they grow
upon him.   He had seen his way dimly, by fits and
snatches, to something of an answer.   Now, as he views
aloof the pageant of life, sees it spread out beneath him,
from the eminence of his solitude, amid the stillness of his
heart, the mists roll away as from a landscape at sunrise :
the veil is lifted; he gazes, and learns.   There, right in
the centre, lies the path whereto each one is called; narrow, rough, ever ascending, with a strain at each step,
with a sacrifice at each turn; but with constant helps also,
secure fences, resting-places here and there.   He sees the
crowds of men, the thronging and various multitudes, pursue their own paths, diverging to the right, to the left,
forgetful of the final cause of their being, unthinking of
the end to which they hasten, never staying to ask themselves why they exist,—all wanderers, and all wrong.
Such was he, and not so long ago.   An exertion of infinite

mercy alone has plucked him back from that miserable company.

Away from the present, he plunges into the future: he will ask himself the same momentous question from thence also. He places himself in imagination on his death-bed. 'Tis but a slight anachronism; he will soon be there: meanwhile he will learn the lessons it has to teach him. On his death-bed, then, he lies; faint, restless with the rackings of the last struggle; the death-sweat on his dizzy brow. All swims around him; but amid the weakness and the anguish, there is one thought that overspreads and overmasters the soul;—the account to be rendered—the life-long trust of a talent to be accounted for. Still that question:—has he fulfilled the end, the one sole end of his existence?

Onward still, from death to judgment. He stands there alone, save that his angel-guardian is on one side, and the accusing fiend on the other. His deeds are about to be cast into the unerring balance. Still the one dread question!

Antoine paused long upon this, returned to it again and again, viewed in its light the details of his former career. How utterly vain; what squandering of time and powers! Was it indeed himself,—the very self that possessed these convictions, that had led that aimless life?

They who are well acquainted with the Spiritual Exercises have learned to admire the solemn and orderly course through which the mind of the *ritirante* is led progressively, step by step, pausing for a definite time, and no longer, before each of those considerations, so simple yet so mighty, so "unknown and yet known," and then taken, as it were, by the strong hand of St. Ignatius himself, and set down before the picture that is next in succession. They will therefore blame our Antoine, and us, for lingering so long upon the threshold. It is true, and we have not forgotten that this meditation on the end of man is but the foundation of all that follows. But in proportion to the breadth and solidity of the foundation is the permanence of the superstructure. And how much need has our poor Antoine of laying, from the very beginning, the basement of his future self! Whatever

17

becomes of him hereafter, he must needs commence, and
he is commencing, to exist to some purpose never yet realized.  Let him alone yet another moment; he is in process of formation.  The earth, wrapt in its fertile soil, car-
peted with pasture-lawns, waving with sunny corn-fields,
laughing, grateful, exuberant, does not differ more from
the slimy chaos out of which it emerged—grim saurians
wallowing in its depths, darkness brooding over it—than
the Antoine of hitherto from the Antoine of a day to come.
That one great question is shaping him; it is becoming
the law of his spiritual creation.  Stir not the surface; let
him crystallize.

&ast; &ast; &ast; &ast; &ast; &ast;

Then, as one day of retreat succeeds another, he passes,
in the light and power of that great generating thought,
through the successive steps of what writers on spiritual
science define as the Purgative, the Illuminative, and the
Unitive Way.  He has first to unlearn affection to sin and
vanity; the ground must be cleared of its encumbering
growths, that the soul's building, which those days are to
accomplish, may rise shapely, unobstructed.

Sin, therefore, is presented to his meditation, that he
may look on it, that he may abhor it.  Sin, and what it
is, and its malice and loathsomeness: the infinite malice,
the unutterable loathsomeness of mortal sin, of each separate mortal sin, of the mortal sin of years past, clean forgotten, unreckoned by the world, but separating the soul
from God, and keeping her still in that dread banishment.
Then sin, as viewed by the light of its punishment; seen
by the flames of hell; the dead soul in the torments of its
everlasting death.  The one momentary sin of the angels
who fell, that thrust them without a second trial down the
abyss, and left vacant a third part of the thrones of heaven.
The mortal sins—perchance the one mortal sin—of some
soul that has sinned less than Antoine's and has already
entered upon its eternity of pain.  He draws near with
awe ; contemplating that soul, remembering himself.  On
the edge of the abyss he leans, he looks down, listens—
ah ! can we go on?  *Misericordiæ Domini quia non con-
sumimur.*

And from this point, is it not enough to say, that, before the days were ended, Antoine's whole being, all that springs from the will and reacts upon it, had received a stamp that will not be obliterated, an impulse that will carry him on unspent to better things? It has been the work of silence, of solitude, and prayer. His soul has been fixed unremittingly upon the interests of eternity; and what is it we need, but to be strong enough to hold at their real value—to keep down in their duo place—the impertinent intrusions and frivolities of time? Vincent has been his constant help and guide. And what more powerful help to us in following upon the good way, which our reason approves, than the personal presence of some well-girt strong-footed traveller upon that narrow road,—some one who has surmounted the steeps, and tracked the mazes, and passed unallured by the seductions of the journey of life? O ye numberless Antoines, who float, unformed and aimless, unconscious of the dormant powers of your own better selves, through the dreary chaos of this world, who shall give you such an impulse, and such a guide? who shall at length show to you your present state, and aid in shaping you anew? Courage, and be but in earnest; true to your own sense of right: the angel shall be sent to you. The advent of that harbinger of good may be at a moment, his presence may be under a form, such as yourselves would not have chosen. But come he shall, unless ye are faithless; and so come as shall be decreed by boundless wisdom, and approved by boundless love. It shall be as a gentle and tender Vincent from without, or as a calm but powerful creative whisper from within.

# CHAPTER XXV.

### AN ANXIOUS EVENING.

*Benvolio.* Supper is done, and we shall come too late.
*Romeo.* I fear too early : for my mind misgives
Some consequence, yet hanging in the stars,
Shall bitterly begin his fearful date
With this night's revels.
But He that hath the steerage of my course
Direct my sail.  On, lusty gentlemen.

*Romeo and Juliet.*

"FOUR to one on the red !"

"I take it, monsieur le comte," answered the young
spendthrift De Brocas, who had run through his fine
estates in Picardy within a couple of years after coming to
them.  "Bonneval, you stake nothing? Grave as a judge,
I protest.  You must have lost, friend, I fear.  Well, I
can afford to lose for a wonder.  See the rouleau that has
found its way to me.  Ha! there it all goes again," he
muttered, as red turned up on the table ; "nothing but
that odious color to-night.  Stockings and hats !  I think
the very cards are turned Mazarins, and declare against
the honest cause."

"Hush, Brocas !" said his friend Gerze, quickly in his
ear, with a glance directed towards the Duke of Orleans,
who, with the cardinal, was playing in the next room.
"Go on with thy betting, beau-sire.  Play is play, and
politics are—"

"The game in which young folks burn their fingers as
well as fling away their money," struck in the Marquis de
Persan, who overheard the remark.

"And elder folks, too, monsieur," rejoined the irritated
De Brocas, "or the *Importants* would have come off
unscathed some few years ago."

There was a good-humored laugh among the knot of loungers who surrounded the table, some engaged in play, others betting on its chances, with that degree of *nonchalance* supposed to be inseparable from gambling in high life ; while others discussed in an undertone the prospects of the late disturbances at court.

The young man's allusion to the cardinal, though sufficiently palpable, passed without further remark. Conscious of his unpopularity with many of the court-party, as well as with the bulk of the middle ranks, and the entire populace, Mazarin adopted, from policy no less than from natural disposition, a mild and conciliatory line of conduct towards his political enemies. Spies were less employed, and speeches therefore freer, than during the late despotic reign of Richelieu. Under that sterner *regime*, such a speech would, beyond all reasonable doubt, have lodged the thoughtless gamester that night in the *Chatelet*.

The Marechal de Grammont, at whose splendid hotel the supper was given this Twelfth-Night eve, mingled with his accustomed high courtesy among the guests who thronged his suite of apartments. Yet there was upon his manly brow a shade of anxiety which he seemed unable, notwithstanding some efforts, to dissipate. He would now and then take a hand at picquet, or stake some broad pieces at one or other of those swifter methods of losing money with which the march of refinement had furnished that generation, in lieu of the patient gambling of their forefathers. He performed, with all the courtly exactness prescribed by the manners of the time, the duties of a hospitable entertainer ; pressed his guests to partake of the slight but luxurious refreshments, handed round at frequent intervals by lacqueys in fanciful and elaborate costumes ; pledged them himself in the rich wines, as he recommended and descanted on the vintage and pedigree of each. Yet at unobserved moments his eye would also steal a glance towards the rich gilded clock that occupied a prominent place among the ornaments of the saloon. It was surmounted by a figure of old Time, a masterpiece of Bernini's workmanship. That imaginary personage had been chiselled by the Italian artist with all the conventional em-

17*

blems that symbolize his rapid flight, and the hopelessness
of recapturing him. There he stood, or rather fled, his
golden limbs glittering changefully in the light of the
waxen sconces, the allegoric forelock floating wild, his
scythe cast back upon his winged shoulder; while, poised .
on one foot, and bending on the spectator a look of mingled
warning and mockery, he shook aloft the hourglass in his
right hand, with all the energetic triumph which the skill
of the artificer had infused into the inanimate metal.

Most men, probably, have at times been conscious of
strong impressions derived from the mute creations of chisel
or pencil, acting upon their own anxious or highly-wrought
minds, and re-acted on by them in turn, until the unconscious object has seemed almost endued with life and meaning. The passionless lineaments of a marble bust, the
warning finger of a statue, have arrested men on the brink
of some act of thoughtless folly or project of guilt; the
reproving inexorable eye of a portrait has followed the
shrinking beholder round the room. Even so did that
small gilded figure, lithe and grim, with so much warning
on the half-open lips, so much energy of flight in the spare
limbs, appear to the marechal as the very embodiment of
one thought that was possessing him amid the careless
mirth of the crowds in his reception-rooms. "Ay," he
unconsciously muttered to himself, as one quarter after
another tinkled clear on the finely-constructed mechanism,
and waking up the chimes of a lively air, sent their silvery
notes through the perfumed atmosphere of the apartments—"ay, ring on, ring on! Ye do but bring the hour
nearer; and the hour must come. God in mercy grant it
a safe issue!"

The anxieties of Grammont (we must do him this justice) were not for himself. He had served with distinction in Flanders and in Germany, and would have scorned,
on the eve of any of his battles, to own to the restlessness
which now made it difficult for him to play becomingly his
part of a courteous and *insouciant* host. His thoughts
during this anxious evening were occupied wholly with the
regent and her royal son. A devoted adherent of the
throne through a life that was already reaching its zenith,

he had now been intrusted, in common with a few other
tried loyalists, with a secret of no small importance to the
royal fortunes.

Once already, within the last few months, Anne of
Austria had found it expedient to adopt the last resource
in times of contention between the several estates of a
kingdom, and to withdraw the young monarch, whose
rights were being invaded by so determined a party among
his subjects. The commotions excited by the arrest of
Broussel, and the success of that day of barricades, which
had first made the popular leaders know their real strength,
had been symptoms too serious entirely to disappear;
though for the moment they had subsided into a deceitful
calm. Accordingly, in less than three weeks after that
eventful twenty-sixth of August, the court had effected
what might be termed an escape out of Paris, and had
retired, first to Ruel, and then to St. Germains-en-Laye.
It is true, that a measure so decided revived for a little
while the decaying spirit of loyalty in a parliament which
had not yet learned to dispense with its sovereign. That
body, in common with the whole city of Paris, became
alarmed at the result of its own resistance to the authority
of the crown. The army of Conde was within a few
days' march of the capital; the forces under Turenne,
many of them Swedes and other foreign mercenaries, with
no interest in the internal factions of France, nor any law
but the will of their military commanders, were at the
beck of the court, and could be brought to bear with irresistible effect upon the insurgent capital. The citizens of
Paris, themselves untrained to war, might well be pardoned for reluctance to the idea of measuring themselves
against the veteran troops which those distinguished
generals could bring against them from the Flemish and
German frontiers. Add to which, that they were unpro-
vided alike in provisions for withstanding a siege, and in
the munitions of active warfare. The two royalist armies
combining in one operation, and advancing upon the
capital from different quarters, had it in their power either
to lay waste the adjacent country, or to appropriate its
stores to their own use, and in either case to surround

the city with the lines of a complete and famishing blockade.

The result of these considerations was a determination
on the side of the Parliament to treat with the queen-mother
and her supporters.   Conde, who from the proud impetuosity that was natural to him, alternately took umbrage at
the demands of the Parliament, and at the court influence
of Orleans and of Mazarin, had hitherto maintained among
the various parties a kind of armed neutrality, and was, so
far, the fittest person to undertake an office of mediation
between the extreme opposing interests.   In this character,
therefore, he now came forward, addressed from Ruel, toward the end of September, a letter to the Parliament, and
invited them to a conference which might adjust the existing disorders of the State.   A deputation from that body
came accordingly to St. Germains ; and their preliminary
debate was succeeded by several after-conferences with
the cabinet council assembled there, which were protracted
through the greater part of the following month.   During
these deliberations, the demands of the parliamentary deputies increased in urgency and firmness, while their personal
demeanor began to lose somewhat of the outward demonstrations of respect.   The insurgent spirit meanwhile increased within the capital ; the execrations against Mazarin
became louder and more vehement ; while the character
and acts of the regent herself did not escape either invec-
tive or the bitterest satire.   The more far-sighted members
of the royal council also began to press upon the attention
both of the queen and of the princes of the blood the
necessity of making some concession to the demands of the
opposite party : the Marechal de Meilleraye, in particular,
urged the deplorable extent of the public distress which
was affecting all classes beneath the actual nobility, and the
bad spirit gaining ground in the capital, which would be
exasperated beyond remedy if all concessions were to be
withheld from the people.   Lastly (though this was a topic
to be delicately handled in a court hitherto so absolute, and
to a regent whom natural character and antecedents had
combined to render so haughtily intolerant of the lesson),
the marechal did not hesitate to point to the neighboring

kingdom of England, and to the warning against an undue disregard of popular claims which was being there inscribed in the blood-stained chronicles of civil war. As to the cardinal, his policy had always been to make the conduct of the regent wear an aspect of severity, in order to enact the character of intercessor, and thus to win some small measure of popularity; and so threatening had now become the aspect of affairs, that neither Orleans with all the vacillation which made him assume any character that suited the moment, nor Conde with all the haughty impetuousness that took fire at every breath of opposition, could be induced by the regent to promise their aid in carrying out her one favorite idea—that of chastising the rebels. The demands of the Parliament, therefore, sifted down through successive interviews, were some of them conceded, others modified, and their final declaration received the royal assent on the 24th of October, the very day on which the ratification of the treaties of Westphalia seemed to promise some access of popularity to the cardinal, while by releasing the forces under Turenne from their German campaign, it gave them leisure to devote themselves to the interests of the court at home.

Anne of Austria was now at liberty, or rather was pledged by the late convention, to bring back the young king to Paris. On All Saint's eve the court returned from St. Germains, and was received by the fickle populace with every demonstration of joy. It soon became evident, however, that these loyal appearances were not too securely to be relied on. A deep spirit of discontent was working in the public mind, and appeared to be fomented underhand by some persons of influence, too cautious to appear above the surface ; seditious pamphlets were again circulated extensively, and though the immediate agents in these acts of disloyalty might be apprehended and imprisoned, the real authors escaped in their *incognito*, while the mischief went abroad extensively, and did its work among the masses. The estrangement of the weak, uncertain, and jealous Orleans from the court grew daily more manifest, and his palace of the Luxembourg became the resort of the disaffected. The house of Vendome represented another branch

of malcontents, and gathered round itself a considerable
number of the nobility who from one cause or other were
prepared to break with the court.

And Conde : where, then, is he amid this confusion of
men and things?   Conde has become an uncertain support to lean upon.   He still remains ostensibly loyal as
before; but his overgrown popularity with the middle and
lower orders is disquieting the regent, and not without
cause.   He has endeared himself to the Parliament, notwithstanding some hasty outbursts—not altogether ungraceful, in their eyes, in a royal prince and a successful
commander—by the part he bore in the late conferences at
St. Germains.   By the populace he is worshipped as a hero
and a demigod ; and his nearness to the throne, his pre-
eminent influence among the high nobility, and the devotion to him of that well-disciplined army, which he had led
to repeated triumphs, seem to unite in his powerful hands
the strings by which almost every class in the kingdom
might be fatally drawn aside.   Thus the prospect of things,
instead of brightening for the young king and the widowed
mother, seems only to darken and close in around them
with gathering gloom.   After much inward disquiet, therefore, and secret counsel with some few trustworthy ones
among those who surrounded her, Anne of Austria has
determined upon a second, and a more disguised, because
now a more perilous move, even in this depth of winter,
to the old deserted palace of St. Germains.

The project on which the whole future of Louis XIV.—
if it be too much to say the future monarchy of France
itself—may hang, is to be executed before to-morrow morning ; and so we return, with a greater insight into the by-
play of the evening, to the revellers and gamesters who
crowd the gay saloons of the Marechal de Grammont, and
who are unconsciously inflicting upon their noble host the
prolonged torture of wearing a laughing mask over a brow
of more than usual anxiety and care.

As the hours wore away, tediously to him, though swift
and unobserved to those whom he was making an effort to
entertain, the marechal had to recall to himself again and
again the vital importance of concealing the bold stroke

that was impending from the suspicions of any dubious observer. No slight risk was to be run that night by the heir of the throne to which De Grammont was so devoted. The citizens had been exasperated in the midst of their alarm by the last evasion of the regent, who had shared largely with Mazarin the odium of the measure. Popularity, indeed, was something undreamt of in the philosophy of Anne of Austria. She appeared very unambitious of that quality, and certainly never attained it. The young king was as yet entirely undeveloped, and incapable of being the object of any personal attachment to his subjects. But Paris looked upon him as public property; and the discovery of an attempt to rob them of their possession of the royal child might involve some rough handling, such as the devoted loyalist shrank from picturing to himself. Then again, the confusion, the darkness, the unprotected state in which the royal fugitives would find themselves, might give occasion to the yet worse-disposed for the perpetration of some frightful crime. No one could calculate upon the lengths to which the seditious spirit now filling Paris might urge the partisans of the Fronde, should the young king be intercepted in his flight.

Filled with such forebodings, De Grammont wore through the hours of that most weary feast. But his trial was now approaching its conclusion. Soon after midnight, Conde, Orleans, and the cardinal, began to detach themselves separately from the circle of the brilliant and careless revellers who still surrounded the gaming-tables. They withdrew from the saloons separately, and at intervals; but with an air of such untroubled gaity, and with so many courteous expressions to their entertainer, that no one could have suspected them to have been all banded together in any preconcerted design.

Mazarin was the last of the three to leave the Hotel de Grammont; and then the marechal drew a long breath. Action suited him better than suspense; and the time was now come when others, at least, were entering upon action in a cause which he could only follow with his anxieties and loyal wishes. No sooner had the six horses of the cardinal's coach drawn that cumbrous vehicle across the paved

court and through the gateway, with all the rumbling and
clatter attendant upon such dignified movements, than the
master of the house, with a more disengaged air than he
had hitherto worn, tapped De Bonneval lightly on the
shoulder, and whispered in his ear: "Return to your
quarters, young lieutenant, and that with speed: you will
find some work there ready to your hand."

## CHAPTER XXVI.

### WE FLY BY NIGHT.

*Oxford.* O brave young prince, thy famous grandfather
Doth live again in thee! Long may'st thou live
To bear his image, and renew his glories!
  *Somerset.* And he that will not fight for such a hope,
Go home to bed, and, like the owl by day,
If he arise, be mock'd and wonder'd at.
                    *Third Part of King Henry VI.*

IT was between night and morning of the Epiphany. But
few, save those communities of religious whose rule called
them to the Church's solemn offices before daybreak, had
yet risen to celebrate the festival. The great world of
Paris, its wants and sufferings, its frivolous excesses and
its crimes, lay hushed and still. A wanderer whose steps
led him abroad in that hour, through the snow that was
mantling street and house-roof in its mute veil, might have
been impressed with a great truth which comes too seldom
across our consciousness amid the ordinary stir of life.
See those lights that are casting a faint gleam into the
frosty air, in contrast with the new-fallen snow and the
deep purple of the glittering night-heavens. They come

from the few wax-tapers that burn on the high altar, where
the discalced Carmelite nuns of the Faubourg Saint-
Jacques are slowly chanting their matin-psalms. And
those gleams of light, and those murmured sounds,—what
lesson do they tell to the heart that comprehends them?
They say intelligibly, that while the vast majority of mankind, of civilized and so-called Christian men, pursue a
headlong course towards the destruction in which selfishness and license terminate, there is at every time a small
remnant here and there, enclosed apart within consecrated
walls, or shrouded beneath an unnoticed ordinary life,
united in one great harmony of design, who live to repair
the forgetfulness of that mixed multitude, and wake and
pray for a slumbering unconscious world.

Those lights are thrown steadily through the lofty
pointed windows of the ancient choir; they burn as tokens
of the tranquil fearlessness which innocence and abnega-
tion of self can bring, even in the most troublous times.
The tumult of the Fronde has never penetrated that calm
abode of prayer. The rudest sounds of earth, all the strife
of passion and turbulence of selfish energy, must needs
die upon the threshold within which a diviner life resides.
Were it not that the Sisters of Mount Carmel are taught
to shape their petitions to heaven according to the varying
needs of the world that struggles and raves without,—
were it not that the victims of that world's conflict, with
broken hopes and gnawing unrest, come to add their
special wants to that wide intention of prayer, kings might
ascend the throne and leave it vacant, empires and revolutions chase one another across the scene, and the matin-
psalms in the Faubourg Saint-Jacques would swell upward
with the same calm deliberation, and the hearts of those
consecrated sisters rise towards the eternal kingdom they
are winning, as tranquilly under the one dynasty as under
the other.

We are on our way to the Palais-Royal, whither Antoine has already preceded us from the Marechal de Grammont's supper. Across the broad open space behind the
Louvre, there lies one unbroken expanse of snow. The
night is piercing cold; it is nearly three hours after mid-
18

night.  See, is there not a dark figure gliding noiselessly
along, now dimly seen in the starlight, now all but hidden
under the shadow of the houses behind which the moon is
setting?   Who can he be, astir and abroad at this hour?
and upon what errand is he bent?   Stand close under the
covert of this massy stone pier that supports the railings
between the *Place* and the inner court.   The figure
approaches; by the cassock, the broad hat, the long ample
cloak, you may tell that it is a priest.   He walks rapidly;
the new-fallen snow crunches under his strides; and now
that he is near, what is it he carries so carefully within
the folds of his cloak?   Hark! what feeble sound was
that?   It is the wailing of a little child.

A little child, whom Vincent of Paul, when abroad this
night on some errand of mercy, had found exposed on a
door-step, wrapped but scantily with any defence against
the bitter cold, is being carried in his arms towards his
house for foundlings.   Infancy and age have met in the
stern winter's night.   Infancy, unconscious of all but the
suffering of the moment, lies cradled warmly in the arms
of age, long-tried, long-refined, by the manifold sufferings
of seventy years, alive only to emotions of charity.   A holy
and tender solicitude, spending and being spent for all who
have the claims of affliction or the needs entailed by sin,
has come out beyond the path of bare ordinary duty, and
caught up as a precious deposit for God what the hard hand
of crime had cast recklessly away.   What more touching
copy of the Good Shepherd, who not only recovers His
strayed sheep from the bramble and the precipice, but
also carries the lambs of the flock in His bosom safely
home, revealing Himself as the preserver of innocence, no
less than as the pardoner of the fallen?   Or what dearer
offering could Vincent make on this holy night to the
Divine Infant whom sages once adored with their gifts,
than to present to Him, not gold, or frankincense, or
myrrh, but that oblation which can be priced at nothing
meaner than His own most precious Blood,—a rescued
immortal soul?

The dead of the night, and the wild desert, and the
lonely sea, bring men together in strange combinations.

Saintliness and unmasked vice both dwell on the outskirts
of ordinary society; and though each mingles with it
occasionally, yet on the whole they range apart, and have
their own objects and methods of pursuit, discountenanced
by the world for its much-cherished comfort's sake.   Thus
the wildest extremes often meet, locally at least, on their
opposite errands; as we have read of solitary travellers
across the desert guiding their camels towards the dark
speck that indicated another wanderer over the waste, and
gazing fixedly upon the stranger, and so passing each on his
several way.   The active forces of good and evil encounter to counterwork one another; and while quiet respectable people sleep, or recreate themselves, and let events
slip by, saints and sinners, as Don Abbondio* so feelingly
complains, are dividing the action of life between them.
Vincent is now abroad, and doing his work, at the same
hour, through the same thoroughfares of the city, as the
secret plunderer, or the pursuer of vice, or the midnight
assassin.

There is another footstep over the snow, lighter, more
active, though not more vigorous than that of the priest.
A young man, dressed in a crimson livery profusely braided,
as becomes his situation of valet to a person of distinction,
is making his way across the open space, and passes within
a short distance of the path of Vincent and his light burden.   If the moon were higher, you would see upon his
left arm the cognizance, or badge, of the house of La
Rochefoucault worked in silver.   It is Gourville; a hero
of whom we have already seen and heard something.   He
occupies a post ranging between that of confidential valet
and *maitre d'hotel* to the Prince de Marsillac.   He is
treated with an intimacy and consideration which elevate
him above the former office ; but for the convenience of
prosecuting the various missions, of great import or small,
with which he is intrusted by his eccentric master, he still
occasionally wears the externals of the condition out of
which he first rose.

Gourville is pre-eminently a man of expedient and intrigue.   A diplomatist of the very first water, fixed prin-

* Manzoni : *Promessi Sposi.*

ciples do not appear to be his *forte.*† Not that he has not
a system of morals, with its great turning-points; for one
of these is faithfulness to his master; another, which he
generally finds coincident with the first, is an attention to
his private interests. He lives amid the Fronde, and
every now and then he comes across Vincent; but religion
and politics chiefly affect him in so far as they affect Marsillac; that is to say (at least as regards the latter topic,)
in a desultory manner, and to no very intense degree.
At present he is hastening upon some errand, whether for
the prince or for himself; but he is not the man to let one
object or pursuit so engross him as to exclude any number
of supplemental ones.  He is many-sided in his method of
conducting business; full of by-play; a very Argus and
Briareus, ever seeing more than was meant to meet his
eyes, and picking up stray information in all quarters.
He worms out some secrets with diligent address, and
stumbles upon others by a happy chance; so that, by dint
of a pretty retentive memory for little things, he knows an
astonishing amount of the private transactions of most persons about the court, and has become a kind of walking
dictionary of other men's affairs.

As Gourville paces along at a light springing trot
through the snow, keeping his hands warm in the lappets
of his livery-jerkin, and whistling through his chattering
teeth the air of a fashionable court-dance, he espies the
venerable priest and makes up to him.

"Good-night, Monsier Vincent," he began, in his usual
tone of frank and imperturbable assurance; "or good-
morning, I should rather say, for I think the day is almost
beginning.  May an unworthy layman ask the cause of
your so late journeying?"

"God's blessing be with you, my friend!" replied the
other, in a tone that effectually repressed Gourville's liberty of speech, while it had in it nothing either haughty
or severe.  "I am carrying home, as you see, a little
houseless one who has had no long experience yet of this
world of sin and suffering."

† See a brilliant and characteristic article upon Gourville in M.
de St. Beuve's *Causeries du Lundi.*

The *maître d'hotel*, court-hardened as he was, and with that species of sensibility only that could throw itself into an attitude at a tender song, or weep maudlin tears over a romance, and remain hard as adamant to actual work-day suffering, stood nevertheless rebuked before the glance of the aged priest. There was something so paternal, so purely disinterested in the act of charity which engaged the other at that moment, that Gourville was startled into one of his very best moods at the sight. Perhaps his conscience smote him for a moment by the contrast presented by their respective errands at this self-same hour. His features altered in their expression, and his manner sank at once into a demonstration of unaffected reverence. Tell it not in Gath! a half-sigh escaped him as he replied:

"Then what I have heard is true; and there *is* one man in Paris to whom day and night are both alike for doing good. Yet tell me, reverend father," he continued, approaching close to Vincent, and looking steadily in his face, in a way that showed the usual carelessness of his demeanor to conceal a character of no small penetration, "do you think this child is the only one who is abroad in the city to-night? Suppose you condescended to take a turn with me now, towards—well, the Palais Royal, we will say— should we have a chance, think you, of meeting any other little ones on the move? And if we did so, you would doubtless offer them a home too? Or should they chance to have a home already, you would think it an act of charity—for children are but children, whatever their rank— to reconduct them thither, and advise them to stay there?"

"I know not what you mean, friend Gourville," answered Vincent, and truly; for the secret of the royal flight had been communicated to very few; and though a vague impression of it had got abroad, yet Gourville's inquiry, on this very night when it was to take place, was the mere chance hit of an active and inquisitive fancy.

"But yes," pursued the old man, half to himself, "there is, on this very night, one child—a child of royal race—" He paused, and Gourville listened with his whole attention. "He is exposed," continued Vincent, seeming as though he had forgotten the other's presence,—"ex-
18*

posed to the inclemency of the winter's night." There
was a second pause, and Gourville remained in doubt, but
watchful for what might still be coming.

"The stars are shining keenly throughout the heavens,"
resumed Vincent, looking upward; "but there is one far
brighter than the rest, and nearer ; and it guides to that
royal Child the princes of a court—"

"Ha!" thought the quick-witted agent to himself,—
"Conde, Orleans, and who beside ?   Are they gone to the
palace thus late ? then something is astir ; yet what can
he know ?"

"Of a court that is truly wise, seeking the one true
object of ambition," continued the priest, his eyes fixed on
the starry heavens, without noticing his companion ; "and
all the while, the infant whom they are approaching with
richest gifts from their distant land suffers, ah ! suffers—"

His hearer's attention flagged ; for he discovered plainly
that the mind of the speaker was very far from the point
to which he had been anxious to lead it.   He waited, however, yet another moment, and as a last chance.

"For us men and for our salvation," Vincent slowly
uttered, with a tone of thrilling love.

Gourville, as having been too long detained, made a
hasty reverence, and departed at his former diligent pace ;
while Vincent more slowly proceeded on his way towards
the House of Foundlings, as though his mind were full of
the thoughts which the allusion of the other to the young
king had casually awakened.

Our wanderings through this night have brought us
acquainted with several phases of human life and will.
We have encountered the holy calm of cloistered prayer ;
and the burning love that urges to deeds of outward charity ;
and the keen intelligence, ready wit, light-hearted selfishness, which are so many attributes of the world.   But our
adventures are not yet concluded.   We are approaching the
precincts of the Palais Royal itself ; and we shall find that
others are now astir besides the Sisters of Mount Carmel,
or Vincent, or the *maitre d'hotel*.   It is scarcely three
hours after midnight, yet the lights that glance here and
there with hurried stealth, appearing and vanishing through

the windows of those apartments occupied by the young
king and his royal mother, have already announced to
some observant eyes in the neighborhood that all is not
as usual in the palace. Two hours later the report will
have circulated through the city, that a great *coup d'etat*
has been executed, and that Louis XIV. has been safely
conveyed from among citizens whose allegiance had long
been growing threadbare to an army still devoted to his
person and cause. Meanwhile we may station ourselves
unobserved near a small postern leading out by a side-pas-
sage to the palace-garden. Two of the royal coaches are
drawn up opposite to this egress; they have been ranged
abreast, so as to present as small a mark for observation
as may be to the curiosity of any chance spectators. The
resinous glare of a single flambeau, held by a dismounted
sergeant of the guard, scarcely struggling through the
wintry mist arising from the river, shows in dim outline
the cumbrous state-carriages, low-hung on their axles,
roomy, and terminating in a solid canopy above, with six
stately Flemish steeds harnessed to either. The gilded
carvings on the panels, and the horses' trappings, return a
faint glimmer in the uncertain torchlight; while champing
the bit, and shaking proudly their long black manes and
jingling harness, the noble animals snort and paw the
pavement of the alley in impatience for their journey.

It was indeed time that the *cortege* should begin to move.
Rumors had for some days past floated in Paris that such
a final resolve was contemplated by the court; and the
suspicion had been but partially lulled by the presence of
mind and calm demeanor exhibited by the regent. Even
on the night which has not yet given place to dawn, she
had maintained the conversation with her ladies of honor
with an air of perfect tranquillity. She had spoken of the
great festival which the morrow would bring, and proposed
to make a visit of devotion to the convent of Val-de-Grace,
her former retreat while she was yet suffering under the
persecutions of Richelieu. She even took part with them
and the royal children in the usual diversion of the
Twelfth-Night cake; made the arrangements for an entertainment to be given two days afterwards by the Marquis

de Villequier, one of the captains of the guard, and insisted
that the little band of violinists in the retinue of the Prince
de Conde should be secured to enhance the pleasure of the
evening.   It grew late amid this seemingly careless talk ;
and towards midnight, the Comte de Beringhen, who held
the office of master of the horse, presented himself in obedience to a summons he had received from his royal mistress.   On seeing him, the regent rose from her seat, and
leaving her ladies for a few moments, took Beringhen
aside, ordered him to have the royal carriages in readiness,
and returned with her wonted calmness to the unsuspicious
circle, who were amusing themselves with the frivolous
conversation usual among court-ladies in their hours of
idleness.

But the arrangements are now complete, and the hour
is come.   The first who emerges from the postern is one
whose form we at once recognize.   It is our friend Antoine, who hurries down the steps of the private staircase,
motions to the soldier who acts as torchbearer to open the
door of the royal carriage, deposits within it something
with which he had been intrusted (for offices and departments of service are rather confused at this hurried moment), carefully arranges some arms in the "sword-case,"
—a portion of the carriage which, in those days, and down
to a much later period, was used for the purpose which its
name implied,—and then giving a glance round the roomy
interior to see that some needful accessories of comfort,
and even articles of food, had not been forgotten, disap-
pears again with an active step into the palace.

After the lapse of a few minutes more, there is a slight
movement on the stairs leading down to the postern.   Several exempts, a trustworthy lacquey or two,—from whom
the secret of this intended flight could not be concealed,—
and then De Bonneval again descend the steps backwards,
mindful, even in that critical moment, of the etiquette of
courts.   They are followed by La Porte, the confidential
valet of the young king.   He carries in his arms the Comte
d'Artois, and leads,—not by the hand, which would be an
infraction of all rule, but slightly holding the royal sleeve,
—Louis himself.   The boy-king has been but just awak-

ened, and made hastily to comprehend the cause of this
sudden move. But there are in his countenance no signs
of fear, scarcely of surprise. Grave and self-possessed are
his noble features, even now at ten years of age; and the
observant composure with which he walks along to take
his seat in the carriage gives an early promise of those
qualities of firmness and dauntless courage that are afterwards to be so much lauded by the panegyrists of Louis
le Grand. Poor boy! you would become a greater man
in that long future for which you are now being preserved,
could you free yourself from the influence of the narrow-
hearted counsellors who surround you. But they will
hinder your fully receiving the severe but salutary lesson
you might else have gained from this bitter January night.

The regent follows, closely muffled, as well for defence
against the piercing cold, as to escape recognition. And
the little party is completed by those three men who come
after, fully armed, and all of them devoted servants to the
royal cause, and officers of the guard. They are Guitaut,
Comminges, and Villequier. It is but a moment ago that
they were informed of the *coup d'etat* in which they are
to bear a part; but they are too old campaigners ever to
be taken by surprise; and they march down the stairs after
their royal mistress with the same deferential composure
with which they would have attended her to a state-ball at
the Louvre.

"To Cours la Reine!" was the order; and as the carriages drove off at a rapid pace, it appeared that, as an
additional precaution, the horses's hoofs had been muffled
in felt. At the rendezvous to which they were proceeding,
a broad alley or drive along the Seine, they are shortly
joined by the Duke of Orleans, with madame and mademoiselle. Then Conde arrives, with his brother Conti; for
the latter of whom the moment is almost at hand when he
will declare for the Fronde. The daughters of the Duke
de Mancini, nieces to the cardinal, and among the chief
favorites at court, come in their turn. Last and least,
Mazarin himself makes his appearance, having been detained till this moment, it is said, by a run of luck at the
gambling-table. The whole future of France awaits the

great and hazardous cast of the die which is now pending ;
but the minister, a gamester of a meaner stamp, could not
endure to tear himself earlier from his cards.

And thus, the *cortege* being complete, they set forth
upon their adventurous flight; and escaping several chances
of being intercepted by the citizens, or, as they might now
fairly be called, the insurgents, who even at his hour were
astir with some uneasy suspicions of the truth, they plunged
into the difficult roads that led westward from Paris, and
arrived on the next cheerless morning with almost an utter
want of ordinary comforts or provisions at the old and half-
dismantled palace of St. Germains-en-Laye.

---

## CHAPTER XXVII.

### BORROWED PLUMES.

"You, sir, I entertain you for one of my hundred ; only, I do not
   like the fashion of your garments. You will say, they are Per-
   sian attire ; but let them be changed." *King Lear.*

SOME weeks have now elapsed since the exiled court of
France has taken up its comfortless winter residence in the
unfurnished chateau to which it has fled for refuge. On
the morrow of their flight, Conde had placed himself again
at the head of the army ; and with a force of nearly seven
thousand well-disciplined troops, advanced to besiege the
insurgent capital. The Parliament of Paris, on their side,
resolute to defend the city to the utmost, organized regi-
ments from among the *bourgeoisie*, appointed generals, and
raised a body of cavalry by means of a house-tax, rigor-
ously exacted. The last measure formed only one of a

series of self-imposed taxations, which ultimately taught the Frondeurs the ruinous expensiveness of revolt. It is true, that on the side of the besiegers also there was scarcity in the extreme; that the young king, the queen-mother, and the court, were suffering absolute want at St. Germains; and that the crown diamonds were of necessity pawned in order to prosecute the war. Still, the army of Conde, small though it was in numbers, had possession of the country bordering one side of Paris, and could draw its supplies from the neighborhood; while it was the prince's great object to hinder, as far as he was able, any provisions from being conveyed into the city. For the military prowess of his antagonists he had a well-merited contempt. Yet, unable to render the blockade of Paris complete, and entertaining some doubts of the loyalty of his great rival in fame, Turenne,—doubts which were soon to be abundantly justified,—he was anxious, by a vigorous prosecution of the siege, to compel the insurgents to terms before any new event should sway the balance in their favor.

We resume the course of our narrative at a moment when young De Bonneval has received notice to prepare himself without delay for an expedition to Paris on a mission of importance. That it will also be difficult and perilous in the execution is evident; but this was a consideration on which our hero was very unapt to dwell. He had lost none of his fearless courage by the mental process he had undergone at St. Lazare; and the inaction to which he had lately been reduced, cooped up within the gloomy and half-ruinous palace, and compelled to witness and to share a misery he could not alleviate, had made him ready to engage with ardor in any new enterprise. Booted and spurred, he now presented himself at the door of the royal cabinet to receive his orders. He was at once admitted by the usher-in-waiting, who drew aside the hangings sufficiently to allow him a passage, merely intimating by an expressive gesture that some unusual and painful communication awaited him within.

The small chamber contained, as our hero had anticipated, only the regent, attended by Madame de Chatillon,

and two or three other ladies of her suite, who had taken
their several opportunities to escape, under more or less of
incognito, out of the city. But in spite of his court-breed-
ing, he started to observe that his royal mistress had made
such changes in her attire as the flight from Paris had left
at her command, and which sufficiently denoted a state of
mourning. Her example had of course been followed by
her attendant ladies. Even as he made the usual obeisance, Antoine's mind ran rapidly over the various possible
misfortunes that could have occasioned this unlooked-for
demonstration of sorrow. They were soon explained to him.

"Yes, monsieur le lieutenant," said the queen, her noble
features evidencing plainly that she spoke with unaffected
concern, "you see us in mourning, and for no such afflic-
tions as those hitherto brought to us by the disastrous
times in which we live. A crowned head has not been
threatened merely; it has *fallen* beneath that scythe which
spares neither prince nor peasant."

The young officer half-raised himself from the respectful
attitude in which,—dropped upon one knee, and his plumed
hat lowered to the mat of rushes that served for all richer
carpeting,—he had scarce touched with his lips the hand
extended to him. An exclamation of surprise and even
horror escaped him, as his thoughts turned instinctively to
that royal child whom a short month before he had escorted
with swelling heart into a kind of dignified exile. Had,
then, anxiety and privation aided the virulent disease from
which the young king had scarcely recovered when the
state of his capital had forced him to that night-march in
an inclement season?

The regent appeared to divine his thoughts, while she
answered with a sad smile and a slight tremor in her voice,
which in nowise diminished the habitual dignity of her
whole bearing: "No, my faithful servant; your king lives
to claim the allegiance of all who, like yourself, have loyalty to remain steadfast in his hour of adversity: thanks
be to Him in whose keeping are the crowns of His an-
nointed! It is our unhappy cousin of England who has
been shorn at once of his crown and life by the base
wretches whom his former clemency—"

She paused. A fearful parallel seemed to unfold itself
before her, as before many other anxious observers of the
times; for the recent tragedy in England had too obvious a
bearing on the state of events in France to escape the most
thoughtless. Her bosom was filled with undefined and
terrible apprehensions that gave a sudden paleness to her
cheek and choked her utterance. Her ladies easily divined
what was passing in the mind of their mistress, and hastened to offer such respectful sympathy as the distresses
and anxieties of a widowed mother would have demanded,
even had that widow not also been a queen. Anne of
Austria, however, possessed the hereditary courage and
firmness of her race; and after a brief pause, she imposed
silence by a movement of her hand, and turning to Antoine, continued:

"Time presses, and your mission, my good De Bonneval,
must be quickly accomplished. It is no very safe or easy
task to which we now send you; but it were a manifest
injustice to doubt either your courage or your readiness to
incur any risks in our service. Answer not," she continued; for Antoine's impulse was to cast himself yet lower
at the regent's feet, and vow to go through any thing for
her lightest behest. "We repose in you the fullest confidence; and it is time, moreover, that you won your spurs,
like a *preux chevalier*, in some adventure worthy of your
name. Go, then: convey safely this small billet to our
widowed cousin at the Louvre. See that it be delivered
into her own hands, or else destroyed. We would not that
the expressions of our condolence should add to the ferocious rejoicings of rebels. And now to horse, good De
Bonneval, to horse. Ride and spur; we are impatient
until that desolate queen shall know there is at least one
heart in France that beats with sympathy for her tragical
sorrows. You will use our name with the loyal unreservedly; for the disaffected,"—her eyes slightly flashed out
from the calm and sorrowful expression hitherto worn by
her matronly features,—"for them you have your father's
spirit and your own good sword. Away then; and your
watchward be Sainte-Genevieve!"

She waved her hand, and the young officer retired with
19

a deep obeisance. He was met, the moment the hangings
fell over the entrance of the chamber, by La Porte, who
now held the office of confidential valet to the young king.
This man had been for many years during the late reign
a trusty agent in secret communications from the queen
to the Spanish court, to the Netherlands, and to her own
intimate friend, the exiled Duchesse de Chevreuse. His
fidelity to his royal mistress had been severely tested during
Richelieu's despotic surveillance over her actions in the
declining years of Louis XIII.: he had even, it is said, been
put to the *question*, or tortured, in the hope of discovering
some treasonable matter in the queen's foreign correspond-
ence. During the regency these bygone sufferings were
abundantly recompensed to him in the unlimited confidence
he enjoyed ; and La Porte, though ostensibly holding an
almost menial office in the court, was in reality no unimportant counsellor of many of its movements.

The old man drew Antoine aside into the deep embrasure of a window in the anteroom through which he was
hastening. "Monsieur le lieutenant will pardon me," he
said in a low and cautious tone, but with an eagerness that
showed him alive to the importance of what he was going
to communicate, "if I suggest to him the full extent of
the mission with which he is intrusted. Condolences and
messages of sympathy from one royal widow to another,—
these are well ; but more remains behind. A messenger
sent into a rebel city under siege must be as close an observer as possible of the state of things he finds there."

"Of course, of course," interrupted our hero, eager to
get to horse and away, "I shall not return without the best
report I can bring. Parliament, Frondeurs, princes, prelates, and populace,—you shall have a sketch of them all."

"Yet stay," continued the experienced depositary of
state-secrets, holding the impatient young soldier by the
cloak, and walking with him out of earshot of any possible
listener ; "for such a purpose, no means,—permit me,—
no disguise must be thought too humble, or even, if need
be, too grotesque. You do not suppose you are going into
Paris in the uniform of the guard ?"

Antoine stopped short. This was an aspect of his enter-

prise for which he was at first hardly prepared. Proud of
the commission he had received, and fired with the love of
adventure, he had scarce allowed himself any other thought
than that of cutting his way through the streets of Paris,
and penetrating to the feet of Henrietta Maria, or dying
in the attempt. La Porte could not forbear smiling as the
young man turned to him a countenance in which a certain
consternation was visibly depicted, and at the same time
of so ingenuous an expression, that it was evident no disguise involving the continued support of an assumed character could easily have been maintained by the wearer.

"A straightforward youngster enough, good sooth !"
Such was the thought of the veteran negotiator, as he half-
muttered it between his teeth with some vexation. "Was
there no more practised hand to be sent on such an enterprise as this ? But we are short of men just now, that is
certain ; and this cavalier has loyalty enough in his heart
to make up for any lack of wisdom in his brains. So let
us e'en to the business. You will not find it over-difficult,"
continued he, again addressing De Bonneval ; "we will
give you no part to play that requires extraordinary
*finesse ;*—you shall be simply a miller's lad."

Of all things under the sun, a miller's lad ! It was now
Antoine's turn to manifest no little vexation. Was there
no other character in which he could make his re-appearance before the walls of that city in which he had been
associating with the noble, the witty, and the gay ? Should
he encounter Marsillac or Fontrailles, to say nothing of
the high-born ladies who had become the life and soul of
the Fronde ? It required a moment's reflection on the
necessity of a thorough concealment, before he could face
the idea.

"I say again, monsieur, a miller's apprentice," rejoined
La Porte almost peremptorily and with perfect command
of feature, though inwardly enjoying the young man's
repugnance ; "and, believe me, no character short of the
Archduke Leopold, or the Spanish commander, at the head
of their forces, could be more welcome at this moment to
the insurgent burghers of Paris. They will be more glad-
dened at the sight of your meal-sprinkled jerkin" (Antoine

winced involuntarily) "than if there appeared before them
the royal herald in his tabard of white velvet powdered
with fleurs-de-lys, who goes thither to-morrow to speak
reason and loyalty to deaf ears.  You understand me ?
they begin to dread famine as well as war ; the price of
bread has been rising almost daily within the city.  Pinched
as we are here, we have the whole country to fall back upon,
and may forage where we will.  Meanwhile, Monsieur le
prince is taking exceedingly good care that not an ounce of
flour, and not a stray hoof of anything to roast or boil,
shall find its way within the circle of the siege ; excepting
always, you know," added he maliciously, "when some
adventurous butcher, or miller, ahem, as the case may be,
succeeds in penetrating the besieging lines, to the wonder
of the grateful inhabitants."

Thus saying, and chuckling inwardly at the grotesque-
ness of the idea, he led the way along the corridor of the
chateau to the door of his own apartment.  At another
moment La Porte would have felt some degree of profes-
sional pride in exhibiting to the young soldier, like a true
master of his craft, the various contrivances at his disposal
for masking every peculiarity of gait or figure, and for
altering "the human face divine."  At present, however,
he proceeded in the most business-like manner to divest
the still-reluctant guardsman of his richly-embroidered
cloak and doublet, his rapier and scarf, and to encase him
in the leggings of tanned leather, and the gray serge jerkin
well dusted with flour, proper to his assumed character.
A broad belt of cow-hide, secured by a coarse iron buckle,
and a plain felt-hat of ample dimensions and rustic make,
besprinkled also with the due amount of corn-meal, completed the equipment of one of the most unwilling masquers
who ever donned for the first time a strange attire.  And
no sooner was De Bonneval thus metamorphosed from
head to heel, than La Porte, standing before him for a
general survey, and giving here and there a finishing touch
to his habiliments, opened his wide mouth, and indulged
to his heart's content in a peculiar kind of noiseless merri-
ment which expressed unbounded satisfaction at his own
ingenuity.  Warned, however, by the flush which instantly

overspread the countenance of the pseudo-miller, that this was an exhibition of feeling rather pleasant than safe, he at once proceeded to what still remained to be done, in order to render the disguise complete and impenetrable. Stepping to a small cabinet, which he unlocked with care, he produced a vial of dark-colored liquid, and with some apologies to our hero, which, we are bound to record scarcely met with a due return, he in a few moments so effectually embrowned the young man's cheeks and hands, and darkened his eyesbrows, that Antoine, glancing at a side-mirror, was forced to acknowledge himself changed by the process into a totally different being. No one, he thought, who was not gifted with unusual penetration, or who had not an intimate acquaintance with his former self, could have recognized him under this strange cosmetic.

"No," said Monsieur La Porte, complacently, continuing the process all the while with true artistic skill, "I do not fear the unobservant faculties of the great majority whom you will meet. (Permit me, I must have your ears as well—there.) With them you will pass easily enough in your assumed character. Even they who think themselves wisest will hardly detect you. (Another touch upon the nose, if you please ; a thousand pardons, that will do.) But there is one pair of eyes in Paris," he continued, a little anxiously, "which I trust with all my heart may not light on you—that inquisitive ubiquitous Gourville! He has a gift of penetration that would read a letter through a deal board. I verily believe he keeps a catalogue in his mind of all the features he ever set eyes on, and of all the secrets of which he has caught the remotest whisper. He has often seen you, of course, with the Prince de Marsillac ?" Antoine nooded. "Beware of him, then, I entreat you; get out of his way by every possible means, or you will do no credit to all my efforts for the decoration of her majesty's guard." So saying, he gave a finishing rub to Antoine's cheek, stroked his eyebrows for the last time with the darkening mixture, and, looking at him with his head on one side, pronounced him perfect, with the air of an artist who is just turning a successful portrait off his easel.

19*

There now only remained the manner and language of
his new character to be adopted; and Antoine, by this time
entering better into the spirit of the part, and amused,
almost in spite of himself, at the kind of double identity he
had gained within the last few minutes, determined to do
this effectually.    He had some acquaintance with the
*patois* of Auvergne; and this he determined to adopt in
preference to hazarding any other.    It would, indeed, involve the task of accounting for the discrepancy of his
approach to the besieged city from the west, instead of in
the direction that led thither from the centre of France.
After a brief consultation, however, on this point, La Porte
advised him not to lose time unnecessarily by skirting the
lines and entrenchments of the besiegers until he gained
the southward side of Paris, but to push in boldly straight
from St. Germains, under pretext of having been forced
from his native province by the distress of the times, and
employed in his supposed calling under a master-miller
near Argenteuil.

"That will not be so improbable a story, after all,"
observed La Porte, musing for a moment; "and to carry it
fully out, you must remember to cross the river at Neuilly,
instead of trying it at St. Cloud.    Pray don't forget, monsieur; it is worth making that little *detour* to gain a character for consistency.    And now the rest must be left to
your own ingenuity and the good chances of the moment.
Mature your plan, and shape it as you see circumstances
arise.    Be bold and unhesitating; swagger it out like any
careless jolly miller who has brought his sacks of flour as
a sample for more that still remain at Argenteuil, and
who is glad meanwhile to see a little of the stir in Paris.
Whatever you have once said, stick to it; for almost any
thing betrays a man less than hesitation.    Be always
making your way towards the Louvre; keep your eyes
sharp about you while your face wears its broadest grin;
and, above all, beware of Gourville!    Well, you grow
impatient; *allons donc,* for the great adventure.    Succeed,
and your fortune is made for you when the tide turns.    If
you should fail, try to pacify them on the first outburst
of their wrath, and you will have a fair chance of escaping

the gibbet. Ten to one, they will but thrust you into some
oubliette, where your friend La Porte," concluded he with
a profound bow, as they reached the lowest step of the
stairs they had been descending, "will undoubtedly seek
you with his heartfelt congratulations, when the good cause
triumphs, and we enter Paris to receive the homage of that
*canaille* parliament and all its myrmidons."

So saying, he again bowed the young miller through a
kind of postern, and waved his hand in adieu as our hero
emerged into the open air.

---

## CHAPTER XXVIII.

### WELL ATTEMPTED.

"As through the bustling streets they go,
    All was alive with martial show;
Page, groom, and squire, with hurrying pace,
Through street, and lane, and market-place,
        Bore lance, or casque, or sword;
While burghers, with important face,
        Describ'd each new-come lord;
Discuss'd his lineage, told his name,
His following, and his warlike fame."            *Marmion.*

ANTOINE now stood upon that unrivalled terrace, which,
extending in a broad esplanade in front of the palace of
St. Germains, stretches for nearly a mile and a half along
the line of the abrupt declivities bordering the southern
margin of the Seine. Its elevation gave him a commanding view of all points of the compass but the west, on
which the horizon was partially intercepted by that exten-

sive forest, whose ancient name, *Silva Ledia*, became perpetuated in that of the palace and town of St. Germains-
en-Laye.   Beneath him the river wound its way, "rolling
in meanders" on its eastward course to the city of Paris,
and in bold reaches and doublings, now hidden by the precipitous banks, now glittering full in sight, resembled the
sinuous motions of some huge serpent with bright scales
coiling and writhing upon its path.   The heights around
were at that time crowned with woods that have since been
shorn of their glories to meet the requirements of a more
extended agriculture.   Here and there, on some favorable
eminence, the picquets of the besieging army might be
clearly distinguished ; while from point to point a solitary
horseman would gallop with orders or intelligence to and
from the head-quarters of Conde and his immediate staff.
In front, but at a distance, and intercepted by the nature
of the ground, appeared one long extent, or rather suburb,
of the city; the pinnacles of its churches caught by the
sun, though the buildings were partly concealed by the
intervening woods of Neuilly.   The expanse of country
that lay between was chequered by such intervals of thaw
as had partially melted away the usual monotony of a winter's landscape.   Patches appeared here and there of a
sombre green, where some upland meadow lay more
exposed to the influence of the sun than the neighboring
tracts ; while through the greater extent the eye travelled
over glittering fields of snow, laced across irregularly with
dark hedgerows of lofty timber, or broken by the intrusion of belts and masses of the leafless forest.   Towards
the left, the tall spires of the abbey of Saint-Denis rose
against the horizon, and crowned a prosperous and a noble
scene with memorials of religion and of death.   It was
assigned as one reason for the dislike afterwards entertained by Louis XIV. for his royal residence of Saint-
Germains, that those ominous spires met his view from the
palace-windows, or on his walks along the terrace.   He
did not relish, amid the luxurious magnificence and the
sensual egotism of his daily life, to be confronted by that
silent memento of the end of life itself.   The vaults of his
ancestors in the ancient abbey formed too stern a commen-

tary upon the habitual frivolities of the court with which
he had learned to surround himself.

De Bonneval had often lingered on this terrace, and
scanned every varied feature of the view. At present,
however, he had other objects before him than to watch
the changing shadows as they floated over the scene, or
darkened the bends of the river. He shaded his eyes with
his hand until he thought he could distinguish the bridge
of Neuilly in the distance. It was but uncertainty; but
he fancied the February sun caught faintly the angle of a
parapet. That bridge lay within the space of ground disputed and traversed by the advanced guards of the opposing armies; it had been a position more than once contested in their skirmishes; and it was now to become one
of the critical points of the adventure for which our hero
was preparing.

Antoine, as we have seen, was not one to look a danger
long in the face before encountering it. At another time,
the beauty of the winter's morning, and the magnificence
of the scenery it was illuminating, might have tempted
him to lean upon the massive stone balustrade of the terrace, and indulge in some of his favorite reveries. Now,
after devoting a little necessary time to tracing from this
elevation his route towards Paris, he turned his steps to
the descending road that led into the town of St. Germains; La Porte having already indicated the spot at
which he could find his horse, and—O shades of all the
barons of Bonneval!—his flour-sacks, too, awaiting him.
He had not made many steps before he saw coming
towards him the spare but vigorous form of an old man
mounted on a horse, whose soiled and jaded appearance
told of a journey of some miles through the miserable
roads, half-mud, half-snow, of the neighborhood. As the
figure neared him up the ascent, Antoine recognized the
man whom of all others he most desired to see. It was
Vincent de Paul.

On the breaking-out of the present troubles, that servant of God had remained at his post in the city. A great
work lay always on his hands in the relief of the miseries,
spiritual and temporal, engendered by those unhappy times;

this work had lately increased upon him tenfold. Vice
and recklessness had long reigned in the capital, and held
him in full employment. It needed but other things to be
superadded, which followed in the train of the Fronde, and
the dark picture became complete.

There were by this time in Paris, the confusions of
civil disturbance; the fury of parties let loose upon one
another; the license of an undisciplined soldiery; the
increased taxation to furnish forth the sinews of war, and
the scarcity attendant upon even the incomplete blockade
which Conde had effected. The city was alive with the
beat of drums, the waving of banners and plumes, the
harangues of the insurgent generals. "Every evening,
those of greatest consideration who belonged to the faction, met to confer in the saloons of the Hotel-de-Ville;
and in these assemblies frivolity had as great a share as
questions of state. Pleasure and business alike employed
them there; the square resounded with trumpets, and the
halls with violins. The free-and-easy manners of the young
nobility, and the grave demeanor of the magistrates, caus-
ing raillery on the one side, scandal on the other; the
cuirasses and military scarfs, the long robes of councillors,
the habit of religious, and the black cloaks of worthy
burghers,—made up a strange medley, and faithfully
represented the confusion then reigning in the councils of
France."*

But side by side with this gay though not attractive
picture were seen the grim and ghastly features of all
those sufferings which the light-hearted freaks in the Hotel-
de-Ville were entailing. The uncertainty, the general
panic and mistrust, had brought trade and employment to
a stand-still. Multitudes of the poorer classes were thrown
out of work, and daily crowded the gate of Saint-Lazare
for a dole of bread. The former horrors that had desolated
the provinces of France—the tragedies of Lorraine, Picardy, and the Duchy of Bar, among which Vincent and
his priests had formerly moved like so many ministering
angels,—seemed likely to be reproduced in this the capital

* M. de Saint-Aulaire, *Histoire de la Fronde*, vol. i, c. 7.

itself. But charity was still there to counterwork the
hardness of selfish hearts, and repair the misery they had
engendered: charity, bold, self-forgetful, yet watchful,
discriminating,

> "Tempering her gifts, that seem so free,
>  With time and place,
> Till not a woe the bleak world see
>  But finds her grace.''

Vincent seemed equal to any emergency. Vincent,—"all
whose undertakings," as it was said of him, "were blessed
by God,"—had met and answered greater needs than even
the present: he needed not to surpass himself to become,
as now he became, the bright spot to which the victims of
that evil day turned amid all their miseries. He was
every where, and armed at all points in his ministries of
good. Want and famine and sin, as they stalked their
rounds through the city, met that unwearied laborer at
every turn; nor ever met him without feeling something
of that blessed influence which floated like an atmosphere
around him.

But this does not suffice the zeal of the devoted priest.
He will attack the evil at the fountain-head. It is Mazarin, detained in office by the queen's fond weakness, and
by his own selfish greed, who causes these disorders. That
one man removed, the barb is gone that rankles in the side
of the state; the enemies of order have lost the master-
topic of their grievances. The regent will see more with
her own eyes, follow more unreservedly the dictates of her
own generous though haughty soul; and the better disposed among her subjects will return at once to their allegiance. For this nothing will avail but the personal interview with his royal mistress. Even then, all the almoner's
saintly character, all his unusual powers of persuasion, all
the remembrances of his past services, will stand, it may
be, a slender chance of uprooting the position of one unworthy man.

It is for this great attempt that Vincent has left Paris
before daybreak, and taken the road to Saint-Germains.
With his usual prudence, he has communicated his plan to

none; only a letter will reach the first president, Mole, an
hour or two after his departure, telling him in a few words
that Vincent felt urged by heaven to go to the court, and
that he had not previously paid him his respects, that he
might be able to assure the queen of his having concerted
with no one what he was about to say.

The city was under arms, and the faubourgs occupied by
picquets of the insurgents. Vincent had to make a long
circuit in order to gain his object; for, like other peace-
makers, he was looked upon with jealousy by the partisans
on either side; all but denounced as a *Mazarin* by the
disaffected, and jealously eyed as a *Frondeur* by some
adherents of the court. It is truth and love and peace that
he pursues with all his singleness of heart; and for those
dear and holy interests he knows neither the names nor
the passions of party-strife.

At length, after much fatigue and some dangers, nar-
rowly escaping the muskets of a patrol at Clichy, all but
swept away at the flooded bridge of Neuilly, the old man
has arrived at the bourne of his charitable pilgrimage.
He recognizes Antoine; and with a kind and cheerful
smile at the young lieutenant's disguise, on which his
innate tact and good breeding taught him to make no
further comment, folded the pseudo-miller in his arms with
paternal fondness.

"Thus, then, we meet again, my dear son," exclaimed
Vincent; "and meet, as it seems, only to part on the spot.
You are bound, I doubt not, on some secret service; good,
you will serve our Master above in serving your earthly
sovereign. I too am bound on a mission in which I trust
to serve both. Farewell, then, till happier and quieter
times. You know always where to find me, and how welcome you are, whenever your duties at court, or," with a
friendly nod, as he glanced at the young man's dress, "any
other honorable employment, allow you to make your way
to Saint-Lazare."

So saying, he waved him a kindly adieu, and continued
his ascent to the entrance of the chateau.

And now De Bonneval has fairly set out upon his adventure. We will not follow him through those steps of his

progress which lay through friendly territory. The road, always bad and neglected, now deep in the mud or half-melted snows of mid-winter, cut up moreover by the baggage-waggons and provision-carts in the service of the royal army, did not allow the sorry jade he was, to his infinite disgust bestriding, to make much progress. The brief February afternoon had therefore closed, and darkness was gathering round him, as, half-numbed with the cold, he gained one of the watch-fires, around which a portion of Conde's line was picqueted. Here he was challenged by the sentinel, and led to the officer of the watch.

Antoine requested to be taken aside by the young man in command of the detachment; and even then felt the color mounting to his cheeks as he announced himself, and declared his mission to Paris. The other seemed for a moment astounded at the intelligence given him; but the tendencies of the great struggle in England had been long foreseen and often discussed. War, moreover, has the effect of inuring men to the contemplation of the most tragic occurrences, and by its constant dangers and its sudden reverses, brings the chance of death so near to each man, that he learns to consider it with much stoicism when it falls to the lot of his neighbor. Kings, however, are not brought to the scaffold every day; and the momentous tidings, fraught as they were with equally grave presage nearer home, sufficed to sober the volatile young officer; who was content, without remark upon De Bonneval's attire, to furnish him with a pass-word that would convey him through the lines of the besieging army.

He passes, then, the outpost nearest the city, and traverses the intervening space unquestioned, until he reaches the very walls. "Certainly," thought the young soldier to himself, "these gentlemen of the Fronde do not shine in their strategic arrangements. A bold *coup de main* now might go far towards putting this rebellious capital in the hands of her majesty: why there is not even a sentinel on the look-out! I have half a mind to ride back and report the state of things at head-quarters. The prince is not a man to let slip a good opportunity, and the night is getting

20

dark enough for petards or scaling-ladders. But no,"
added he, on second thoughts, "my present commission is
distinct, and I have no choice. *Allons !* let me execute
it with as much expedition as I may ; perhaps there may
be time on my return to suggest a surprise, and I may see
the fun and share it."

Just then the noise of his horse's hoofs attracted the
notice of a drowsy sentinel ; for the Frondeurs, unskilful
as they were in military defence, had not left the walls of
the city wholly unguarded ; and the services of the rude
militia they had hastily formed were furnished with a degree of zeal which supplied in some measure for want of
science. *"Qui vive ?"* shouted the bourgeois soldier from
his station over the gate.

Antoine gave a feigned name, and stated his errand.
He had come from his master, the miller at Argenteuil, a
devoted partisan of the Fronde, who had sent him with a
sample of the flour with which, from his own and the
neighboring mills, he could supply the besieged on a short
notice.

We cannot do our friend the credit of saying, that he
delivered himself of this statement with a very good grace.
The acting was not first-rate by any means, and the
speaker felt his ingenuous cheek burn while he uttered,
even as a *ruse de guerre*, his first deliberate lie. So, with
an ungracious half-sullen manner, he went through the
form of words almost mechanically, and stood silent before
the sentinel.

But the latter was an unobservant *insouciant* mortal, a
small shop-keeper near the Halle des Bles, before the disorders of the times had forced him into the glories and
perils of the military state ; and Antoine's surliness, far
from attracting suspicion, seemed rather a guarantee for the
truth of his story. His message was a most welcome one
in the actual state of Paris, where every little assistance
would turn the edge of a pressure for food that was
beginning to be acutely felt. The messenger was alone,
unarmed, and of peaceful guise ; the sacks of flour at least
were genuine, well-filled, and spoke for themselves. In a
word, after a few brief whispers with the rest of the guard,

whom the sentry had summoned to aid his deliberations,
the young miller, still mounted on his sorry steed, was conducted in a sort of ovation towards the residence of the
Prefect of the Markets, there to state more explicitly the
means of relief he was prepared to offer.

This was a distinction with which Antoine would gladly
have dispensed.  His great object was to watch for some
opportunity to slip aside unobserved, and execute his real
mission.  He might even have escaped by dexterity and
speed from a single guard; and he who had stood the
chance of so many hostile shots in the forest of the Bourbonnais, in a rash attempt to effect his escape, would now have
risked much greater dangers in the service of the regent.
With no such hope, he found himself carried along in the
midst of armed men, attracting the gaze of every passenger or idler in the streets of Paris, and stung by a thousand
rude jests as his conductors with vociferous triumph pursued their way.  He, a devoted loyalist, was rejoicing the
hearts of insurgents with the prospect of relief!  Moreover, unpractised in stratagem or disguise, he could not but
believe himself in danger of discovery every moment.  He
was pretty well known in the city as an attendant on the
queen; had been seen constantly on public occasions; and
he seemed to forget for the time that his acute and mor-
tified sense of his own personal identity tended in no
degree to reveal to those around him the young guardsman
through the miller's attire.  It seemed, to his sensitiveness,
as if every chance eye that gazed listlessly or curiously into
his face was fraught with suspicion.  A man of far less
nerve and greater habit of concealment would have borne
himself better through that trying passage than our dauntless and ingenuous young friend.

Meanwhile, as they penetrated further into the city,
the throng of horsemen and foot-passengers increased, and
Antoine found himself amid a state of things as turbulent
and disordered as he might have anticipated.  Paris was,
in fact, convulsed from end to end by the faction, or rather
the rudely-united cluster of factions, that had undertaken
to free it from one despotism by substituting another yet
more grievous.  The parties of Beaufort, of Conti, De

Longueville, and others, bickered over their plans of
defence with but a poor semblance of merging their private
differences in the common weal. De Retz had figured
better as a restless agitator than as a general of division :
his military attempts had made him the butt of many a
humiliating and indignant pasquinade. The license of a
dissolute half-trained soldiery, impotent in warfare, but
intolerable when not engaged, was exhausting the patience
almost as much as the resources of the burghers. And
as, in public confusions, the evil-disposed of every class
are sure to break loose from restraint, and profit by the
disorder to push their schemes of plunder and violence,
the disturbing forces we have enumerated were further
quickened by interludes upon a minor scale, whenever
individual passions could find a vent in some fresh deed of
wrong, perhaps of blood.

So it was, that as De Bonneval proceeded on his unwilling embassy to the Prefect of the Halles, he saw
scenes enacted around him which fired his indignation at
every turn, while they only excited the amusement or
applause of those who constituted his guard of honor.
Here was a house, once the residence of a small religious
community, bearing unmistakable marks of violence and
pillage, and with rude caricatures scrawled upon its walls
with charcoal. A ruffian soldier, his foot dangling over
the window-sill, was seated smoking in a room on the first
floor, laughing at some ribald jest with his comrade who
lounged against the doorpost below; while a bundle of
red rags, fashioned into a grotesque effigy of Mazarin,
swung from the end of a pole thrust through one of the
chapel-windows, and fluttering in the night-air, tempted a
salute of stones or a handful of mud from every vagrant
urchin or zealous Frondeur. There, on the other side,
another rude scene is exhibited by torchlight : a citizen,
aided by his neighbors, is endeavoring to expel from
his house a half-drunken party of the same rude militia
for some wanton insult, and in imminent danger of having their throats cut in the attempt. That shout in the
distance, which draws rapidly nearer, announces a full
chase down the street of an unfortunate lacquey attached

to one of the loyal families who have not effected their escape from the city, and who remain barricaded within the precincts of their hotel in a state of siege, almost of starvation. The lacquey has been sent out to forage for provisions; his livery is recognized, and he has to run for it. Close at his heels comes on a mad rabble, some urged by party hate, some by mere ferocious love of mischief, all pressing onward with clubs, hurling at him stones and other missiles. Lucky will it be for him if he escapes without shot or stab. See how he strains every nerve, making for his goal, a handsome *porte-cochere* some twenty yards in front of Antoine and his attendants. The wicket is slightly ajar, held from within by the strong hands, peered through by the jealous eyes, of his fellows, waiting to admit him. A few more strides and the runner is safe. But no; the foremost pursuer fetches a sweeping blow with his staff; just catches him on the ankle. He trips, staggers forward some paces, is dashed by the violence of his own momentum almost against the very door. Then his friends rush forth; a halberd or two keep his assailants at bay, and secure him for a moment from further injury. He is seized, disabled as he is, dragged forcibly within, and the wicket immediately closes, while the baffled rabble thunder against it in vain.

During the excitement and din of this last incident, Antoine was not aware that he had become in his turn an object of keen and earnest scrutiny. Turning, when the escape of the wounded lacquey was secured, he almost started to find a young man, whose features he recognized, with a hand on the arm of one of his guards as if to stay him, and apparently asking some question in a low tone, but keeping his gaze fixed upon our hero himself. Yes, there was no mistaking that sharp observant eye and that mocking lip. It was Gourville, and no other.

Antoine was conscious of such a thrill as even the brave may know without shame when in the presence of a danger from which no exertion of their own can deliver them. He felt at once that he was in the hands of the fowler.

To Gourville's question the sentinel who held the young man's bridle made some muttered reply.

20*

"From Argenteuil!" pursued the questioner, in a tone
of mock surprise, and still fixing upon the supposed miller
his penetrating glance. "Or is it not rather from St.
Germains? A miller, saidst thou? Nay; learn greater
respect, friend, for her majesty's guard! And let me, in
quality of equerry, assist Monsieur de Bonneval from his
horse."

So saying, with a ceremonious reverence, he held Antoine's stirrup, and proffered to him his hand.

A crowd had by this time gathered round them. Gourville was pretty extensively known in Paris, and his rich
livery, with the cognisance of the house of La Rochefoucault
emblazoned on it profusely, aided by his own good appearance and somewhat showy manner, procured for him a sort
of deference among the bystanders. None of them, fortu-
nately for our hero, had caught the words with which the
*maitre d'hotel* had saluted him, or Antoine would infallibly
have been torn to pieces on the spot. Nothing so infuriates
a mob as even the suspicion of having a spy among them.
The action itself, however, was suspicious; and angry murmurs and questions were beginning to rise on all sides.
Gourville, whose ready invention was rarely at fault, hailed
an old coach that was rumbling and jolting by; and after
a whisper with the driver, who seemed well known to him,
opened the door, and without more ado quickly transferred
De Bonneval to the interior, signing to two of his guards
to take their places by his side. Then turning to the unsatisfied bystanders, he threw himself into an attitude, and
delivered himself with the utmost fluency as follows :

"A little affair of the Prince de Marsillac, my friends.
He is not quite pleased with the price at which some of the
purveyors have been letting him have flour lately for the
troops ; and therefore sent for this youth, the nephew of a
worthy friend of mine, to bring in a sample at a lower rate.
I am glad to have met him ; and to secure his getting to
my lord's secretary as soon as possible, I myself shall
follow with the flour-sacks. You will present the prince's
respects to Madame Piancourt Hugues," added the ready-
witted dissembler, turning to the coachman, "with thanks
for her benefit to the public service by the loan of her

vehicle. And now move on, till we meet this evening over a bottle of hippocras." He stepped close to the hammer-cloth, and whispered in the man's ear, "To the Bastille; drive for thy life!"

---

# CHAPTER XXIX.

## THE BASTILLE.

> "Ye horrid towers, th' abode of broken hearts,
>    Ye dungeons, and ye cages of despair,
>    That monarchs have supplied from age to age
>    With music, such as suits their sovereign ears,—
>    The sighs and groans of miserable men!"          *Cowper.*

THE old uneasy coach rumbled doggedly on, as though it shared somewhat of the gloomy determination of those into whose hands De Bonneval had fallen. Now the wheels jolted on the irregular disjointed paving of the streets, which had been partially torn up to form the too celebrated *barricades* of the preceding autumn, and either not replaced, or hastily and loosely thrown in upon its former bed. At other times the crazy machine plunged and ploughed amid the deep mire of more neglected thoroughfares, such as occurred not seldom during its devious progress through the Faubourg Saint-Antoine. At such moments, the change from pavement to aboriginal mud was announced by jolts which shook to its centre the unwieldly carriage, making its timbers crack like those of some distressed vessel in a gale of wind, and seeming to forebode its speedy and utter dismemberment,—an event not so very unusual in the town and country progresses of even the highest personages of the day.

The young captive's heart, however, was too much downcast at the prospect now before him to admit of any

great sensitiveness to such bodily discomforts. He maintained an unbroken silence, poising himself in the best
manner he could, so as to avoid the extremity of the rude
concussions to which he was so unwillingly subjected. But
even his youth and high spirits could only derive some
momentary distraction from the half-ludicrous, half-painful
incidents of this uneasy land-voyage. His thoughts brooded
on the well-known features and dark traditions of that
gloomy fortress, which he was so soon to enter as a prisoner, and in the hands of men apparently as pitiless as its
own massive stones and bars. Or they reverted to the gay
scenes in which he had taken part in this very city; or to
the royal circle, self-exiled at St. Germains, where he had
left wretchedness, it is true, and the utmost penury, but
sweetened by the consolations of liberty and hope. What
would be the progress of the struggle of which he had but
witnessed the outbreak? In what condition would he himself exist during its continuance; or what fate awaited him
at its termination? Deeds of valor and loyalty would
doubtless be performed by his comrades in defence of the
person or in assertion of the rights of his sovereign. And
he, all the while, debarred from the opportunities of distinction now open to those more favored companions in
arms, would be lying forgotten in some obscure dungeon,
measuring the lapse of time by the feeble waxing and waning of day through the bars of a grated loophole, and
only hearing from afar the report of the cannon that
announced a momentous struggle in which he could not
share.

These painful reflections were interrupted by an object
that suddenly presented itself through the front windows
of the coach before the anxious eyes of the prisoner. High
over surrounding buildings of more modern date rose in
frowning majesty two towers of massive strength, united
by a curtain-wall of nearly equal height with themselves.
This again extending to the left, carried on the eye to the
dimly seen outline of similar towers, scarcely distinguish-
able in the darkness. Here and there, at intervals, from
that quarter of the heavens where the young moon struggled among driving clouds, an uncertain gleam was cast,

faint and pale, against the lofty masses of squared masonry, and showed Antoine a narrow barred window, or battlement, or the rounded projection of a tower, and then was shrouded again. But it needed no second glance to assure him that he had now reached the dreaded termination of his journey. An involuntary feeling of heart-sickness, for which at another time he might severely have tasked himself, overpowered the young man's spirit; while every jolt of the carriage seemed to cast him, as by the action of a resistless engine, nearer and nearer to the dim-seen prison that loomed before him, awaiting and looking down upon its prey. He gazed upward with a look of hopelessness at the pale sullen towers of that fortress, crowning the *cachots* and *oubliettes*, in which so many of the brave, the high-born, and the gifted had dragged out an existence, till they sunk in despair or drivelling idiotcy. Many and many, thought he, as the recollection flashed irresistibly upon him, have entered the grim circuit of these walls, and left hope for ever behind. The iron portal has jarred behind them, the heavy bolts have been drawn-to; and then years afterwards their names may have been casually uttered amid the gay heartless mirth of some brilliant saloon; while their nearest in kindred and affection knew not whether they still breathed in a forgotten cell, or whether the grave, not more inexorable, had closed over their bones in the prison-court. Then his thoughts took one backward sweep, and lighted on the rocks of Auvergne, with the Chateau de Bonneval full in view: forms were looking on him from the window, in the clear October sunlight, and voices in accents of love were uttering farewell. But he tore himself hastily from *that* remembrance before it had unmanned him.

One of the ruffians at his side appeared to divine in some measure what was passing within the prisoner's thoughts. "Ay," he broke in, with a deep harsh voice, which sounded frightfully in Antoine's ear, from its near approach to savage laughter, "true enough, young master of mine, many's the bird of gayer plumage than thine, and of stronger wing too, that has been caged in this pretty aviary, and never heard to sing again. We shall have

thee tame enough soon, and thankful for the crumbs thrown
to thee, I'll warrant."

Antoine made no reply to these consolatory suggestions;
and the carriage, now deviating to the right, tottered
round a projecting angle of the outer buildings already
mentioned, and in a few minutes stood before a *corps-de-
garde*, or advanced outpost to the fortress.

When the "royal castle of the Bastille," as this dreaded
prison was styled, remained in the hands of its rightful
master, a sentinel was posted on this spot by day and
night, as well to give notice of any approach to its jealous
precincts as to cut off the last possibility of escape to any
prisoner who might have been desperate or skilful enough
to pass the other barriers of the prison. But this was a
chance scarcely imaginable; and, so far, the outer sentinel
might be looked upon as a precaution altogether super-
fluous. At the present, watch was maintained before the
guardhouse by a volunteer of the municipal guard, who,
with a matchlock carelessly swung over his shoulder, and
an old ill-fitting buff coat, which had not succeeded in giving to his lounging figure the true military air, drew up
on the approach of the carriage; and after performing a
few evolutions with any thing but soldier-like exactness,
called out the guard.

Under happier circumstances, Antoine might have been
entertained by the style in which this body now made its
appearance, and dressing itself in an awkward line, displayed accoutrements on whose details the critical eye of a
lieutenant of the Garde Royale would have found much
to exercise his loyalty in the way of contemptuous laughter.
But other reflections were now engrossing our hero, and
he scarcely noticed the few brief words that passed
between the ruffian who had made himself spokesman and
the officer in command of the outpost.

"Give the watchword." "Rights of the Parliament."
"The countersign?" "Broussel." "Pass, on, citizens,
and deliver your prisoner."

The words, though unheeded by him whom they chiefly
concerned, produced an immediate effect upon his movements; for the two men, taking each a firm grasp on his

collar, dragged De Bonneval without further ceremony
from the carriage, and conveyed him up to a gate which
was opened without delay by one of the guard. This led
out upon a drawbridge, at the further end of which appeared a second gate, studded and plated with iron. Then
came another door, or rather postern, admitting the party
to the *Cour du Gouvernement*, an irregular area, surrounded
by the buildings assigned to the governor of the fortress
and certain of the officials. Traversing this court in grim
silence, the conductors hurried their prisoner upon a second
drawbridge of much greater length than the former, crossing at an elevation of some thirty feet the deep and wide
fosse that surrounded the fortress. Finally they came to
a stand before a narrow Gothic gateway that opened between the two flanking towers which had caught Antoine's
eye on their first approach to the Bastille. Dating from
the fourteenth century, and the reign of Charles V. of
France, this narrow entrance, with the twin-towers erected
for its defence, had formed the Porte Saint-Antoine, the
most important entrance into Paris from the southern side.
Having from the commencement served the double purpose of a fortified entrance to the city and a prison, the
latter gradually predominated over the former use; until
within twenty years after its first erection, the addition of
six other towers, uniform with the original two, and united
together by a lofty curtain-wall of unusual massiveness,
had converted the Porte Saint-Antoine into a fortress of
formidable strength at the entrance of Paris. The public
thoroughfare was at the same time turned aside, and conducted round the entire building instead of passing through
it. The eight towers, with their connecting walls, were
surrounded by a dry ditch of considerable depth, strengthened with hewn masonry; and thus the fortifications of
the Bastille were rendered complete.

Through this ancient gateway had ridden in former days
the knight in mail, attended by his esquire and men-at-
arms; and the narrow horse-litter used by ladies of the
fourteenth century had also passed and repassed without
difficulty through its straitened limits. It would, indeed,
have been inaccessible to the unwieldly carriages in vogue

three centuries later; but long before that period, as we
have said, the entrance had been closed to all except those
who sought admission into the fortress.  Ponderous and
ill-hung from age, the massive gate now swung heavily
inwards to allow Antoine his involuntary passage: the
chains by which it was secured from within clashed against
bolts of a massive size, and studs and plates of solid iron,
laid on with a profusion and rude contrivance of workmanship that aimed at making the grim assurance of the
prison-house doubly sure.  And finally, when the captive
thought himself at the termination of all these multiplied
defences, he found his progress stopped by a strong *grille*
of open timber-work plated with iron, too high to be
scaled, and running up into spikes that would almost to a
certainty have impaled any one adventurous enough to
attempt to escape.

    "So," gruffly ejaculated the former spokesman,—for
Antoine's left-hand conductor seemed to think silence a
proof of stoic wisdom, and had acquired in a high degree
the difficult art of holding his tongue,—"so, here we usher
thee into all the liberty of the great court of the Bastille ;
that is, into so much liberty as his worship the governor
may think good for thy delicate constitution.  'Tis true,
the air is somewhat confined, and maybe a thought chilly
to butterflies that have been used to bask in the sunshine
of the Palais Royal; and the exercise is not to be taken
at all times in the day, haou, haou! for the king's lieutenant, you see, is out of the way just now, and can't
regulate these matters.  So there you have the prospect
at a *coup-d'œil*, not quite so extensive, perhaps, as from
the terrace at Saint-Germains, haou, haou, haou!"  But
by no combination of vowels can we convey to our gentle
reader the tone in which this consoler of the downcast
testified the enjoyment he derived from his own brutal
remarks.  They were responded to by noiseless chuckling
grins from the votary of silence on the other side.  And
now the amiable pair, feeling that their prisoner was
beyond possibility of escape, vouchsafed to relax their hold
upon him, and stood, with folded arms and countenances
of grim satisfaction, watching the effect which a first full

view of his place of detention would produce on the young
officer.

It was indeed a sight that might have quelled a stout
heart. The feeble light of a few dim oil-lamps, hanging
in cressets at four several points of the prison-yard, just
enabled the sentinels to discern the figure of any person on
the flagstones with which it was paved, and crept a certain space up the smooth-jointed masonry of the walls and
towers, leaving the remainder of the elevation soaring into
the darkness overhead. The great height of the walls
excluded any ray from the moon, which had not yet risen
sufficiently to penetrate into the court; and it was only at
intervals that the night wind, tearing a gap in the heavy
snow-clouds, threw a faint and dubious light upon the
upper portions of the fortress, and showed the battlements
of the turrets and the parapet of the lofty curtain-walls,
dimly traced for a moment against the sky. All the space
that intervened between the dim lamp-light brooding over
the pavement, and those still more ghostly revelations
above, lay shrouded in impenetrable gloom. It might
almost have seemed as if the one visible portion of the
building were floating detached in the murky air, above
the other, like some watchful bird of prey that hovers
motionless over its quarry beneath.

Antoine, however, had no greater leisure allowed to
him than sufficed to scan the principal features of this dismal scene. The sentinel who was slowly pacing the
further end of the great court had not returned twice upon
his walk, when another of the garrison, who had been sent
forward to advertise some one in authority of the entrance
of a prisoner, appeared again. He beckoned to them from
a doorway opening in the centre of a curtain of buildings
later in date than the towers, running across the area contained in the enceinte of their connecting walls, and screen-
ing off one-third of the whole space as an inner court,
known, from the name given to one of its corner turrets,
as the *Cour des Puits*. Into the silence of this inner
court, as De Bonneval was given to understand by his
grim companion, none who were not prisoners were ever
permitted to enter; a restriction that derived a gloomy

21

mysteriousness from the fact, that even the larger and
outer court had so little to enliven or cheer the mind of
any visitor.

His guides now hurried our hero across the court towards
the door in the *corps de logis* that faced them.   The sentinel challenged the party on its approach ; and receiving
the same passwords that had been given before, motioned
the three silently to advance.   A few massive stone-steps
led into the *corps de logis*, and the door was immediately
closed behind them.   A short passage opened through a
vestibule into a small chamber, called the *Salle de Conseil;*
and here, in an ancient high-backed chair, behind a table
covered with papers, some loose and some carefully folded
and ticketed, sat the man in whose custody Antoine was
now unresistingly placed.

The revolutionary captain of the Bastille, Louviers, a
kinsman of the president Broussel, was at that moment
away from his post.   It was therefore the lieutenant-gov-
ernor of the fortress into whose presence De Bonneval was
led.   On the first entrance of the prisoner, that functionary
bent on him a glance which the other recognized in a
moment.   He stood in the presence of the man who
had captured him the preceding autumn on the road to
Bourges.

From whatever motive, however, this personage gave
no token of recognizing our hero.   De Bonneval could
not doubt that the keen full gaze which the lieutenant-
governor instantly bent upon his countenance detected him
under the mere accidentals of dress and the artificially
embrowned complexion.   But the look he was now encountering was precisely what it had been in the forest on
the night of that adventure—calm, piercing, and severe ;
and as Antoine, recovering from his first surprise, thought
it well to preserve silence on his part, and leave all recognition to come from the other, so it was that no syllable
now passed between the two men who had spent so many
hours of one night in varied and friendly intercourse, and
had on the following morning so nearly been to each other
the slayer and the slain.

After a pause of a minute or two, during which the

arbiter of Antoine's fate continued reading the young man's
countenance with the grave and considerate calmness that
distinguished him, he turned to a huge volume at his elbow,
containing a record of the prisoners confined in this formidable fortress, and dating back to a much earlier period.
Had the Bastille continued under the dominion of Richelieu, or even of Mazarin, the new-comer would have been
subjected on the spot to a rigorous cross-examination, and
his name, age, residence, and offence, together with a
description of his height and appearance, been carefully
entered in the prison-calendar. At present, it seemed to
be referred to chiefly in order to ascertain the vacant dungeon to which he was to be consigned; for the robber-
captain (so let us still call him, notwithstanding the change
of dress and his present position) soon raised his head from
the volume, and with his finger laid upon the page, briefly
interrogated Antoine's conductors. The deep full tones of
his voice thrilled upon the young man's ear, so intimately
linked were they to his last eventful interview with the
speaker. The rude sentinels who had him in charge made
the best reply they could, which amounted to little more
than that the prisoner had been given in charge by Gourville, acting under authority of the Prince de Marsillac.
They were proceeding to give some account of the circumstances of De Bonneval's arrest, and their own suspicions,
when they were cut short by the man they addressed, in a
tone which admitted of no questioning.

"Enough," he said; "you have done your duty, and
shall be well reported of. The prince will be here himself ere long; if not, I will examine the prisoner on my
return to Paris, two days hence. You, Gilles," he continued, turning to a grisly hard-visaged old *porte-clef*, or
turnkey, who stood by his side, "escort these worthy citizens with their charge, and relieve them of him when you
get to the *Tour de la Bertandiere*." He referred again for
a moment to the register-book, and repeated, "*La Bertandiere*, first story. I will not condemn you, young sir,"
—and the slightest imaginable smile passed over his features, which would have satisfied Antoine, had he doubted
it, that he was recognized,—"in this inclement season, I

should be loth to condemn you to one of the *cachots*. Yet stay; was it not in that cell that the prisoner Gaultier Tricot died last week of jail-fever ?"

Gilles grimly nodded assent.

"Hast had the chamber purified, thou varlet, since then ?"

The same unamiable functionary shrugged a surly negative, with a kind of dogged assurance, which fell, however, before the steadfast authoritative look of his superior.

"See it be done, and soon. Meanwhile, to the *Tour de la Liberte ;* the *calotte* there is vacant."

And to the *Tour de la Liberte*—misnamed abode, where all around spoke of bondage and constraint—the ponderous keys clanking at old Gilles's girdle, as he hobbled onwards to conduct the party, Antoine was accordingly ushered, without further remark or ceremony.*

* In addition to the description of the Bastille incidentally given in this and the following chapter, it may be well to state that each of the six towers composing the fortress had its peculiar name. The two original towers, the first stone of which was laid in 1369 by Hughues d'Aubriot, provost of Paris, in the reign of Charles V., were the *Tour de la Chapelle*, and that of *Du Tresor ;* the latter so named, because it was afterwards employed as a strong room for specie by Henri IV. These two flanked the ancient Porte Saint-Antoine, and were used for the incarceration of prisoners even before the enlargement of the fortress, like the New-Gate prison in London, and many other examples. This gateway was soon additionally strengthened by the erection of two other towers, apparently the *Tour du Coin* and the *Tour de la Comte ;* and by the year 1383 Charles VI. had added four more, behind the four already mentioned, and parallel with them—the *Tour du Puits, De la Liberte, De la Bertandiere,* and *De la Basiniere.* These were united with each other by enormous walls of squared stone, six feet in thickness, forming the enceinte of the fortress, and rising as high as the towers themselves, which reached a measure of more than seventy feet. Terraces ran along the summit of these walls, connecting tower with tower, and widening into platforms for the purpose of defence. Each tower was closed at the basement by double doors, shod with iron. These led downwards to the *cachot*, or subterranean *oubliette*, with which each separate tower was furnished ; a damp and horrible dungeon, nineteen feet below the pavement of the court, and five below the fosse outside, from which it received air through a small opening. A glimmer of light was perceptible in some, but others were in total darkness. In the infected atmosphere of the *cachot*, swarming as it did with noxious

# CHAPTER XXX.

## A LOOPHOLE.

"Stone walls do not a prison make,
    Nor iron bars a cage ;
Minds innocent and quiet take
    That for a hermitage."                    *Lovelace.*

STRETCHED on the miserable couch which formed the only
furniture of his *calotte*, or pacing the stone-floor with impatient strides, while his spirit alternately chafed and sank
within him, like a wild bird, that beats against the wires
of her cage, and then lies panting with exhaustion from
the fruitless effort, poor Antoine wore through the long
hours of his first night of captivity.  The morning broke
upon him, late and pale, and as it seemed reluctantly,
slanting through a narrow embrasure that pierced the
thickness of the tower.  A ray of light, first doubtful,
then more strongly defined, straggled in, and told of a wintry sun mounting above the houses of the Faubourg Saint-

reptiles, and dripping with damp, no prisoner could long exist.
Above the dungeon, and reached by a winding staircase, were three
stories of small prison-chambers, irregular polygons of about fifteen
feet in diameter, and from fifteen to twenty in height.  Lastly,
came the *calotte*, or highest chamber in the tower, which, from its
elevation, and probably from its leaden roofing (like the *Piombi* of
the Venetian prisons), exposed its occupant to great suffering from the
extremes of heat and cold.  This was lighted by a loophole, pierced
in the thickness of the wall, narrowing (towards the light) to a
mere slit of two or three inches in width, and guarded, moreover,
by heavy iron stancheons, so as scarcely to admit a glimmer of the
day.  Each cell was secured by two doors of oak, from two to
three feet thick, shod with iron and furnished with heavy bolts and
ponderous locks, which resounded throughout the whole tower
when closed or unfastened ; and, as an additional security, each
tower was closed at the basement by double doors of the same
formidable kind.  See *Memoires Historiques de la Bastille, &c.,*
Paris, 8vo., 1789.

21*

Antoine, and began to creep tediously through its contracted span upon the prison-floor.  In the captive's half-
vacant thoughts, exhausted as he was by excitement,
indignation, and vain struggling, a something grew up that
almost approached to languid interest in the mere listless
watching of this change of light upon the rude freestone
pavement.  It seemed like the monotonous murmuring of
a slow-paced rivulet, that blends with, while it also carries
on, the reveries of the listener, though not to any thing
very definite, yet away from all that is present to the
senses, into the regions of fancy or memory or affection,
suggestive of what is beyond, and scarcely obtruding its
own presence on his consciousness.  So did that wan contracted ray of sunshine, for the few hours during which it
visited Antoine's cell, become to him a kind of welcome
companion, simply because it was a thing that stirred and
progressed, and by its semblance of life claimed some
attention from a mind that would otherwise have been
riveted upon its own misfortunes.

Yet with this, amid the utter uncertainty that possessed
him as to the period of his durance, there came the almost
maddening thought, that at some distant day he might still
be gazing on that beam of light, but gazing upon it in
vacant idiotcy.  Frightful traditions were current in Paris
of the effects of prolonged and hopeless imprisonment
within these very walls upon the minds of some who had
once been known as ornaments of the court, and even
sharers in the administration of government.  Men, in
the fullness of life and all the vigor of intellect, with their
capacities of joy or suffering quick and keen within them,
had crossed the very drawbridge over which Antoine had
been hurried some few hours before; and, like the souls
condemned to enter the dread portals seen in the poet's
vision, had ''left hope behind.''  Years had rolled over
them in the monotony of their dungeon-life, and brought
as little token of their existence to the world without as
the billows that welter over the drowned seaman tell of his
whitening bones within their deeps.  And when a late
reversal of the sentence, or the fall of a tyrannous minister had proclaimed them free, the messenger of joyful

tidings had arrived only to view the wreck which hope long deferred, and a grinding sense of present misery, had completed. Reason has fled for ever from the ruined mind; and the courtier, the soldier, the satirical poet, he who had charmed the brilliant circles of Paris by the grace and keenness of his wit, now raves disjointed folly, wears a coronet plaited from the straws of his pallet-bed, or clanks his chains with a stride of fancied military triumph.

Such thoughts as these haunted the new prisoner during the first hours of his solitary captivity. To the world without, those hours had been but as any other night and day. There had been the masked ball, the gay *reunion*, the concert of hautboys and violins; the scandal, the flutter, the mirth and laughter;—there had been also the sinking heart-weariness, and all those darker passions lurking behind the painted mask of fashion—the gnawing tooth of envy, the basilisk eye of hate;—these had filled up for many an undying spirit in that great city the self-same night and morning. They were marked in their calendar with neither a darker nor a whiter stone than those that went before, or those that followed after. It was but another fresher bubble, rising and breaking on their stream of life as it hurried on; fretful or musical, but hurrying on—Whither? that was the one topic untouched by the wit, except to give an occasional edge to his profaneness. And wherefore? that was the one problem unattempted by the theorist, except to deepen the selfish epicurism of his boasted wisdom of the moment.

Antoine's world meanwhile had become contracted within a much narrower span. His outer world was of a sufficiently monotonous character; and as it relieved the inward thoughts by few interruptions, gave scope for that action of the unquiet mind upon itself, which alternated between a dull sense of wretchedness and paroxysms of agony or of rage. Shortly after he had been so unceremoniously thrust into his cell, a great clock from the adjoining tower, struck by the hand of a sentinel stationed there for the purpose, tolled out the hour of seven. Stroke after stroke the harsh iron sounds smote upon the air, reverberated with a booming echo round the smooth masonry

of the prison-court, shot off from the points of junction
between the towers and the wall, and rattled and quivered
along the battlements before they would absolutely die.
To the excited nerves of our hero, who started impatiently
from his seat at these unexpected sounds, it seemed as if
the official charged with this duty performed it with a
degree of deliberation that betokened something of stern
enjoyment, so measured, so inexorably loud, his mallet
crashed on the great bell, breaking in upon the meditations
or the repose of the unfortunate listeners.    But when
another weary fifteen minutes brought a renewal of the
infliction, and not the quarters merely, but the full hour of
the night, was struck as loud, and bellowed in at his grated
loophole, as hoarsely as before, Antoine fairly rose and
cursed the unwelcome sounds; for they renewed his first
horrible forebodings, and seemed the very type of a time—
perhaps a life—of dull, hopeless, reasonless imprisonment
to come.

"Ay, one day," groaned he forth, with clenched hands,
as he strode despairingly through his cell,—"one day shall
I be shouting back to the din of yonder strokes in frantic
madness!    One day—and how soon—but, merciful Heaven!" ejaculated the unhappy youth, while better thoughts
came over him, and he sank on his knees, and buried his
face on the pallet, "save me; spare me that last direst
infliction of Thine avenging hand!    Much I have deserved; ah, very much, for a life misused; and I resign
myself to meet it.    But may the punishment fall upon the
frail body, and leave untouched the immortal spirit—Thine
own best gift.    Any thing, every thing, but to lose that
intelligence, which I have, alas, too little employed in
learning to know Thee, to love Thee, the Bestower of
all!"

Calmer thoughts now possessed him, and with all their
humiliation, brought with them such emotions of penitence
as are ever the surest harbingers of inward peace.    From
the broken and troubled slumbers of that dreary night he
had now arisen to renew the fervor of yesterday's prayer;
and thence his mind passed into a contemplation, earnest
indeed, but no longer bitter or hopeless, in which he

reverted to the past with a heartfelt intention of atoning for its errors, if a future should still be permitted to dawn upon him. It was now that the interval of retirement he had spent at Saint-Lazare told upon him with a blessed influence. Those eight days had formed a kind of parenthesis in his life ; they had been preceded by much worldliness and guilt, and followed again by a return, at least outwardly, to his former occupations. But they had given him a new standard by which to measure both duties and misfortunes. He felt that, were the uncertainty of his fate once cleared up, he could meet and encounter whatever might come with a courage more unshaken, because emanating from a higher source than the mere natural hardihood that had formed the mainspring of his actions hitherto. Nay, more. Let even the gloom of doubt, and the sickening trial of a hope long protracted, and growing fainter every day, hang over his weary life, yet would he not be deserted by that same grace, which can take the shape of resignation and patient conformity to the Divine will, no less than that of outward energy. In every event, therefore, as our poor prisoner was beginning to say to himself, he possessed in the well-remembered meditations of his retreat a remedy against utter hopelessness, and a clue, by following which he might attain to patience at least, if to nothing more.

Antoine remained for a considerable time on his knees. At intervals he prayed for patience, and aimed at making acts of resignation, which, if broken and imperfect, were at least sincere. Then again he would fight against the intolerable thought that came forcing itself in upon his mind, that this stone cell might be to him the scene of a prolonged, perhaps a lifelong, captivity. Who could foresee the end of that struggle which was agitating Paris, and, through her, France entire ? The Fronde might ultimately prevail, and he remain a state-prisoner in this den, which was fitted alike to the cruelties of a faction and of a despot. Or if the siege were successful, and the kingly power reestablished, what security had he for being sought for with much diligence by his former friends ? His fate would be an uncertainty to them ; they might suppose him to have

perished under the hands of the populace or the rebel soldiery. There would be much to do, many pressing interests to settle, many claimants on the attention, not over-
active, of a selfish government. If he remained here,
unknown and forgotten, under a restoration, which, after
all, was but problematical, he would not be the first victim
whom a similar fate had accompanied to the end. The
ear of man's sympathy grows dull to the groans of his
fellows when they do not strike upon it with too startling
nearness. Antoine felt at such bitter moments that the
promise which La Porte had given of seeking him out was
almost the only thread on which hung his hopes of future
liberation.

He was aroused by sounds from without. It wanted yet
some time to the hour of the scanty morning-meal which
was to reinforce the morsel that had been thrust into his
cell yesterday evening by a grim-visaged gaoler; yet Antoine's quick ear became aware that steps were now ascending the stone-stair of the turret. Upward they came from
story to story; and as they approached, he distinguished
more than one tread, together with the clanking of the
ponderous keys that were always attached to the girdle of
his warder. On the landing outside the door of the cell
there was a momentary pause while the right key was
selected; then it was thrust into the massive rusty lock,
and turned slowly with no small effort. As the door
opened, the rough head of the *porte-clef* appeared above
the shoulders of two other men, to whom he pointed the
way, merely saying, in a harsh voice, but with some rude
attempt to be accommodating:

"One quarter of an hour, if you please, messieurs, and
no more. Such are the orders; and I must execute them
to the letter."

He withdrew; and Antoine's unexpected visitors entered.
They were young men, and both dressed in the habit of
ecclesiastics. The imperfect light would scarcely have
allowed him to see their features distinctly, even had they
removed the broad hats which they continued to wear on
their entrance into his cell. This latter circumstance
piqued our hero, accustomed as he had been to the punc-

tilious manners of the court. Advancing with an air of
rather formal courtesy, he began to inquire to what circumstance he was indebted for the honor of a visit so unexpected. This address was soon interrupted by one of
the two supposed abbes, who now took upon himself the
office of spokesman:

"Hist!" ejaculated this personage in a cautious tone,
placing his finger upon his lips, and then pointing through
the narrow embrasure towards the clock-tower, which was
beginning again to reverberate with its loud harsh warning. "Time is precious, monsieur, as you hear, and we
have not much of it to spend in complimenting. Before
that clock sounds again, our good friend Gilles will be
coming back to look after us. A quarter of an hour is
more than we shall need for our little arrangements;
nevertheless, there is no use in loitering. So now to business."

Thus saying, he stepped to the door, which had been
again doubled-locked by Gilles on his exit. The now-
comer applied his ear to the large keyhole, and listened,
without drawing breath, for a minute. This scrutiny apparently satisfied him; for he now advanced again towards
De Bonneval, who had remained watching his movements
in a surprised and not very complacent mood. The manner of the young officer seemed in no wise to disconcert the
*sang froid* and easy self-complacency of the other, who
began, in a light careless tone:

"There he goes, muttering and cursing, down the stairs;
he will not be in a hurry to come all the way up again before his time. And now, monsieur," stepping closer to
Antoine, and assuming a certain demureness of look and
manner, "have I the honor of being known to you?"

Antoine looked at him steadily, but was unable to
identify either the features or the voice of the speaker. It
was one of those flexible countenances that seem capable
of such alterations of expression and character at the will
of their possessors as to render it no easy matter to recognize them when they are purposely disguised. Such a
characteristic is said to have belonged eminently to that
versatile copyist of the peculiarities of his fellow-men,

Garrick ; and it was shared in no mean degree by one to
whom we must assign considerable dramatic talent—the
present speaker, Gourville.  It might have been thought
impossible that after Antoine had met this adroit intriguer
so lately, and under circumstances so deeply affecting himself, he could have been easily deceived by him under any
disguise.  Yet so it was.  There was the quick restless
eyes, now composed into what was intended for an ecclesiastical gravity and recollectedness of look.  The rest of
the features were slightly lengthened and drawn, so as to
make him appear several years older than in their ordinary
expression.  His abbe's dress was unexceptionably correct,
and worn without either foppery or slovenliness.  In short,
he might have passed for the very quiet respectable cure of
any of the parish-churches of Paris.

About his companion there was nothing particularly to
attract comment.  He too looked just the abbe, and in
nothing further remarkable ; and as Gourville from the
first took both talking and arrangements wholly on himself, we are relieved from the duty of further describing
his companion.

"Ah, well," said the lively *maitre-d'hotel*, when he had
allowed Antoine time to peruse his features, and breaking
into a light laugh; "it is plain that if I had been the
young miller, and Monsieur de Bonneval his present humble servant, a certain recent capture might have been more
easily avoided.  There is nothing like practice in these
matters.  It was the first time monsieur had attempted to
personate any one but himself ; whereas I have been so
many different people in my day, that I sometimes feel to
have let slip my personal identity altogether.  That is
nothing to the present purpose.  My master, the Prince de
Marsillac, out of his old friendship for you, sir, has charged
me to adventure myself into the Bastille, and leave my
worthy fellow-servant here, François Dideron, quietly in
your place ; that is, if you have no more invincible repugnance to becoming an abbe than a peasant for a few hours,
and if you will accept so unworthy an escort through the
streets of Paris as that of Gourville."

De Bonneval, after the first moments of surprise, instantly closed with the offer; and the ingenious agent, who had so recently effected his capture, and was now charged with his escape, proceeded to make all the dispositions thereto with a readiness that showed him to be accomplished in the resources of manœuvre and disguise. The exchange of garments between De Bonneval and the lacquey Dideron occupied but a few minutes. The man had been selected for his present uncomfortable—perhaps even perilous—service, owing to a certain similarity to our young hero in make and stature; and Antoine soon appeared in black hose and doublet, high-heeled buckle-shoes, cloak, and bands, as a young, good-looking, though much-embrowned abbe; while François, in all the externals of the miller's apprentice, certainly looked the part more naturally than De Bonneval had succeeded in doing while he had worn that brief disguise. Gourville in the mean while actively assisted both parties in their transformation; not, however, intermitting the small talk, in which he indulged with the greater zest from its being unnecessary for the moment to support his assumed character.

"Ah, monsieur," he rattled on, "in these stirring and changeful times we enact strange parts, not only in our own persons, but (what is more) in our conduct towards our best friends. To-day we assist in conveying them to prison; to-morrow we undo our own work, and help them out again. Who knows? it may still be my lot to have the honor of escorting you to the Chatelet, or, by a little tour into the country, as far as Vincennes. Well, there you are, as far as mere garments go; and now for the face, a nobler and a more difficult subject. Your complexion has suffered considerably, it must be owned, during your absence from Paris. What *artiste* put on all these uncourtly tints? La Porte, I will make a shrewd guess?" Antoine merely nodded assent; for his cheeks and chin were already under Gourville's manipulation. "I guessed as much; and tolerably done, too. La Porte and I have played at cross-purposes with people's faces before now. There was once a courier—(Allow me to beat and dust your hair a little; there is not much flour remaining in it: you have beaten it wildly yourself,—eh, monsieur?—since your acquaint-

22

ance with the Bastille. One should learn to take these
things philosophically, though ; there is no wall without a
chink in it, if we will but watch for the daylight.) Well,
this courier having important despatches—(Thank you, we
will leave the eyebrows alone ; they are much the same
color as that beetle-browed Dideron's there. Now for the
hands ; and then I think we are complete.) He having
despatches to Normandy—"

Just then the first stroke of the iron knell that announced the expiration of the quarter resounded through
the prison-chamber. Antoine started at the harsh summons, as bringing with it the crisis of his fate. Dideron
too, his scarce willing substitute, moved about a little un-
easily in his miller's dress, as stroke after stroke crashed
on the ear. But Gourville was not so easily discomposed.
His nerves had been practised in more hair-breadth adventures than the present ; and his confidence in his own
ready wit, that had borne him scatheless through so many
trials of address, maintained him in the same buoyant and
seemingly careless spirits, which he knew how to exchange
at a moment's notice for any manner, or set of manners,
suitable to the work in hand.

"Let him come," said he, laughing, but rather more
cautiously than before ; "we are now ready for him. The
actors are dressed, the little drama will not occupy three
minutes, and will be enacted before a very uncritical audi-
ence. It must be confessed that we friends of liberty, and
that sort of thing, have not succeeded in giving to our
prison functionaries the adroitness of their more loyal pre-
decessors in office. If we can but keep clear of those
searching eyes of friend Saron, I have no anxiety about
any one else. There comes old Gilles up the last flight :
listen !"

And slowly was heard the tramp of the gaoler, as he
mounted step after step of the stair, his heavy keys clanking, and the strong sword he wore as a defence against any
attempt from his prisoners ringing on the freestone steps as
he mounted them towards Antoine's cell.

"Françuis," whispered Gourville, fully on the alert,
"now is the time, man. Quick! lay thee on the pallet-

couch; turn thy face to the wall; cover it with both hands.
Thou art in the deepest grief, remember. Bungler!"
added Gourville, stepping nimbly to the bed, and arranging
the passive François in what he considered an attitude of
the most natural despair; "lie still as thou art; if thou
stirrest, I shall forget my character of abbe, and kick thee
outright! And you, monsieur, are to utter no word;
you are merely in attendance upon me: a very easy part,
you see. Isn't it beautifully natural?" he continued, surveying, with his head on one side, the success of the *pose
plastique*, and appealing to Antoine with as much careless
gaiety as if they had been standing together in the Hotel
de Marsillac, though at that very moment the key was
thrust by the gaoler from without into the heavy prison-
door.

Gilles entered, with his dogged and downcast look, to
announce that the allotted quarter of an hour had expired;
and he saw—O sublimated quintessence of dissembling!—
he saw a young abbe standing in the midst of the cell,
his features composed yet kind, and full of gentle sympathy, his quiet eye resting in pity on the form of the man
in miller's garments, who, lying on the pallet, with his
face averted from the light of the open door, appeared to
be absorbed in the deepest grief.

"Take courage, then, my dear son, said Gourville, in
measured tones, and waving his hand as if to enforce a
parting admonition; "and above all, take patience. It is
true, we have been hitherto unsuccessful in our applica-
tions on your behalf, but we shall not therefore desist. In
the mean time, this worthy man," slipping into Gilles'
rough hand a piece of gold, "will, I am sure, treat you
with all the leniency consistent with the prison regulations.
Look forward to seeing us again with better news; and in
the mean time, farewell!"

So did he exhort, with all the tokens of a benevolent
and placid sympathy, the captive he was leaving. Motioning Antoine to precede him down the stairs, he turned
as if to take a parting look at the prisoner, but in truth to
assure himself that Gilles was still unconscious of the de-
ception that was being practised upon him, and then fol-

lowed De Bonneval closely, addressing a few words to the
gaoler as they descended.

Though the deputy gaoler was undoubtedly a novice in
his trade, and none of the keenest or most observant of
beings in any capacity, it must be allowed that more practised eyes and wits than those of Gilles might have been
at fault in detecting Gourville's *ruse*.  There could be no
question as to the identity of the more prominent of the
two visitors, Gourville himself.  As a young abbe of
engaging mien, he had entered the Bastille. furnished with
an order from Marsillac, countersigned by Conti, generalissimo of the Fronde ; and now, after a brief visit, the same
engaging young abbe was leaving it again.  With regard
to the ecclesiastic who accompanied him, he had been silent
and undistinguished from the first ; and Antoine, in spite of
his intense eagerness to escape, had sufficient self-command
to remain entirely passive, and allow Gourville, as he had
himself requested, to do all.  The task of doing all was,
in fact, this man's province ; and well did he now sustain
it.  By continual, though not obtrusive questions, ranging
from one subject to another, sometimes quaint, always to
the purpose, he kept the attention of their conductor so
fully on the stretch, that by the time they had crossed the
court on their way to the outer gate, he seemed almost to
have forgotten the existence of the subordinate visitor.
Antoine was a mere *umbra*,—a silent walking shadow, a
humble friend in attendance on the active, inquisitive,
entertaining, somewhat puzzling abbe, who seemed to
claim the whole attention of every one that came across
him : who bustled by the sentinels, with a careless word for
each ; jested blandly, and with a *debonnaire* graciousness,
with the turnkey as he opened the heavy *grille ;* discussed
for a moment the subject of weapons, and the duration of
the watch, with the guard before the drawbridge ; and
finally, on leaving the gloomy fortress, bade them expect
him again the following day to pay another visit of consolation to the poor mistaken young royalist in his captivity.

"Not so fast, monsieur ; not so fast,, if you please,"
whispered Gourville to our hero, as they walked away

through the narrow antique street that led beyond the
enceinte of the Bastille, but still within view of the outer
gate ; "you must restrain yourself until we have turned
the corner. There I have a coach waiting for us ; and,
the blinds once drawn, we may proceed at a round gallop.
Meanwhile, a stray warder might be looking at us from
one of the towers, and you would be greeted with a bullet
to moderate your speed. It wasn't so badly done, after
all," pursued the *maître-d'hotel*, with a quiet chuckling
laugh ; "though that stupid old Gilles was too easily
blinded to win me much credit. I am glad we did not
fall in with Saron, however. He is about the only man
in Paris from whom I could not hope to disguise myself,
or you either. And now," added he, as they entered a
coach which was standing, with a lacquey beside the open
door, at the first turn in the street, "whither shall I take
you, monsieur? You have all the length and breadth of
Paris to choose from ; and I am bid to conduct you where-
ever you will."

"To Saint-Lazare !" he exclaimed, on receiving Antoine's answer. "Well, I confess that would have baffled
my calculation."

He remained for a minute in unusual silence as the
vehicle proceeded. Then he said, more thoughtfully than
was his wont :

"There is something strange, it must be allowed, in
the fascination of that old Monsieur Vincent! What magnetic power does he possess to attract a young blade like
you, sir, to his house in preference to any other? It is
beyond me. I am afraid I am of different metal,—mere
sounding brass, or something of that nature ; and the load-
stone of such an influence has no power over me. And
yet who knows?—as one began to draw towards the end
of this bustling empty life—

"Well, we are not there yet," he resumed, with all his
usual rattle ; "nor near it, I hope. And meanwhile we
have arrived at Saint-Lazare. There is old Alexis, the
porter, who grins a recognition to you. He would not
receive me half so complacently ; for it was once an adventure of mine—but no matter. *Au revoir, monsieur,*

22*

and under happier circumstances. Keep close here for the present; and you may chance to see no more of your humble servant Gourville until Paris and the court both return to their senses, and we have minuets and hautboys once again, instead of all these trumpets and counter-marchings."

## CHAPTER XXXI.

### STRUGGLES OF THE WORLD WITHOUT AND THE WORLD WITHIN.

"So we'll live,
And pray, and sing, and tell old tales, and laugh
At gilded butterflies, and hear poor rogues
Talk of court-news; and we'll talk with them too,—
Who loses, and who wins; who's in; who's out."

*King Lear.*

THE progress of the Fronde had not remained unwatched by the foreign powers against which France, while united in herself, had been successfully engaged. Spain, her ancient rival and enemy, saw the army of Catalonia, which had been harassing her frontier with various success, withdrawn to aid the royal cause at home, and herself left free to commence active operations in her turn. These she could now best pursue by combining with the insurgent parliament and city of Paris. Accordingly, a secret envoy, who passed under the name of Don Joseph Illescas, was sent from the Archduke Leopold to the French capital, where he resided *incognito* for some weeks, in order to seize any opening that might present itself for declaring his mission.

Illescas, however, found Paris divided into factions, whose mutual discords and jealousies made any unanimous prosecution of the war impossible; and still further precluded a measure so overtly disloyal as that of treating with a foreign and hostile power. The parliament hoped for important permanent concessions from the treaty of the preceding October; and a gracious message of the regent, conveyed to them by Omer Talon and Jerome Bignon, who had been deputed to wait upon her at Saint-Germains, the more disposed them to make overtures for peace. On the other hand, the high nobility, as little prepared to endure the authority of a parliament as to submit to the dictation of a minister, sought in the continuance of the present troubles the re-establishment of their former influence in the state. Many of them, too, had placed themselves, in a spirit which then went by the name of chivalry, at the commands of those ladies of rank whose caprice and ambition induced them to wear the colors of the Fronde. The Duke of Beaufort and the Marquis d'Hocquincourt were blindly subservient to the Duchesse de Montbazon's lightest bidding. The Prince de Marsillac had vowed himself to the service of the sister of Conde and Conti, the Duchesse de Longueville,—that beautiful and gifted being whose vanity, whose intriguing ambition, whose vices, alas! had become sufficiently notorious to make her long and earnest after-repentance the more signal exhibition of triumphant grace. The selfish aims of other persons of rank had taken a different turn, equally opposed to the interests of public peace. They laid claim to posts of honor and profit, the government of the fortresses and provinces of France; or, with a more undisguised simplicity of view, to the immediate replenishment of their private coffers. Among these last, the Duke d'Elbœuf became entitled to a conspicuous place, having, on joining the party of the Parisians, abstracted forty thousand crowns from the public chest, on the plea of raising troops for the cause, though neither horse nor man ever appeared as the result of the transaction.

The Duke de Bouillon and the Coadjutor maintained their former prominence on this distracted scene; and their

several views armed them in mutual opposition. Bouillon
had never lost from view the great end of his ambition, the
recovery of Sedan, that hereditary princedom of which he
had been deprived by the jealousy of Richelieu. A true
representative of the ancient feudal spirit of France, his patriotism (remarks a calmly-judging historian of the period)
was concentrated in the interests of his house and family ;
and for the re-acquisition of this long-regretted prize, he
would have consented to deliver over France to the Spaniard, and Paris to the violence of the mob. For the magistracy and the middle classes he entertained a repugnance
which he did not care sufficiently to disguise. The nation,
according to his political theory, was composed of men of
gentle blood, together with the military. Happily, however, this lordly view was counteracted, when it would
have advanced into action, by the no less determined line
of the Coadjutor.

De Retz, on his part, clearly saw the importance of the
parliament at this crisis, as a bulwark against the conflicting but selfish aims of individual nobles, and the blind
headlong impulses of the populace ; and refused, therefore,
though closely urged, either to lend himself to any treaty
with Spain, or consent to rouse the lower orders against the
magistracy.

It resulted from this universal disunion among the
leaders of the Fronde that the Spanish envoy, introduced
into the chambers to exhibit his credentials at the moment
when the message from Saint-Germains had likewise been
reported to the assembly, remained simply to witness a
declaration which remanded the letters of credit brought
by him from the archduke for the consideration of her
majesty. All parties were by this time wearied with their
mutual dissensions ; and, as usual in such cases of exhausting political strife, their thoughts turned with longing to
the well-remembered tradition of a legitimate and a settled
throne. As the men of Israel, taught wisdom by the mis-
rule of an usurper, sought their remedy in the restoration
of the prince whom their factions had exiled, so had this
period of agitation, of fruitless absurd attempts at warfare,
disappointment in the character of their leaders, decline of

commerce, and increasing misery, disposed the rebellious
Parisians to welcome back the regency, even with Mazarin
appended thereto as a necessary condition. "All the people were at strife in all the tribes of Israel, saying : The
king delivered us out of the hands of our enemies, and he
saved us out of the hands of the Philistines ; and now he is
fled out of the land for Absalom. . . . how long are you
silent, and bring not back the king ?"

No wonder that, with such dispositions among the many,
and only a minority of malcontents with any influence or
consistent plan, a conference at Ruel between the regent's
immediate council on the one side, and Mole and De
Mesme at the head of a few parliamentary deputies on the
other, should at length have terminated what may be
called the first war of the Fronde. A treaty was signed
by the deputies, even at a moment when a dawn of success
appeared to gleam on the arms of the insurgents ; when
Bouillon, in spite of his rival, had succeeded in exciting
the populace against the pacificators ; when the Duke de
Longueville was leading his troops from Normandy, and
the Duke de la Tremouille ten thousand men from Poitou ;
and when Turenne himself, seduced from his allegiance,
partly by the influence of his elder brother, partly (it is
said) by a less worthy motive, announced to the Prince de
Conti, generalissimo of the Fronde, that "he had passed
the Rhine with his army, and was coming to offer himself
to the parliament for the service of the king, and of the
public, against the unjust oppression of Mazarin." It is
true that Mole and the rest, having thus compromised their
constituents, in their zeal for the desired accommodation,
by signing it on their own authority, were greeted on
returning to Paris with a general discontent. The life of
Mole himself was placed in danger by the violence of the
populace ; and even the example of England began to be
quoted, and the cry, "A republic !" heard in the streets of
Paris,—a word startling enough, one would have thought,
to summon the awful shade of Richelieu again upon the
scene. But the calm intrepid dignity of Mathieu Mole, his
consistent view of the interests of his country, his dauntless exposure of himself to danger while speaking reason

to infuriated men, and the conviction of his entire disin-
terestedness, gradually stemmed the tide that threatened
to engulf him.  In the stormy debates which ensued, he
was able to make head against the several influences of
Conti, Bouillon, Noirmoutiers, and their inferior agents;
and, with much opposition and some delay, to carry the
consent of the chambers to the propositions of Ruel.  These
had in the mean time been considered in detail by the deputies on either side, modified in part, and finally adjusted.
A private treaty made by some of the generals with Spain
was disavowed by the parliament.  The archduke, who had
already entered France, withdrew his forces precipitately
into Flanders.  Turenne, whose army had been secured
in their loyalty by largesses from the minister, found himself now a deserted solitary traitor; and was compelled to
escape over the frontier of Holland, to save himself from
arrest.

The return of their majesties to Paris, in the middle of
August, 1649, formed a brilliant spectacle of triumph.  It
had been brought about at the last through the influence
of Conde, whose destiny still maintained him true to the
dignified post that so well became him, as pacificator between the interests of crown and people.  He now appeared
with his young cousin and the regent in the royal coach, to
spread around the former the ægis of his own renown, and
usher him back to his capital.  For the moment it seemed
as though all the bitterness of past faction was lost in one
universal joy*.  An immense concourse of citizens had
advanced to Le Bourget, two leagues beyond the walls, to
greet the august personages against whom they had so
lately been in arms.  The Duke de Montbazon, as "pro-

* "The court was received," says the Cardinal de Retz, in his
*Memoirs*, "as kings have always been, and always will be; that is
to say, with acclamations, which mean little enough to any save
those who seek to delude themselves.  An insignificant king's attor-
ney of the Chatelet, a kind of crazed person, hired a dozen women
or so, who, at the entrance of the Faubourg, when they saw Mazarin in the king's coach, cried, 'Long live his eminence!' and his
eminence forthwith believed himself to be master of Paris.  At the
end of four days, however, he found that he had lamentably deceived himself."

vost of the merchants," together with the sheriffs, the guilds
and corporations of the city, awaited them in the Faubourg
St. Denis; the great officers of state, the principal nobility,
the heads of the magistracy, and the parliamentary presi-
dents, were assembled to pay their homage at the Palais
Royal. Even Mazarin—object as he was of general detesta-
tion, despised by all in the day of his crying adversity, and
now mistrusted and feared by many on his return to power—
came in nevertheless for his share of the popular greet-
ings, as, seated by the side of the prince, he completed
the number who had the privilege of the stage-coach on
this auspicious day. Conde, too proud to be influenced by
any such demonstrations of his own popularity as were
showered upon him from the masses who swelled around
the progress of the royal *cortege*, turned a deaf ear also to
the cardinal's protestations of unalterable gratitude. It
was not difficult to foresee that in the impetuous haughti-
ness of that young commander the elements of new dissensions were already working; and that the war of the
first Fronde, whose wayward career had now been brought
to a close, might at no remote date be followed by a second, in which he might be led to take a part less worthy
of himself than that which he at present sustained.

All this while De Bonneval is in Saint-Lazare. Factions have been raging; schemers plotting and disappointed; treason has been brewed and come to naught
again; and it seems to concern him now no more than the
wind that strews the last year's leaves over the walk along
which he is pacing. Not that he has lost any of his loyalty, or his real interest in the welfare of his royal mistress,
or of France; but for the present he has a nearer, a more
engrossing subject of thought before him. He is still
occupied with the efficient means of securing his salvation;
and that "one thing needful" may well put aside for a
while the thousand other secondary things amid which he
has hitherto sought the interests of his life.

The return of the court to Paris, however, recalled Antoine to his immediate duties as an officer of the guard.
His capture first, and then his escape into a place of concealment, had made his absence from those duties unavoid-

able; and he had spent some time in close retirement before
it became possible to leave the city, or even to show himself
in the streets.   One of his first objects had been to con-
trive some mode by which he might still execute the commission with which the regent had intrusted him.   But the
Louvre might at that time be said to be in a state of siege,
and all ingress had become impossible.   The commanders
of the insurgent forces, knowing the personal good understanding subsisting between the royal ladies, kept strict
guard round the residence of the English queen, to prevent any information of the state of affairs within the city
reaching Saint-Germains from thence.   It was but darkly,
and by vague rumors, that the terrible truth at length
penetrated through the twofold circle of siege and counter-
siege, and was whispered in the court of Henrietta.

That such a tragedy as the public murder of Charles I.
had been assuming shape and likelihood, none who had
watched even distantly the progress of events in England
could fail to see.   The heart of Henrietta-Maria had been
tortured during the suspense of the last few months with
alternations of feeble hope, to which she was still fain to
cling, and the darkest forebodings regarding the fate of
her royal husband.   Soon after the siege of Paris had
commenced, intelligence reached her that the trial of the
king had been determined upon, and the tribunal on the
eve of being appointed.   Faithful and devoted to him in
this hour of extremity, as she had been throughout his
chequered reign, Henrietta had written to the Count de
Grignon, ambassador of the French court in London, and
also to General Fairfax, suing for the necessary passports,
and the sad permission to re-enter England and share the
fallen fortunes of the king.   The ambassador performed
his part; but when Fairfax transmitted the letter to the
Commons, it was contemptuously cast aside, with the comment, that six years ago the queen had been declared by
that house to be guilty of high treason.

Her request thus answered, the exiled Henrietta, now
almost a widow before the axe had fallen, was left to the
dread suspense which ensued upon the sending of her despatches to London.   This sombre silence continued for

upwards of a month, and aided the extreme penury and
destitution endured by the royal personages in the Louvre,
in converting those vast and now silent apartments into an
abode of twofold gloom. It was broken at the end of
those long weeks by the last and worst tidings, with which
De Bonneval had been unsuccessfully charged; and which
it now fell to the lot of Lord Jermyn to communicate, as
gently and gradually as the case admitted, to the widowed
queen.

His mission first rendered impossible to himself, then
discharged by another, Antoine had been left free to prosecute the great absorbing object to which his whole mind
was now devoted. Not that the victory over his own worse
motives had yet been completely gained. There were
many returns to the old lingering wishes of enjoying life,
of advancing himself in the world. The work of the
retreat, in changing the bent of his will, advanced, indeed,
upon the whole, but with checks and counteractions from
that former self, who would not resign the empire without
a struggle. Still he never really wavered in his purpose.
He had made a fair experiment of the worldly life. The
knowledge he had gained of its perils and seductions
enhanced, indeed, the respect he could not but feel for
those rare examples of men who, plunged in the midst of
it, yet breasted its waves manfully, and gained the shore.
But he felt this was a task above his own measure of
strength. He must leave the court, or he would more
than probably lose his soul.

This conclusion once reached, several after-questions
presented themselves. And first, his father? The worthy
old baron was perhaps at that moment rejoicing himself
with the thought of his only son's career, his courtly or
his military success. How could Antoine endure to disappoint him? It was not so much his anger, though a
father's anger is always terrible to witness—more terrible
to bear; but the deep sorrowful disappointment with which
he would hear that Antoine had thrown up all his prospects, and would now return upon his hands; this was
the bitter cup; and our friend began to taste it by antici-
pation.

23

Return upon his hands? Why no:· that was not going
to be the result. Antoine would not abandon one phase
of self-pleasing life merely to recommence another; nor
be an idler at home, and nothing more, after the stirring
life he had led in Paris. His father should never have
that ground of complaint or disappointment. His mind
wavered among several plans for the future. He might
ask to exchange into some regiment now on active service.
Young officers were to be found in abundance who would
gladly occupy his position in the guard. There was a
noble career open to him under Lascaris, Grand Master of
the Knights of Malta; and he might join the squadron
sent yearly from that island to the relief of Candia; or
take service among those chivalrous volunteers who, under
Louis Comte d'Arpajan, had banded together in the name
of Christendom for the defence of the order against the
attacks of the Grand Signior, Ibrahim, and his infidel
forces. Or he might turn to some entirely new career;—
try his fortune at the bar, and belong to *la robe*, after all.
Nay, rather than that, he would join the other adventurous
spirits who had carried their energies to the island of Mad-
ágascar, or some other of the foreign French settlements,
and carved out for themselves under another sun the fortune from which untoward circumstances debarred them at
home. With such a fair choice of paths before him, why
might not young De Bonneval be light-hearted at his prospects? It is true that all this while he had had a revelation made to him of his future. There was one picture
in the sorcerer's dark glass with which the reader has not
been made acquainted; and this might have been supposed
to decide the question. But Antoine had either learned
to disbelieve those insights into futurity, and, in the light
of his late spiritual exercises, to regard all that had been
shown him in Lomelli's chamber as the delusions of a jug-
gling fiend; or else, he reasoned, that as he had been
absolved from the guilt of that dread adventure, so he
might possibly be able to remould the future there announced to him. Certain it is, that while he now anxiously forecast the various paths in life that might open to
him upon his quitting the court, that particular event,

whatever we may hereafter discover it to have been, recurred to him only as one out of several destinies, and not perhaps the most likely, after all.

## CHAPTER XXXII.

### THE RESOLVE FAIRLY TESTED.

*"Fabian.* A coward, a most devout coward ; religious in it.
*Sir Andrew.* I'll after him again, and beat him.
*Sir Toby.* Do ; cuff him soundly, but never draw thy sword."
*Twelfth Night.*

AMID these balanced questions, the time arrived for our hero to seal his resolution, and to lay his sword at the feet of the royal lady whom he had hitherto, though for a brief period, served so faithfully. Vincent de Paul had already paved the way for his doing this with a good grace, and prepared the regent to receive him as favorably as could well be expected. Her mind was not of a character to be much alive to the reasons which made such a step desirable to the young guardsman. In Anne of Austria a good deal of habitual devoutness co-existed with, or rather was overlaid by, the counter-influence of two dominant faults. Pride, less, perhaps, personal than the pride of caste and station, disposed her to take for granted that men and things were better than they actually were, because of the fact of their belonging to her court and government. And indolence, no less fatally, withheld her from taking such measures as might serve to purify and reform the condition of the society around her. In the assertion of her rights, in resisting and thwarting the encroachments, nay, the just demands, of the commons, she had shown

264 ANTOINE DE BONNEVAL:

herself energetic, and even impetuous. But in banishing
unworthy favorites, in a conscientious search after worth
and virtue to fill their places, she was culpably supine.
And it resulted from this twofold error, that the personal
good example of the queen went little way towards reform-
ing the manners of the time. Scandals appear to have
abounded even within her own circle, in no very marked
contrast to the open and systematic profligacy of the suc-
ceeding reign.

Even Vincent, therefore, had not gained his point without some difficulty. His influence had ultimately carried
the day, though it had failed to convince her that young
De Bonneval's retirement from the court, if not altogether
from the world, was to himself a matter of spiritual necessity. Antoine's qualities had produced in the mind of the
regent a degree of sincere regard for him; and to this,
since his capture and imprisonment, had been added a
sentiment of gratitude for all he had ventured and undergone in her service. His devoted loyalty, his chivalrous
courage, his courtly manner and appearance, all tended to
make his royal mistress sincerely regret young Antoine's
determination. Added to this, came a certain proud surprise that he should voluntarily cast away the advantages
which his present position held out to him. These had
not been exaggerated by De Montauban in his remon-
strances; it was quite true to say that Antoine was looked
upon as one of the most promising young officers then
about the court. We have seen him, it is true, rather put
to confusion among the learned and literary at the Rambouillet; nevertheless he had not entirely neglected such
branches of study as might forward him in his future
career. The celebrated Blondel had given him lessons in
military architecture and fortification; one of Antoine's
few competitors in that select class being the young Vau-
ban, afterwards the distinguished engineer in the campaigns
of Louis XIV. Abraham Fabert, the future marquis and
marechal of that name, and preceptor in strategy to the
young king, had instructed him in the art of war, and
already counted him amoung his foremost pupils. He had
made some little way in Spanish, so useful an acquirement

at that period to the soldier or the diplomatist; and had even been adventurous enough to attack both German and English, though these he successively abandoned in despair. His use of the rapier and poniard, whether on horse or on foot, had gained him a more than average reputation as a swordsman. Young Louis, his most frequent antagonist in these exercises, had laughingly declared that he should avoid with all care any such quarrel as would lead to Antoine's practising his weapons upon him in earnest. In dancing, twin-sister to these more martial accomplishments, he was equally proficient, whether it were the intricate *branle* or the lively *corante* in which he made his appearance. Lastly, he had commenced thrumming the guitar, with a good deal of perseverance, and some reasonable hope of final success.

Why, then, was the young lieutenant to abandon a career in which so many things united to beckon him forward with flattering promises? We have already given Antoine's answer to the question; but it was asked by the queen, more than once, while Vincent de Paul was pleading for his neophyte's release from his court-engagements. Why could not Monsieur de Bonneval make an occasional retreat of a few days for his spiritual welfare? She was herself accustomed to spend a short period of retirement at Val-de-Grace in preparation for the great festivals of the Church; would not such a measure as this content him? Could he not use the world without abusing it; and prosecute at once the honors and employments to which he seemed to be destined, as well as secure his ultimate salvation?

No; Antoine was resolute, and still respectfully solicited the favor of a day on which he might come from Saint-Lazare and resign his commission into the hands of Anne of Austria herself.

It was at length notified to him that on a certain morning, after a council to be held in the queen's own withdrawing-room, she would grant this interview.

The ex-guardsman—for he now considered his commission as virtually revoked—did not prepare for the moment with all that calmness he had promised himself. His
23*

mind seemed to have become the sport of a thousand conflicting motives, which raged the more vehemently because
they were so near to their final solution. It was the
darkest hour with him, for it drew towards the dawning of
a better day. How more than ever did he appreciate the
wisdom and charity of the venerable superior of the house
in which this his last struggle was being undergone! Vincent devoted to him all such portions of time as he could
spare from his many pressing occupations, or steal from
his too scanty rest. Calm, considerate, and tender, urging
little and weighing all, his ready sympathy overflowed at
once from his full heart; while the practical wisdom of his
views seemed drawn from the remoter depths of a life-long
experience. He had watched Antoine through the first
fervors of his repentance, and cautioned him against forming any resolution while under their sway. He had seen
these decline again, and had then supported his young
disciple under the period of dejection and wavering that
followed. He had strengthened his motives, reminded
him of his first good resolutions, and had finally been consoled by seeing Antoine arrive at a firm determination to
secure his soul at any cost, and do the one thing which he
felt to be safe for himself. Yet all Vincent's tenderness
and consideration, and his firmness too, were needed to
crown the good work, on the very morning when he took
Antoine with him to the palace.

The council was over; and young De Bonneval, introduced into the cabinet by Vincent himself, found the regent
still seated at the table, on which lay several petitions and
public documents. These were being collected by La
Porte, now no unfrequent attendant on the discussions of
the queen, the minister, and the princes, as a kind of secretary and universal go-between. This intelligent court-
dependant eyed our hero on his entrance with a peculiar
expression, which brought to Antoine's mind the parting
words at Saint-Germains, in which he had encouraged him
to hope for no mean advancement as the issue of the
adventure then in hand. But Antoine had already counted
the whole cost of the sacrifice he was now about to make;
and there was nothing in the glance of La Porte—semi-

reproachful and perhaps demi-semi-contemptuous as it was—to re-awaken in him a struggle in which he had already triumphed.

"*Eh, quoi ! le jeu vaut-il bien la chandelle ?*" whispered the confidential secretary to our young friend as, having gathered up the papers and made his profound reverence to the queen, he passed close to our hero, and disappeared through the door.

"Yes," thought De Bonneval to himself, "as surely as the soul is the most precious of things, and eternity outweighs time, it is worth all it costs me now, and through my life to come."

With no return of his former vacillation, he remained kneeling on one knee until the regent should address him. His heart throbbed indeed, for he was no stoic; and he knew the extent of the sacrifice he was thus making, absolutely on the threshold of life. But he had learned to see, and trusted hereafter more fully to realize, his present act in the light of eternity.

Orleans, Conde, and Mazarin, had risen from the council-table; and now, withdrawn into the embrasure of a window, seemed to be continuing among themselves a discussion which engrossed them altogether. The manner of the prince was haughty and reserved; there was a flush on his usually pale cheek, and a fire in his eye, which told plainly that some outbreak of that impetuous spirit was either impending, or had scarce passed away. The duke, on his side, exhibited the demeanor of a man resentful for something that had just been uttered by the other. Mazarin, standing in full robes between them, and turning alternately to either, was employing all his powers of conciliation to prevent a more open rupture between the two men on whose co-operation depended the stability of the throne no less than his own continuance in power. Their conversation was carried on in suppressed tones, interrupted at times by a proud or impatient gesture on the part of the belligerent princes, or a deprecatory wave of the hand from their half-successful peace-maker.

Of the remaining members of the council, the chancellor, Segnier, remained still seated at the table, his pale

thoughtful brow supported on one hand, while he pondered
intently over some columns of figures on a paper of sta-
tistics or finance before him.    None of these, therefore,
had leisure to notice a young lieutenant, who was come on
what they would probably all have considered a fool's
errand, had they condescended to bestow a thought upon
it.    There remained only the Abbe de la Riviere, who
had been lately made a minister of state through the
influence of his patron Orleans, certainly not for any qualities of his own.    He had felt awkward and out of place
during the important discussion in which the council had
been engaged; and now, glad of the diversion afforded by
the little episode which concerned our hero so nearly, he
stood leaning over one of those straight high-backed chairs
that are reckoned in our degenerate days rather as instruments of torture than as articles of furniture.    His inex-
pressive features were composed into what he intended for
a look of keen observation of human nature; but he was
only so far successful as to gain an air of ludicrous and
magisterial self-importance.

Meanwhile Vincent had advanced, and spoken a few
words in an undertone to the regent, who now turned and
said to Antoine, in a tone in which pride and a certain
degree of offence were struggling with her habitual deference for the young man's intercessor :

"So you are determined to leave us, Monsieur de Bonneval ?   I had hoped otherwise ; but we will not now speak
of that.   Monsieur Vincent has told me all you would say ;
and you have our leave to retire from the guard, in which
you have served your king faithfully, though not long.
We owe you thanks and recompense for your late special
service, moreover.   You are not experienced enough," she
added, her manner relaxing a little from its first stateliness,
"to be made governor of the Bastille, with whose interior
you have already made acquaintance on our behalf; but
any more fitting post which you may hereafter solicit shall
be yours.   This we promise you, in token of our gratitude
to your loyal devotion, and of our unfeigned respect"—
she inclined towards Vincent as she spoke—"for him who
has undertaken your cause.   And now," added the queen,

drawing from her finger a ring set with emeralds, "keep this little trifle from us as a memorial of the days of your vanity spent in the palace, and which you appear to have found too much for you. You can wear it," she added with a smile, "at least until you become a cordelier; and whenever that event shall take place, I expect to receive it again, in token that you will remember me in your prayers. And now go, monsieur, and all good be with you. You are in the best of hands; that one circumstance withholds me from saying that I think you are committing an error. Monsieur Vincent, you must be good enough to trust your pupil out of leading-strings for a while. The Archbishop of Auch is almost *in extremis*; and, as usual, there are some who think us under obligation to them, and are already soliciting his mitre for their sons and nephews. Remain with us to discuss their claims, and some other matters on which we desire your opinion."

So saying, she extended her hand to Antoine; and with a manner more gracious than at first, once more thanked him for his services, and bade him farewell. The young man, still kneeling, bent lower as he respectfully touched with his lips the royal hand; and when he rose, and, with a deep reverence, retired backwards to the door, it was with the lightening of heart of a man who has gone through his trial and known the worst. La Riviere had accompanied this brief scene with a self-important attention, and bowed obsequiously at every pause in the regent's address. It was with the most patronizing air that the abbe now gave a parting nod to our hero over his shoulder, as one who did not quite venture to approve, yet would not wholly condemn. The chancellor was still absorbed in his calculations; the conversation, or dispute, between the princes at the window continued without intermission; and Anne of Austria had now motioned Vincent to a chair by her side, and was conversing with him in a whisper. De Bonneval, just before leaving the apartment, caught a glance from the eye of Conde, who possessed the true military faculty of being conscious of several things at a time. He bestowed on our hero a slight token of recognition; and there was something in the expression of that keen glanc-

ing eye which made Antoine feel that, excepting only Vincent, no one then in the presence-chamber was as capable
as the lofty and generous Conde of appreciating the motives
of his present act.   Ah, if only they who have the faculty
to value great and good things at something of their worth,
—to see their intrinsic beauty, and in passing moments to
feel their power,—had also the courage to respond to such
a call !   This earth of ours would not then be the "drone-
hive strange of phantom-purposes," the scene of fleeting
impressions and talents recklessly squandered, it is to-day !

And now calmly, and even with a certain buoyancy of
soul, the young man measured back his way through the
suite of state-apartments which he was probably treading
for the last time.   Those lofty saloons had again and again
re-echoed to the sound of music, as he had stepped their
polished floors through the mazes of many a court-dance,
one of the gayest and most graceful of triflers among all
the graceful and the gay.   At present they resounded
sullenly to his solitary footfall ; and to a superstitious
fancy, their dull echoes might have seemed to reproach the
ungrateful favorite of fortune who was wilfully abandon-
ing at once the pleasures and the advancement he might
have enjoyed by remaining still their denizen.   But Antoine was in no such mood.   He already began to taste
that calm, that joy, which is the present repayment of
every sacrifice made for God, as well as the foretaste of its
ineffable rewards to come.   His step was never firmer or
lighter ; his heart had never drunk a deeper measure of
happiness ; his lips had never smiled a more unconstrained
smile, than now, in these last moments of his farewell to a
life of emptiness and glitter.   He felt as far removed from
misanthropy as from any wavering or regrets ; he judged
not his brother-men ; he was but providing for himself as
best he might ; and he seemed unconsciously to realize
that great and serene ideal sketched by one of the most
thoughtful of our poets.   He was the

> "Philosopher, despising wealth and death,
>   Yet docile, childish, full of life and love ;"

while in the exuberant fullness of his heart, seeking to
vent its unbitter and thankful emotions, he began to hum

the first air that came into his mind, and checked himself,
half-startled, at finding that he had fallen without pre-
meditation into the long-drawn cadences of the hymn for
the departed.

De Bonneval had reached the last chamber of the suite,
leading out upon the landing of the great staircase. A
*mousquetaire* of the guard, a loitering groom of the chambers, or court-page, had been the only occupants of the
saloons through which he had hitherto passed. But he
was not fated to accomplish his departure so easily. He
was passing through the open door of the ante-room, and
emerging upon the hall, down which the wide-sweeping
staircase wound, when he came full upon another young
man, in the rich uniform of an officer of the guard, sauntering up the steps, carelessly swinging a tasselled cane in
one hand, while with the other he stroked the long waving
locks that escaped from under his plumed hat. A long-
drawn sonorous yawn seemed to tell a tale of the most
desperate ennui on the part of the lounger. It was Louis
de Montauban.

Of all his acquaintance, this one was the person whom
Antoine would have most wished to avoid. He had prepared himself for offence on the part of the queen, and for
haughty surprise and disdain from any who might immediately surround her. But satire and ridicule, such as he
was now sure to encounter from an equal and former companion, was a far more trying prospect. He nerved himself for it, however; and, after a first movement of dis-
agreeable surprise, stood face to face with the professed
satirist.

De Montauban awoke in an instant from the expression
of languor with which he had completed the ascent of the
great staircase. His eye lit, his lip curled; he seized
Antoine by both shoulders, and forced him, half-jestingly,
though by no means gently, backwards until they were
both in the ante-chamber from which the latter had just
come forth. The two young men stood opposite one to
the other in the midst of the apartment: Louis hard, caustic, merciless; Antoine steady, grave, collected, slightly
displeased. There was sarcasm in the eye of the one, and

firmness on the lip, though a slight flush on the cheeks, of
the other.

After a minute, Louis flashed out: "And this is my
pupil in the art of life? Truly, he does me credit. He
cannot taste the sweets of imprisonment for a couple of
days, but he must fly back to gratings and bars like a
tame linnet when he has once been fairly freed, and pass
from the dungeon to the cloister! But no, pupil of mine,
I must liberate you in spite of yourself; so please to turn
back with me towards her majesty's cabinet, for I am
going to relieve De Fleury in the charge of the door. I
will expound to you on the way all the weighty reasons
that may induce you to return to a sounder mind."

"Louis," replied the other firmly, "spare yourself the
trouble. I have obtained my dismissal from her majesty,
and am retiring from the guard and from the court.".

"You are retiring?" exclaimed De Montauban, opening his eyes wide, and staring Antoine insolently in the
face;—"retiring, like a fastidious unmannerly guest, before the feast has well begun! Impossible, Antoine!
either you are jesting with me, or you are a fool."

Our hero had determined with himself that he would
maintain, during this last interview, a calmness and patience that should be in keeping with the great sacrifice he
had just completed. The words of the other touched him
to the quick; his color heightened; his lips were more
firmly compressed together. Still he looked De Montauban steadily in the face, with no unkindliness, and repeated
with a deliberation that might have impressed any one who
was open to better feelings:

"I am leaving you; I am leaving the court. My resolution has been taken and declared; my lieutenancy is
vacant."

Certain it is that they who are thoroughly bad, not only
revolt from any token of the supernatural workings of
grace in another, but are absolutely transported by it into
fury. They can look on with complacency at the ordinary
doings of those who, like the fallen angels described by
Dante, live neither in overt rebellion nor sterling fidelity

to the Divine Will, and simply for themselves.* But the presence of any thing above this average self-pleasing standard appears to lash the wicked into a paroxysm of hate. It is as though the evil spirit cried out with rage and gnashing of teeth when brought into unwilling contact with that Power, all divine, though working in frail human subjects, by which it shall one day be confounded and hurled into the abyss. It is "tormented before the time," and raves with the agony of a despair already kindled and burning fiercely. So was it now with De Montauban. His eyes flashed fire, his cheek became livid with rage; and it was rather with the gesture of a demoniac than with aught that resembled even the wildest moods of his former self, that he shook his clenched hands in Antoine's face, and shouted,

"Traitor and coward! thou leavest us because thou darest not face the contests that are at hand! Go, hide thee in the cloister, and sing psalms while braver spirits are waging the battle of life. Get thee hence, and take with thee a memorial from one who still deems it his honor to wear a sword!"

So saying, he drew off his long military glove, struck De Bonneval a violent blow with it across the face, and, with a stride and gesture of contempt, was passing inwards to the further door leading to the regent's apartments.

Quick as thought, Antoine had sprung after him and grappled him. The previous insulting words of his brother-officer had tried him to the uttermost; and this last outrage was too much. He seized Louis with an infuriated gripe by the scarf that covered the breast of his doublet, his right hand sought the hilt of his own rapier, —another moment, and their swords would have been crossed in deadly strife,—when the door of the inner saloon opened, and there appeared the calm yet commanding form of Vincent de Paul.

"Peace here, within the royal palace!" exclaimed he, somewhat sternly; "Monsieur de Montauban," he instantly

* " . . . . quel cattivo coro
   Degli angeli che non furon ribelli,
   Ne fur fedell a Dio, *ma per se foro.*"          *Inferno.*

24

added, "I need not remind you of the consequences to
yourself if your quarrel is pursued in these apartments.
It needs but the first clash of your weapons for the halber-
diers in the nearest saloon to transport you both to the
*Chatelet*.   And you, my own son," pursued the old man,
turning to Antoine, "are these to be the first-fruits of your
new resolutions ?"

The two young men remained motionless, still glaring
on each other with looks of fury, while Vincent stood
where he had strode between, his arms extended to part
them.   Antoine was the first to recover himself.   His eyes
sank to the ground, while the thoughts returned that had
possessed him at Saint-Lazare, and had brought him here
this morning.   He then raised his countenance to that of
the old priest, flung himself suddenly upon his bosom, and
pressed his flushed convulsed face hard against that paternal heart.   De Montauban turned on his heel with a light
and scornful laugh ; and merely saying, "If Monsieur De
Bonneval ever acts for himself, and wishes to return the
compliment he has just received, I am always to be heard
of, and at any hour," he passed on his way through the
door by which Vincent had entered, and hummed to himself, though not with all the composure he strove to attain,
the air of a minuet.

Vincent said nothing, but led Antoine forward to the
staircase, the young man's head still drooping on his
bosom.   There was a tumult raging in the breast of the
brave high-spirited youth.   It was the enemy's last chance,
and powerfully did he ply it.   The stainless honor of his
name ; the long line of ancestors, who would each have
washed out a far less insult in blood ; the contemptuous
laugh of his adversary that still rang in his ears ; the
thought of his father, of Louis's future version of the
story, of the finger of scorn that would be pointed at him
wherever he turned, of the jests of Fontrailles and the
light sarcasm of Marsillac, that would spread his dishonor
through the court, through Paris, and would be repeated
at Bonneval ;—such were the images that arose before his
soul, and did battle against the better spirit within.

They reached the landing of the stair in silence.   As

Antoine's feet fell upon the steps, slowly and heavily, he raised his head, and would have spoken. Vincent stopped in the prayer in which he was silently pleading for him, and whispered, as he pressed him closer to his bosom, "Peace, my son; not a word at this moment. I feel for your hard struggle, while I foresee your victory. You will rise from it a stronger man. Have you not this day enlisted in the service of Him who said of Himself: 'I have given My body to the smiters, and My cheeks to them that plucked them; I turned not My face away from them that reproached and spat upon Me?'"

## CHAPTER XXXIII.

### SAINT-LAZARE.

"And while thou notest, from thy safe recess,
Old friends burn dim, like lamps in noisome air,
Love them for what they are; nor love them less,
Because to thee they are not what they were."

*Coleridge.*

FIVE years have nearly elapsed since that day when the love and dread of the world on one side, and those new-born higher affections on the other, held their decisive wrestle in De Bonneval's breast. The course of time has scarcely brought greater changes to himself, than to the chequered scene of politics in which he once had some share. Nearly all the principal actors in the troublous days of the Fronde have changed their parts; some led to it by the weariness of struggle, some from interest, others from higher and worthier motives. Conde has quarrelled with Mazarin, and in his personal pique has lit again the

torch of civil war.  He has been arrested, with his brother
Conti and the Duke de Longueville, and imprisoned at
Havre.  Mazarin, in turn, has found the tide run against
him with resistless power; the provinces have been in revolt
in consequence of that *coup-d'etat* by which he imprisoned
the princes of the blood.  The chivalrous romance of Bordeaux has been enacted by Clemence de Maille, Princess
de Conde, a heroine worthy of her husband; and has
enlisted popular feeling on the side of the princely captives.
De Retz, at the head of the popular party, is manœuvring
with all his skill against the cardinal.  The populace and
the middle classes rise against the hated foreigner.  Mazarin escapes from the Louvre in disguise; the discovery
is hailed with delight; his departure is a public deliverance; the Parliament obtains from the queen a declaration
that he is gone to return no more, and immediately
registers it as a decree.  He fixes his place of exile at
Cologne; the liberated princes make a triumphal entry
into Paris.  The Coadjutor raises a new Fronde, persuades
the people and the adherents of Orleans that the regent
meditates again escaping out of the capital with the young
king, and sends a tumultuous armed mob to the palace.
Anne of Austria's haughty calmness and intrepidity avert
the storm.  The doors of the royal apartments are flung
open, and the foremost of the populace see their young
king sleeping, or feigning to sleep, in all tranquillity.
But though the rude multitude are thus silenced, Conde on
the one hand, the Coadjutor on the other, remain as permanent movers of disorder; both hostile to the court, each
incensed against the other.  De Retz obtains the cardinal's
hat which was to have rested on the brow of Conti; his
power grows by the extravagant pride and ambitious pre-
tentions of his rival, but accompanied by a state of public
disorder which nearly entails his own assassination.  The
conflict between parties advances to the verge of wholesale
bloodshed, even in the halls of the parliament, and the
galleries of the Palais de la Justice.  In the midst of this,
Louis XIV. is proclaimed, soon after entering his fourteenth year.  Conde breaks into open revolt, urged by his
sister, who is urged by Marsillac, now Duke de la Roche-

foucault. Conde, become an acknowledged rebel, secures the assistance of Spain, and seduces the loyalty of Anjou, Poitou, and Guyenne to join him against his royal cousin. Mazarin, who from his exile at Cologne had been watching events, and continually aiding the regent by his counsels, raises a small army of adventurers, leads it into France, is joined at his head-quarters on the Loire by several detachments of the royal troops, by the queen-mother herself, with the young king, and by the great Turenne, now returned to his allegiance. Paris again becomes a scene of factions and counter-factions. The parliament issues a decree of proscription against both Mazarin and Conde, and sets a price of fifty thousand crowns on the head of the former; this, with several other of its proceedings, does but furnish matter for public ridicule and pasquinade. Conde falls suddenly upon a portion of the king's forces, defeats them at Bleneau, and nearly surprises the court; but Turenne, by a masterly movement, saves the royal cause from further reverses. These two great generals, who had so strangely exchanged sides within a short interval of time, encounter each other again under the very walls of Paris. The battle of the Faubourg Saint-Antoine declares in favor of Turenne. He is, however, prevented from following up his success by the cannon of the Bastille, fired upon him by Mademoiselle de Montpensier, the haughty and adventurous daughter of Orleans, who had assumed the command of the fortress, and thus rendered it practically a drawn engagement.

The public anarchy, the public misery, are complete. The scenes of lawless violence between factions in the capital, and of famine and death in the provinces, have been equalled by few passages in the history of that century. The parliament openly decrees Orleans lieutenant-general of the kingdom, and Conde commander-in-chief of the armies. But it is by this time found impossible to reawaken the popular interest to very active exertion in aid of the princes. An insurrection, indeed, is organized either to enable or to compel the parliament to raise fresh troops, and renew the war. During its progress, several of the magistracy meet with a violent death at the Hotel de Ville.

24*

Some touch of remorse for the blood of peaceful men shed
in the interests of a faction that no longer commands
public sympathy, together with the general weariness,
desolation, and ruin which the progress of the Fronde had
involved, puts a final stroke to the lingering and changeful, but undignified struggle.   De Retz, who at its very
outbreak, on the Day of Barricades, had endeavored to
mediate between the opposing parties, now, perhaps with
greater sincerity, certainly with better success, carries in
the name of the Parliament a supplication to their majesties that they would return to their capital.   Accordingly,
on the 24th of October, 1652, the court once more makes
its entrance into Paris, where Mazarin soon joins them
from his separate exile.   Orleans, whose inconstancy and
cowardice had involved the death of many better men
than himself, is sent for life to Blois; Conde, remaining
stubborn in his disloyalty, is declared guilty of *lese-majeste*,
and, in his absence, condemned to death.   The Dukes of
Beaufort, La Rochefoucault, and De Rohan are banished
the kingdom.   Gondi himself is imprisoned at Vincennes.
Conti effects his reconciliation by allying himself with a
niece of the cardinal's.   Madame de Longueville at length
finds the true end of her existence, the reparation for a
wasted and guilty past, in a life of devotion, sincere and
penitent.   The power of the French monarchy is firmly
re-settled for more than a century to come ; and Conde
himself, when he returns, after the Peace of the Pyrenees
in 1659, will appear once more at that court which he
always adorned, as the most loyal son of France, no less
than her first subject.

   And Antoine—he too is changed, as time has rolled by.
Or rather, as it is the wear and working of the heart, and
the contention of opposite motives in the little world
*within*, far more than the mere flight of years that ages
us, he has matured more rapidly than the lapse of time in
itself would have seemed to warrant.   The vicissitudes he
has encountered, the experience and deep convictions they
have wrought, have left abiding traces on him, and brought
out and consolidated a character hitherto unformed.   There
is less of mere buoyancy about him than before he had

made the great experiment of life; but there is no loss—
rather is there a palpable increase—of activity of mind,
range of thought, and braced energy of will. Fancy has
not died within him—let us not say it; it has passed into
something more, as youth passes into fully-developed manhood. It lives, but is transfigured, and has become a
power of realizing the unseen, of appropriating it as a motive of action, of resting in it as a consolation under labor
and trial. He is "walking by faith, not by sight;" and
the precious faith which is now the loadstar of his course,
beams upon him as his great present reward, while it mar-
shals him forward to a day of yet brighter recompense in
store. His old courage has not waxed faint; nay, it is
now sublimed and intensified. It has ceased to be a mere
impulse, onward, unreflecting, such as is shared even by
the ranks of inferior animals; it has become steady and
enduring, by allying itself with Christian self-denial. That
man fears nothing who aims at nothing for himself; and
he who sits loose to present ease or advancement is ever
the foremost to face onsets of whatever kind, to mount the
breach with any forlorn hope, to stand steadfast under the
press of any imminent peril. He is unhampered by the
pledges which other men have given to fortune, and which
bind them perforce to a secure, if not a timid, line of action.
Antoine, we have seen, has learned the courage to remain
tranquil under an unprovoked insult; and that day placed
him on a path which would have conducted him, had Providence so willed, to the martyr's high-souled endurance,
and the martyr's radiant crown.

Thus our dear Antoine—for dear he has become to us,
and we trust our readers are not wholly indifferent to him—
is still himself, yet almost another. He was fanciful, and
disposed to be fastidious; he now possesses an imagination
solidly stored with the sublime realities of the Church, who,
while she meets every demand of the intellect for truth,
affords ample satisfaction to the soul's yearnings after
beauty. He was gentle and affectionate: he craved human
sympathy; the appeals of friendship, the voice of attachment, were powerful—alas, over-powerful—to his natural
heart. And now these impulses, all refined, have found

their true centre in the one master-motive—an energetic
self-renouncing charity. He was bold and fearless, with
all the courage of a young soldier, with all the high blood
of a noble of France. But there is now about him a yet
more braced and constant daring; for he can grapple with
that enemy within his own breast, the demon of self-love,
who, in a long course of triumphs, has subdued so many
a conqueror, flung to the ground so many a hero. De
Bonneval has tried some decisive falls with that ancient
enemy. The wily wrestler, oiled and slippery, like the
athletes of old, has more than once eluded his grasp, and
tripped him unawares. He has fawned upon him under
the mask of seductions and pleasure; he has grinned at
him fearfully with the wrath and contempt of the world.
But Antoine has at length become his practised antagonist.
Slowly and wearily, with uncertain resolution at first, but
gathering strength as he proceeded, slipping back here and
there, with sometimes a fall, with errors not a few, he has
won his way. And now he is a tried—were it not for his
years we might say a veteran—champion in that arena,
the battle-ground of the hardest, most protracted, and
exhausting, but most richly-crowned struggle the soul of
man can undergo; the life-long struggle against the
tyranny of self.

Shall we look in upon him again? There was one revelation made to him in Lomelli's chamber before which we
have not lifted the veil. Our sagacious readers may or may
not have divined it; but the time is come. Antoine's fifth
birthday had found him an innocent child, receiving into
his soul heavenly inspirations by his mother's knee. On
his tenth he was a boy of promise, spirited, untried, with
every budding hope for his future manhood. His fifteenth
was the day on which that soul was espoused to its Redeemer; supernatural strength imparted to it; and the
Divine life infused, as a pledge and foretaste of heaven to
come. His twentieth saw those glories tarnished, that fine
gold dimmed, under the tainting breath of the world, the
world of Paris in the mid-course of the seventeenth century. What is his twenty-fifth? Let us answer that, and
our task is done.

The scene is in Saint-Lazare, as the title of our chapter has announced. That house, whose walls have sheltered him during more than one crisis of his existence, contains him still. The time is between nine and ten in the morning, when meditation and Mass, and the acts of thanksgiving which follow it, are over, and a brief recreation is part of the day's rule after the slight morning-meal. It is a fine spring morning; and forth he comes to breathe the fresh air, in his cassock, a breviary in his hand.

A priest! And they who have been taught to associate with that name a train of dark malignant shadows have already closed the book, in distaste at what is to them "a lame and impotent conclusion." Antoine a Lazarist priest! the young, generous, ardent spirit, in whom they have taken some little interest, confined for life within the cold trammels of such a vocation! victim of the solitude of celibacy, a servant to the will of others, surrounded no longer by the gaiety, the refinement of a court, with no sphere for the romance and imagination of his nature, no future for the energy whereby the inner being impresses itself on the outward world.

No sphere, no future? Hear what our friend himself feels upon this subject.

"Yes, dear Henri," says Antoine to the other young priest, who is walking by his side, "it was a great struggle, I will own; and there were times when I thought I must have given in. Now that it is over, and I can look back upon it calmly, it seems like the traveller returning in the morning to trace the path he had trod by the precipice during the dark night before; wondering how he ever got through it safely, how no false step had hurled him down. There were so many chances against me: temperament, education, flattering promises, all beckoning me back to the danger. And then, then—my father—nay, even now *that* almost tries my calmness; and he speaking of my mother, too, and of her grief, and surprise, and disappointed hopes! O friend; you who have been dedicated, like Samuel in the temple, and have worn your cassock before you would have assumed your *toga virilis* in the world, can hardly realize, with all your power of sym-

pathy, the terrible hindrances which these things offer to
a man's simply pursuing his vocation. To disappoint
those who gave one being, tended and trained one fondly,
with care and pride, and looked in the course of years for
a return in kind; to witness their parental anger, or still
worse, their speechless sorrow—the proud tear he dashed
from his eye at our last interview, ere it lit with the scorn
that bade me leave his presence;—no, nothing but grace
could have brought me through!"

Henri pressed his arm, and they walked some paces in
silence. "*Alerte!*" then cried the other gaily; "it is not
that you have left the army, Antoine. You are a soldier
still, with much of the uncertainty and vicissitude of a
soldier's life. Tell me—monsieur le baron would willingly
have parted with you, had you been called to serve against
the enemies of your country, would he not?"

De Bonneval nodded, with a smile.

"Well, then, your own thoughts supply what I would
say. Do you know that I have a touch of the military
about me too, though you give me credit for having been
such a cleric in long-clothes? Yet, in truth, the two things
touch upon each other in more points than one. I remember the refrain of an old ballad which I caught from one
of the soldiers billeted upon us here during the troubles,
while you were still wearing rapier and plume; it expresses,
in a profane sort of way, what I mean. The soldier (so it
runs) is a being who sits loose to all ties of earth; let him
go; don't stop him! He has no time for such things. His
destiny is a rapid one, it drives him on; places are indifferent to him; no rest awaits him any where. He sups
with his best friend to-night, and rides over his dead face
to-morrow—"

"Stay there," interrupted De Bonneval, who had re-
gained his spirits, "and acknowledge that in that respect
the priest has a manifest advantage over the soldier. You
and I are never likely to find it a part of our duties to
trample one another down. But I catch the spirit of what
you mean; it has more than once occurred to my own
mind. In going through the Spiritual Exercises, that
meditation on the Two Standards has always come home to

me with a special force. Yes, friend, in the blessed call
which has been given to us, demanding so much, yet
repaying so richly, I recognize the fulfilment of all my
boyish imaginings. You will smile at me—you, who,
instead of dreaming, have ever lived by faith—if I were
to tell you what a dreamer I have been in my day. I have
awoke; and it is a glorious reality, above romance, above
the highest reach of fiction."

"Demanding much, repaying more!" he repeated to
himself, walking along, with his eyes half shut, while his
step, firm and elastic, resumed something of its old military
tread. Then, after a pause: "Only let us take care that
the soldier's courage, the soldier's discipline, is linked with
humility and kindliness from first to last, gentle though
brave, *sans reproche* as well as *sans peur*, and all will be
well. So now, shall we say Sext and Nones together?"

## CHAPTER XXXIV.

### NEWS OF AN OLD ACQUAINTANCE.

"*Siward.* I could not wish him to a fairer death;
And so his knell is knoll'd.
*Malcolm.* He's worth more sorrow,
And that I'll spend for him.
*Siward.* He's worth no more :
They say, he parted well, and paid his score :
And so, God be with him."                    *Macbeth.*

*To our Reverend Father Vincent de Paul, Superior of
the Congregation of Missions at the Maison de Saint-
Lazare, Rue du Faubourg Saint-Denis, Paris.*

BOJEYA, ALGIERS, this 20th day of May, 1653.

WITH tears of joy, in the midst of natural regrets, I write
to you, dear Father in Christ. Thankfulness and triumph
mingle with our weeping for a most dear soul taken away

from us; and you will share in both.   Your prayers have
been again heard; the blood of one of your spiritual
children has bedewed this heathen earth for the faith of
the Lord.   Yes, we have another member in heaven, and
the Church another martyr on the roll of her intercessors.
Who? you will eagerly ask.   O miracle of grace! it is
that child for whom you wept and prayed so long before
his final conversion.   You have now guessed, and your
guess is a reality—the lay brother, Claude Saron.

    His blessed body is even now laid out in our church;
the faithful crowd around it, and ask permission to touch
with their rosaries his pale hands, as they lie crossed,
clasping the crucifix on his breast.   There are tears and
sobs among them; but they are rather those of devotion
than of personal regret, for he was little known beyond
the walls of this house.   From the moment of his entrance
among us, as I have written to you formerly, he was
remarkable only for a staid and sedulous performance of
duty.   You never saw in him a token by which to divine
what he might have been in the world.   Remember,
father, that I am unacquainted with the circumstances of
his former life.   I have had discretion enough to avoid
any question that might indicate a wish to learn them;
but whenever, on observing his regularity in all our community offices, I have speculated on his antecedents, I
have been completely baffled.   That his past life, whatever it may have been, was not without cultivation and
refinement was obvious.   The simple dignity and perfect
ease of his manner, his grave self-restrained courtesy,
might almost have seemed to trench upon the humility
and plainness of a religious, but that it was relieved by
his ready, though somewhat measured smile, and lowly
unquestioning obedience.   His whole demeanor, too, attested a complete self-forgetfulness, an absorbing intention
to fulfil his duties as perfectly as might be; nor did he
ever manifest any repugnance, even the slightest, to the
most menial office imposed upon him.   He never alluded
in the most distant manner to the past.   Once only, I
remember, when one of the suite of the Spanish envoy had
come to our house for confession, and had laid aside his

rapier while he went into the church, brother Claude chanced to enter the guest-chamber, where it was lying on the table. I was also there at the moment, waiting for a Mahomedan catechumen, who was forced to visit us by stealth. I remarked the eye of the lay brother glance upon the sheathed weapon, which was of superior workmanship. He raised it for a moment from the table, poised it, measured it with his eye; then, as if some train of recollections had carried him away altogether, he flourished it with a practised hand in the air, and with the evident ease and grace of a master of defence. Another moment, and he had replaced the weapon upon the table, and with a head bent lower than usual, left the room with the air of a man humbled by the consciousness of a fault.

I remember, too, *inter scribendum*, that some time after he joined us, I selected him one day to accompany me on my visit to the Christian captives who were working in their chains. We found among them a poor man on the verge of despair. He had been lately torn from his native France and from his family; captured by an Algerine corsair as he was returning from Marseilles to Toulon in a small coasting-vessel. He had undertaken this voyage, always dangerous in a sea infested with pirates, in order to repair the little fortune which had been diminished by a sum of money taken from him by robbers a few years before. He mentioned to us the exact time and place of his misfortune. I was turning to make some remarks to brother Claude upon this history, when I observed his eyes riveted intently on the speaker, with an expression, not of mere sympathy, in which (it was one of his few faults) we had sometimes thought him rather deficient. His lips were compressed; he shaded his brow with his hand, but said nothing. Only I thought, as the poor captive occasionally looked at him during the recital, there was a wondering puzzled expression in *his* eyes also, as if he thought that, but for his religious habit, he could have recognized brother Claude. Nothing further passed; but the next time it fell to the turn of Father Felix, who confessed the novices and lay brothers, to visit the poor galley-slaves, brother Claude asked permission to accom-

25

pany him, and at the same time urgently requested that he
might take a considerable sum of money with him from
the funds of the house.    It was a sum that would have
been more than enough, at the average rate which the
Algerines exact, to redeem a captive from slavery.    I
naturally demurred to so unusual a petition from one
whose rule was poverty; but there was something so im-
ploring about his manner, and moreover he had so amply
endowed our house on his first entrance, that I did not
feel justified in refusing.    He took the money, therefore,
with an expression of humble thankfulness; nor did I ever
afterwards hear him refer to the subject.    His cell being
near mine, I could not avoid knowing that for some time
after this occurrence he took the discipline, which he
always did with great severity, more frequently than the
rest.    Could it, then, be, I asked myself—but no; it would
have been uncharitable to entertain such a thought.
Whenever the remembrance of that poor injured captive
and of brother Claude have come together (as they often
would) into my mind, I have checked myself in drawing
any inference from the story I heard.

How am I wandering all this while!    You will forgive
me, father, for you loved him well; and you know, too,
how much he deserved the charity with which he inspired
us.    He is now among the blessed, and each memory of
him is precious.    I have mounted to my room to write to
you, after having assisted in chanting the Office for the
Dead by his peaceful holy corpse.    Those features are still
before my eyes, as I saw them a quarter of an hour since,
shown by the light of the funeral tapers; so calm and
grave, as if he were but dreaming some thoughtful dream,
except that the overhanging dark brow remained somewhat contracted, as of one who had suffered much in dying.

But why, you will ask, did we thus perform his obse-
quies, instead of singing a *Te Deum* for him as for a
martyr?    It is true, there is not one in our community
who doubts that his death was for the faith; yet we desire
to copy the caution of holy Church, whom we know to be
circumspect, even to slowness, in enlarging her calendar.
And as she has demurred to the canonization of holy

priests butchered at many a gallows in England half a
century back, because, though martyrs in the sight of
Heaven, they were executed in the face of the world on a
political pretext, so do we abstain from pronouncing judgment as to our dear and happy brother, except the involuntary jubilant thankfulness that escapes us, when we
contemplate such a death, as crowning nearly four years of
so holy a life.

The facts are as follows; you will gather from them
what cause we have for joy. Our brother, from the time
when he passed out of his noviciate, and began to be employed in a share of the external works of the community,
manifested, I will not say an attraction,—for attractions
and repugnances seemed scarcely to exist in him,—but
rather a special gift, for aiding in the conversion of the
Mahomedans around us. You are aware of the peculiar
difficulties which beset this branch of our labors. Any
one among these men who should betray a wish even to
inquire into the Catholic religion, or address himself to a
priest, becomes jealously watched by his brother infidels.
He is a man marked and suspected; and, should he per-
severe in his inquiries after the truth, would be exposed to
relentless insults and persecutions from all to whom he had
been nearest, yea dearest, hitherto. To commit the final
offence of abjuring the creed of the false prophet would be
followed by a public accusation; and one of the iniquitous
tribunals to whom the Dey gives his sanction would almost without question sentence the culprit to be impaled
alive. Under such inducements to maintain the tradition
of their elders, it is no great marvel if the number of our
Mahomedan converts has been but small. Instances there
are, thanks be to the Giver of all strength; but they are
rare, and for the most part secret. Some of these visit us
by stealth as catechumens; others have already been admitted to the Sacraments, and are practising their religion
with edifying patience, and under difficulties as great as
those of the primitive Church in the Catacombs. Others,
more blessed still, whose steps have been traced to our
church by the jealous vigilance of relatives, or who, from
their refusal to join in the sinful practices around them,

have become known as Christians, have been added already
to the white-robed army who surround the King of Martyrs.   We have been anxious in many of these cases to
obtain materials for the process of their canonisation; but
the infidels, with the perverse malice exhibited by the
heathens of old, have jealously secured the secrecy of the
martyrdom, and destroyed every vestige or record that
might have come to our hand.

Of this class of happy souls was a youth named Abdoul,
who had been educated carefully by his family, with a view
to his embracing the profession of a moullah, or expounder
of the Mahomedan law.   At the age of sixteen, Providence
brought him in the way of brother Claude, who was one
day proceeding to a *temar*, or farm, at some few miles distance, to obtain provisions for the community.   Claude, as
I have said, was especially successful in his intercourse
with the unbelievers.   There was a grave and natural dignity of manner about him which harmonised with their
own demeanor.   His piercing dark eyes and whole expression arrested the attention of men who value so highly
the quality of unmoved calmness, and impress it so strongly
in the education of their youth; and we used sometimes to
remark to him laughingly at recreation, that in this respect
he had more of the barbarian than the Frenchman in his
composition.   In consequence, he soon obtained a great influence over Abdoul, who was himself a staid and thoughtful youth.   Claude had acquired sufficient of the Algerine
tongue to express himself in it with some facility; and
Abdoul's thirst for instruction led him to make frequent
opportunities for conversing with our brother, even at personal risk to himself.   He would often watch near the convent, as the hour arrived for his instructor to set out upon
some external duty; and it was moving to see the unaffected
joy that beamed in the eyes of the young Moor as he hastened to meet the tall form of the other issuing from the gate,
and walked away with him, plying him with questions, and
drinking-in every syllable that dropped from Claude in
reply.   To the other members of the community Abdoul
was friendly and respectful; but it was to Claude, though
he knew him to be a layman, holding an inferior place

among us, that he turned as a child in the faith to his
spiritual parent. They were Claude's words to which he
listened as to a sacred oracle; Claude was the appointed
instrument of his salvation.

Our dear brother, on his part, seemed to open his whole
heart to respond to this touching spiritual affection. Detached as he had been from his first entrance among us,
deadened to mere human sympathy as he seemed, attaining with some difficulty to the true measure of fraternal
love, there was something in his manner towards the young
Abdoul which betokened a tenderness of sympathy he had
seldom exhibited before. It was as if some new thing had
happened in his existence, that a young and ardent soul
should thus attach itself to him, hang upon his words, and
respond to his thoughts; and sometimes, as I have seen
from my window the two walking away together, I could
not but fancy that brother Claude, who always retained a
degree of undefined and impenetrable dignity, if not command, of manner, had perhaps often in the course of his
life been obeyed and even feared, but never so *loved* as
now he was loved by his simple neophyte.

The good work proceeded, and young Abdoul was
fully convinced of the truth of our holy faith. Claude
had placed him in communication with one of our priests,
who perfected the instruction he had so well begun. It
was then Abdoul's delight to seize every spare moment to
talk over with his cherished friend those sacred truths which
were absorbing his every thought. The day of his baptism was fixed; he insisted that the name of his new birth
should be that of his benefactor. His soul expanded with
joy at the prospect before him; his tread was lighter, his
very form dilated, and his eye glistened, as though body
and soul were exulting together on the eve of their regen-
eration. And so he departed from the convent-gate, on his
last walk with brother Claude before the happy hour when
he might indeed hail him as his brother in Christ.

Meanwhile Abdoul's movements had been watched by
one of his school-companions, who bore a hatred to the
Christian name that seemed preternatural for his early
years. He had awaited the moment when he might de-
25*

nounce him as a Catholic without the possibility of a denial.
The fact that young Abdoul had frequently sought our
society, would not of itself have formed a sufficient proof;
for not only were the Christian captives accustomed to send
for us in their need by Moorish messengers, but other
youths of promise besides the young convert had frequented
the house for occasional instructions in astronomy, medi-
cine, and algebra. We had encouraged this to a certain
extent, in the hope of some ulterior benefit to themselves;
and the cases of conversion among the well-educated classes
of Mahomedans were so rare, that the lessons proceeded on
the whole without much suspicion on the part of the unbelievers. This day, however, Abdoul's enemy, Ibraim, obtained proof positive of the young man's Christianity, and
was not slow to use it.

The catechumen had quitted me; he had just finished
making his general confession preparatory to his baptism
on the morrow. Never have I seen such an expression of
youthful joy, such determination to endure all and give up
all for Christ, as irradiated his beaming face when he
kissed my hand and bade me farewell for the last few hours
of his unbaptised life. I committed him to Claude's com-
panionship with a full heart; for I well knew their conversation would be of God, and of the blessed morrow.
Some feeling more than ordinary prompted me, when I
gained my own room in the upper story of the house, to
look out upon them again as they went down the street.
Whether it were an undefined presentiment, or a whisper
from the guardian-angel of our dear brother, that if I would
ever see them again in life, I must take that opportunity,
I know not. But I obeyed it, and stood gazing at them
from the window with strange and mingled feelings.
Swiftly they paced along, though the powerful sun made
them keep carefully to the shaded side of the narrow street;
for Claude never let any thing stand in the way of the
duty on which he had been sent, and the young Moor
clung to his side with almost a bounding step, and was
speaking to him eagerly with his whole soul. I well knew
the deep earnestness of his character; otherwise his man-

ner might have seemed almost too playful for one who stood upon the turning-point of his existence.

When they had passed a sort of blind alley that opened out into the street, and were pursuing their way under the wall of a garden overtopped with cypress-trees, I saw Ibraim, with a stealthy gesture, emerge from his hiding-place behind them. He had evidently been watching their whole interview from that concealment; and it was proba-bly not the first time that he had stationed himself there to gain proofs against Abdoul. I marked the fiendish malice with which he riveted his eyes on his schoolfellow, as though he was endeavoring to guess from every movement of the young convert the subject that so much interested him.

At that moment the evening *Angelus* sounded from the clock-turret of our church. Claude and his disciple stopped, turned toward the sound, and with closed eyes recited the prayer, signing themselves with the sign of the cross. This was enough for the accuser; the action was unmis-takable, the proof was complete. He waited motionless, with eager exulting eyes, till they had turned to pursue their way; then, with a wild laugh and a frantic gesture of triumph, dashed off in another direction.

"God and his holy angels keep them!" said I involun-tarily, as I turned from the window. And it was so. They were indeed both kept and blest on that evening, beyond my utmost wish for them; kept from the peril of falling away at the last, blest with the blessedness of that higher conformity to our Lord, which is the privilege of His martyrs. The lay brother was to close his earnest life of self-sacrifice by a crowning act that transferred him to his place in heaven. And he who had longed so ardently to enrol himself among the baptised, was to receive in exchange the baptism of blood that should be his safe pass-port into the Church of the first-born.

Nearly an hour had elapsed, and all I had witnessed made me more uneasy than I should otherwise have been at their prolonged absence. Suddenly I became aware of some confused sounds, as of many persons speaking at once, that rose, and drew nearer to the house. There was the wailing of women, mingled with fiercer tones, and the

authoritative voices of some who strove to maintain order..
Turning the corner of the street, and running towards the
mission, while they wrung their hands in uncontrolled.
grief, came two or three of our young catechumens, and.
some of the Mahomedan boys who had attended our classes.
They loved brother Claude dearly; and the moment I saw
them, my heart foreboded something concerning him.   Nor
was I left in suspense; another minute, and there came
round the corner a procession of natives and Christian
slaves, five or six of whom bore gently and slowly a rude
bier of planks; and on that bier lay, in the composed attitude of tranquil death, our dear brother!

His habit had been torn by the violence of his murder-
ers; there was dark blood oozing from his brow; but what
an image of peace was he, spite of these rude accidentals!

A few words declared all.  The traitor had hastened to-
some of Abdoul's fanatic relations, who had taken with
them others, and gathered still greater numbers as they.
rushed in fury after the young convert.  They had come-
upon him as he was returning with Claude from his even--
ing walk, and assaulted him with stones and staves with
such vehemence that he fell under their hands bathed in.
blood; nor did their rage end there.  They leaped upon-
him with frantic gestures, flung themselves upon his pros--
trate body, ground him into the dust; and while his soul.
was rejoicing among the Saints, nothing was left of him-
upon earth but an indistinct horrible mass of sand and
blood and torn garments, retaining scarcely a semblance of:
the human form.

Claude might have escaped; but in that moment of
rage all distinctions were forgotten.  He was indeed a-
born Christian, and belonged to a house under the protec-
tion of the Dey; but then he was the converter of Abdoul.
He never raised a hand to protect himself; but when the·
first assault was made on his friend, he threw his own
body before him, and received several of the blows aimed
at the youth.  The fanatics pushed him aside, and threw
him, notwithstanding his strength, to the ground; but not·
before a stone had struck him on the temple, which must·
in a few moments have deprived him of life.  I was as—

sured by some, who are concealed Christians, and who watched the whole scene from a distance, that his only thought seemed to be to save the young neophyte from death. But what could we desire better for either of them than the disposition of Providence, which has removed from us a hopeful catechumen and a beloved and edifying member of our community, only to add to the number of free and happy adorers before His throne, and of intercessors for ourselves? For I am well assured that neither Claude nor Abdoul forget us now in heaven. Many things call me away; indeed, I have sent you an account of these events rather proportioned to the degree in which they preoccupy my heart than to the time I ought to have bestowed upon them; remaining, however, always,

   Dear and réverend father,
    Yours in the bonds of Jesus Christ,
       AUGUSTIN-MARIE DESLORGES,
        *Superior.*

## CHAPTER XXXV.

### THE LAST PASSAGE ALL UNLIT.

"If thou think'st on heaven's bliss,
Hold up thy hand, make signal of thy hope,
He dies, and makes no sign : O God, forgive him !"
        *King Henry VI.*

"RING, ring, ring !" cried the lay brother at Saint-Lazare who had charge of the gate, his good-humor waning into a shade of natural impatience. A third hasty summons on the porter's bell had reached him before he could descend the stair from the chapel to the entrance of the house. "And who may *you* be ?" he pursued, in no very amiable tone, sorely tempted to walk a little slower by the impetuousness and perseverance of the summons from without,—"who may you be, that cannot wait five minutes till folks have finished their rosary, but must ring them up from their prayers to attend upon you ? Some would-be penitent of Father Antoine's now, I'll be bound, with your perfumed love-looks and jingling chain, mincing— ah, there you go again!—mincing your words, with scarce half an eye to bestow on any one but the father himself. There again, louder than ever. Wait a bit, my gallant," continued the old man, hobbling on his way: "I've shown many a ruffler of your sort out at this gate a deal humbler than when he clanked in, with his spurs and—"

"Come, brother Alexis," interrupted Victor, the under-porter, already at the gate, "let us have the key without more ado. You know how the pere has charged us never to refuse him to any comer, however late, lest good purposes, as he says, should cool by standing; and here is more than one outside, I tell thee. I hear the shuffling of feet, and whisperings from one to the other. What if it be some such visit as we used to have from gentlemen of the Fronde not so many years back ? Well," added he, as the lock of the wicket yielded, "they will find nothing here but a good will to help their souls, and poverty in all beside."

It was no hostile party, however, that became visible through the opening gate by the dim light of the under-porter's lantern. A cavalier, in hat and plume, concealing as much of his face as he could in the lappet of his walking-cloak, might indeed have seemed a suspicious visitor at that late hour. But a second glance showed behind him three stout serving-men supporting a fourth figure, which lay as a dead weight in their arms.

A ray of the lamp, directed towards their burden, glared on the countenance of a man of perhaps seven-and-twenty, deadly pale, and contorted with agony, though at that moment exhibiting no token of consciousness. His rich doublet was streaked with blood, which, during the few minutes the party had been waiting at the gate, had formed a dark pool on the outer pavement. The right

hand hung powerless; the left was feebly clenched on the
chest, as though in his death-struggle he still sought to
withdraw the fatal weapon, as in the first moment after the
thrust that had laid him low.

An exclamation of horror from both the good brothers
of Saint-Lazare was cut short by the cavalier heading the
party; who, stepping at once within the wicket, explained
in a few hurried words that his friend had just been seri-
ously wounded in a personal rencontre; and before his consciousness left him, had desired to be carried quickly to the
Pere de Bonneval.  He added his own urgent request that
no delay might retard what ministrations from that father
the nature of the case admitted.

No delay was thought of.  Victor, lighter of limb than
his senior, flew at full speed up the staircase, and along
the quiet corridor, with a few devout aspirations under his
breath that all might not be too late.  He then knocked
hurriedly at a door on which was neatly inscribed, "R. P.
DE BONNEVAL," and rushed in to summon the father.
Alexis, his better nature roused at once, and breaking
through the rude crust that sometimes concealed it, lent
his aid with almost a woman's tenderness to bring the
bleeding burden gently through the wicket of the porter's
lodge.  The wounded cavalier was laid upon some cloaks
hastily arranged on the table of the guest-chamber that
opened to the right of the entrance.  For some minutes
no sound broke the fatal stillness, except the deep and convulsive breathings heaved from the sufferer's chest, and the
few muttered words of those employed in supporting him,
who endeavored to recover him from what threatened to be
his death-swoon.

Our hero—we still cling from old association to that
title, though he would now be the first to disclaim the ideas
attached to it—was reading quietly by the light of a small
shaded lamp at the close of a wearying day.  The Paschal
season had commenced, and brought more than ordinary
anxieties to the zealous confessors of Paris, and to Pere
Antoine among the number.  It was not the fashion in
France at that day to incur the Church censures awaiting
such as neglected to present themselves for Communion at

Easter-tide. Men came; with many exceptions, indeed;
but the rule was to come, and at least to offer themselves
to the judgment of the clergy. Then arose the dilemma.
How to admit them, with antecedents often so little fit;
with a purpose of amendment often so unsatisfactory?
How to refuse them, when this might extinguish the last
spark of grace still flickering around the cold heart, and
cast them back irretrievably into the gulf of recklessness
or of despair? It was grave work to adjust and hold the
balance between such alternatives; work demanding more
than the firm nerve and keen quick eye of the operator in
sciences that merely affect the bodily weal. The stake was
immeasurably greater; the trust reposed in a poor human
instrument higher beyond compare. And it is some such
consideration as this, that has made the Pere de Bonneval
lay his volume of theology gently on the table, and, leaning his brow on his pale thin hand, gaze fixedly before him.

He has not many minutes to pass undisturbed. The
repeated knocking at the gate has not, indeed, broken in
upon his thoughts; he is engaged upon a problem more
absorbing than wrapt Archimedes while the storm of war
was bursting into Syracuse. But he will be summoned
almost before we have had time for our last tranquil glance
at him in this silent study-hour; when an air of repose so
deep and holy is cast around him; when all is at rest and
still, save the energetic brain, as it balances the eternal
interests of his fellow-men—save the humble, trustful
heart, that raises that voiceless aspiration for guidance to
the Source of all!

He is slightly older than his years might warrant; that
is our first impression from looking at him. But he is
happier now than before; he has made trial of life, and
risen from it taught, matured, but gentle and loving; with
no soured hopes, no cynicism, or lonely pride—that is the
next thing we read in his face. That premature streak or
two of silver in the wavy hair (who knows but, after all,
'tis the mere lamp-light that deceives us?) may come from
intense study and thought; all the intenser because he has
come to it later than others, and done his duty by making
up lost ground. Or it may be that, sensitive as we have

always known him, he has felt in all their keenness—felt too keenly we dare not say—the anxieties which agitate noble natures, none the less because they concern others rather than themselves; and arise from responsibility more than from grief or peril. However it be, there is that in the clear steadfast eye, in the unruffled brow, and ready unconstrained play of the lip, to assure us that our Antoine's being has found its true centre, and settled down upon it. Yes, he is happy, inwardly, deeply—as happy as is good for him on this side the grave—as happy as they can be, or wish to be, who are sent upon a mission to the manifold distresses of a sin-smitten world; who, in measure as they now sow in tears, shall reap in joy, and bring in their sheaves exultingly to the Great Harvest-home.

A hurried knock at his door, and Victor rushes into the room.

Antoine is accustomed to be disturbed at all seasons; but when the lay brother stood there in the middle of the apartment, gasping for breath to tell his message, pale with the horror of the sight he had left, the Father rose instinctively to answer some call more importunate than common.

"A cavalier, *mon pere*"—panted forth the breathless messenger; "brought in—run through in a duel—begged to be carried to you; so they have him in the *parloir*; but now, I fear, poor gentleman—"

Antoine had not waited to hear so much. Grasping a violet stole that lay beside him, he had rushed from his room, and was already half-way along the corridor.

Mingled with the anxiety of a zealous priest for one who stood in extremest need of his ministry, came the boding sense of a personal anguish awaiting his own heart, that curdled his blood as he ran. It was some time since he had heard any tidings of Louis. His rapid conjectures now concentrated irresistibly upon the long-estranged companion of his court-life. As the imagination flashed across him of the wounded man lying below, they were the features of Louis that he seemed to see convulsed in the throes of the death-agony; it was the faint accent of *his* expiring

26

voice that sounded in his ear. With an almost frenzied
gesture he flung himself down the broad stairs, and burst,
with something of the impetuousness of his former self,
into the little parlor, which so brief an interval had transformed into a chamber of death.

Yes! in that moment were realized his darkest fears.
They that were busied around the table fell back on his
entrance. There, extended before him, returning to some
consciousness, opening those eyes, languid and agonized,
full upon him—there lay the evil companion who had won
his untried heart, the tempter that had well-nigh made
over that heart to the evil one, the causeless aggressor who
had still kept his unmerited place in it—and he, dying
apace !

How strange are the powers of action and self-mastery
that lie dormant within us, till a great occasion comes to
evoke them ! Had any one assured Antoine de Bonneval
—even calmed and consolidated as he is become—that he
could minister with unshaken firmness at the death of his
early friend—and *that* a death so horrible, and with a hope
so faint—he would have deemed the assurance unreal. But
now he has become suddenly equal to the task demanded
of him. The priest has triumphed over the mere man.
For an instant he stood without motion, as though gathering into his soul the full import of the truth that had burst
upon him. All—all ; *who* it is that lies there, and the
greatness of his needs, and that a few moments more will
send him to his irreversible doom—Antoine has realized it
all. He tests it : it is *not* merely a dark dream. Then he
gives himself wholly, with energy, to what is to be *done*.
By his rapid clear directions the wound is laid bare ; he
examines it ; alas ! it needs no very practised eye to pro-
nounce. There is nothing to be done *there ;* the minutes
of the sufferer are numbered. Then, for the soul ? Listen :
the dying man moves to speak ; and the Pere de Bonneval
stoled and ready, motions to a distance all who had been
around them, while he bends his ear to those pale faint lips,
to catch some fragment of confession. His arm encircles
the neck of his dying friend ; his throbbing heart pleads

with all its power that the grace of contrition may descend upon him in this last wrestle with the enemy.

There is again a dead silence in the chamber, except from the corner where Alexis is murmuring prayers, broken by suppressed sobs, that come from the very depths of his rough chest.

"Antoine!" falters the unhappy man, in a tone scarce audible, but which rose-to a hissing gasp—"Antoine—art there?"

A gentle pressure on the clammy hand answers that every breath is listened to.

"Dearest Louis," he replied, in a whisper clear and steady, "I am here, close; but not so near to you as God!" and he pressed the crucifix to the open, bloodless lips. "Speak to me again," he urged, in a more agonized tone—for the gleam of consciousness seemed passing; "tell me but *one* sin—alas! one out of many; the first you can think of. Rouse, rouse yourself, my Louis!" he almost shouted in his ear: "one little act of contrition—one; while I absolve you!"

There was no response. Nothing but a deep gurgling sound, which brought the attendants hastily to his side. Twice or thrice, while Antoine, agonized with grief, murmured for the passing soul that conditional absolution which the Church's tenderness provides, where she "hopeth against hope"—twice or thrice came that hollow gurgling sound. It was followed by a convulsive sigh. And the gray shadow of death is creeping over those sharpened features. And the spirit that had bartered itself for the phantoms of evil passion and the dream of the world, has passed—passed to stand its trial by a code that errs not, nor spares where it does not save.

THE END.

KELLY & PIET, PRINTERS, BALTIMORE.

www.ingramcontent.com/pod-product-compliance
Lightning Source LLC
Chambersburg PA
CBHW060547030726
47498CB00005B/1303